Tragedy at Welcome Inn

Robert W. Gregg

Copyright © 2014 by Robert W. Gregg

ISBN 978-1-4958-0014-6
ISBN 978-1-4958-0015-3 eBook

Printed in the United States of America

Published May 2014

INFINITY PUBLISHING
1094 New DeHaven Street, Suite 100
West Conshohocken, PA 19428-2713
Toll-free (877) BUY BOOK
Local Phone (610) 941-9999
Fax (610) 941-9959
Info@buybooksontheweb.com
www.buybooksontheweb.com

Other Crooked Lake Mysteries by Robert W. Gregg

A Death on Crooked Lake
The Man Who Wasn't Beckham
Setting the Stage for Murder
The Scarecrow in the Vineyard
The Cottage with Too Many Keys
The Haunting of Hawk's Nest
In the Chill of the Night
Death Comes on Silver Wings

This book is dedicated to all the people who have helped me find an audience for my Crooked Lake mysteries, especially Pam Knapp and Jim Long

I owe a debt of gratitude to the following people who have helped to make the book possible: Brett Steeves, who created the cover picture; Laura Gregg, who took the photo on the back cover; forensic pathologist Melissa Brassell, who advised me on issues related to the death of the victim; and Lois Gregg, who provided much needed editing of the manuscript.

CHAPTER 1

Carol looked at her watch and then back at the people who had come to the Southport library to hear her discuss her job as sheriff of Cumberland County.

"I was told that we had an hour, and it looks as if we have run over by almost ten minutes. I'm sure the staff would like to close up and go home for the night, so I think I should thank you for coming out this evening and being such a wonderful audience. If you have a question I didn't have time for tonight, don't hesitate to give me a call at my office."

There was a hearty round of applause, and then the unexpectedly large crowd began to break up. Carol moved away from the lectern to shake hands with several people who obviously wanted to say goodnight or perhaps pursue an issue that had been raised earlier. It was after 9:20 when she stuffed her notes in her briefcase and prepared to leave the nearly empty room. It would have been empty except for Alice Lent, the assistant librarian, who had been charged with locking up, and the lone remaining member of her audience, a man in the last row of chairs, a man she didn't think she had ever met.

"Thank you, sheriff," Ms. Lent said. "It was a successful evening, don't you think?"

It was a thoughtful thing to say, but the librarian looked as if it might be an even more successful evening if she could turn off the lights and call it a night.

"I do, and I want to thank you for giving me the opportunity to share my thoughts with all these people."

Carol debated going to the back of the room to say hello to the last of the evening's crowd, but he made it unnecessary by suddenly getting to his feet and leaving by a door at the other end of the room.

It had been a pleasant event. While Carol had expected no more than 20 or 25 attendees, there must have been at least 50 people on hand. And they had been a respectful audience, no one with an axe to grind. Nor had anyone said anything about the frequency with which murder had become part of Carol's responsibility as sheriff of Cumberland County. She congratulated herself for accepting the library's invitation to speak, an invitation she had initially planned to decline.

The library had been warm, but when she stepped out into the night air she was reminded that it was unseasonably cool for June. They were just four days past the solstice, and although lake summer wouldn't really begin until the Fourth of July, summer had officially arrived. Carol set off down the street. The small library parking lot had been full when she arrived, so she had had to drive a long block to find a parking place. The lights in the library went off behind her. It was turning into another quiet, sleepy night in Southport.

Although she hadn't heard a footfall, Carol was suddenly aware that someone was walking down the street behind her. She slowed down and looked back toward the library. It was as she thought. A lone figure was on the sidewalk. Could it be the man who had been sitting in the last row, the man who had been the last to leave when she finished her talk? If so, perhaps he had a question he wanted to ask, a question he had been reluctant to ask in front of all of the others in the room. She called out to him.

"Hello there. Didn't I see you in the library this evening?"

The man, for it was a man, walked slowly toward her. As he came into the pale pool of light from the sole streetlight in the area she recognized the black windbreaker he'd been wearing and the heavy growth of dark beard that covered his face. He wasn't smiling, nor did he seem inclined to speak.

"I was right," Carol said. "You were present for my little talk. I don't believe we've met. I'm Sheriff Kelleher, but of course you know that."

She extended her hand. The bearded man accepted it, albeit tentatively.

"I'll bet there's something you wanted to ask me," she said. "I'm sorry we ran out of time."

"No, I don't have any questions." When he spoke, the man's voice was low, almost inaudible. Carol wondered if he was embarrassed. If so, she didn't wish to further embarrass him.

"Well, then, thanks for coming, and have a good night."

She extracted her keys from a jacket pocket and the lights of her car flashed, announcing its presence a short distance ahead of them. When she gave the stranger a slight wave as she slid into her car, he hadn't moved on. Nor did he wave back. There had been a brief moment when she considered offering him a ride, but decided against it. If he lived in Southport, he wouldn't have far to walk. If he lived elsewhere, he would surely have come by car.

As Carol drove back to the cottage, she was feeling good about her meeting with the local citizenry. It was not until she was almost at the pull off on Blue Water Point that she realized that the stranger she had just recently talked with so briefly reminded her of someone she knew. He hadn't mentioned his name, and no name now came to her as she parked the car. But she had a feeling that she had met this man somewhere. Why had he come to her talk and not introduced himself? Why had he been the last member of the audience to leave? Why had he followed her down that dark street in Southport? For she was sure the heavily bearded man had been following her.

CHAPTER 2

Carol was reflecting on what she had said in her talk the night before as she drove to work the following morning. 'An Evening with Our Sheriff' was the way it had been advertised in the *Gazette* and on notices posted around town. It was an open ended and decidedly non-specific title for a speech, and she had chosen to keep her prepared remarks brief and then shift to a Q & A format. She had been surprised, and then pleased, that the questions had focussed less on her than on what policing the county entailed. For the most part they had been practical questions, and it had occurred to her that most of her officers could have answered them as well as she could. Perhaps even better. As she thought about it on the way to the office, an idea came to mind which caused her to smile to herself.

Ms. Franks had the coffee pot bubbling, so it was with coffee cup in hand that she cornered Deputy Sheriff Bridges and asked him to join her in her office for a few minutes before squad meeting.

"Sam," she began, "do you feel up to taking over for a few days?"

From the look on his face, it was obvious that she had surprised him.

"Is there some problem?" he asked. "You're not sick, are you?"

It was a reasonable question. Carol was almost never sick, and there had been no intimation that she might be having some kind of a problem.

"Quite the contrary, I'm feeling like I could run a marathon before lunch. No, that's not quite true, but I'm fine. It's just that I have a plan, and I need your help."

"Well, sure, whatever you say." Sam's puzzlement showed.

"It really came to me last night, although I don't think I was aware of it until this morning. You know I gave that talk down in Southport, don't you?"

"How did it go?" he asked.

"It went fine, but what mattered wasn't what I said, it was the questions people asked. And the more I thought about it, the more I realized that I spend too much time here in the office, writing reports, giving you and the men things to do. Making policy, I guess you'd say, insofar as we law and order folks have any leeway to make policy. What I don't do is get out and implement policy. When did I last issue a ticket? Investigate an accident? Break up an argument? Go out on water patrol? You know what I mean."

"Oh, come on, Carol. You're a doer, not a sitter. You were involved in that Mobley case 24/7. And what about that guy Stearns? Or the priest who became a scarecrow?"

"I know, but I'm not talking about one of those big cases that kept us all jumping. I'm thinking about the day to day stuff. Anyway, what I want to do is get out on the road, see what it's like to do what Barrett and Grieves and all the rest of you guys do day in and day out. I'm only talking about a week, not the rest of the summer."

"You're the sheriff, so it's your call. And I'm to sit there at your desk, is that the idea?"

"Something like that," she said. "I can't issue an order that makes you the sheriff, you understand. I'm still the one who's responsible. But I need to see what it feels like, and I propose to start this morning at the squad meeting. I'll get us started, then turn things over to you. Just be yourself."

"I'm supposed to give you your assignments?" Sam asked, sounding doubtful.

"That's right, and don't make it look like you're giving me any of the cushy stuff. Okay? Now let's get over there or they'll start to wonder what we're up to."

"I'm already wondering about that."

The squad meeting was something of a recapitulation of Carol's and Sam's conversation, except that she cut off debate about her plan before it started. Only Bill Parsons, her most senior officer, flashed a knowing smile when she spelled out her intentions. The others showed varying degrees of uncertainty as to how they should respond, but none of them said anything. I'll hear from someone in due course, she thought to herself, but I'm sure that they're all wondering if I have a hidden motive. She was thinking about what hidden motives her officers might be attributing to her when the meeting broke up.

Sam had responded to her instructions by putting her on highway patrol down county, between Southport and the Pennsylvania border. The rest of the morning proved to be uneventful. If the drivers she encountered were disposed to speed, the sight of a sheriff's department car had the effect of slowing them down, at least for a mile or two. By lunch time, she had logged more than one hundred and fifty miles and neither ticketed nor warned anyone. It occurred to her that much of policing in Cumberland County was simply boring. Necessary, but nonetheless boring.

She had driven a rectangular box shaped network of roads, and by 12:30 she was within seven miles of Southport again. Time for lunch, and the place where her men typically stopped was the diner on the square. Others apparently had a similar idea, because the parking spaces in the immediate area had all been taken. When she finally found a space, it turned out to be quite close to where she had parked the previous evening for her library talk. All the booths in the diner were occupied, but there were two or three spots at the counter, and she took one of them. Carol didn't know those on either side of her, and they showed no inclination to strike up a conversation. She placed her order for a club sandwich and iced tea and studied the occupants of the booths with the help of the mirror behind the counter. There were a few recognizable faces, but nobody she knew by name.

Carol had given herself twenty minutes, and her lunch hour was nearly up when a man with a dark beard and wearing a black windbreaker entered the diner and slid into a seat at the other end of the counter. It was the stranger from the back row at the library. She had been absent mindedly observing the lunch hour crowd, but she was now suddenly more interested in the newcomer. The presence of two waitresses back of the counter made it difficult to see him clearly in the mirror, but as they moved back and forth, taking and serving orders, Carol was able to get a better look at 'black beard' than she had the night before. 'Black beard.' Why was she thinking of him that way? Perhaps she should stop when she left, say hello, and ask him his name.

After she had paid her bill and deposited a tip on the counter, it became apparent that the stranger had spotted her. In fact it was likely that he had been aware of her presence as soon as he entered the diner. After all, it was a small place, and she was the only person in the room wearing a sheriff's department uniform. He was staring at her, or rather at her reflection in the mirror. Carol self consciously looked away, but when she looked back he was still staring at her. The expression on his face gave no evidence that he recognized her. She smiled. He continued staring.

It was an uncomfortable moment. The man was being rude, whether consciously or not. Perhaps she should not stop to talk with him on her way out of the diner. But curiosity prevailed.

"Hello, again," she said as she passed behind him. "First the library, now the diner. I don't believe we've met."

It was an invitation for him to introduce himself. He didn't do so, but for a second time he did speak.

"I enjoyed your talk last night."

"Thank you." Okay, Carol said to herself, no reason why she shouldn't ask. "I don't know your name."

"There's no reason why you should." He spoke quietly, much as he had the night before. "Excuse me, but I think the waitress wants to take my order. Have a nice afternoon."

'Black beard' turned his attention to the waitress and Carol, aware that she had been dismissed, walked out of the diner, wondering once again what that had all been about. When she got to her car, she climbed in but sat there for several long minutes, thinking about the uncommunicative stranger. Last night she had, for a few fleeting moments, thought that he reminded her of someone she knew. But she had dismissed the thought. Probably just a superficial resemblance to someone she had seen somewhere. Now she was revisiting the idea that he was somebody she had known. Try as she would, however, she couldn't place him. When she started the engine and pulled away from the curb, she had resolved to put the matter out of her mind. 'Black beard' was simply someone who was socially inept and uncomfortable making small talk. She had more important things to worry about, such as seeing if she couldn't catch a speeder before the end of the day.

CHAPTER 3

"I'm home," Carol called out as she came into the cottage. It was 5:30, and she had completed her first day as Sam Bridges' underling and was anxious to tell Kevin all about it.

"So I see," he said as he came out of his study to greet her. They kissed and it was then that he realized that something was different. "You're all wet!"

"It's just sweat. Good, honest sweat. Let me change and I'll explain."

"I thought you worked with your brain, not your brawn."

"I do, most of the time. And I don't think brawn is quite the right word. Just give me a few minutes to shower and make myself respectable."

When she reappeared, Carol had traded her uniform for something which looked considerably more comfortable. Kevin had uncorked a bottle of Chardonnay.

"So how did you manage to work up a sweat?" he asked.

"Changing a tire on the upper lake road," she told him.

"I thought you guys kept your vehicles in tip-top shape."

"We do. It wasn't one of my tires. I'm now a highway patrolman, and sometimes it necessitates playing Good Samaritan."

"You must feel very virtuous, but what is this highway patrolman business?"

"I've got a new job, effective this morning," Carol said, a broad smile on her face.

"Okay, you've got my attention."

So she told him of her decision to spend a few days on the road, taking stock of how her officers spent most of their days. Kevin listened with barely concealed amusement.

"You don't really have to do this, you know," he said when she finished her story. "I doubt that Sam and the gang will give you many brownie points for it."

"I'm already doing it, Kevin. One day down, five to go. Besides, I'm sure Mrs. Neukirk has already given me a few brownie points."

"Neukirk. She must be the lady with the flat tire."

"She is. Old enough to be my grandmother, God bless her. And she didn't think I'd be able to do it. I told her it wouldn't be a problem, but if I ran into trouble I'd call my husband."

"You didn't!"

"I certainly did."

"Well, I'm impressed. But tell me, will I be allowed to make out tonight with a highwayman instead of a sheriff?"

"I believe you mean a highway patrolman. Highwaymen were known for robbing travelers."

"Highway patrolman, highway patrolwoman, whatever. You haven't answered my question."

"Why don't we see what develops? In the meantime, are we having supper?"

"Of course. If you're going to change tires, the least I can do is put food on the table. Nothing fancy, just a big Cobb salad with that left over chicken and things I picked up at the farmers' market."

"Sounds good," Carol said. "Then I can tell you about a new man in my life."

Kevin, who had started to get up, sat back down.

"Wait a minute. Another man in your life? What was his problem? Did he want you to jump start his car?"

"I'll tell you after we eat."

"You know perfectly well you can't spring something like that on me and then expect me to talk about the weather or the Yankees over a Cobb salad. Come on, out with it."

Carol conceded the point and went to the kitchen to retrieve the Chardonnay.

"It's kind of weird," she said as she refilled their glasses. "I wasn't even going to mention it, but I can't quite get it out of my mind. It started last night at the Southport library. You do remember that I gave a talk there, don't you?"

"Of course. I even said hello when you came in, but I'd gotten hooked on an old movie and you said you were going to hit the sack."

"That sounds about right. Anyway, we had a good crowd, or should I say I had a good crowd. Much better than I anticipated. There was a chap who sat in the far back of the room, didn't say anything, and was the last one to leave other than the librarian who was closing up. I didn't give him a thought until I realized he was following me when I was on my way to my car."

"He was following you?" Kevin sounded alarmed.

"Well, it looked that way. He was maybe twenty feet behind me and going the same way I was. So I stopped to wait for him. I had no idea who he was, but I figured I should thank him for coming, ask him if he was new in town. He was polite, but he made no attempt to introduce himself, so we didn't really have a conversation. And that was it until this noon."

"He was still following you this noon?"

'No, nothing like that," Carol said. "I was having lunch at the diner in Southport when he walked in and took a seat at the opposite end of the counter. He was easy to recognize. He has a heavy black beard, and he was wearing the same dark windbreaker he'd had on at the library. There's not much more to tell, except that he began staring at me almost from the minute he sat down. I stopped and said hello as I was leaving. I even asked his name. He didn't want to talk this time either, and he declined to give me his name. Like I said, it seemed weird."

"Probably just a real introvert."

"That makes sense. But do introverts stare at other people like that? He had to know I was aware he was staring at me."

"It sounds as if he lacks what we think of as the social graces. Or perhaps he's retarded in some way. I wouldn't give him another thought."

"That was my feeling, but for some reason I can't get him out of my mind."

Kevin tried to lighten the conversation.

"You know what? I'll bet he's got a uniform fetish. He's fascinated by you because you wear a uniform, but he's shy and can't admit it. If he did, you'd think he's weird."

Carol smiled, but she didn't laugh.

"I do think he's weird, but I never heard of anyone having a uniform fetish. Let's dig into your salad."

"Coming up. Thank goodness we don't have to set the table for your black bearded friend."

They had reason to remember Kevin's remark several days later. It would not be as funny as it seemed at the time.

CHAPTER 4

Carol chose not to mention 'black beard' to Deputy Sheriff Bridges, much less to the other members of her department. They would either assume that she was too quick to magnify the significance of such behavior or that she might actually be putting herself in harm's way. Sam would probably fall into the latter camp and urge her to abandon the plan to take her turn at patrolling the highways of Cumberland County. Ironically, however, it was Sam who first raised the issue, although he didn't realize that he had done so.

As they had agreed, he once more took charge of the squad meeting and gave everyone his assignments with dispatch. Then he caught up with Carol before she left and asked her to join him for another cup of coffee.

"What's the problem?" she asked as she resumed her seat.

"I'm not sure there is a problem. But I didn't want to bring this up in front of the guys."

"You're sounding very mysterious, Sam."

"I know, and I'm sure it's nothing. But I owe you a heads up. Yesterday afternoon a phone call came in from a man who didn't leave his name. In fact he called twice. Asked for you both times, but never told JoAnne what he needed to talk with you about. Said it was personal. But he did ask for your home address and number. She didn't give it to him, of course, and I guess he was upset, said you'd want her to help him reach you. When he called a second time, he insisted JoAnne put him through to her supervisor. I guess that's me, so I heard him out, explained our policy, told him I'd be glad to take a message if he'd give me a name."

"And he didn't."

"Right. He kept telling me he was a friend of yours and needed to find you, but for some reason he refused to tell me who he was. It was weird."

Weird. That had been Carol's term when she told Kevin about the man with the black beard who stared at her and had twice declined to introduce himself.

"Anything else?" she asked. "I mean can you describe him? Like his voice. Or whether he used abusive language. Did he sound agitated? Worried? I'm just trying to get a handle on what his problem might be."

"Kind of funny, when I think about it. He clearly wanted to get in touch with you, but I didn't have the feeling it was an emergency. He was kind of soft spoken, and you'd think if it was so important he'd have raised his voice. But he didn't."

Carol kept digging for clues to the man's identity.

"Did he have an accent of some kind? Not sure how to put this, but did he use proper English? You know, no 'ain'ts,' things like that."

"It was a pretty brief conversation, Carol. Not much chance to learn much about his educational background. But he's definitely a native speaker, and I'd hazard a guess that he's up on his grammar."

"Hmm." Carol was thinking.

"You have any idea who this guy might be?" Sam asked.

"I have no idea who he is," she said, "but I have an idea that I've met him. Like yesterday."

She didn't hit the road for another half hour, spending it instead telling Sam about her strange encounters with the man with the black beard and black windbreaker over the previous two days. As she had expected, he found her story alarming, especially when coupled with the phone calls to the office. But they agreed that they might be talking about two different people, and that it takes all types to make up this crazy world. When they parted, however, they also agreed to monitor closely all further efforts to contact the sheriff.

Unlike the day before, when the only challenge she faced concerned a flat tire, Carol did have to contend with several minor problems, including an underage driver, an out of date license plate, and a collision between a tractor and a sports car. But there was still time to reflect on 'black beard,' and she did a lot of reflecting.

For the first time since she had wrapped up her talk at the library, she found herself thinking that someone might be stalking her. It didn't seem likely. She ran through in her mind every kind of stalker she could think of: someone who can't accept rejection, someone who harbors a grievance, someone who is infatuated with another person. She couldn't imagine herself as the target of a stalker who fit any of these descriptions. But that didn't rule stalking out. After all, what do we know about what goes on in the minds of others?

By the time she had dealt with the underage driver and the car bearing an expired license plate, she had also poked a few holes in the stalker scenario. In the first place, it was really a stretch to call someone's presence at a public lecture an instance of stalking. It was, to the best of her knowledge, the first time she had ever seen the man. Moreover, the fact that he was the last member of the library audience to leave had many an innocent explanation. Somebody is always last out the door, and since when is that person thereby a prospective stalker? It was also true that it was she who had initiated the conversation on her walk back to her car. For all she knew, he was doing exactly what she was doing, returning to his car, which happened to be parked on the same street as hers.

And what about the fact that he had had lunch in the same place where she was eating the next day? Probably pure coincidence. How would he have known that she would be in the diner at that precise time? Because a sheriff's department patrol car was parked nearby? No, she was the sheriff, and the odds were that she would be in her office, not lunching in downtown Southport. Yes, but he had found her and he had stared at her. So what? For all she knew, so had others in the diner. A uniformed officer of the law probably draws attention wherever he - or she - goes. He probably had stared at her because he had only seen her the day before from the last row in a crowded room and on a dark street later that evening. He was curious, just as she was.

Carol idled at the stop light in Dickerson, waiting for a chance to turn east. Her thoughts turned to the phone calls and the fact that the caller, like 'black beard,' had not divulged his name. But that, too, could easily have been a coincidence. Two phone calls certainly don't constitute a pattern. Had she instead of JoAnne and Sam spoken to yesterday's caller, she might have a better idea of whether he sounded like 'black beard.' But she hadn't heard his phone voice. All in all, the more she thought about it, the stalker idea seemed a bit far fetched. Sam had told her just the previous summer, when she had been fixated on the Mobley case, that she tended to make mountains out of molehills. Actually, that wasn't quite the way he had put it, but she understood his point. She tended to become so invested in a case that she found problems where no problem existed. And here she was, almost a month into what had so far been a quiet summer, and there was no case on her agenda. No case, yet she was worried that she was being stalked. Was she trying to make a figment of her imagination into a case? A case in which she herself was a principal character?

CHAPTER 5

It was day four of Carol's self-imposed exile to highway patrol, and day five of Kevin's effort to overcome the writer's block that had begun to make him feel like Jack Nicholson in Stanley Kubrick's film *The Shining*. For Carol it was an uneventful day. For Kevin, on the other hand, it was not only another day devoid of inspiration, but one marked by constant interruptions.

The first of those interruptions came mid-morning when their neighbor, Gloria Snyder, called. That in itself was unusual, inasmuch as she lived next door and had long made it a habit to drop by unannounced rather than use the telephone.

"Kevin, it's me."

Kevin knew who 'me' was without asking. Nobody but Gloria Snyder managed to make everything she said sound as if she were about to share a momentous secret.

"Hi, Gloria, what's up?"

"I didn't dare come over because I thought he might see me. But I want you to go to a window and look out across your backyard. Be careful. Don't let him see you there - just sort of stand back of the curtain. Know what I mean?"

"I'm not sure I know what you're talking about. Who am I looking for?"

"For that man who's been hanging around. Didn't I tell you? Go take a look, but don't let him see you."

"You're talking about somebody in my backyard?"

"No, of course not. He wouldn't be as brazen as all that. Just take a look before he takes off. I'll stay on the line."

Kevin had no idea what this was all about, but he laid the phone down and went out to the kitchen window. He positioned himself behind the curtain, as Gloria had suggested. What he saw was his Toyota, a lawn that needed mowing, several cotoneaster shrubs he'd planted because they were alleged to attract butterflies, and the grill on which he had cooked their burgers the night before. In the distance, on the gravel road which provided access to the cottages on the point, sat a gray car which he thought was a Ford. A man was sitting at the wheel, and although Kevin could not be sure, he seemed to be studying a map. Or perhaps he was fiddling with the dial on the car radio. In any event, after only a few seconds the car began to move slowly down the gravel road in the direction of Meadowbrook.

True to her word, Gloria had stayed on the line.

"Did you see him?" she asked breathlessly when Kevin picked up the phone.

"You're talking about the man in the gray car?"

"Yes, just like yesterday. Do you know him?"

"I doubt it, but at that distance I couldn't tell. You've seen him before this morning?"

"Like I said, he was out there yesterday. I didn't think anything about it then. Figured he was just looking for a cottage and not sure of its number. But now he's back again, and both times he stopped right behind your place. You sure he doesn't look familiar?"

"I'm afraid not. He never left the car, and he didn't seem to be paying any attention to our place. He's probably lost, can't find the place he's looking for. I should have gone out to see if I could help."

"Well, I think he's suspicious. I'd be careful if I were you."

———

Kevin had briefly found himself wondering if the driver of the Ford might be the man whom Carol thought might be following her. But he quickly dismissed the thought. He could think of no reason why anyone would be resorting to such behavior. More likely that the man in the Ford was lost and trying to get his bearings. Kevin chided himself for going along with Gloria Snyder's fantasy when he should have gone out to the road and offered his assistance.

He returned to the study and tried to find inspiration that would free him from writer's block. He had made a couple of false starts when, at 3:20, the phone rang.

"Hello, this is Kevin."

Silence.

Another of those recorded solicitations, he thought, as he waited for the delayed sales pitch. But he heard nothing and hung up. It was at a quarter to four that the phone rang again.

"Kevin Whitman speaking," he said. Once again no one acknowledged him. But someone was there. Either that or he was imagining that he heard breathing.

"This is the Whitman residence." Perhaps the caller was hard of hearing, so he raised his voice. It did no good.

This time Kevin showed his frustration by returning the phone sharply to its cradle. Moreover, his interest in the article he was writing had suddenly disappeared. He would have to do something about these unwelcome robocalls. If they were robocalls. When the phone rang again for the third time in less than an hour, he was in no mood to be polite.

"Yes?"

When confronted again with silence, Kevin lost his temper.

"I don't know who you are, but I don't appreciate what you're doing. If you don't leave me alone, I'll report you."

He wasn't sure how reporting these calls would solve the problem. He wasn't even sure that someone had been on the other end of the line and had heard his probably meaningless threat. But he felt better. He also, and for the first time, felt that there might be something to Carol's story about being followed. The word that came to mind was stalker. His wife, the sheriff of Cumberland County, was being stalked.

CHAPTER 6

Carl Keller stared at himself in the mirror. He didn't like what he saw. What he saw was a failure, a 45 year old man who had never come close to achieving what his high school yearbook had predicted for him: Most Likely to Succeed. If proof were needed that he had fallen far short of becoming his graduating class's golden boy, it could be found in the room in which he was at that moment trimming his beard. It was the bathroom of a third rate motel, struggling to stay in business after construction of the Hopewell bypass. By comparison, the Bates Motel looked like the Ritz.

The paint on the walls was peeling, the plumbing was old and unreliable, and it was obvious that the owner was not about to spruce the place up. Carl was not staying at the *Welcome Inn* because it was welcoming. He was staying there because it was cheap. It was also close to Crooked Lake, although it was closer as the crow flies than it was by the roads he had to traverse in order to get there. He had been in the *Welcome Inn* now for seven days, and in that time he had shared the motel with only four others, and none of them had stayed for more than a night.

He put his shaving gear back in his dopp kit, cupped his hands under the faucet and splashed water on his face, and returned to the bare bones sleeping and sitting room, where he flopped down on the bed. It was too soon to head back to the lake, and he wasn't even sure just what he was going to do when he got there. He turned on the TV and punched the remote until he located ESPN. The room to which he had first been given a key had a malfunctioning set, but the owner, or whoever it was who registered guests, had apologized and let him try other rooms. Number 8 was no better than its neighbors in other respects, but at least he could watch television.

Unfortunately, Carl had never been an athlete nor was he very much interested in sports. He had turned to ESPN simply because he couldn't stand the insipid morning fare on shows like *Good Morning America* and *Today*. After watching five minutes of replays of walk off home runs and fielding gems, he switched off the set and closed his eyes. And contemplated his own life.

He had done it many times, and he always began at the beginning. The reason was clear: his early life had been, or so it seemed in retrospect, idyllic. He had been an only child on whom his parents had lavished not only affection but gifts that had made him the envy of his playmates. Good grades had come easily, and he had become an eagle scout before his fifteenth birthday. Best of all he had won deserved praise in high school for the leading roles he had played in virtually every play the drama club had staged, ranging from Shakespeare's 'Midsummer Night's Dream' to Wilde's 'The Importance of Being Earnest.' He had even won the county's prestigious speaking contest in his senior year for his delivery of Hamlet's famous 'To be or not to be' soliloquy.

He had always been good with words. He remembered thinking that when he spoke, even archaic language became intelligible to others.

Hamlet's words, still familiar after all these years, came to mind, and he found himself silently reciting them.

To be or not to be - that is the question.
Whether 'tis nobler in the mind to suffer
The slings and arrows of outrageous fortune
Or to take arms against a sea of troubles
And by opposing end them. To die, to sleep -

He knew what came next, but he didn't say it. Not even to himself. He opened his eyes and sat up on the bed. And cursed Hamlet.

Replaying the newsreel of his life was always a pleasant experience until he reached the point when he earned his law degree and became a member of the New York bar. It actually wasn't bad for the first few years thereafter, but he knew that those first few years had simply been stepping stones which led to his joining the firm of Morgenstern and Brauchli. And that had been a disaster. It was all because of Morgenstern and Brauchli that he had come to Crooked Lake and was holed up in a miserable motel, trying to screw his courage to the sticking point and take action to regain control of his life. But his courage had failed him. He was paralyzed by indecision. He had used Hamlet's memorable words to win a coveted prize when he was only 17. Now he was 45, and the Dane's great character flaw, captured in those same words, had become his own.

He did not feel like reviewing the events which had led Morgenstern and Brauchli to sack him. For that matter, the fault did not lay in the hands of those two gentlemen, both of whom had died well before he had been hired by the firm. It had been the current senior partner, Francis Foster, who had shown him the door. And Carl knew that he himself was not entirely blameless. But he not only no longer had a job; his prospects for resuming the practice of law had been reduced to close to zero. His situation could hardly be worse had he been disbarred. A grave injustice had been done, and he should be doing something about it.

That he had come to Crooked Lake was due to an irony. His name was very similar to that of another member of the Albany law firm, something he had discovered the day he joined Morgenstern and Brauchli. She was Carol Kelleher, he was Carl Keller. He had initially found this amusing, as had she. But it provided an excuse for them to see more of each other than might otherwise have been the case, considering that she had been with the firm for several years and he was its most junior member. Unfortunately, Ms. Kelleher disappeared less than three months after he arrived, having accepted a position as sheriff of Cumberland County. He had been puzzled by her decision. The practice of law in a prestigious firm seemed much more attractive to him than trying to maintain law and order in the rural hinterland of western New York state.

But that had been almost a decade ago, and he had pretty much forgotten about it until this spring, when events conspired to place his career in jeopardy. He had run across her name on a case he was researching several weeks earlier, and it occurred to him that he might track her down and enlist her help. By the time he got around to doing so, however, it was late June and he had wasted valuable time. It had been no problem ascertaining that she was still serving as sheriff, and he should have called her, reintroduced himself, and made plans for them to meet. Instead, he had once again dithered. It was not until he had moved into the *Welcome Inn* that he finally became proactive, and that came about because he spotted a poster in downtown Southport announcing that Sheriff Kelleher would be speaking at the local library.

When he took a seat in the library's meeting room that evening, it had been his intention to say hello to his former colleague at the end of the evening. To his surprise, he reacted to her presentation in a way he had not anticipated. He had expected her to be well prepared, at ease as she explained what it was like to do her job, and she had not disappointed him. But he wasn't just impressed. He was awed. In the span of little more than an hour Carol Kelleher had not only become someone who might help him with the great problem of his life. She had, paradoxically, become a person he knew he would have trouble talking to.

All of a sudden he knew that he could not approach her, tell her what had happened to him, seek her legal guidance. He was sure he would make a fool of himself. She would be polite, even pleasant, but she would wish him well and move on, leaving him much more miserable than he had been when he took his seat in the back row of the library meeting room. For a few brief minutes at the end of her speech he had stayed seated, trying to find the courage to approach her. It hadn't worked. He had followed her as she walked to her car, but he did so without a plan, and when she stopped and spoke to him he had experienced a moment of sheer panic.

She had not recognized him that night, nor had she done so the following day when he happened upon her in the diner in Southport. The heavy beard, which he had adopted a year earlier, provided a good disguise, and she would remember him dressed in a suit, not Levis and a windbreaker. His efforts to learn more about her - whether she had a husband, where she lived - had initially been unsuccessful, but in less than two days he had discovered that she was married to a college professor and that they lived in a cottage on the West Lake Road. His curiosity as to what the professor looked like had not yet been satisfied.

Enough of this, Keller thought. He was still playing Hamlet, doing nothing that would either rectify what had happened at the law firm or bring Carol Kelleher back into his life. He would accomplish neither objective unless he got the hell out of the *Welcome Inn*. He poked around in his suitcase until he found a clean shirt, and ten minutes later he climbed into the grey Ford and set off for the lake. What he would do when he got there, he hadn't decided.

CHAPTER 7

His indecisive and ineffectual pursuit of the sheriff came to an abrupt and embarrassing end that very day. It happened because both he and Carol Kelleher were not quite themselves that morning. Normally attentive to such things as the state of his gas tank, Carl Keller was preoccupied with other matters, with the result that the tank ran dry on the upper lake road about six miles short of Cumberland. In the sheriff's case, she was completing the week in which she and deputy sheriff Bridges had swapped places. While her former colleague at Morgenstern and Brauchli was sitting behind the wheel on the roadside, cursing his bad luck, she was rolling west on the same road, regretting that she had ever had the bad idea of seeing what highway patrol felt like.

As Carol came around a bend in the road just west of Kelly's Corners, she saw a car on the opposite shoulder ahead of her. The vehicle didn't appear to be in distress, so she made no attempt to slow down but waved good morning as she passed. It wasn't until the car was almost out of sight in her rear view mirror that she remembered Kevin's story of the night before about Gloria Snyder and the gray Ford. The car she had passed was gray. It was also, unmistakably, a Ford. There was no reason to go back, of course. Gray Fords must be a dime a dozen, and both she and Kevin had gotten a laugh out of Gloria's overheated imagination. Nevertheless, Carol, as always, was preternaturally curious.

She used the nearest farm road to turn around. The Ford, less than half a mile away, was still on the shoulder. The driver, who had probably only pulled off the road to enjoy the scenery, might be alarmed to see the patrol car approaching again. But it was too late to change her mind. She slowed to a crawl and eased in behind the Ford.

"Good morning," she said in a cheery voice as she came along side the open window on the driver's side. "Everything okay?"

The words were no sooner out of her mouth than she realized that the person at the wheel was the black bearded man she had seen in the library and the diner. Seen and spoken to.

The look on his face was one she doubted she would ever forget. The driver was in a state of panic when there didn't seem to be any reason why he should be. The fleeting thought that he had drugs stashed in the trunk crossed her mind, but she put the thought aside and resumed her role as a friendly local cop.

"I believe we've met," she said. "Didn't you attend my talk at the library in Southport the other night?"

Carol chose not to mention the diner and the fact that he had rudely stared at her over lunch.

"Yes, I did hear you speak," he admitted. "It was a nice talk. Look, I'm all right, I just ran out of gas. Stupid of me. Maybe you can tell me if there's a gas station close by, close enough I could walk to it."

It was obvious that the black bearded man wished to take care of his problem himself. It was equally obvious that he knew that the sheriff would insist on giving him a ride to a gas station.

"Bad luck, huh?" she said. "No need to walk. Hop in and I'll give you a lift."

"It's not necessary. You're busy and I'm not."

"Come on, get in. It's about six miles to the nearest station. Besides, my department exists to help people."

He knew better than to make an issue out of it. Reluctantly, he got out of the Ford, locked the door, and started to climb into the back seat of the patrol car.

"Not back there," Carol insisted. "Up here. Much easier for us to talk."

It was going to be just like the other two times she had spoken to him. Unless, that is, she didn't let him get away with it.

"I take it you're not from around here," she said as they set off for Cumberland.

"No, just visiting." He lapsed into silence.

Visiting from where? Visiting whom? Who are you? It was going to be like pulling the proverbial hen's teeth.

"You know, you don't have to be shy where I'm concerned. People around here think I'm an easy conversationalist. Try me. Why not tell me your name?"

"You wouldn't know me. I'm from Albany, and that's a long drive on the thruway."

"I know Albany," Carol said, encouraged by this bit of information. "In fact, I used to live there."

And then it came to her. She did know this man, or at least she was willing to bet that she did. Perhaps it was that it was a warmer day and he wasn't wearing the black windbreaker. In any event, Albany was the connection. When her companion in the front seat didn't add to the fact that he lived in Albany, Carol decided to confront him with what she thought she knew.

"Funny thing, but I had a feeling the night we met - after the talk at the library, that is. I had the feeling I knew you, but I just couldn't think how or where. But it was in Albany. When I was with a law firm there. And you were, too. Tell me, aren't you Carl Keller?"

Carol rarely took her eyes off the road ahead of her, but at that moment she violated this important first rule of safe driving.

It was Carl Keller. He didn't say so, nor did he nod in the affirmative. But she knew she was right. The only question was why he was so reluctant to admit it, so reluctant to make an effort to renew an old relationship, especially one which had been friendly, even if it had also been brief.

When he didn't speak, Carol tried an approach which she hoped would encourage him to open up.

"It's been quite a few years, hasn't it? We were just getting to know each other when I decided to try sheriffing over here on the lake. I remember the coincidence of our names. So close, weren't they? And still are, for that matter. It's the beard that fooled me."

Carl shifted his position, the better to observe her.

"I didn't want to take advantage of the fact that we'd known each other," he said. "That was almost like another lifetime. You'd moved on, I hadn't. Ten years is a long time."

"But those years have gone by awfully fast," she said. "I used to think that I'd traded in an exhausting job for an easy one. You know, 80 hour work weeks, keeping Mr. Foster happy. But being sheriff's not a breeze. By the way, is Foster still riding herd on you guys?"

She thought that he had relaxed a bit, that he was now willing to have a conversation. But he didn't answer her question. It occurred to her that perhaps he, too, had left the firm, was now doing something else with his life.

"Sorry. I was assuming you're still with the firm, but maybe I'm wrong. What are you up to now?"

"Let's not talk about the firm, okay? I'm not practicing law any more. Not a big deal. I'm sort of between jobs at the moment."

There was something in the way that he spoke that made 'between jobs' sound like something less than a carefully thought out career change. It might even explain his reticence to talk with her, although she couldn't imagine why. Carl Keller was certainly not acting like the same extrovert she remembered.

By the time they reached the gas station at the western edge of Cumberland, the conversation had drifted into inconsequential small talk. Carol had abandoned her effort to get him to talk about himself, although her curiosity had not abated. Quite the contrary. Had Carl Keller been the one who had twice called her office but declined to give his name? Had he been the one whose car had idled out back of the lake cottage on two different occasions? Had he been the one who had been ringing up the cottage and then saying nothing when Kevin answered the phone? He had certainly followed her down a dark Southport street after attending her library talk. He had certainly come into the Southport diner where she was having lunch and watched her from his stool at the end of the counter.

Had he been stalking her? It made no sense, yet if, in addition to the library and diner episodes, he had been the one making the phone calls and sitting in his car behind their cottage, he might be a stalker. But why? What he said on the trip back to the Ford with a container full of gas was even less revealing than what he had said on the way over to Cumberland. When Carol left him to resume her last day on highway patrol, she had made up her mind that the first thing she was going to do when she got back to the office was to call her old law firm in Albany and make inquiries about Carl Keller.

CHAPTER 8

Carol got back to the office too late to place a call to Morgenstern and Brauchli. She was sure somebody would be there. Several somebodies were always there after hours when she had been with the firm, she herself frequently among them. But she didn't want to talk with just anybody. Chances were that if she waited until the following morning she'd be sure to find Gretchen Ziegler, her best friend from the Albany days. Gretchen had been of some help when she was dealing with the case of the priest who had ended up as a scarecrow, and she would be most likely to speak candidly about why Carl Keller had left the firm.

She would have liked to have Gretchen's report in hand when she told Kevin about Carl Keller, but she knew he would be intrigued to hear that she now knew who her 'stalker' was, even if she didn't know why he was following her. In fact, Kevin might actually find her story more interesting if Keller were still, like Churchill's Russia, a riddle wrapped in a mystery inside an enigma. It would give him more opportunity to let his imagination run wild, something he tended to do annually when something out of the ordinary happened on Crooked Lake.

To her surprise, when she got back to the cottage she found that her husband was in what for him was a grumpy mood. His welcome home kiss seemed more perfunctory than usual.

"You okay?" she asked.

"I guess so," he told her, but it was not a reassuring answer.

"How about something to drink? I need a pick me up, and it sounds like you may need one, too."

That got his attention.

"You had a bad day, too?"

"Not exactly, but a strange one. I'll share it with you if you tell me what happened on the home front."

"I'm sorry, Carol. And I'm really okay. But somehow today I realized for the first time just how old I am."

"Oh, come on. You just recently crossed the fifty threshold. That's young by contemporary standards."

"Feelings trump facts. You know that. It's all because of Jennifer Laseur."

Carol scowled.

"Jennifer Laseur? You're feeling old because of Jennifer Laseur? Who's she?"

She had a suddenly uncomfortable feeling that she'd been taking Kevin for granted.

"You remember," he said, sounding weary, "she was that girl who was my teaching assistant, the one who had a crush on me. The one who tried to break us up. It was the year after we met, the year when that woman's body was discovered up in the ravine."

Carol was thinking back to a time when their relationship was on much less solid footing than it was today. She remembered the dead woman in the ravine, and the murderer who wasn't Beckham. She hadn't remembered the name, but she had no trouble recalling that Kevin's teaching assistant had tried to undermine her relationship with him. What is it? Had she come back into his life?

"So what's up with you and this Jennifer person?"

"Nothing, except that she reminds me of my age."

"Is she mounting another attack on our relationship?" She tried to make a joke of the question, but she only managed to sound anxious.

"Nothing like that. I'm sure she's forgotten all about me. But a colleague down at the college called to inform me that he read that Miss Laseur is making her Carnegie Hall debut next month. How's that for a downer?"

"A downer? It sounds like she's making good."

"Yes, and at a ripe young age. She can't be more than 25."

"What's so remarkable about that? I thought you once told me Mozart was writing operas when he was barely into his teens."

"I know. There are child prodigies and then there's Jennifer Laseur. She was my student, my t.a., just a few years ago. Now she's about to become a world famous violinist. In a year's time everybody in the music world will know who she is. And how many people in the music world know who I am? Twenty? Twenty-five? All I do is teach and write papers that nobody reads."

This was a Kevin Whitman that Carol didn't know.

"Come on, Kevin, why so hard on yourself? You're good at what you do. You're even a good sleuth, and you never took a degree in sleuthing. How many people outside of Cumberland County know who I am? And you're not old. Are you listening? Repeat after me, I'm not old, I'm not old."

"But I am, and we both know it. Old and stale. Even if I could smuggle a course on rock opera past the dean - you know, stuff like Pink Floyd's 'The Wall' - I'd lay an egg. The kids all know it - Whitman thinks opera died with Puccini, and he's been gone for almost a century."

Carol had had enough of this.

"If you'll excuse me, I'm going to change out of this uniform. When I'm more comfortable, I'd like to tell you about what happened to me today."

Without another word, she scooted down the hall and into the bedroom. When she came back, she was wearing a pair of black shorts and a bright yellow tank top.

"Now come here and sit down and I'll tell you all about the guy who's been stalking me."

"You found out who he is?" Kevin sounded surprised.

"I did, and if you'll forget about little Miss Laseur for a few minutes I'll bring you up to date. In fact, you'll be the first to hear who's interested in your wife, because I haven't said a word to Bridges or any of the guys."

"How about something to drink?" Kevin said, sounding somewhat more animated this time.

"I thought you would never ask, and the answer is yes. I'll have whatever you're having."

For some reason, he selected beer rather than wine.

"Thank you. Now sit down and we'll talk about Carl Keller rather than Jennifer Laseur."

For the next half hour, Carol recounted the story of the man in the gray Ford who had conveniently run out of gas on a road she was patrolling. By the time she had finished her report, Kevin looked to have gotten out of his funk.

"He didn't say anything at all to give you a clue as to what he's doing?" he asked.

"Not a word. But I think in some funny way he wanted to get my attention, wanted me to know who he was. Like I said, I hope to know more after I talk with Ziegler, but I've got a hunch that he's in some kind of trouble and has latched onto me as a way out of his trouble. I may be dead wrong. Maybe he's really been stalking me. But we'd both found the similarity in our names amusing. It had unquestionably brought us closer together when we were in the firm. Of course that didn't last long."

"Did you date this guy Keller back then?"

Carol smiled to herself. Kevin wondering about what role Keller had played in her life, just as she had wondered about Jennifer Laseur's role in Kevin's life.

"Sorry to disappoint you, but he never asked me out. We were just two busy attorneys, racking up billing hours for the firm."

"Do you plan on trying to get reacquainted?"

"I have no idea. It depends on what Gretchen tells me. In any event, he never told me where he's living - or staying. If he now lives in this area, he might turn up in the phone directory. Tell you what. Why don't you see if you can find if Carl Keller's listed?"

"Good idea."

Kevin went into the study and leafed through the slim volume containing phone numbers of people in the surrounding communities.

"Several Kellers, but none of them go by Carl," he announced.

"That's what I figured. But I'm not sure what if anything it proves."

"We were just talking about the Beckham case," Kevin said. "Remember that you had me scouring the phone directory for him, too?"

"Actually, the way I remember it we didn't know whether we were looking for a Beckham or a Becker or something along those lines."

This got them reminiscing about the case of the woman in the ravine, the second murder to bring them together. By the end of the evening, Kevin didn't feel nearly as old as he had earlier. And Carol had a much better sleep than she had expected to have when Kevin started talking about Jennifer Laseur.

CHAPTER 9

Carol had said good-bye before Kevin was fully awake the next morning, but she had tried to make it clear that she would not tolerate any more of his 'old and stale' complaints that evening.

"Do you hear me?" she had said as she shook her husband.

"Whatever you say, dear," had been his mumbled reply.

"No, it's not what I say. You say it!"

"Okay, I'll be young again." He then rolled over and pulled the blankets up around his head.

As she drove to Cumberland, Carol shifted her focus to what she needed to say to Gretchen Ziegler. She realized that she hadn't been in touch with Gretchen in almost five months, and that she should be doing a better job of maintaining contacts with old friends who had dropped out of sight.

Whoever answered the phone at Morgenstern and Brauchli was not someone she remembered from her years with the firm. There had probably been considerable turnover. While waiting for Gretchen to pick up, she found herself wondering whether any of the young attorneys she had known had made partner, and if so which ones. This train of thought was broken up by a loud, cheery voice.

"Carol! Long time, no hear from you. Of course, I haven't been any better. How are things over there?"

"Things are fine. Not all the people are, however, which is why I'm calling. By the way, how is your mother doing?" She had almost forgotten that Gretchen's mother had been hospitalized the last time she had talked with her.

"So so. At least she's out of the nursing home, and her spirits are much better."

They chatted briefly about personal matters, but apparently Gretchen had to be in court at 10, so Carol turned to the reason for her call.

"I'm interested in Carl Keller," she said. "I ran into him yesterday, which in itself is surprising. I wasn't sure what he was doing in our neck of the woods. He tells me he's no longer practicing law, but he didn't elaborate. He seemed reluctant to talk about why he left the firm, so I thought I'd ask you for an update."

"He didn't tell you anything?" Gretchen asked.

"I'm afraid not. In fact, I now realize that I'd seen him on a couple of other occasions recently, but frankly, if you can believe this, I hadn't even recognized him. He'd grown a heavy beard, and - well, you know how it is. It's easy not to recognize people you don't know all that well, especially when you aren't expecting to see them."

"Would it be all right, Carol, if I called you at home tonight about this?"

"Oh, I'm sorry. You've got a court date."

"No, that's not it. I'd just feel better not to be talking about Carl while I'm here in the office. You understand?"

Carol wasn't sure she understood, but she had no intention of pressing Gretchen on it. Obviously, this was a sensitive subject, one not to be discussed when and where others might overhear.

"Of course. I'll be home all evening." She gave her her cell number, told her she appreciated the call back, and said good-bye. Not surprisingly, she spent most of the rest of the morning thinking about the fact that Gretchen hadn't wanted to discuss Carl Keller from her law firm office. She tried to rein in her imagination, but various explanations for Carl's strange behavior and its relationship to his leaving the firm kept popping into her mind. It was an unproductive use of her time, and eventually she turned her attention back to the affairs of Cumberland County. It was her first day back from highway patrol, and while Sam had taken care of business, a few issues had arisen that he had deferred until she resumed her proper role.

When she arrived back home, Carol found Kevin in a much better frame of mind than he had been the night before.

"I see you're young again," she said as they retreated to the deck.

"I deliver on my promises." He stood up and performed a bad pirouette. "Notice anything different?"

"Only that you have no balletic talent."

"I was trying to show off my new outfit. New duds for a new man."

It took Carol only a few seconds to realize that she hadn't seen his polo shirt before.

"You went shopping," she said, "and you decided that being young means being gaudy."

"You don't like it?"

"Let's just say that it's rather loud. But it goes with your smile, so I won't complain."

"Good. I also picked up a new pair of swimming trunks. They're loud, too."

It wasn't until eight o'clock that Carol's cell rang. It was, as promised, Gretchen Ziegler.

"Excuse me," she said to Kevin. "It's Gretchen. I'll take it in the den."

She settled into what was usually Kevin's chair and put her feet up on the ottoman.

"Thanks for getting back to me. I gather that Keller's a sensitive subject at the firm."

"Definitely. You said that you've seen Carl several times but that he's in disguise."

"I have no idea whether the beard is a disguise. I suppose that would depend on whether he's pulling some kind of disappearing act. Anyway, I've seen him three times. He came to a talk I gave at a public library, and then he had lunch at the same diner where I was eating. I spoke to him briefly both times, but I didn't recognize him and he didn't seem to want to talk. Then I saw him yesterday, and he had no choice but to talk. I happened to spot him where he'd run out of gas, and drove him to a gas station. That's when I finally recognized him, and when he told me he'd given up law. So all I know about Carl is that he's in the Crooked Lake area, that he's no longer with the firm, and that he's been following me."

"Following you but not explaining why?"

"Following me but obviously not wanting me to know he was doing it." She explained the mysterious phone calls and the car idling behind the cottage. "What's the problem with Carl and the firm?"

"It's a complicated story, Carol. It'll take awhile. In fact, I think we'd do better if we could get together to discuss this. I'd suggest that you come over to Albany and join me for lunch, but I know you're busy. If you're really worried about what Carl is up to, and it sounds like you are, we really should talk. What if I could come over there

48

this weekend? I'd love to see you, and while I doubt I could explain Carl's behavior, I could bring you up to date on what happened to him at the firm."

"I hate to impose on your time, but if you think you can get away, I'd be grateful. I've never been stalked before, and while I'm not really worried, I'm sure puzzled."

"You actually think Carl's been stalking you?" Gretchen sounded concerned.

"That's probably too melodramatic, but what he's been doing is definitely not normal, considering that I thought we were friends when I left the firm."

"Would it be okay if I came over Sunday afternoon? You pick the time."

"How would a late lunch be, say two? You could meet my husband, bring along a bathing suit if you'd like to. The lake's only a hop, skip and a jump from the cottage."

"Sounds good. I may not be able to solve your puzzle, but I'm sure you'll be interested in why Foster fired Carl."

CHAPTER 10

Carol met Gretchen in the yard when her car pulled in next to the Toyota and gave her a big hug.

"You look like lawyering's still agreeing with you."

"Most of the time," Gretchen said, "but you'll notice a little gray at the temples."

"It happens to all of us," Carol said, "even us blondes. We just hide it better, and longer. Come on in and I'll introduce my professor."

At that moment Kevin stepped out onto the back porch.

"Ms. Ziegler," he said. "At last we meet."

"Hi." He put out his hand, but she brushed it away and gave him a hug. "You look every bit as good as advertised."

Kevin blushed at the compliment. Their visitor also lived up to Carol's description. Tall, slender, raven hair, a perfect face marred only by a port wine birthmark beneath her left ear. He was willing to bet that opposing lawyers didn't like to be pitted against her in court.

"It's been a long drive, so how about a swim before lunch?" he asked her.

"That's an offer I can't refuse. Glad you suggested I bring my suit," she said to Carol.

It wasn't long before the three of them were enjoying the lake off the end of the dock. Carol finally had to remind them that the afternoon would be gone before they got around to Carl Keller if they didn't get out of the water. It was close to three when they sat down to a cold lunch and first addressed the reason for Gretchen's trip from Albany.

"You understand that you're free to say anything in front of Kevin," Carol said. "He's a gifted keeper of secrets."

"I never doubted it," their visitor said. "I suspect you wouldn't have married him otherwise."

"Actually, I kept him at arms' length for five years just to make sure."

It was at about this point in the conversation that Kevin might have raised a question about Gretchen's husband, had not Carol given him a heads up that men weren't her thing.

"So," the lawyer began, "I'm supposed to disentangle the knotty tale of Carl Keller's departure from Morgenstern and Brauchli. And it is knotty, and, to be quite honest, delicate. It's really a case study in how not to practice law, or something like that. The unfortunate thing, for Carl at least, is that while he's the sacrificial lamb, there's a lot of blame to go around. I'm sure you can't imagine what I'm talking about, but I think you'll see why I decided that a face to face conversation would be much better than the telephone."

"This doesn't sound like the firm I knew, always so staid and buttoned down."

"Well, I guess it just proves that life is full of surprises. Even at old M & B. I doubt that what happened to us is ever going to be a the subject of some law school lecture, but it's certainly a cautionary tale. You want to take notes?"

"I hope it isn't quite that complex," Carol said. "I'll trust Kevin to keep track of names."

"Okay. Let's start with Randall Truscott. He was charged with aggravated assault back in the late winter, and Carl Keller got the assignment of defending him. Truscott's a pretty well-to-do 40-something with a reputation for having a quick temper. Something got him all riled up and he took it out on his girlfriend. Her name's Donna Sugar and rumor has it that she may have been a highly successful call girl. Keep that in mind - I'll get back to it later. I never saw her, but Carl told me she's a stunner, except for the fact that her face was a mess after Truscott got through with her."

"What made the charge aggravated assault instead of the ordinary kind?" Carol asked.

"Apparently he didn't use a weapon, but he did break ribs and caused internal bleeding. Anyway, the trial was slow getting off the ground, like they usually are, but it seemed to be moving right along until Carl decided to go after Sugar's reputation. He'd done some research, figured that she was no angel. You know, it takes two to tango. Unfortunately, the judge put a quick halt to that strategy when he ruled that the evidence Carl wanted in was either prejudicial or hearsay. Mostly both. Carl, of course, was upset, but he made matters worse when he kept right on looking for ways to get that evidence on the record. Eventually, the judge cited him for contempt of court, and then the fat was really in the fire."

"By the way, who's this judge?"

"Sorry, I should have mentioned his name, because it turns out to be pretty important. Lindsay Hartman. Remember him?"

"I sure do," Carol said. "If you liked him, he ran a tight ship. If you didn't, he was a mean old bastard. I don't know it for a fact, but I think I recall that he owns a summer place here on Crooked Lake. Do you know anything about that?"

"I'm afraid not. Anyway, it wasn't long before Carl found himself between the proverbial rock and a hard place. Not only was Hartman down on him. So was our good friend Francis Foster."

Carol interrupted to tell Kevin that Foster was the senior partner who managed the law firm.

"What was Foster's problem?" she asked.

"He made it clear that his people weren't going to be cited for contempt of court. 'We're not going to make a habit of alienating judges,' was the way he put it. And he has a point. But it's more complicated than alienating any old judge. Hartman happens to have been a classmate of Foster's at Harvard Law, and they've remained good friends. So Carl not only got under Hartman's hide. In doing so, he irritated his boss at M & B."

"I'm beginning to understand why Carl is no longer practicing law," Carol observed.

"The jury convicted Truscott, and Hartman sentenced him to three years. But the most interesting thing about this whole affair is that Keller kept right on digging, and he decided that Hartman himself might have had an affair with Sugar, the lovely call girl, back before she took up with Truscott. I won't pretend to comment on that, but whether Carl's right or wrong, Foster had had enough of him to send him packing. So I think you can see how things lined up. Carl thinks that Hartman might have ruled against him to protect his relationship with Sugar, and that Foster kicked him out of the firm to protect Hartman."

"Life must be really exciting over in Albany," Carol said. "It sounds like you're living in a hornet's nest."

"I think most of us are keeping our heads down," Gretchen said. "Foster will never win a popularity contest, but everyone knows which side our bread is buttered on. Besides, Carl was stupid to antagonize the judge. Not to mention the fact that if he were to go public with this allegation about Hartman and Sugar, it would be very hard to prove. If he wants to take down the judge, you were in this business long enough to know that the dice are stacked against him."

"Do you know anything about Carl's so-called evidence?" Carol asked.

"Nothing at all."

"When did Foster give Carl his walking papers?"

"I don't know whether Carl ever took his idea about Hartman and Sugar to Foster. In any event, Carl was gone before the rest of us heard anything about the judge and the Sugar woman."

Kevin spoke up for the first time since the gazpacho.

"Did Keller say anything to you about his firing before he left?"

"What happened was that Foster sent us a memo which simply said that Carl Keller had resigned and that Morgenstern and Brauchli wished him well. Carl said nothing, other than good-bye when he cleaned out his office. It was obvious that he was steamed, but he chose not to talk about it. None of us were fooled. We knew he'd been sacked, and, as you can imagine, it was very awkward."

"No word as to what he was going to do?"

"Nothing. He was there one day and then gone the next. I remember thinking if you'd still been there, Carol, he might have shared some of his thoughts. As it was, it was the quickest exit I've ever seen."

"I've been thinking about the fact that Judge Hartman has a place on Crooked Lake," Carol said. "At least I think he does, and I'll check into it tomorrow. That could give Carl his reason for hanging around over here, although I'm not quite sure what he thinks he's going to accomplish."

Gretchen considered the idea.

"It's possible that he thinks he might enlist you in his campaign to expose Hartman."

"If that's what he's up to," Kevin said, "he's certainly going about it in the wrong way. I wouldn't think you'd be stalking the person whose help you're seeking."

"Is that really what he's been doing?"

"I don't know," Carol admitted. "But if he wants my help, he's got a funny way of saying so. In light of what you've told us, I can imagine that he might be stalking the judge. But why me?"

"So what are you going to do?" Gretchen asked.

"I guess I'd like to get him to sit down with me and tell me what he's up to. Trouble is, I have no idea where he's staying, how to reach him. For all I know, he'll be even harder to smoke out now that he knows I know who he is. So much for Keller and Kelleher striking up a special relationship."

The conversation drifted away from Keller, Hartman, and the Truscott case and back to recollections of old times at Morgenstern and Brauchli. By the time that Gretchen Ziegler left for her return trip to Albany, it was obvious that she wouldn't make it until after dark. Carol and Kevin talked about what they had learned that afternoon until it was time to hit the sack. They both agreed that it was interesting, but that it hadn't explained the strange behavior of Carl Keller.

CHAPTER 11

Tony Ferraro sat on the edge of the couch in the living room of his apartment. He looked at his watch for the third time in five minutes, wondering if he was going to be stood up by a prostitute. He mentally corrected himself: by a call girl. Of course call girls are really prostitutes. He knew that. But he also knew that he wouldn't be sitting here, nervously awaiting a knock on the door, if the person he was expecting were an ordinary prostitute. Tony was nervous because he had never done something like this in his 47 years on earth. Until recently the thought of doing what he was about to do would have been unthinkable. He had always been a devout Catholic, and until the previous fall he had been happily married to his high school sweetheart. But Karen had surprised him by announcing one beautiful September day that she wanted a divorce. The announcement had floored him, but after three sessions with a marriage counsellor and a lot of painful thought he had given his consent and the result had been a no fault divorce settlement. Their two children, now young adults, had already left the nest, and at the moment were elsewhere, starting their own lives.

His watch now told him that it was 9:23. They had agreed on 9:15. Perhaps this was what call girls did, arriving when it suited them, perhaps doing it intentionally to keep the men in their lives off balance. If so, this one was succeeding. He had seen the evening as an adventure, an opportunity to break out of his months long celibacy, to do something daring. The idea had come to him when he and Carl Keller, a fellow attorney at Morgenstern and Brauchli, had taken a break to step out for a cup of coffee. Carl was just beginning to recover from the conviction of a client for aggravated assault and his own citation for contempt of court by the judge in that case.

The suggestion of a coffee break that day had had the purpose of trying to cheer Carl up. Carl had been giving vent to his feelings about Judge Lindsay Hartman when he suddenly went off subject and began talking about Donna Sugar.

'She's really something else,' he had said. 'She'd sit there in court, a smug look on her face, while the prosecution made mince meat of my client. I tried to level the playing field, and she still had that same look on her face.

'She was cocksure which way the jury would decide. I think she was laughing at me all the way. And what do you do with a witness like that? Five feet tall, maybe ninety pounds. Dressed to cover up her physical assets. And then that face, still looking like she'd had a close encounter with a door. She winced every time she stepped in or out of the box. I'll bet she'd practiced that until she had it down pat.'

Tony had listened patiently while his colleague got his frustration with Sugar off his chest. It was obvious that Keller disliked the woman, but he himself had reacted differently. She sounded poised, intelligent, attractive if one discounted the lingering discoloration of her face. It wasn't until Keller disclosed his hunch that the judge might have had an affair with Ms. Sugar, however, that he had surprised himself by asking if Carl knew how he might get in touch with her.

'You want to call her?' Carl had asked. 'Why, for God's sake, would you want to do that?'

'I'd like to meet her, that's all. She sounds interesting,' had been his response.

'If I were you, I'd stay away from her - far away,' Carl had said. 'She's poison. Look where my client ended up.'

But Tony had not been deterred. The fact that she might have shared a bed with a judge only made the prospect of spending a night with her even more attractive. He'd been living in a rut for months, and here was an opportunity to get out of that rut. But where was this woman who was going to recharge his batteries?

When the knock on the door finally came, Tony almost upset the highball he'd been nursing. He took a deep breath, collected himself, and made his way to the door.

"Mr. Ferraro, I presume," said the diminutive woman as she stepped into the room. It was a familiar greeting, although Tony couldn't remember the context. Carl hadn't done justice to Ms. Sugar. She was beautiful. Whether her face had fully recovered from Randall Truscott's battering or she had carefully masked the bruises with makeup, he didn't know. Or care. What he did know was that he was in the presence of a striking woman and that he had done the right thing to ignore Carl's admonition to stay away from her.

"Please call me Tony. And may I call you Donna?"

"You may. There's no need to be formal. You have a lovely place."

This wasn't true, but it was nice of her to say so. He had never done much to replace the things that Karen had taken with her when she moved out. But this evening he had kept the lighting low and he had put on what he thought of as seductive music.

"What can I get you to drink?" This was the first time he had been on what used to be called a date in at least thirty years, and in spite of the thought he had given to what he should say and do, he was nervous. He hoped she would make it easy for him.

"I'll have whatever you're having. It looks like scotch, but bourbon would be fine, too."

"It is scotch," Tony said, "a nice single malt. Please make yourself at home. I'll be right back."

When he reappeared with her drink, Donna Sugar had kicked off her shoes and taken a seat on the couch.

"I'm making a guess that you live here alone, but that it wasn't that long ago that you shared with somebody. A wife?"

"We divorced last fall. What made you think so?"

She smiled and complimented him on the scotch.

"Like I said, a guess. And maybe a woman's intuition. What do you do?"

So this is how we do it, he thought. We make small talk for awhile, maybe have a second drink. No rush to the bedroom. Conversation is our foreplay.

"I'm a lawyer, wouldn't you know."

Donna Sugar's smile vanished for a second, then returned.

"Let me hazard another guess. You're in corporate law."

"I'm afraid not. If I were, I'd be living over on the Heights in one of those gated communities. It's a general practice. I tend to handle divorce, the occasional malpractice case. Mostly civil law. How about you?"

"Let's see. How should I answer that question?" she said, feigning serious thought. "I rather like to fit into other people's imagination. So why don't you tell me what you'd like me to be?"

Tony wasn't sure whether to play her game or be serious. He opted for the former.

"What about fashion designer?"

"That's good. And flattering. I am a fashion designer."

Tony knew that Donna Sugar was not a fashion designer, but he found himself enjoying the game.

"What if I'd said that you were a physical therapist?"

"I'd have congratulated you for your perspicacity. I am a therapist."

"Oh, come on. How many fashion designers who are also physical therapists can there possibly be?"

"I'm not sure, but you are looking at one. And I'm here tonight because you need therapy. Right?"

She's good, Tony thought. He was willing to bet that she would have told him she was a therapist even if he hadn't suggested it.

"Why do I need therapy?" he asked, curious as to how she would answer the question.

"You're lonely and probably have been ever since she left. You need company. Somehow you found me and invited me over. By the way, how did you find me?"

"A fellow attorney. He knew you, or knew about you."

"Really. Does he have a name?"

"Sure. Carl Keller."

Tony knew instantly that he'd made a mistake. He had seen his mentioning Carl as his source as a way to rev up the element of excitement in what he was doing. Sugar didn't react as he'd figured she would. Her smile disappeared. The casual banter came to an abrupt end.

"Mr. Ferraro, you are a son of a bitch," she said, biting off the words. "You think you're going to be Keller's surrogate, don't you? He tried to screw me in court, and now you're going to screw me for him. Well, think again. And it better be fast, because I'm leaving."

Sugar slipped her shoes on and got to her feet.

"No, no, you don't understand," he said, his voice revealing his anxiety. "Keller didn't want me to call you. It was my idea. You sounded like somebody I'd like to know."

"Well, now you know me. Not in the biblical sense of the word. Let's be clear about that."

"I'm sorry about you and Keller, but it has nothing to do with you and me. Please sit down."

Tony tried to guide her back to the couch, gently touching her shoulder. She shook him off.

"Just how is it you know Keller?" she asked.

The question offered the hope that she might be induced to stay.

"We work in the same office. But it's a large firm, and we aren't close."

"I should hope not. He was hell bent on dragging my name through the mud, just to get some sympathy for the man who assaulted me."

"I'm afraid that's what lawyers do. They have to work for their client, even if he's a real bastard. Even killers are entitled to a defense."

Sugar sat back down. He wasn't sure she did so because he'd persuaded her to or because her display of righteous anger had only been a bit of play acting.

"How would it be if I freshened your drink?" he asked. "We might even change the subject."

She stared at him as if trying to decide whether she could trust him.

"I'll have some more of your scotch," she announced. She didn't appear to have made up her mind about whether she'd consent to anything else.

When he returned with her drink, she made it clear that they weren't finished with Carl Keller.

"Did Keller talk much to you about the Truscott trial?"

Tony saw this as a dangerous question.

"Not much. Like I said, we weren't friends, just professional colleagues. Like all attorneys, he didn't like to lose a case. But he knew his client was a loser. I think he admired you."

It was a lie, but in the circumstances a useful one. Gradually, Tony Ferraro and Donna Sugar resumed a civil conversation that didn't focus on Carl Keller and edged slowly but inevitably toward the moment when she said she'd like to see the rest of the house. The inspection ended in Tony's bedroom.

CHAPTER 12

When Carol awoke the morning after Gretchen Ziegler's visit, she almost immediately found herself trying to thrust Carl Keller out of her mind. She had fallen asleep mulling over the questions she wanted to ask him, then pondering how she could first find him so that she could ask those questions. Cumberland County was one of the more sparsely populated counties in the western part of the state, but it was a good sized piece of real estate and she hadn't the slightest clue where to begin her search for Keller. It was while she was showering that she decided not to look for him, but rather to let him come looking for her. After all, that's what he had been doing last week. Could he be counted on to do it again? If not, she'd simply write him off as somebody she hadn't known as well as she thought she did.

Little did she know that finding Carl Keller would not be difficult.

She had no sooner arrived in her office than JoAnne buzzed her with word that somebody named Marty Reese needed to talk with her. Urgently.

Carol had no idea who Marty Reese was, but JoAnne quickly solved that problem by identifying him as the manager of the *Welcome Inn.*

"Good morning, Mr. Reese. I understand that you have a problem."

"I do, and so does the man in room 8," he said. "He'd dead, and what's more he's had his throat cut."

She had been staring out the window to where a small crew was resurfacing the parking lot. She quickly pivoted back to her desk.

"Let me get this straight. One of your guests is dead in his room. How did you happen to discover that he was dead?"

"I'd gotten a phone call for him, but he didn't answer his phone when I tried to reach him. His car was there, so I assumed he was in the shower or something. I went down to 8 and let myself in. It was terrible."

"I'm sure it was. You found him, what - just a few minutes ago?"

"That's right. No idea how long he's been dead."

"Mr. Reece, please keep a watch on that room, but don't touch the door handle or anything else. I'll be there as fast as I can." Chances are, she thought, that he'd already touched the door handle and heaven knows what else.

Carol hurried out of the building, telling JoAnne to have Sam take the squad meeting and send the first officer to arrive over to the *Welcome Inn* a.s.a.p.

She was halfway to Hopewell when she remembered that she hadn't asked Mr. Reece for the dead man's name. Had it been a different motel she'd have thought of Keller. But he wouldn't be staying in a flea trap like *Welcome Inn*, an old, run down place that should have been razed when the bypass was put through. When she turned into the motel's rough parking lot, however, she realized that she had been wrong. There in front of room 8 was Mr. Reece, sitting on a bench, and in front of him was a grey Ford that was almost certainly the one Carl Keller had been driving when he ran out of gas.

––––––

By the time that Officer Byrnes joined her, she had confirmed that the man with his throat slit was indeed Carl Keller. As Reece had reported, his throat had been cut, although it seemed not to have bled much. Reece had said that the door had been locked, which meant that Carl had either let his killer into the room or that the killer had managed to jimmy the lock. The latter was unlikely. The locks on the doors were the only sign that *Welcome Inn* had undergone any recent maintenance. They were brand new and looked as if they would be a real challenge for someone bent on breaking and entering. In all probability Carl had known who his killer was. Perhaps they had an appointment, an appointment with death.

She tried to sort out her feelings. She had known Carl some years ago when they had briefly worked together in the Albany law firm. They had had a good relationship. But after she left the firm they had drifted apart. In fact, they had not written or talked in seven years, and when their paths had again crossed, only a week ago, Carl had made no effort to say hello and she had failed to recognize him. Now he was dead, less than a day after a colleague at the firm had brought her up to date on the end of his association with Morgenstern and Brauchli. There were so many things she had wanted to talk with him about, so many questions she had wanted to ask. They would never have that conversation. She would never ask those questions.

Instead, she was confronted with yet another murder, in this case the murder of a former friend she no longer knew.

By eleven o'clock she and Officer Byrnes had closed *Welcome Inn* and turned it into a crime scene, shipped Carl Keller's body off to the hospital in Yates Center, and converted the office into a temporary headquarters. Marty Reece had readily accepted the news that his motel would have to be shut down; he had even volunteered to post a No Vacancy sign. Carol finally got around to having a chat with Reece.

"How long has Mr. Keller been staying with you?" she asked.

"Nine nights. It's not hard to remember. Business is slow here, nobody stays more than one night. Except Mr. Keller, that is."

"Did he ever tell you what he was doing here? Why he needed to be here for so long?"

"I thought about it, of course, it being so unusual. But I figured it was none of my business. Besides, he wasn't a talker. Never said much."

"Did he ever have visitors?"

"Not that I know of. It's possible somebody came by after I'd gone to bed or had to run an errand, so I can't be sure. It's obvious that he had company last night."

"That seems to be the case. You didn't by chance hear a car in your parking lot, did you?"

"Wish I could say I did, but I'm a sound sleeper."

Carol changed the subject.

"During the day, what did Mr. Keller usually do? Hang around the motel? Leave early? Did he seem to have a routine?"

Marty Reece hesitated before answering. Probably doesn't want to look like he spends his time spying on his guests, Carol thought.

"Hard to say," he finally said. "Of course he'd have to go out for breakfast. All I provide is coffee. But he seemed to be up and out by mid- morning most days."

"And nights? Was he gone most evenings?"

"Some of the time, I think. I usually watch TV after supper, so I really can't say."

Carol wondered why Carl had chosen the *Welcome Inn*. Was it because he wanted the greater privacy of such an out-of-the-way place? Because he was hurting financially and *Welcome Inn* was cheap?

"What do you charge for a room, Mr. Reece?"

"I know," he said, regret in his voice. "We can't afford to compete with the newer places. Here it's just $75 a night, all except for room 12, which is a sort of suite. That one goes for $90."

Carol was surprised that Reece could get even that much for the dingy rooms and no breakfast.

"What did he pay with?"

"Cash, which was fine with me."

She had expected this. In any event, Carl's wallet was gone as were his car keys. The Ford was unlocked, other than the trunk, but the glove compartment and the door pockets contained nothing except for a few CDs and evidence that the car had passed an emissions test in Albany some six weeks earlier. Byrnes had gone through the small suitcase and the few clothes that were hanging in the closet. He had discovered nothing of interest, not even a piece of paper that could tell them where he had eaten, left his dry cleaning, filled his gas tank. No cell phone, no pocket calendar, nothing.

Whoever had slit Carl Keller's throat had done a thorough job of removing everything that might be of some help to a police investigation. They would get into the Ford trunk, of course, and they would dust the car and room 8 for finger prints. But Carol was convinced that they would find nothing.

It was while she was giving the room another once over lightly that it occurred to her that she had no idea whether Keller was married. She recalled that he had been divorced shortly after he joined the firm. She would have to get back in touch with Gretchen. Somebody at the firm would know whom to contact. In the meanwhile, Carol had no idea where to start. All she had to go on was what she had learned from Gretchen, and she found it difficult to picture any of the people who had been involved in the Truscott case driving over from Albany to slit Carl Keller's throat.

As usual, Carol was getting ahead of herself. She knew absolutely nothing about Carl Keller's relationships except the ones that had come into play in the Truscott case. For all she knew he had other problems, perhaps even more serious problems. He might be a pedophile. He might have been having an affair with a neighbor's wife. He might have run afoul of some shady characters or welched on a bet.

When Carol left the *Welcome Inn* in the good hands of officers Byrnes and Barrett, she felt a headache coming on. She was about to embark on a murder investigation of somebody she had known and once considered a friend. An investigation that had begun with a puzzle: Carl Keller's throat had been slit, but there had been no blood on the bedding.

CHAPTER 13

Carol's first order of business when she got back to the office on Monday afternoon was to call Gretchen Ziegler. Not only would she need to hear about the totally unexpected murder of their former colleague at Morgenstern and Brauchli. It was possible that she would be able to answer a few of Carol's questions, questions that it hadn't even occurred to her to ask the previous day.

Fortunately Gretchen was in, and the reason for the call was so pressing that Carol felt no need to apologize for interrupting whatever it was that she was doing at the moment.

"I'm sure you didn't expect to hear from me so soon," Carol said. "And I didn't expect to be calling less than 24 hours after you left the lake yesterday. But this can't wait. Carl Keller was murdered last night."

"Oh, my God!"

"Unbelievable, isn't it? We were talking about what got Carl fired, and now, before I'd even digested your news, the question is who killed him and why."

"If you'd told me the president had just declared war on Iran I wouldn't be more shocked. What happened?"

"I got a call this morning from the manager of a nearby motel, the place where Carl had been staying. He found him dead, his throat slit."

Carol told Gretchen what she knew, which wasn't much, and then asked a few questions.

"It never occurred to me yesterday that it might be important, but was Carl married?"

"Not unless he and Lisa tied the knot without telling anybody. He used to be married. You may even have known his wife. Mary Louise, I think it was. But they've been divorced for years. He's been living with a woman named Lisa off and on now for awhile. I don't think I've ever heard her last name, and I only met her once. Carl didn't talk about his personal life, at least not with me."

"So you don't know whether there have been problems with this Lisa woman?"

"There may be someone here who would know, but not me."

"Could you do me a favor and see if you can find out what Lisa's name is and how I can get ahold of her? Married to Carl or not, she should be notified that he's dead. I need to talk with her."

"Sure, I'll do it this afternoon and get back to you."

"If you were to recommend somebody in the firm who might be able to help me get a picture of Carl's private life, who would it be?"

Gretchen gave this question some thought, and then suggested Tony Ferraro.

"Sorry, I've never heard of him," Carol said.

"He came aboard after you left. I mention him only because he and Carl spent some time together working on a case recently. I think Ferraro was taking over some of Carl's cases after he was fired."

"But they weren't close, is that what you're saying?"

Gretchen sighed.

"I don't think I'm going to be much help, Carol. I don't pay much attention to office relationships."

"I may have to talk with Ferraro. But right now I've got a problem, and I hope you can help me out. There's no point in pretending you don't know about Carl's death. I wish I could be there to observe how people react to it, but that won't be possible. Do you suppose you could be my eyes and ears? Especially with Foster. I've really been blindsided by this, and I'm going to need all the help I can get."

"You can't imagine Foster had anything to do with Carl's death, can you?"

"No, of course not. Heads of prestigious law firms don't go around killing people. Neither do distinguished judges. But right now the only people I know of who may have had a grievance with Carl are Foster and Hartman. So I'd appreciate it if you could let me know how Francis deals with the news. I don't know what to do about Hartman, although it shouldn't be too hard finding out whether he's at his lake hideaway."

"Okay, I'll keep my antennae up, see what I can pick up from water cooler gossip. In other words, I'll try to put myself in your shoes. Do you think you'd like to come by and question our people?"

"I'm not sure just what I'm going to do. There's no point in making it look as if someone at the firm might have had something to do with what happened. I'm only trying to get a better picture of Carl Keller's life, all of it, not just the Truscott case and his skills as an attorney."

When her conversation with Gretchen ended, Carol felt restless. She couldn't expect Gretchen to function as her surrogate in Albany, although she knew that her friend would do what she could. She also knew that making contact with Lisa was important, and that she would almost certainly have to visit her and go through Carl's things, hoping that there would be something that would offer a lead to his killer.

Before the afternoon was over she had briefed Sam on the murder of her 'stalker.' She had also learned that Byrnes had gained access to the trunk of the Ford only to find nothing of interest there. Finally, it had been established that Judge Lindsay Hartman was enjoying a brief vacation at his Crooked Lake cottage, although an effort to reach him there by phone was unsuccessful. It was at 5:22, as Carol was about to leave for the day, that Gretchen Ziegler called back with information about Lisa.

"Here's the scoop on Lisa," she reported, "at least as much as I've been able to dig up so far. The office log still has his name, and it says to call Lisa Simmons in case of an emergency. Got something to write down her cell number? There's no landline."

"Go ahead." Carol jotted the number down and stuffed it in her jacket pocket.

"I called her. She's one of those people who leave their cell on - like I should but don't. Anyway, she picked right up. I figured you'd want to be the one to provide the details, so all I told her was that we'd had a call from the authorities over in Cumberland County telling us that Carl was dead and asking us to contact next of kin."

"Thanks. That couldn't have been easy. How'd she react?"

"She certainly didn't go all to pieces. Her first question was 'where's this Cumberland County?' Then she made quite a point of making it clear that she wasn't his next of kin. She's either a born stoic or she and Carl weren't as close as we thought."

"Did she ask for a number to call?" Carol asked.

"No. I gave her your office number, but she didn't seem that interested. She probably assumes that you'll be in touch with her in due course. I suppose if I'd told her Carl had been murdered, she might have responded differently, but I thought I should leave that to you."

"She never asked what had happened to him? You know, heart attack, car accident, things like that?"

"Another no. They may not have been ready to head to the altar, but you'd think she'd have been a little shaken up by the news. It was almost as if she wasn't surprised."

"Maybe she wasn't. Look, I appreciate your having taken care of this. I'll try to reach her this evening, and I'll keep you posted. Now how did people at M & B react to the news?"

"About as you'd expect," Gretchen said. "Everybody was shocked, a few sounded genuinely sad. I didn't ask anyone for a theory as to who might have done it or why, and nobody volunteered an opinion. As for Foster, he was the only one to wonder if it might have been a case of suicide. He was obviously thinking about the fact that it had happened so soon after Carl had been fired. Maybe he was experiencing a bit of remorse. But I assured him that the Cumberland authorities, a.k.a. you, were sure it was murder."

"Francis' response seemed genuine?"

"I'm not sure I'm a good judge of such things, but, yes, it didn't look rehearsed, if that's what you mean."

"Well, keep your eyes open. And I really do appreciate your help, Gretchen. If you weren't so busy practicing law, I'd deputize you."

"Glad to be of help. And good luck."

After hanging up, Carol did some thinking about her facetious remark about deputizing Gretchen. In view of the fact that the investigation of Carl Keller's death was likely to involve quite a bit of attention to Albany, she would probably have to seek the cooperation of police in the state capital. Or, alternatively, send Sam or someone from her own force over to Albany. There was, of course, a third possibility. She could deputize someone other than Gretchen, thereby avoiding the need to put more strain on her own limited budget. The obvious person for such an assignment was someone who would relish the job. That person was, at that very moment, waiting for her with a chilled bottle of Chardonnay at their cottage on Blue Water Point.

CHAPTER 14

Kevin was as shocked by the news of Carl Keller's horrible death as Carol and Gretchen had been. The day before Keller had been a possible stalker. Today he was a murder victim. By the time Carol had given Kevin all the details of this dramatic turnabout, the sun was setting behind the cottage and they hadn't eaten dinner.

"Still hungry?" he asked.

"Not really. I think I'll settle for a piece of that rhubarb pie we didn't finish yesterday."

"Sounds good to me. I'll get it."

The pie finished. Kevin turned the conversation back to Carl Keller's unexpected demise.

"What's your game plan?"

"Don't fall off your seat when I tell you this," she said, "but I think it's going to be our game plan. There's a lot to do both here and in Albany, and some of it can't wait. I believe there's a law of physics that says I can't be in two places at the same time. What's more, my budget is tight right now, and I'm not sure whether I can send one of my officers to do what needs doing in Albany."

"I'm reading between the lines, but does this mean you want me to take to the thruway?"

"It does. As the old 'Mission Impossible' lead in would have put it, your mission Kevin, if you choose to accept it, is to get yourself over to Albany and perform a few feats of derring-do on my behalf."

"What if I don't choose to accept it?" Kevin asked with a straight face.

"I know you, and you will accept it."

"I appreciate your confidence. I'd have thought you'd be calling in the Albany police department."

"Not this time. This is too personal. It involves people I know, and I'm not sure I could get the PD over there to do it my way."

"And it isn't as if I don't have some experience, like Chicago in the Beckham case. I think I did you some good in that one. Not to mention Brighton when you were in the hospital last year, or that town in Massachusetts where the little priest had had a parish. And let's not forget that I've been your gumshoe in Albany before. Remember that former student of mine who worked in the state legislature?"

"Yes, yes," Carol said. She stood up and took a deep bow. "If it hadn't been for you, murderers would still be running wild around Crooked Lake."

"Oh, come on. I think I'm a better sleuth than I am a teacher."

"I won't tell your dean you said that." Carol smiled. "You're pretty cocky for someone who doesn't even know what I'm going to ask him to do."

Carol proceeded to tell Kevin what she would like him to do and when she would like him to do it. The what depended in part on a couple of phone calls she had to make, the when on whether the people she wanted him to see would be available. She hoped it would be tomorrow.

"Let's get the ball rolling. According to Gretchen, Lisa Simmons has been living with Carl. You find something to do while I give her a call."

Ms. Simmons answered her cell phone so fast that she must have had it in her hands when the call came through. Her voice had just a hint of a Boston accent.

"Yes, this is Lisa Simmons speaking."

"Hello, Ms. Simmons, this is Carol Kelleher. I'm the sheriff of Cumberland County, and I believe someone from Carl Keller's old law firm talked with you earlier in the day about the fact that we found Mr. Keller dead this morning."

"This is about Carl?"

That seems pretty obvious, Carol thought.

"Yes, I'm calling because I understand that you and Mr. Keller are sharing an apartment on Woodmere Road. I thought you would need to know what had happened to him."

"I don't live there anymore."

"Oh, I must have been misinformed. But you and Mr. Keller are friends - I should say were friends. Isn't that right?"

"I knew him, but it was awhile ago."

Why is this woman so reluctant to talk about Carl? Gretchen didn't really know Lisa, but she wouldn't have spoken of her sharing an apartment with Carl if it was merely unsubstantiated gossip.

"Ms. Simmons, I don't know anything about your relationship with Mr. Keller, and that's not why I'm calling. We are investigating his death, but we don't know much of anything about him. So we're contacting people in Albany who we've been told are close to him, and you are one of those people."

"And it was his old law firm that told you to call me?"

"That's right. It seems he had listed you as the person to call in an emergency, and while he is no longer with the law firm, I think you could call this an emergency. So, please, try to remember when you last saw him, when you last talked to him."

"I think I moved out of the apartment about two weeks ago," she said. "Is the date important?"

"Probably not. Before you left, did Mr. Keller talk about his plans?"

"His plans?"

"Yes. He was no longer practicing law, but had he taken another job or spoken about what he was going to do?"

"No, and frankly that's why I moved out. He'd changed. He used to be easy to live with. He could even cook. But when he quit the firm he sort of went into his shell. He talked about getting another job, but he didn't do anything, just sat around all day. I know changing jobs can be hard, and I'd have stuck around if he had taken me into his confidence. But he didn't even try."

"Did he ever talk about why he left the firm?"

"No. I know he'd just lost a case, but he'd lost cases before and he always bounced back. He used to say 'win a few, lose a few,' and then he'd be his same old self. But not this time. I think he decided he just didn't like what he was doing anymore."

"So he didn't share his work much," Carol said.

"No. He always complained that it would just be boring to non- lawyers."

"And you aren't a lawyer?"

"No. I run a small boutique store over near the university. You wouldn't know where that is."

Actually, Carol said to herself, I do.

"Sounds interesting. What's it called?"

"*Treasure Chest.* Not very original, is it?"

No, Carol thought, but I doubt that Kevin will find it hard to find.

"Actually, I like it. Thanks for putting up with my questions, Ms. Simmons. I hope we get to the bottom of this very soon."

She thought it was interesting that the woman had not asked about how Carl had met his death. She either didn't care or, and it was far less likely, she already knew. She now had enough to send Kevin to Albany for a face to face conversation with Lisa Simmons. Hopefully, it would be more productive than the last ten minutes on the phone had been.

But the good news - or what Carol hoped was good news - was that Carl's apartment had apparently been empty since he had left for Crooked Lake. Of course Lisa may not have told her the whole story. She knew, however, what she had to do next. She had to call the Woodmere Road apartments.

It was getting late, and Carol had feared that she had waited too long to place the call. But to her relief someone answered at the front desk.

"Good evening. I'm sorry to be bothering you so late. This is Carol Kelleher, I'm the sheriff in Cumberland County over in the Finger Lakes area, and I'm calling about one of your tenants. Or perhaps he owns an apartment there. Do you know Carl Keller?"

"Sure," came the answer. "He's a lawyer, lives on the third floor, apartment 33."

Carol wasn't sure who the deskman was, but he was obviously knowledgable about who's who at Woodmere.

"I'm afraid that I have some bad news. Mr. Keller is dead. We found him in a motel just west of Crooked Lake this morning, and I'm going to have to ask for your cooperation."

"Mr. Keller is dead?" The deskman was obviously shocked by what he had heard.

"That's right. My request is somewhat unusual, Mr. - I don't believe I have your name."

"Turner. William Turner."

"Thank you, Mr. Turner. It is important that no one other than a representative of my department be allowed into the apartment. A deputy of mine - a plainclothes officer named Whitman - will be arriving sometime tomorrow morning. On my instructions, he will need to search the apartment. When he leaves, it may be necessary to keep people out of the apartment until we have completed our investigation."

"This sounds serious," Turner said. "What happened to Mr. Keller?"

"That is what we are looking into. We are particularly interested in why he was over here on Crooked Lake when he died."

"You're on the lake where that woman from the state legislature was found, aren't you?"

"You have a very good memory, Mr. Turner. Unfortunately, that case was in my jurisdiction, and so is this one. I assume that someone else will be on duty tomorrow. I'd like to entrust you with making sure that my instructions are given to that person, and I'd prefer that you tell him, not just leave a note."

"Absolutely," Turner assured the sheriff. He sounded pleased to be working with the people who had brought the assemblywoman's killer to justice.

The sheriff hung up and set off down the hall to where Kevin was watching TV.

"Okay," she said when she got his attention. "Now let's talk about what you're going to be doing in Albany tomorrow."

CHAPTER 15

Kevin had left Preemption Road behind him and was now rolling east on the thruway, Albany still some two hundred miles and three hours ahead. He was thinking of the last time he had gone to Albany, and that was because Carol had wanted him to talk with a former student of his, Princeton Elliot, who was then a staffer in the state legislature. Elliot, he remembered, had been a brilliant student, one of the best he had ever had in class. But he had gone to see him not for old times sake, but because he had apparently become something of a stud in the world of Albany politics. More particularly, he had been one of several lovers of the woman whose body had been found in the attic of the Hawk's Nest mansion on Crooked Lake. As it turned out, Elliott had had nothing to do with her death, but his outsize ego had changed Kevin's mind about him. They had never spoken again.

This time he was traveling to Albany not to visit an old acquaintance, but to learn what he could about a former legal associate of Carol's, a man named Carl Keller, who had been found dead with his throat slit in a seedy Cumberland County motel. Kevin was well aware that his interest in playing sleuth was typically the subject of friendly banter with Carol. But today's trip was a serious matter. She needed his help, and she trusted him to be both perceptive and thorough. Had she had more resources, her fellow officers would be the ones on their way to Albany and he would be sitting at the computer fighting off writer's block as he tried to finish a paper he was working on. But she lacked those resources. Moreover, they had lived together for so long and had worked together on so many cases that they thought of themselves as a good illustration of the old idiom that great minds run in the same channel. The 'great minds' might be a bit of hyperbole, but he knew that this was one of the reasons that Carol had entrusted him with the trip to Albany.

It was when he had gone beyond Syracuse and Utica and was approaching the exit to Herkimer that Kevin began to think seriously about his mission. His main task was to take a good look at Keller's apartment. What he would be looking for was anything that could explain what had sent the ex-lawyer to Crooked Lake. Not to mention anything that could shed light on the life he'd been leading since the Truscott case, as well as people he'd been seeing, talking to, or thinking about over recent weeks. The odds were that he'd find nothing that would be helpful, but he wouldn't know that for sure until he'd given the apartment a thorough going over. His other major purpose was to visit Lisa Simmons' boutique, probe further into her relationship, past and present, with Keller, and more generally form an impression of the person who was presumed to be his closest friend. Carol had also asked that he stop by Morgenstern and Brauchli and have a chat with somebody named Ferraro. She had promised to alert Gretchen that he would be dropping by the firm.

Kevin had no idea how long it would take to discharge these obligations. He might be on his way back to the lake by the end of the day. On the other hand, he might have to find a motel for the night and finish up his rounds the following morning. Either way, he was looking forward to what he'd be doing. It promised to be more interesting than the paper that had been frustrating him for the better part of a week. Much as he enjoyed teaching, he knew that he was no scholar, that the papers he delivered at conferences periodically were hardly cutting edge pieces of research. Maybe he should abandon the pretense that he could contribute to the world's storehouse of knowledge about opera and try his hand at a memoir about his life as a sometime sleuth. That thought occupied his mind for about five miles before he ruefully rejected the idea. He knew that Carol would counsel him to keep his priorities straight.

It was close to noon when he pulled up in front of the Woodmere Road Apartments. The visitors parking area appeared to be full, but a station wagon pulled out of a space just as he was prepared to circle the lot again. In less than five minutes he was talking with Joseph Hurley, the deskman on duty. Hurley had been expecting him, and didn't seem to need him to produce evidence that he was who he said he was, a plainclothes officer representing the sheriff of Cumberland County.

The door to the apartment bore no name, but the key he had been given by Hurley let him into a living room that was darker than he had expected because the blinds had been drawn. In fact, the entire apartment was gloomy for the same reason. It also smelled of cigarette smoke. Kevin pulled a blind aside to see what the window looked out upon. He was disappointed. Not fifteen feet away was the wall of another building. Carl Keller's apartment would not have been one of the more expensive ones at Woodmere.

He left the blinds down, but turned on several table and floor lamps. It was an undistinguished place. The walls were largely devoid of pictures, the living room carpet had a conspicuous stain where something had long ago been spilled. The bed in the bedroom had been made up, but not very well. The kitchen, a narrow galley, was superficially neat, but it was quickly apparent that it was poorly stocked. Indeed, the contents of the refrigerator consisted primarily of beer and frozen pizza. Only in what was obviously a study was there any evidence that Keller had lived more than a transient life. A bookcase contained evidence that he had, indeed, been a lawyer. The other books were mostly paperbacks, but they gave no evidence of his principal reading interests. Kevin spotted John Grisham and David Baldacci, but there was also an old copy of *The Hitchhiker's Guide to the Galaxy* and some indication that Keller had an interest in American history.

Before tackling the study, he decided to work his way around the small apartment more methodically. He searched under the bed, emptied wastebaskets, went through the dresser and the bedroom and hall closets. Eventually he got back to the study, and while it looked lived in, it contained little to suggest what Keller did there. There was no computer. Kevin assumed that he used a laptop and had taken it with him. If so, the killer had absconded with it along with his wallet, his keys, and his cell phone. The only items on the desk were a portable landline phone, a printer, a pad of yellow stickies, half a dozen pens, a small cactus plant that had seen better days, and an unwashed coffee mug. He picked up the phone, but there were no messages. There was a file cabinet under the desk, and Kevin went through it carefully, but it told him nothing which seemed relevant.

Kevin sat back in the desk chair and thought about what he had found and, more importantly, what he had not found. Too many things were missing, things which should logically be on or in the desk or file cabinet. There was no check book, no record of checks cashed, bills paid. There was no address book, no list of phone numbers or e-mail addresses. They could be in the laptop, wherever that might be, but it was disappointing that not a single name or number had been jotted down on the pad beside the phone or anywhere in the apartment. Kevin felt frustrated. There was nothing more to be accomplished here. He'd stop at the desk to return the key and see what USPS had left for the occupant of apartment 33.

The deskman seemed pleased to hand over the mail that had accumulated, and for the first time since he had entered the Woodmere Road Apartments, Kevin felt that he finally was in possession of tangible proof that Keller had actually been in contact with the outside world. Most of the mail that had been held for him was junk, but he decided to take all of it with him.

Once in the Toyota, Kevin thumbed through the mail. He set aside five fliers and an appeal for a contribution to a fund raising drive by his college. Two bills, one from a cable company and the other from the company that carried his automobile insurance policy, proved to be equally unhelpful. There was but a single letter that was personal, and it, too, turned out to be irrelevant. It came from someone with a New Hampshire address who identified herself as Carl's Aunt Sylvia and reported the sad news that someone named George Kerchner had passed away after a long illness. Kevin slipped it into his jacket pocket. Carol might want to notify Sylvia of Carl's death; she might even want to use her as a source of information about his next of kin.

There was still plenty of time to catch Lisa Simmons before she'd be closing her boutique. So he sat quietly, trying to exorcize his frustration. From where he sat he could see people going into the apartment building. He found himself absent mindedly guessing which ones lived there, who were visitors, who had business to conduct. One man wearing a baseball cap stopped near the entrance and snuffed out his cigarette and dropped it into a large earthen pot containing an unfamiliar plant. The man looked around, furtively Kevin thought, before entering the building; perhaps he's not sure he should have put his cigarette butt in the pot. Kevin remembered the smell of cigarette smoke in apartment 33, and then another thought came to him. What if things he had expected to find in the apartment were missing not because Carl Keller had taken them with him to Crooked Lake or because he was simply a man of strange habits? What if they were missing because somebody had visited the apartment after Carl had left and made off with them because he didn't want them to be found there?

He got out of the car and went back into Woodmere Road Apartments.

"Mr. Hurley," he said when he reached the front desk. "There's something I forgot to ask you. Has anyone been in apartment 33 since Mr. Keller left?"

"Not to my knowledge, but I'm only on during the day, and not even every day. You'd have to ask my colleagues."

"If people visit here, are they allowed to go straight up to an apartment without first having whoever's on duty check to see if it's all right with the resident?"

"Oh, no. Visitors must sign in, and we call ahead to be sure it's okay."

"So I wouldn't have to ask your colleagues if somebody had been in Mr. Keller's apartment while he's been away. It would have been impossible because it's against Woodmere's rules."

Suddenly, Mr. Hurley looked uncertain as to what he should say.

"Well, I'm not sure I'd say it's impossible. Just not very likely."

"I'm confused," Kevin said. "Mr. Keller wasn't there to tell the deskman to send a visitor up, so the visitor would not have been allowed to go on up. Isn't that right?"

"Yes, technically."

"Technically?"

Hurley was now obviously uncomfortable.

"I know it's a rule, but sometimes when the visitor is a good friend or a family member, we don't bother with a call. It would seem kind of unfriendly, like we're just doing it to give them a hard time. You know what I mean?"

"I understand what you're telling me, but it also means that somebody could have been in apartment 33 even if Mr. Keller was away."

"Like I said, you'd have to ask the others."

"By the way, would everybody who worked the desk have known that Mr. Keller was away and when he left?"

Once again, Hurley hesitated.

"I'm not sure. I mean people who live here don't have to tell us when they're going away, although many of them do. You know, because of their mail and things like that."

"You said that visitors have to sign in. What is done with those sign- in sheets?"

"You want to see who signed in to see Mr. Keller?"

"I'd think that would be easier than making appointments to talk with the others who cover the desk here at Woodmere."

Kevin realized that he might be pushing the envelope just a bit too far. He certainly didn't want to create a problem for Mr. Hurley or any of his co-workers. But he was now concerned that perhaps somebody had visited Keller's empty apartment.

"Truth of the matter is that I don't know who keeps the sign-in sheets. We turn them in each day to the house manager. Maybe he files them, but for all I know he shreds them."

"I'm sorry to be such a problem, but my instructions from the sheriff are to learn everything I can about Mr. Keller, and that includes his visitors here at Woodmere."

"Turner says Mr. Keller's dead. Do you suspect someone of killing him?"

Hurley had put two and two together.

"We have no idea what happened to him, but we're in the process of investigating his death."

He comforted his conscience with the thought that half of that statement was true.

"Maybe you should speak with Mr. Abato, but he won't be in until nine o'clock tomorrow."

"Good. I'll be back at nine. Shall I come here to the desk, or how do I go about seeing Mr. Abato?"

"I'll be here when you arrive, and I'll show you."

"Many thanks, Mr. Hurley. You've been most helpful. My job would be a lot harder without the help of people like you."

As Kevin left the Woodmere again, he wondered whether he should tell Carol what he had just said. It was arguably the biggest lie he had told in quite some time.

Once back in his car, he made a decision to postpone Lisa Simmons until tomorrow. He would have to stay in Albany to see Abato and Ferraro anyway. Why not make it three interrogations? It would give him more time to hunt down a decent motel. And find a restaurant that served a more balanced dinner than pizza and beer.

CHAPTER 16

While Kevin was canvassing Carl Keller's mostly bare apartment in Albany, Carol was seeking help from Judge Lindsay Hartman in recreating the Truscott trial that had led to Carl's departure from Morgenstern and Brauchli. The judge would be in the best position to give her a picture of just what had transpired at the trial. The picture he drew would not, of course, be wholly objective, least of all when it came to the matter of holding Carl in contempt of court. But she needed his assessment of the participants, especially Truscott and Carl, who was in charge of Truscott's defense. She would like his impression of Donna Sugar as well, although that might pose a problem if she had once had an affair with Hartman, as Carl seemed to believe.

Her first problem, however, would be to get the judge to talk with her. For all she knew, he made it a habit never to discuss his cases with anyone. If, on the other hand, he was not averse in principle to doing so, he might not wish to have such a discussion with her, inasmuch as she had been a colleague of the man he had held in contempt and a member of his friend Francis Foster's firm. But she was very anxious to meet with the judge, and hopefully Carl Keller's death might be the bait that would persuade him to talk with her.

Officer Byrnes had ascertained that the judge was in residence on the lake, which was fortunate. He was reputed to spend many weekends a year at his cottage, but it seemed that he was currently taking a whole week of vacation. Carol had known that he owned a place on the lake, but had no idea where it was. She couldn't recall having ever seen him in Southport or Yates Center. Perhaps his wife did all the shopping and he simply spent his time fishing or writing his memoirs. In any event, he answered the phone himself when Carol called.

"Judge Hartman, this is Carol Kelleher. I'm the sheriff here in Cumberland County, but you may remember me from the time I practiced law with Morgenstern and Brauchli."

"Oh, yes, I remember. I think you appeared before me as counsel on more than one occasion. And needless to say, everybody who spends time on the lake knows all about you in your latest incarnation as sheriff."

"I'm sure you are taking some well deserved vacation time, but I'm calling to see if it might be possible for me to come by your cottage and talk with you for a few minutes. It's about the Truscott trial, and I'm interested in it because the attorney for the defense in that case was found dead yesterday in a motel not far from the lake. It's in my jurisdiction, and I'm afraid I'll be the one investigating his death." Carol paused. "The problem is that he didn't die of natural causes. He was murdered."

"That's terrible news. You're talking about Carl Keller?"

"That's right. I wouldn't be bothering you except for the fact that his life seems to have gone into a tailspin after the Truscott case. I don't know much at all about that case, and I'd be grateful if you could review for me what happened in your court. Might that be possible?"

"Well, now, let's see. I have to be back in Albany by the end of the week, and my daughter's family is coming for a short visit tomorrow. It looks like it will have to be today. Could you make it by, say, 4:30?"

"That's very kind of you. I'll be there."

"I'll open a bottle of sherry by way of celebration," he said. 'Do you know where to find me?"

Carol had made it a point to learn where the cottage was, but she chose to be in need of the judge's directions.

"I'm afraid not."

"We're about five miles down from Yates Center on the East Lake Road. You should be watching for a sign telling you that Dogwood Point is off to your right. Take that road and we'll be the fifth cottage on the lake side. It's yellow with brown shutters."

Carol relaxed in her desk chair. She needn't have worried that Judge Hartman wouldn't see her. It remained to be seen how frank he'd be when they met.

The afternoon dragged by slowly. Finally at 3:50 she stopped in the restroom to look at herself in the mirror. She wasn't pleased with her appearance, but there wasn't much that could be done about it at that hour. She couldn't remember if the judge had been a bear on one's attire in the courtroom, but he was aware that she'd be in uniform.

The cottage was exactly where both Byrnes and the judge had said it was, and it looked to have been well maintained. In spite of her effort to slow to a crawl over the last mile, she was still five minutes early. But she remembered Hartman as a stickler for promptness; he'd hardly fault her for arriving before the appointed hour.

Mrs. Hartman, who looked better in shorts and halter than most women her age, met her at the back door.

"Do come in, sheriff. I'll get Lindsay. He's down on the dock fishing for those little blue gills."

They walked through the cottage to the lakeside porch.

"She's here," she called out. Her husband, who had made no effort to dress up for their meeting, waved back and reeled in his line.

In another five minutes the judge had produced the promised bottle of sherry and they had made themselves comfortable.

"You look just as stunning as you did when last you stood in my courtroom," he said. "The life of a sheriff must agree with you."

Carol had no idea whether the judge's compliment was an honest one. Perhaps he was simply accustomed to flattering the ladies. But it didn't really matter.

"I enjoy what I'm doing, and to be quite frank about it, the lake makes it easier to relax than Albany does. When I get a chance to relax, that is," she added with a smile.

"I'll agree with that. I'd rather fish than sentence miscreants. But tell me about Mr. Keller. I can't believe he was murdered. Things like that shouldn't happen in our little corner of paradise."

She was sure that the judge knew all about the rash of murders that had visited Crooked Lake in recent years, but she was not about to raise that issue.

"There isn't really much I can tell you. I hadn't seen Mr. Keller in years, and then to find him here. And dead. I had actually seen him briefly just a couple of days earlier, but he didn't seem to want to talk about his life, other than to say he was no longer practicing law."

"Did he tell you what he was doing on Crooked Lake?"

"I'm afraid not. I had remembered him as fairly loquacious, but for whatever reason he'd changed. That's why I wanted to talk with you. Maybe what happened during the Truscott trial could shed some light on his problems."

She thought it best to leave it there. There was certainly no reason for her to focus on the contempt citation. She hoped the judge would bring it up.

"How did you hear about the Truscott case? It can't have been a big enough story to have stirred the Crooked Lake grape vine."

"I talk occasionally with Gretchen Ziegler. She's still with Morgenstern and Brauchli, and we compare notes occasionally."

Judge Hartman considered this and then took a sip of his sherry.

"You're interested in whether Keller's defense of Randall Truscott might have something to do with the subsequent changes in his life. I'm obviously in no position to make that connection. All I can do is tell you what transpired at the trial. I never talked with Mr. Keller after it was over, so I guess I'm as much in he dark as you are."

"I understand," Carol said, hoping that Hartman would not leave it at that.

"But about the trial," the judge went on, "it was an unfortunate one for Mr. Keller. He'd been dealt a losing hand. Truscott had clearly battered the Sugar woman. If you'd been there, you'd have seen how uneven a match it was. He's a big guy, has the build of a linebacker. What's more, he looks like one of those guys you'd best be careful not to cross. He was on his best behavior in court, of course, but there are people who look and sound menacing even when they're on their best behavior. Truscott's one of them. The woman in the case, Donna Sugar, she's a little thing. She's petite any way you look at it, but next to Truscott the contrast is really striking. Any jury looks at the two of them, the defense's got two strikes on it from the get-go. I know that that doesn't guarantee a finding of aggravated assault. But the pictures of Miss Sugar, her face, her throat - she looked like she'd gone fifteen with Mohammad Ali. And that doesn't include her internal injuries. The medical report made it clear that she had broken ribs, some bleeding in her lungs. Even by the time the trial got underway, she still looked awful. To put it bluntly, Keller didn't have much to work with."

"It certainly sounds that way," Carol said.

"Keller did the best he could, at least to start with. He pointed out that Truscott hadn't used a weapon, and the prosecution admitted that there'd been no gun, no knife. But they claimed that Truscott's hands qualified as a weapon. The jury got to see those hands, and the prosecution did a good job of reminding the jurors what big, hard hands like that did to Sugar's face and her throat. The prosecutor even said she was lucky she hadn't been strangled to death. Where Keller got himself in trouble was when he tried to argue that Sugar was equally to blame, that this began as a nasty verbal fight in which she gave as good as she got, even biting and planting kicks on his legs throughout the struggle. But like I said, you only had to see Truscott and Sugar side by side to realize how hard that would be to sell to the jury."

Hartman drained his sherry and shrugged, as if to say the outcome was a foregone conclusion. It looked as if he wouldn't be bringing up the contempt citation. Carol decided to take the plunge.

"I understand that you held Mr. Keller in contempt."

The judge smiled.

"I had to," he said. "Keller kept trying to steer his questioning into areas he should have known were out of bounds. He thought if he could malign Miss Sugar's character, the jury might back off a bit. It was obvious that what he wanted to bring up was based entirely on hearsay, and I instructed him to leave it alone. But he wouldn't. He didn't give me much choice."

The judge looked thoughtful.

"I suspect that a lot of lawyers think we're always looking for a reason to charge them with contempt," he continued. "Fact is, I hate to do it. Counsel has to do his best for the client, we all know that. I like to think that when I hold somebody in contempt it's to keep him from unintentionally hurting his client's case. Does that make sense?"

Carol wasn't sure she could buy Hartman's logic, but she wasn't about to say so.

"The word I get from Morgenstern and Brauchli is that they let Mr. Keller go because of the contempt citation."

"I'm not privy to their reasoning, but I think that's unlikely. If every attorney who's been cited were fired, there'd be a lot of shorthanded legal firms. Anyway, you'd have to talk with Francis Foster."

I expect I'll be doing that, Carol thought.

"I'm not sure whether what you've told me can help, but I appreciate your willingness to talk with me. Frankly, this is a case I'd have preferred be someone else's responsibility."

"I understand. Do you have any theory about Mr. Keller's death?"

"None at all. It just happened night before last."

"Has it occurred to you that he might have been over here at the lake because he wanted to see you? After all, you were once colleagues."

"True, but that was years ago."

"The way I look at it, there wasn't much of anywhere to turn in Albany. Word that he'd be sacked by his firm would get around pretty fast. So he starts thinking where to turn for advice, and he remembers you. Just an idea, and I could be dead wrong."

"We'll never know, will we?"

As Carol drove back to her own cottage, she thought about what Hartman has said. It closely paralleled her own thinking. But it did not explain why Carl had been so reluctant to talk with her. Nor did it explain why he was now dead, his throat so horribly slashed.

CHAPTER 17

Kevin and Carol had a relatively brief phone conversation that evening, catching each other up on what they had managed to learn as they went about the incipient investigation of Carl Keller's death. They had agreed that they needn't talk the evening away, so by shortly after eight Kevin was in the process of getting ready for bed and a Peter Lovesey mystery.

The motel was a considerable improvement over Carol's description of the *Welcome Inn*, but it gave him no pleasure. It reminded him of his city apartment, where he spent many a long and lonely month without Carol's company. Of course it was only early July, and he still had two months with her at the cottage to look forward to. But whenever he crawled into bed alone he couldn't help but think about the only downside of their marriage.

He mentally recapitulated his agenda for the next day. He'd be seeing a Mr. Abato, the keeper of visitor sign-in sheets at the Woodmere Road Apartments, at nine. Then he would drive over to Lisa Simmons' boutique, the *Treasure Chest*, to get a better picture of her relationship with the late Carl Keller. Finally, he'd pay a visit to Carol's old law firm to quiz Tony Ferraro, who, according to Gretchen Ziegler, might be able to help reconstruct Keller's private life. If he didn't learn more from these meetings than he had from his time in Keller's apartment, his trip to Albany would have been a waste of time. But there was no point in anticipating trouble, so he propped up his pillow and picked up Lovesey's latest Peter Diamond novel.

As promised, Paul Abato was in his office at Woodmere at nine. He had obviously been informed of the purpose of 'the detective's' visit, and was both curious and anxious.

"I understand that one of our residents has been found dead and that you're investigating his death," Abato said. "From what our deskman tells me, there seems to be something mysterious about his death, and that is why you've been in his apartment."

"That's right. It's Carl Keller we're talking about, and I'm particularly interested in whether anybody has been in his apartment since he left on a trip over a week ago. I understand that you maintain visitor sign-n sheets."

"We respect the privacy of everyone who lives here at Woodmere, so there's really no reason to maintain a list of their visitors. The only reason we ask people to sign in is for our residents' protection."

"Yes, that's what Mr. Hurley told me. But like I said, it's important that we know who's been in Mr. Keller's apartment recently."

"Did Hurley say that somebody had been in the apartment?"

"No, he didn't." Kevin found Abato's evasiveness frustrating. "Look, all I want to do is take a look at the sign in-sheets for the last two weeks."

"This is highly irregular," he said, obviously unwilling to admit that there may have been exceptions to house protocol.

"Perhaps it is, but I am investigating a possible crime. Mr. Keller is dead, and were he alive, I'm sure he'd want us to know whether someone had been in his apartment in his absence."

"I see," Abato said, drawing out his words as if to say that he finally understood what the stakes were in this conversation with an officer of the law. "Let me see if we still have those sign-in sheets."

He went through the motions of looking in the desk drawer.

"Aha," he feigned surprise. "This could be what you're looking for."

Abato took out a bunch of papers, each bearing a heading entitled 'Visitors List' and followed by a list of dates, times, signatures, and a check list which presumably indicated that the person being visited had given permission for the visitor to proceed to the apartment.

Kevin did not know, nor did Carol, the exact date on which Keller had gone to Crooked Lake. But he was quite sure that it was less than two weeks but more than a week ago. He picked out the lists that he assumed were most likely to be relevant and scanned them for a reference to Keller and apartment 33. There were two such entries. One of them contained the name of Lisa Simmons. It was dated June 28th at 9:17 pm. The other was dated June 30th at 11:42 pm. The name was Richard Keller.

He knew who Lisa Simmons was, and he'd be asking her about this visit within the hour. He had never heard of a Richard Keller.

"Do you know who this Richard Keller is?"

"No, but it sounds like a relative to me. Probably a brother."

In other words, somebody for whom an exception to house rules could be made.

———

Half an hour later Kevin located the *Treasure Chest* and found a parking place half a block away.

There were two women in the shop, and he had no idea which of them was Lisa Simmons. He asked the tall blonde with a Virgo tattoo on both arms, and she pointed him toward a shorter woman with jet black bangs and purple lipstick who was arranging things in a display case.

"Good morning, Ms. Simmons," he said. Lisa looked puzzled, but she shook hands. "I'm Kevin Whitman, and I'm working for the Cumberland County sheriff's department. You talked with the sheriff just the other day, and I'm here to ask a few more questions about Carl Keller. We understand that you've been living with him in the Woodmere Road Apartments."

"I think I told the sheriff that I'd moved out of Carl's apartment some time ago. I haven't seen him in weeks."

"That's what she told me, but I still need to talk with you. Do you have some place where we could talk privately?"

Lisa looked uneasy.

"If it'll only take a few minutes, we could duck into the stock room. It's right this way."

She led him to a door with a full length mirror in the back of the shop. There was very little space to sit down, but Kevin took the room's only chair and Lisa pushed aside some boxes on a table against the rear wall and scooched herself up onto the table. It was, to say the least, an awkward moment, inasmuch as her skirt was short and provided very little protection from indecent exposure. It didn't seem to bother Lisa, however. What obviously did bother her was that these people from wherever it was that Carl had died were persisting in asking her questions.

"I don't know what you want," she said. "Carl and I are through, like I told the sheriff. I have no idea what happened to him. Of course I'm sorry, but I can't see how I can help you."

"I think you can. How long have you known Carl?"

"I'd say about two years. Off and on."

"Had you moved into Woodmere, or did you just spend time there?"

"Mostly I stayed over. You know, for a few days or a week from time to time. But I moved some of my stuff in last fall. I guess we really lived together for only five or six months."

"Would you like to know what happened to Mr. Keller - sorry, to Carl?"

"If you'd like to tell me."

"He had his throat slit."

"No!" Kevin was sure that her colleague in the shop had heard that.

"Yes, Ms. Simmons, it's a cruel way to die. You seem to be the person who knew Carl best. Perhaps you can tell me who might be most likely to have done this terrible thing."

"Oh, I wouldn't have a clue. Carl didn't talk much about people."

"You and he didn't socialize?"

"Not much. We definitely weren't part of any crowd that hung out together."

"So he never talked about anybody that had given him a problem, anybody he didn't like?"

"Not that I remember."

"How about the people in his law firm?"

"What about them?"

She's either dumber than she looks or she's uncomfortable with this conversation, Kevin thought. Perhaps both.

"Did he talk about them? Can you remember the names of some of his fellow lawyers?"

"It's like I told the sheriff, he didn't like to talk about what he did for a living. He may have mentioned a name or two. It's hard to remember."

"Let me try a couple. Foster? Francis Foster?"

"I don't think so."

"Tony Ferraro? Gretchen Ziegler?"

"The first name sounds vaguely familiar, but I know he never talked about some woman," she said.

Okay. Time to ask the $64,000 question.

"When were you last in the Woodmere apartment?"

"I thought I already told you that."

"You said some time ago. I'd appreciate it if you could be more precise."

"One day's like another, I guess. But it was at least as far back as the middle of June."

"Let's try that again. How about June 28th?"

"No, no, that's not possible."

"Actually, your signature is on the Woodmere's sign-in sheet for that date. 9:17 pm is when you signed in."

Lisa was clearly shaken by this bit of information.

"But that can't be," she said. It was almost a whine. "It must be somebody whose name sort of looks like mine."

"I'm afraid that won't do, Ms. Simmons. I looked very carefully at that list, and there is no question that the name is yours. Unless, that is, there have been two Lisa Simmons seeing Carl Keller at Woodmere, and I think we both know that that isn't the case."

Suddenly, Lisa's face brightened. She has an idea, Kevin thought. He doubted that it would pass muster.

"I just remembered," she said, almost breathlessly. "When I moved out, I forgot some jewelry. Nothing very valuable, mostly ear rings and stuff from the store here. But it wasn't doing Carl any good, so I went over to get it."

"I thought the Woodmere didn't allow visitors to an apartment unless they checked to see if it was okay with the resident?"

"Oh, that. It's a rule for real visitors. I wasn't a visitor. I lived there."

"So you kept your key to the apartment when you broke up with Carl."

"I did. It wasn't intentional. We just didn't think about it the day I packed up and left."

"Tell me, what was the condition of the apartment when you were there. Did it look like you remembered it?"

"What do you mean?"

"Was everything in place, or were things missing?"

"How would I know? All I was there for was to get the jewelry, and it was right where I'd left it in the bedside table drawer."

"Did you take anything with you other than the jewelry?"

"Are you accusing me of being a thief?"

Kevin let that pass.

"One final question and then I'm on my way. Did Carl smoke?"

"No. He had a thing about cigarettes. He couldn't understand how people could smoke them, knowing they'd kill you."

"How about yourself?"

"I did when I was a kid in high school, but I quit years ago."

"I said that would be my last question, but another one just occurred to me. Did Carl have a brother named Richard? Or perhaps a cousin?"

"He never said much about his family."

"Do you have any idea whom we should talk with about claiming Carl's body?"

"I think his parents are still alive, living somewhere near Boston. I think it's Stow." Lisa climbed off the table. "Why don't you believe me about the jewelry?"

"I haven't said I don't believe you. I'll have to think about it. But I want you to take that key to apartment 33 and leave it with the man on duty at Woodmere. I'll be calling him tomorrow and asking if the key has been returned."

"Please don't do that," Lisa said. "I don't have the key anymore. I lost it."

"You lost the key to Carl's apartment?" Kevin's tone of voice made it clear that he didn't believe her.

"I must have. I can't find it anywhere."

"I'd suggest that you keep on looking. And thinking. You don't suppose you gave it to Richard Keller, do you?"

"Who?"

Kevin was suddenly very tired of Lisa Simmons.

"Find the key," he said, and turning on his heel he walked out of the stock room, said good-bye to the tall blonde with the tattoos, and set off for his meeting with Tony Ferraro.

CHAPTER 18

It was barely noon, and Kevin was once more on the thruway, heading back to Crooked Lake. That he had gotten such an early start was due to Tony Ferraro's bad luck. He had had an emergency appendectomy operation that morning and was obviously in no condition to talk with anybody except the duty nurse. Chances were that Carol would be sending him back to Albany when Ferraro was up and about and ready to talk about the late Carl Keller.

As he drove, Kevin was doing some mental arithmetic. He toted up the cost of the motel and thruway tolls, then added a modest fraction of what he had paid for meals. The total came to about $235. It would have been higher had he included the full cost of meals, but that didn't seem fair inasmuch as he would have eaten at home if he hadn't been in Albany. In any event, the $235 in expenses would be coming out of their pocket, not the county budget, and that had been the reason Carol had asked him to make the trip rather than one of her officers. Or had it? After all, $235 didn't sound like a very large sum considering that the purpose of the trip had been to move the investigation of Carl Keller's murder along. Not that it had accomplished much, although he hoped Carol would see it as having made a small beginning. But Kevin liked the idea that Carol had sent him on this trip less to save money in her discretionary account than because she thought he would be better able to charm a few people into speaking candidly than Sam Bridges or one of her other colleagues would.

The early start brought him back to the cottage in time for a relaxing swim and let him put together what he thought of as a pretty good supper with which to welcome Carol home.

If she thought he was back from Albany earlier than she had expected, she didn't say so. When she walked through the back door she immediately tracked him down in the study and gave him a big hug.

"One night and I've already been missing you," she said. "Let me get out of this impossible uniform and then I want to hear all about it."

It wasn't long before they were comparing notes on what each of them had been doing and what they had learned. Carol was unusually upbeat about what Kevin told her.

"I suppose the downside is that bare apartment," she said, "but I think Carl's friend Lisa is going to be an interesting player in this case. And Richard Keller. He could be even more important. It's a safe guess that he's a relative of Carl's, and I'm going to be shaking Carl's family tree tomorrow. Finding out who he is shouldn't be hard. You certainly had a more productive couple of days than I did. The judge didn't tell me anything I hadn't heard from Gretchen. Except, of course, that the Sugar woman was no match physically for her boyfriend, Truscott. She'll probably turn out to be a red herring. How seriously can you take a woman who's last name is Sugar? I'd be more suspicious if her first name were Sugar."

"Maybe, if she is indeed a call girl, she changed her name from something like Smith or Brown to

Sugar. It'd be more likely to attract gentleman callers."

"Whatever. I'll put Byrnes on her as well as Richard Keller. Wouldn't it have been nice if Carl had shrugged off his reticence to greet me like a long lost friend and told me what was going on in his life. We might not have been able to save him, but we'd have a better idea about what we're up against. There had to be a reason why he was following me but not ever coming right out and telling me what the problem was."

"On the other hand," Kevin said, "there may be no connection at all between his following you and the fact that he was killed. Maybe he had a sudden crush on you but couldn't quite bring himself to be up front about it. Maybe Carl also had an enemy who took advantage of the fact that he was skulking around Crooked Lake, a love sick man having a middle age crisis, to kill him."

Carol looked at Kevin as if he had a screw loose.

"Your imagination is in overdrive again, Kevin. Why on earth would Carl be having a crush on me? We worked together for about three months almost a decade ago, and haven't exchanged even an hello since then until a few days ago. He also knew that I'm married. And we know nothing whatsoever about his enemies, if indeed he had any."

"If he didn't, why did a casual acquaintance slit his throat? That's not something casual acquaintances do, unless they're on Prozac or something and go berserk."

The thought seemed to please Kevin.

"Hey, maybe it wasn't an enemy after all. Maybe Carl's killer is trying to quit smoking and has been taking Chantix. The commercials say that it can have severe side effects. Anyway, I'm not saying that his killer, if he's ever found, will prove to be either an enemy or somebody who's going to plead the Prozac defense. I'm just throwing out ideas."

"So I see. While you're doing that, I think I'll start searching for Richard Keller and Ms. Sugar. For all I know, you're going to be making more trips to Albany. First Ferraro, then people who've been known to hate Keller because he bullied them in grade school. Even smokers who can't handle Chantix."

"Now you're making fun of me," he protested, "just when I've spent $235 of our hard earned money to drive to Albany, spent a fruitless day in a depressing apartment, and tried to get an immodest young woman to tell me the truth. That's not fair."

"What's this about an immodest young woman? You haven't told me about that."

"It wasn't worth mentioning, but Keller's ex-girlfriend contrived to give me a peek at her panties while I was questioning her."

"What kind of interrogation technique are you using, for heaven's sake?"

"It's called staying focussed, ignoring distractions. I think I do it well."

"I should hope so," Carol said. "Do you think she was trying to distract you?"

"No. If so, she lacks the necessary finesse. I can't imagine what Carl saw in her."

Supper finished and the dishes put away, Carol asked Kevin what he planned to do with the rest of the evening.

"I started a good mystery last night, but I don't think I'm up to reading. How about you?"

"Last night I was watching an episode in a series about the ancient Romans. For some reason I'm not in the mood tonight."

"Which leaves us where?" Kevin asked.

"I was thinking of trying immodesty. With finesse, of course."

"Now that's a great idea. Let me get into something more comfortable."

"Me, too."

CHAPTER 19

Francis Foster normally put in a ten to twelve hour day, a price he willingly paid for the privilege of being the managing director of a prestigious law firm such as Morgenstern and Brauchli. At the present time, his responsibilities were momentarily greater because the firm was seeking another attorney to replace the recently released Carl Keller. Francis was not by nature a delegator, and he was particularly concerned to maintain control over the selection of Keller's successor. Of course he would have had no need to worry about replacing Keller if he had not summarily fired him. But he had not liked the fact that Carl had been cited for contempt of court. Even more importantly, he hadn't liked the fact that he had been cited by Judge Lindsay Hartman. He and Hartman had been close for years, and he knew that Hartman would not appreciate it that he had had to cite a member of the Morgenstern and Brauchli law firm for contempt. The judge would have expected him to keep his colleagues in line, rather than letting them go Rambo.

The decision to sack Keller had not been difficult. Friendship demanded nothing less, especially in view of the fact that Hartman had contacted him and had politely made it clear that Keller's courtroom behavior was simply intolerable, not to mention a personal affront to the judge. 'Take care of that man Keller of yours,' was the way Hartman had put it.

Lindsay might have said more, Francis thought, but he knew that he didn't need to. His memory is very good, and he knows that mine is, too. He had been friends with the judge since their days at Harvard Law School. That friendship had survived not one but two impulsive and potentially self-destructive acts of his. In the first place, he had misrepresented himself and his credentials when he applied for admission to the law school. Had he not doctored his application, it is doubtful that he would have been admitted and thus able to claim a Harvard degree. His second mistake had been to cheat on exams in both his torts and constitutional law classes. Moreover, his cheating had not been a minor matter; it had been blatant. None of this would matter today, years after the fact, had he not shared the details of these devious violations of the academic code of ethics with Lindsay Hartman.

Why had he been so stupid, he wondered, knowing that the answer was simply that at that time he had been a bit of a hellion. He ran risks and got a perverse pleasure from doing so. And if that weren't bad enough, he got a kick out of sharing his 'little crimes' with others. No, he had to correct that: with *one* other, his best friend, Lindsay Hartman. He could remember the feeling that he had beaten the system, but if no one else knew about it, beating the system was a rather hollow triumph. So he had bragged to Lindsay about what he had done.

In retrospect, that had been the ultimate act of bravado, for Lindsay was something of a 'goody two shoes.' He had liked him, but found it hard to believe that someone could be so virtuous, so unrelievedly proper. But one of Lindsay's virtues had been that he wouldn't betray a friend, so while he always greeted these tales of moral brinkmanship with disbelief, he never told anybody about them. Francis had even come to the conclusion that Lindsay rather liked having as a friend somebody who was so different from himself, somebody who was so charmingly reckless.

The two of them had gone off in different directions after Harvard, but it was only a dozen years after graduation that they both found themselves in Albany. They had quickly resumed their friendship, and in time had both become pillars of the state capital's legal fraternity. I've outgrown my irresponsible youth, Francis said to himself, but Lindsay hasn't forgotten. He hoped that he also hadn't forgotten that friends keep their friends' secrets, which was one of the reasons he had been so anxious to do him the favor of firing Keller.

And now Keller was dead. Gretchen Ziegler had spread the word around the office. In fact, she had seemed almost delighted to be doing so. He was worried about Gretchen. Was she too close to their former partner, Carol Kelleher, now the sheriff in the jurisdiction where Keller had met his death? He had no cause to sack Ziegler, but she made him uneasy and he realized that he'd have to watch her carefully.

Francis was also worried about the investigation that would be unfolding into Keller's death, especially now that it was known that he had been murdered. The sheriff would certainly be thinking about whether it might have had something to do with his being let go by the firm. Kelleher was too smart not to consider a possible relationship between the two events. Which meant that sooner or later she would be wanting to talk with him. She couldn't, of course, consider him a suspect in Keller's death. That would be inconceivable. Or was it? He hadn't paid much attention to the careers of former colleagues at Morgenstern and Brauchli, but he'd heard enough about Kelleher, much of it from Judge Hartman, to know that she had a deserved reputation for tenacity.

CHAPTER 20

Carl Keller's problems with his law firm began when he took the case involving the charge that Randall Truscott was guilty of aggravated assault. From Truscott's point of view, his problems began when he chose Keller to defend him. Now Keller was dead and Truscott was in jail. In fact he had already served three weeks of his three year sentence, and he had hated every minute of it.

Randall was a man who was used to having his own way. He was someone who usually found a way to brush aside those people whose presence in his life was annoying or an inconvenience. He had skated close to the margins of the law on a number of occasions, but he had always managed to survive those troubling encounters, thanks both to his ability to charm people and his ability to make them nervous about pushing him too far. He also had friends who were in a position to intercede on his behalf, even go to the mat on his behalf.

Sitting in his cell one day, bored and restless, he took some pleasure in recreating in his mind some of those situations in which he might have ended up in jail but had not. There had been more than one bar brawl in which he had given worse than he got and might easily have landed in the pokey. But he had been able to demonstrate that the instigator of the fight had been the other guy, in one case several other guys. Or to be more honest about it, his lawyer, a clever dude named Gus Crenshaw, had been the one who had managed to saddle the other guys with responsibility for what had happened. He might have come even closer to serving time for a fracas with his wife, back when he'd had a wife. But he had been at his charming best in court; he was certain that two of the women on that jury had been swayed by his manner. He still regarded the way he had played eye contact with them as among his finest hours. Of course Melanie had not helped herself with all of the inconsistencies in her testimony.

And then along had come Donna Sugar. How had he ever let himself fall into her trap? Unfortunately, he knew just exactly how it had happened. He had dropped by *The Lounge* one night, and there she was. *The Lounge*, a ridiculous name for an upscale hangout whose only purpose was to facilitate hooking up for guys and gals on the prowl. He had been there before, and had usually returned to his apartment alone, the options at *The Lounge* not to his liking. But on this particular night, a petite brunette had caught his eye almost from the minute he walked through the door. She was sitting at the bar, talking with a man who struck Randall as out of his league in the place. Perhaps he was filthy rich, but he was certainly unprepossessing. Short, overweight, sporting a mustache which only served to make his face look misshapen, his chances of scoring with the brunette looked to be close to nil. Randall decided to make sure that his chances would indeed be nil.

There had been no vacant seat near her at the bar, but he had positioned himself behind her, flashed a smile, and in the process of ordering a drink inquired as to whether she'd like another. She had pointed to the half full glass in front of her, but he had resorted to some cliched line like 'the night is young' and she had accepted his offer. The two-way conversation between the brunette and the man with the misshapen face had quickly turned into a three-way conversation, and within a relatively few minutes the other man had excused himself and Randall had slipped onto the vacant bar stool and swiveled around until his knees touched those of the woman.

They had spent a stimulating hour in conversation. She proved to be well informed and whip smart, and he decided that he would like to know better - much better - this package of beauty and intelligence. As it turned out, Randall and Donna Sugar did not go to bed that night. She had told him that she wasn't in the habit of being picked up, but she gave him her card and suggested that he give her a call. He did so the following day, and within a week they had spent two nights together at the apartment. By the end of the month, they were in effect living together, although their arrangement included the occasional night out for Donna. A night out, he understood, meant that she needed, for 'professional reasons,' to share her sexual favors with a few other men. The quid pro quo was that she charged him less than her going rate in return for his covering some of her other expenses.

It worked for awhile, but it didn't take long for Randall to learn that there was more to Ms. Sugar than he had bargained for. It gradually became apparent that she was more than a good conversationalist and a good lay. She was also a selfish little bitch, not to mention an occasionally dishonest one. He remembered the fight they'd gotten into. It was all her fault, her wanting to set the rules of the relationship, her wanting to wear the pants. Well, no goddamn woman was going to wear the pants in his apartment. He could have killed her right there in the bedroom, the scheming little naked tart. It's lucky he hadn't or he'd be doing time for something much more serious than aggravated assault. Anyhow, she was probably out there right now, luring some other guy into the sack and setting him up for heaven knows what kind of a fall.

Meanwhile, here he was doing time. And it was all because of those idiots in the criminal justice system. The judge, a sanctimonious bastard. A jury which had lined up like a bunch of suckers on behalf of that manipulative Sugar. Worst of all his own defense counsel, a mealy mouthed milquetoast whom he hired only because Crenshaw had moved to Oregon. Well, at least Keller, his incompetent attorney, had met his maker. Truscott smiled at the thought. Word had reached him the day after it had happened. See, he had said out loud to his deaf cell walls, you think you've gotten rid of me. But I'm Randall Truscott. So fuck you!

CHAPTER 21

Officer Byrnes had no trouble producing the information on Carl Keller's parents that Carol had requested.

"Once I knew they lived in a Boston suburb called Stow, it was a piece of cake," Tommy explained when Carol looked surprised. "They're Patrick and Mildred, live in the Falmouth Garden Apartments there."

He handed Carol a sheet of paper with the pertinent data, neatly typed, phone number included.

"Thanks. Now I have no excuse to put off notifying the next of kin. I hate this part of my job."

If it hadn't been for Lisa Simmons, they might still be searching for the next of kin. The Simmons woman didn't seem to know much about the people in Carl's life, but at least she had known where his parents were living. Carol wondered if Carl himself had been a Bostonian. They hadn't known each other long enough or well enough to compare backgrounds.

She retreated to her office, closed the door, and steeled herself for another 'I'm sorry to be the bearer of bad news' telephone calls.

In all probability the Kellers were retired. She wasn't sure how old Carl had been, but she was reasonably certain that he was pretty close to her own age, which meant that his parents would be somewhere in their 70s - Carol caught herself in mid-thought and dismissed this pointless speculation on the age of Patrick and Mildred Keller. What difference did it make? They had just lost a son. He might have been the love of their life, or he might have been the black sheep of the family. Either way, she would be passing along news, not only of his death, but of he fact that he had been murdered in a motel in a place his parents had probably never heard of. She dreaded the call.

The phone at their residence rang seven times, and Carol was experiencing a sense of relief that they weren't home when someone answered.

"Hello, this is Pat," a deep male voice said. "Sorry to be so slow getting to the phone. We're not as swift as we used to be."

"Hello, Mr. Keller. My name is Carol Kelleher, and I'm the sheriff of Cumberland County in New York state. I'm afraid I have bad news for you and Mrs. Keller."

She wasn't sure why she paused. Perhaps to let Mr. Keller sit down, perhaps to give him a chance to summon his wife.

"You are Carl Keller's father, am I right?"

"Yes, I am. Is this about Carl?"

"It is. Your son is dead, Mr. Keller."

When she next heard his voice, he wasn't speaking to her.

"Mildred, come here. It's about Carl."

Carol heard another voice, less distinct. Mrs. Keller was making her way to wherever it was that her husband had taken the call.

"It's Carl?"

"No, it's a woman. Carl is dead."

"Who is this woman?"

"She says she's a sheriff." It was at this point that Mr. Keller spoke into the phone again.

"What is it that's happened to our son?"

"This is very hard for me to say, Mr. Keller, but somebody killed Carl. We do not know who did this or why, but we are investigating his death. I would have called sooner, but we didn't know who his next of kin was until yesterday."

This was where it always became difficult. She wasn't where she could see the reaction of the people she was talking to. They would almost certainly be devastated. At least most people were. She wanted very much to ask them questions, but she was reluctant to do so when they were coping, or trying to cope, with such terrible and unexpected news.

It was apparent that a conversation was going on between Carl's mother and father, but Carol could not understand what was being said. Mr. Keller must have covered the phone with his hand. After a long minute, she heard his deep voice again.

"Sheriff, I'm going to put my wife on the phone. She'll handle this better than I could. Here's Mildred."

"Hello, sheriff, I'm Mildred Keller, Carl's mother. I appreciate it that you called us. Something like this must be difficult for you."

"Yes, of course, but you're the ones who have suffered the loss, not me. It's hard enough that you've lost a loved one, but I hate to tell you that he didn't die of natural causes."

"The news is a shock. I shan't pretend it isn't. But I have to confess that Pat and I haven't seen Carl in more than two years. When he was young, we were very close, but - well, things changed. We weren't exactly estranged, but we haven't seen much of each other. So if you need to talk to us about what has happened to him, I doubt that we can be of much help."

This was awkward. Carol supposed that it was better than trying to comfort a sobbing mother, but she hated to hear that families had drifted apart, lost touch, no longer thought of family members as loved ones.

"I suppose I called for two reasons, Mrs. Keller. As his next of kin, you needed to be informed of his death, and I wanted to share with you my condolences and inquire as to what you wanted to be done with his body. Inasmuch as we know almost nothing about him, we were also wondering if you might help us understand the strange circumstances of his death. Do you know where he had been living and what he had been doing?"

"The last time or two we spoke he was in Albany working for some law firm. When he was married, we knew more about him because Mary Louise kept in touch. But they divorced several years ago. She tried to pretend Pat and I were still family. But you can't expect something like that to continue, can you? I'm afraid she disappeared from our life quite a long time ago."

"Do you have any idea where she is now? In case we need to contact her."

"Last we heard she was living in Pittsfield, but like I said, that was quite awhile ago. If it helps, her maiden name was Gallagher. Mary Louise Gallagher. She kept using Keller for a time, but for all we know she remarried, could be living most anywhere - Worcester, Burlington, heaven knows where."

"Did your son ever talk about someone named Lisa Simmons?"

"Who is she?"

"She's the person who told us that you lived in Stow. I don't know about her relationship with Carl. They weren't married, but they seemed to have been seeing each other in recent months. Did Carl ever mention any of his colleagues at the law firm in Albany?"

"If he did, I've forgotten them. Carl didn't make friends easily. I guess I should say he didn't keep friends easily either."

"Let me mention a few names and see if they sound familiar. How about Francis Foster?"

"I don't think so."

"How about Tony Ferraro? Gretchen Ziegler? Carol Kelleher?"

"I've never heard of any of them. You can see I'm not going to be of much help."

"By the way, Mrs. Keller, I'm Carol Kelleher. I worked in the same law firm as Carl for a few months. It was years ago, but I remember him as both a nice guy and a good lawyer. It's one of the reasons I'm so anxious to find the person who killed him."

Mildred Keller didn't seem to know how to respond to this hint that somebody had once thought highly of her son.

"I'm glad you knew him," was her laconic comment.

"We need to talk about what you'd like done with Carl's body. But I have two more questions. Did he ever write or say anything about a man he recently defended in court, Randall Truscott? Or about the Truscott case?"

"Not that I recall. Was it a big case?"

"I suspect that within legal circles it's not considered a big case. But for Carl it was definitely a big case. It was because of it that he lost his position in the law firm where I met him. As for my other question, do you have another son Richard?"

"No. Carl was an only child."

"But about Richard. Is there a Richard Keller in the family, like maybe a cousin of Carl's?"

"No, there aren't any Richards. It's a funny thing, but both Pat and I only had sisters, five of them in all, and the ones that got married only had girls."

Well, she thought, I was wrong about that. There was no Richard Keller in Carl's family, which meant that whoever had used that name to get into his apartment had almost certainly been up to no good.

In the end it was agreed, reluctantly, that Carl Keller's body would be shipped to Stow, Massachusetts after the autopsy and that his parents would make appropriate arrangements. In view of the nature of the relationship between Carl and his parents, Carol had no idea what appropriate arrangements would consist of.

It had been a strange and depressing conversation. The Kellers had not asked where their son had been killed, much less how it had happened that he had been there instead of in Albany. Nor had they inquired as to how he had met his death. Carl's mother had claimed to be shocked, but she hadn't sounded shocked. She hadn't even sounded curious. Her husband, Carl's father, had said even less. The words that stuck in Carol's mind were those he had spoken when he handed the phone to his wife: 'She'll handle this better than I could.'

But the more serious problem was that she now had to worry about an unknown somebody who had spent time in Carl's vacant apartment. Who he was and what he wanted from the apartment, she had no idea. Discovering the answers to those questions promised to be an exceedingly difficult task. She hoped it wouldn't be impossible, but she wasn't optimistic.

CHAPTER 22

Carol's efforts to question Tony Ferraro, Gretchen's candidate as Carl Keller's best friend, had so far come to naught due to his emergency appendectomy. They almost took another hit when Sam Bridges dropped by her office that afternoon.

"I hope you have a minute," the deputy sheriff said, "because I have a problem."

"Of course, but I hope it's nothing serious."

"It depends on how you define serious. It's about this man Keller. Or rather its about our effort to discover who killed him."

Sam hesitated, then took a seat across from Carol's desk.

"I'm not exactly sure how to put this, Carol, but I'm concerned that you sent Kevin over to Albany to interrogate people who might know something about Keller. And you did it without saying anything to me about it. I suppose it's not all that big a deal, but somehow it doesn't seem fair."

Carol suddenly felt very uncomfortable. This was a subject that had come up before when she'd asked Kevin to tackle a problem that properly was the responsibility of the sheriff's department. Sam had taken offense on a couple occasions, suspecting her of having more confidence in her husband than she did in him. But she thought that they had put the issue behind them. At least Sam hadn't brought it up in over a year.

"Oh, Sam, I'm so sorry," she said. "I should have said something about Kevin's trip to Albany.

It had nothing to do with you or any of the other men. As usual, it's a budget problem. I figured Kevin and I could eat the costs of going over to the capital to talk with people. Better that than dipping into my contingency fund."

"Carol, you know me. We've been together for nearly ten years. All you had to do was tell me things were tight and I'd have paid for my own gas and tolls."

"I know you'd have been willing to do that, but in good conscience I couldn't have let you. It was either Kevin or the Albany PD, and I wanted to keep this business about Keller in our hands. I'd rather have had you do it, but that being impossible, I knew that I could trust Kevin. Frankly, he pictures himself as a cop. He's got a good head on his shoulders, and he's no screw-up. But he's not a cop, and he should spend more of his time concentrating on his own job. I'm always telling him that."

Sam laughed, but it was a wry laugh.

"Funny thing, isn't it? You used to be married to your job, and now it's your husband. You're having a tough time balancing the two."

"Not really, Sam. I'm having a tougher time balancing the department's budget. Let me see if I can make it up to you. There's another guy over in Albany we've got to talk to, and I don't want to do it over the phone. Give me half an hour with the books and I'll see if I can find a way to give you the green light to make the trip."

"I have a hunch I shouldn't hold my breath."

"Come on, be my glass half full deputy."

It was more like two hours before Carol asked Sam to stop by the office. He stopped in the doorway, looking skeptical.

"Please, sit down, and I'll give you your marching orders. I think I've tweaked the budget enough so that you can be the one taking the next trip to Albany. It wasn't easy, but considering that you're the beneficiary of all that tweaking, I'd say it was worth it."

Sam wasn't sure whether to thank the sheriff or ask how she'd done it. He did neither.

"I've made a call to a man named Tony Ferraro," she continued. "He's a partner in my old law firm. At the moment he's recovering from an appendectomy, but he's quite able to have company and you'll be that company, providing that you can get away tomorrow."

In view of his recently expressed opinion about Kevin's recent trip to Albany, Carol was confident that Sam would have no trouble getting away.

"Sounds good to me. What am I supposed to do?"

"Ferraro is alleged to have been Carl Keller's best friend, at least in the law firm. How good a friend, I'm not sure, but we need to start somewhere. At least the two of them have worked together on cases, and Ferraro could be in a good position to tell me what was going on in Keller's life recently. So what I want you to do is sit down with him, get him to talk about Carl. Don't take 'I don't know' for an answer. If he sounds like he really can't answer a question, ask him to tell you who can. We need to know about the women in his life, about anybody he's had trouble with, what he does after office hours. We're particularly interested in anything Carl told Ferraro about the Truscott case and the people who were involved in it. That means Truscott himself, the attorney for the prosecution, Judge Harrtman, the woman Truscott assaulted - her name's Donna Sugar. Did he say anything about witnesses at the trial? Get him to talk about the people in the firm. How did he get along with them? If he didn't, why not? I'm assuming Ferraro will know something about Keller's being fired. What did Keller say about it? About Foster, the managing partner who gave him his walking papers? About what he planned to do next? And where. In other words, just pump the guy as hard as you can."

"What if Keller turns out to have been pretty closed mouth about everything? I mean, maybe Ferraro wasn't all that close to him. Then what?"

"Let's start with the assumption that Ferraro knows things about Keller, even if he doesn't think he does. He'll have impressions, gut feelings. You're good at this, I know because I've seen you work. By the way, I don't suspect Ferraro of anything. That's not why you're grilling him. But keep your antennae up. I'm interested in what you make of him, as well as what he seems to make of Keller."

"Have you already scheduled a time for my visit with this Ferraro guy?"

"I have. You're to be at his apartment at 11:30. He'll be expecting you. Here's the address and a sketch that takes you off the thruway and into that part of the city. And a phone number in case you get lost."

"I never get lost."

"I know. The number is just in case you do."

———

"There's been a change of plans," Carol told Kevin when they settled down on the deck for the cocktail hour. "You're to scrub your return trip to Albany. I've put Sam on it."

"Why did you do that?"

"Because he's my deputy. You're my husband."

"But you told me the budget was too tight. I thought this commute to Albany was coming out of our pockets."

"Well, I decided that there comes a time when it's necessary to overlook budgetary constraints. Sam needed an ego boost."

"Don't tell me he thinks I'm usurping his role?"

"It had occurred to him. I assured him it isn't true, but letting him interrogate Tony Ferraro was more convincing than a mere verbal assurance. Besides, I want you to publish, not perish, so consider it as a gift of time in which to write that paper you promised your dean."

"You're much too kind, Carol."

CHAPTER 23

Sam Bridges had long assumed that lawyers were typically wealthy. Perhaps not as wealthy as titans of Wall Street or heart surgeons, but still among the most well heeled professionals in the United States. He wasn't sure where that idea had come from, but there it was, lodged somewhere in his bank of unexamined assumptions. Carol, of course, had been an exception, due in all probability to the fact that she had grown up in an area where ostentatious wealth was frowned upon and where she came from a family of modest expectations. The fact that she had abandoned a career in law to become a poorly paid sheriff only proved the point.

But Tony Ferraro's apartment surprised Sam. He had expected plush furniture, expensive looking paintings on the walls, well crafted art objects on the tables. Instead he found himself looking at a living room that was less attractive than the one he himself went home to every night back in Cumberland.

"So, you've come to learn something about the late Carl Keller," Ferraro said. "Please have a seat. Would you like coffee?"

"Sure, if it's no trouble. Just a little cream, although milk will do."

He watched as the man he had come to see padded back to the kitchen in slippers. Otherwise, he was fully dressed in tan cotton slacks and a polo shirt that looked like an advertisement for Hawaii.

"I understand you'e recovering from an appendectomy," he said when Ferraro handed him his coffee cup. "You look like you'e doing pretty well."

"I am. People don't spend a lot of days healing from surgery anymore. I expect to be back at the daily grind in another day or two. The boss probably wonders why I'm not there already."

"Well, if my experience is worth anything, I wouldn't rush it."

"You've had a bad experience?"

"It's not important," Sam said, waving off the question. "It's just that I once did some stupid things too soon. I appreciate you seeing me like this. I think the sheriff - I'm her deputy, by the way - gave you a heads up on why I'm here. We're investigating Carl Keller's death, and word has it that you and he were friends. We don't know much about him, so we're asking around, hoping to get a picture of him that might explain why he was killed and why it happened over in our neck of the woods."

"I must have misunderstood," Ferraro said. "From what I heard, I thought he and your sheriff were good friends."

"They knew each other about ten years ago when the sheriff was a member of this firm. But she left the firm to go into police work just a few months after Keller came aboard. So, no, they were never good friends. But you, you've been here how long?"

"Close to four years now. Which means I knew Carl longer than the sheriff did, but to be honest about it we weren't really friends."

"How would you characterize your relationship?"

Ferraro thought about that and gave Sam a shrug of his shoulders and a wan smile.

"Frankly, we aren't exactly a close bunch here. We get along, but we all have our own cases, go our own ways. I can't think of a single social friendship among the lawyers at M & B."

"You're telling me there's nothing distinctive about you and Carl? That you didn't work together on cases? Share stories about days in court? About clients?"

"Well, of course there was some of that. There always is. But it was mostly fleeting things. You know, one of us would have a case that took an odd twist, so it was natural to share it. Or we'd get frustrated trying to find a way out of a legal cul-de-sac. But that's not friendship. More like sharing a joke or griping about the Yankees blowing one."

"You knew, I assume, that he lost his last case here. Truscott, I think that's the name of the guy he was defending. And then he left the firm shortly thereafter. Did he ever discuss that one with you?"

"Not much. Carl was always pretty closed mouth."

"Yes, but did he share his feelings about the case with you? Talk about his client, the judge, any of the other participants?"

"Some. I think he was bitter."

"Bitter because he lost or bitter about the fact the judge cited him for contempt?"

"He didn't dwell on it, but I know he was pissed with the judge. Of course Carl knew he had a tough case, but he didn't like the way the judge handled it. Hell, when you're cited for contempt of court, how'd you feel?"

"Did he ever talk about the judge?"

"He may have said a thing or two. I had the feeling he thought the judge should not have taken the case. Conflict of interest, although Carl was vague. After the case was over, he did say something one day that he was going to keep after Ms. Sugar, although I wasn't sure just what he meant. She was the woman who had accused his client Truscott of aggravated assault. At first I thought maybe he was interested in making a play for her, but that made no sense and he later told me that she was poison. Or something like that."

"So Carl did talk with you about both the judge and this woman Sugar," Sam said, thinking they may now have gotten to something important.

"We didn't really talk about them. It was more like throwaway lines. But he didn't like either of them. And as long as we're talking about people Carl didn't like, we can add our senior partner. But that's understandable, because Foster's the one who sacked him. I guess you could say he hated everything about that case."

"Why don't you take a deep breath and tell me about those throwaway lines. Try to remember everything you heard him say about the people who were involved in the Truscott case. Even if you think it's a throwaway line."

Now Ferraro was uncomfortable.

"One of my colleagues is always telling me to be careful what I say about people and cases. You know the problem, somebody will hear you, misunderstand you, and the next thing you know you'll be in trouble."

"Probably good advice when you're where you can be overheard. But there's just you and me, and I'm investigating Carl's murder, so please, don't be shy."

"But what if -" Ferraro paused, apparently reluctant to suggest that whatever he said could find its way into an interrogation of Francis Foster. Or Judge Hartman.

"I don't think we need to worry about what ifs," Sam said. "I'm sure you're most concerned about Mr. Foster. If he could take offense at what Carl had done and give him his walking papers, he could do the same with you. Okay. Let's leave Foster aside for a minute and take an easy one. Tell me what Carl said about Ms. Sugar."

"Didn't I say he called her poison?"

"You did. Why would he be saying that about her?"

The conversation was taking a turn that Ferraro wasn't happy with. Sam wondered if he might know about Carl's suspicion that Sugar had been in a relationship with the judge.

"I'm not sure it was wise," Ferraro said, "but I spent some time with her."

He did not elaborate.

"Want to tell me what that means?" Sam asked.

"All right, I had her over to the apartment. Here, where we're sitting."

"I'm not the morals police, Mr. Ferraro. I think you mean that she was sleeping with you. Occasionally? Regularly?"

"Yes." He didn't say whether he meant occasionally or regularly. But if they had established a personal relationship, it might mean that Ms. Sugar had unburdened herself of other relationships. Such as one with the judge in the Truscott case.

"Okay. Now answer me this, and it's important. Did Ms. Sugar say anything to you about Judge Hartman? About how well she knew him?"

Sam leaned forward as he asked the question. It was clear that he expected a straight forward answer, not obfuscation.

"That's a funny thing," Ferraro said. "Carl thought she might have had an affair with the judge. He didn't have any proof, just a hunch. Anyway, the idea that Sugar might have been sleeping with Hartman was sort of like catnip, if you know what I mean. I know it's crazy, but it sort of made me more interested in her. I never asked her about it outright, at least not at first. Figured it might turn her off. But along about the third time we were together, I casually dropped a rumor I'd heard about her and the judge. She just laughed."

"So she didn't admit it was true?"

"No, but I'm not so sure."

"What makes you think so?" Sam asked.

"It doesn't prove anything, of course, but it was the way she responded. 'Would it make any difference to you,' she asked, 'if I'd been doing it with the judge?' How do you think you'd interpret a question like that, sheriff? Anyway, I told her it wouldn't matter to me. She wouldn't talk about it, said that we should just enjoy the here and now."

Sam didn't agree with Ferraro that what Sugar had said more or less constituted an admission that she and Hartman had had a relationship. But Carol would be interested.

"Did you talk with her about her affair with Truscott?"

"What would be the point of doing that? That was one arrangement she'd have regretted, and I didn't want to remind her of it."

"So, what's the status of your relationship with Ms. Sugar?" Sam asked.

"Pretty much a dead end. Neither of us has said so, but it's been nearly two weeks since I saw her last. I never expected it to be more than a little adventure. Too expensive. Besides, she's probably got a list of guys as long as your arm, and who am I to monopolize her time."

"So what's the bottom line, Mr. Ferraro? How would you rate Ms. Sugar? Honest? A reliable witness if she ever turned out to be a party of interest in the case of Carl Keller?"

"I wish I knew. I'd say her first concern is looking out for herself, and she seems to be pretty good at it. All except for that one mistake with Truscott. Tell you one thing, though. That won't happen again. She's smart, and she's wary. Not poison, like Carl said, but I wouldn't want to mess with her."

CHAPTER 24

There had been no talk of Sam doing more than questioning Tony Ferraro when he hit the road for Albany that morning. But the fact that he now knew that Ferraro had become another of Donna Sugar's bed mates dictated that he should see whether Carol would grant him a twofer. He was aware that the sheriff wanted to quiz the call girl herself, but if he were to do it it would save another round trip on the thruway and hence more of the department's limited funds.

As soon as he got back to his car he took out his cell and made the call to Cumberland. JoAnne reported that Carol was away from her desk, but that she expected her to be back within ten minutes.

"Tell her to buzz me as soon as she's back, and let her know that it's important."

There was no reason to leave the parking space he currently occupied, so he put in one of his favorite country CDs and began to make notes of his reaction to what he had learned from talking with Ferraro. It was almost exactly ten minutes later that Carol called back.

"I hope Ferraro didn't stand you up," she said.

"Far from it. But I'm calling because I think it would be a good idea if I stuck around over here for a little longer and had a conversation with little Ms. Sugar."

"I was planning on doing that, Sam. What makes you interested in seeing her?"

"My interest is purely professional, Carol. The fact is that Ferraro surprised me by letting me know that he's been seeing a lot of her lately. That makes it three people who seem to be on our radar these days - the guy who's doing time for pounding her face into a pulp, the judge who sent him up, and now a member of your old firm. And what do they have in common besides Sugar? Carl Keller! Sounds like a trifecta, doesn't it?"

"Agreed. But -" Carol paused to consider 'but what,' then asked a more practical question. "You don't know that she's even where you could see her. For all we know, she's having a roll in the hay with somebody up in Saratoga Springs."

"If you'd give me her number, I could find out in about five minutes. Odds are she earns her living at night, not in noon hour quickies."

Much as Carol had wanted to be the one to question Sugar, she could see the logic of what Sam had proposed.

"Tell you what," she said. "Let me give you the number I have for her and a few questions which I'd put to her if I were over there. I presume that what Ferraro told you gives you some idea as to how to approach her."

"It sure does." Sam sounded ebullient. "And Carol, thanks a lot. I'll break down her defenses."

"Be careful. We don't know that she has any defenses that need breaking down. She's not a murder suspect, just someone who knows people who knew Carl."

"Yes, and knew them intimately."

They talked for several more minutes, and then Sam made the call to Donna Sugar. He crossed his fingers, hoping she would pick up.

It was a sleepy woman who answered on the seventh ring. A sleepy and irritable woman. Sam had to sound authoritative, patient, and charming all at the same time, but eventually Sugar agreed to see him at 1:30, by which time she'd have gotten dressed, had her morning coffee and biscotti, and devised a strategy for coping with the deputy sheriff of Cumberland County.

———

Sam didn't know Albany, but after a wrong turn or two he located the address and occasional pad of Donna Sugar. As he parked, he found himself remembering the first and only time he had visited a prostitute. It had not been the typical assignation, but an attempt to check on the alibi of a suspect in the murder of a wealthy vintner on Crooked Lake. Carol Kelleher had been the sheriff for less than a year at the time, and the murder would prove to be the first of several with which she would have to cope in the years they had subsequently worked together. Sam could recall many demanding assignments, but he could not recall any which had made him more uncomfortable than that visit to a tough and dishonest hooker in an old brownstone down in the city. Hopefully, today's meeting would not be so unpleasant.

The woman who met him at the door did not look tough. Her life might be hard, but she looked soft, as if she were made to melt in your arms. She was, as he'd been told, diminutive, but the proportions were right. She had a beautiful face, no longer marred by the beating which had earned

Randall Truscott three years in jail. What is more, her face wore a big smile, as if she were greeting a favorite squeeze, not a uniformed officer of the law.

"Officer Bridges," she said as she took his hand. "This is a pleasure."

He knew better, but appreciated the compliment.

"Thanks for finding time for me on your schedule," he said, immediately regretting how this would sound to Ms. Sugar.

"No problem. Come on in."

Her apartment was less impressive than she was, but that presumably had something to do with the fact that she typically met her men where they lived, or in hotel rooms, rather than at her own apartment.

"I know this isn't a social visit, but if you like I can find vodka or cognac in one cupboard or another. Or if you prefer, coffee."

"Coffee will be just fine," Sam said.

When Sugar returned with the coffee and sugar and cream, she proceeded to take charge of the conversation.

"I'm sure you'll forgive me, but it's rare when I'm asked, without notice, to make myself available for a police interrogation. This must be very important."

"My apologies. It just happened that I was in Albany, and I hoped that you might be able to give me a few minutes."

"As you see, I've done that. You said it had to do with the death of Carl Keller. I barely know the man, although I had an opportunity to watch him in court for several days. You will not be surprised that I'm not that fond of him. After all, he did his best to make me responsible for what Randall

Truscott did to me. But that's now history, and from what I hear Mr. Keller is no longer with us. I assume you are investigating his death. How may I help you?"

"I'm not interested in going back over the trial, which must have been difficult for you. Our concern is that Mr. Keller was killed - violently, I may add - very soon after the trial ended and Mr. Truscott was sentenced.

"Of course there may be no relationship between what happened in court and Mr. Keller's death. But I'm sure you can understand why we have to consider the possibility that the two things are related."

"And I'm sure you can understand that I have no idea whether they are related. I never talked with Mr. Keller. My attorney may have, but that's beside the point. I know enough about these things to know that it wasn't surprising that Mr. Keller tried to make me look like the provocateur. What other choice did he have? Anyway, Randall lost, as he deserved to. What any of this has to do with what happened to his attorney I can't say. He didn't deserve to die like that, but it really has nothing to do with me."

"It is our understanding that Mr. Keller was pursuing a strategy in court which threatened to reveal that you and the judge had an affair. The judge put a stop to it by holding him in contempt of court. I'd be interested to hear what you have to say about your affair with Judge Hartman?"

Donna Sugar crossed her legs, took a sip of her coffee, and smiled.

"I take it that you would like me to tell you that I had an intimate relationship with Judge Hartman.

I'm sorry to disappoint you. I'm sure you are aware of how I make my living. In the course of a career in modeling I have probably dated a number of men. It is not unusual today. In fact, I have probably been more monogamous - or, if you prefer, less promiscuous - than the great majority of young women. I have never kept a score card. That would be tacky, don't you think?"

Sam realized that he was dealing with a clever woman who was not likely to be caught off guard.

"The reason I brought it up was because I had an interesting conversation this morning with a local attorney you may know. His name is Tony Ferraro. He quite casually admitted that you and he had been in a relationship. He didn't resort to euphemisms. He said you had been sleeping together for awhile, and he intimated that you and the judge might have had a similar relationship."

Donna Sugar was not going to be riled.

"Really? Mr. Ferraro has a very rich imagination. He's a nice boy, but one whose ego benefits from the idea that he is sharing something desirable with a celebrity. Perhaps that term is excessive. Let's just say that he finds fulfillment when he imagines himself to be playing in a league of his betters. As I said, Mr. Ferraro has a fertile imagination."

"So you deny that you were sleeping with Judge Hartman?"

"I come from a generation that does not regard sex as some sort of ultimate taboo, Officer Bridges. I like men. I have taken a few of them to bed. And I do not ask whether they preside in court when they put their pants back on in the morning. But you have asked about Judge Hartman. He saw to it that justice was done in my case, which I appreciate.

And that is the extent of our relationship. What more can I say?"

"You might say that the judge issued his contempt citation to silence Mr. Keller and thus protect his reputation from the charge that he'd had an affair with you."

The smile had vanished from Sugar's face.

"Mr. Deputy Sheriff, I think you are carrying this exercise in speculation way too far. And I'm also mildly offended by the thought that anyone's reputation might be jeopardized by an affair with me. Mr. Ferraro, who seems to be your source, has no idea what he's talking about. Perhaps he thinks he's getting back at me for terminating our relationship. In any event, I'm sure that whoever killed Mr. Keller had a more urgent motive than saving the reputation of a middle aged judge."

When Sam got into his car and headed back to Crooked Lake, he found himself reluctantly admiring Donna Sugar. She had handled herself superbly. He wondered how Carol would have reacted to the woman's cool and confident performance. He knew that she would be intrigued by what he had to report.

CHAPTER 25

Gretchen Ziegler had just come from a brief meeting of M & B's 12 attorneys, the purpose of which had been an update on the firm's quest for a replacement of Carl Keller. Francis Foster had, as usual, been in charge of the meeting, and he had been in an uncharacteristically sour mood. The search was not going well. At least that was Foster's view; nobody else seemed to think that it was a serious problem. After the managing partner had reported on two upcoming interviews, he turned his attention to another matter that was bothering him.

"I want all of this backstage speculation about Carl Keller to stop," he said. "There is no reason why M & B needs to become a rumor mill. We know absolutely nothing about Mr. Keller's death, and finding his killer is not our responsibility. I've overheard at least three overheated conversations about the matter since Ms. Ziegler sprang the news on us, all of them uninformed and none of them related to what we do here at M & B."

Foster looked at Gretchen as he spoke. His message was clear: she may have meant well, but she had done the firm no service by distracting attention from its raison d'etre.

"I'm also troubled by the fact that too many of you are in the habit of taking unscheduled leave days." This time he looked at Tony Ferraro. "You seem to be the worst offender, Mr. Ferraro."

Rarely had Foster singled out a member of the firm for criticism in front of his colleagues.

Surprised by this exception, all eyes around the conference table turned toward Ferraro.

Then, as if embarrassed by what he had just said, Foster sought to pour oil on troubled waters.

"Sorry, Tony. No capital offense. But all of you, let's make M & B priority number one. I know I'm a bit out of sorts, so bear with me."

Later that morning Gretchen ran into Foster in the coffee lounge. She had been with the firm long enough and had enough seniority that she thought it safe to say something.

"Francis, I want to apologize for stirring things up regarding Carl Keller. All I intended to do was let everyone know that a former colleague had met a bad end. I guess the story has gotten out of hand since then."

"I didn't intend to sound off about it, but it's been getting me down. No one has said it in so many words, but I suspect that some of our colleagues think Keller would still be alive if I hadn't sacked him."

"But that doesn't make sense," Gretchen said. "Why would he have been murdered because you let him go?"

Foster chose not to get involved in a discussion of Gretchen's logic. Instead, he asked her a question about their former colleague, now the sheriff of Cumberland County.

"It's my impression that you've remained a friend of Carol Kelleher since she left the firm. How's she doing?"

"I wish we were closer, but yes, I like to think of myself as a friend. As to how she's doing, she seems to thrive on her job. It helps that she's got a wonderful husband who, incidentally, also loves police work."

"He's in law enforcement, too?"

"No, he teaches music down state at Madison College. But he fancies himself a sleuth."

"Because Keller was killed over in her jurisdiction, she'll be in charge of the investigation into Keller's death. Does she talk to you about how it's going?"

"Not a lot. We're both busy, and she hasn't had much time to get things off the ground."

"But you have discussed it, haven't you?"

"Sure," Gretchen said, wondering where this conversation was going. "Like I told you, I found out about Carl's death from Carol. We've just had one brief phone chat since then."

"I take it she knows about Keller being fired?"

"She does. I believe I'm the one who told her, although she ran into him shortly before his death and he said he was no longer practicing law."

"May I assume then that she is also familiar with the story of the Truscott case?"

Gretchen was becoming concerned that Francis Foster might not be pleased that she had spoken so freely with the sheriff. But there was no point in pretending that she hadn't.

"Yes, she is. I didn't think of it as privileged information, just a matter of catching her up on what was going on in the lives of people she knew when she was with the firm. She had liked Carl, and I thought she'd be interested in what had happened to him."

"No, of course it isn't a matter of privileged information. I just wouldn't have wanted her, or anybody for that matter, to have the wrong impression of my decision to let Carl go."

Foster didn't ask the question that Gretchen was expecting: had she expressed an opinion as to why he had let Carl go? Instead, he again changed the subject, raising an issue that Gretchen knew nothing about.

"What do you know about Tony Ferraro's relationship with Carl Keller?"

"Their relationship? I'm not sure what you mean."

He shook his head.

"No, I'm not referring to any sexual peccadillos. Ferraro is, as I'm sure you know, one of the more aggressively heterosexual men around here. I'm simply asking what you know about their professional relationship. Did they seem to talk together much? About - well, let me be quite frank about it - about legal ethics? I'm afraid I don't pay as much attention to such things as I should."

Gretchen was once again puzzled. The words 'legal ethics' raised a red flag in her mind.

"I thought of Carl as a bit of a loner, and it seemed to me that Tony was as close to a friend as he had. In the firm, I mean. But that's only because I saw Tony in Carl's office from time to time. Obviously, I never heard what they were talking about. Probably just one or the other's case de jure."

"Either one ever tell you what they were discussing?"

"No, and I never saw a reason to ask."

"Well, that's understandable. But I'm afraid Ferraro wasn't a friend of Keller's. Quite the contrary. Tony came by my office a day or two after you told us that Keller was dead, said he knew something he ought to share with me. It seems he'd discovered that Carl had violated his fiduciary duty to a client in a recent case. Apparently the matter was quietly resolved, so with Carl now dead, Tony figured there was no point in making the matter public."

"That's interesting. And surprising. But why did Tony tell you this if he had no intention of doing anything about it?"

"What he said was that he had supported my decision to sack Carl, and thought I should know that there was an even better reason for doing it than his citation for contempt."

"May I ask why you are telling me this, Francis?"

"That's a fair question. I hadn't planned to, but here we were talking about Carol Kelleher, who was something of a mentor of Keller's when he joined the firm. Knowing you're her friend, I thought you might want to let her know that Carl wasn't the fair haired boy she remembered."

Foster had apparently said what he wanted to say to Gretchen. He excused himself, and set off down the corridor to his corner office. It took Ms. Ziegler the better part of half an hour to put their conversation out of her mind. The managing partner had clearly been interested in Carol Kelleher and her investigation of Carl Keller's murder. And he had thought it important to share with Carol Tony Ferraro's story that Carl had had feet of clay. It had been an interesting ten minutes, and she wasn't sure what to make of it. It was obvious, however, that she would soon be placing a call to her friend over on Crooked Lake.

CHAPTER 26

Officer Parsons was due to have his patrol car serviced, and he always liked to make it presentable before taking it in. He was by nature tidier than most of his colleagues, so making it presentable was not a big challenge. There would be none of the hamburger wrappers and related junk that made Officer Grieves and his car the butt of jokes among his colleagues. Nonetheless, Bill was going through the vehicle, collecting a few things which had escaped his attention earlier.

To his surprise he discovered a receipt for gas tucked down in the side pocket beside the passenger seat. He could not imagine how it had gotten there, inasmuch as he always filled the tank himself and, consistent with department rules, was careful to keep the receipts in the glove compartment. Moreover, the amount of the bill was small; he couldn't remember ever putting so little gas in his car. And then it occurred to him that he had loaned his car to the sheriff one day when she was learning what it was like to be ticketing speeders. Her car had needed to have its tires rotated, and inasmuch as he was scheduled for water patrol that day he had let her take his.

He caught Carol in her office after squad meeting and decided to kid her about the receipt.

"I see you're in the business of topping off the gas tank," he said.

Carol, of course, had no idea what Bill was talking about.

"Topping off the tank? Where did you get that idea?"

"I was cleaning out my car and found a receipt for the grand total of $4.76. That kind of money doesn't buy you much gas. And then I remembered that you'd borrowed my car one day last week, so you must be the culprit."

"That's crazy. I make it a practice never to run out of gas, but I -" She stopped mid-thought. "Wait a minute. Let me see that receipt."

Bill handed it to her, a knowing smile on his face.

"Somebody's written something on the other side," Carol said. She tried to read it, but it was both badly smudged and looked as if the writer's pen had run out of ink. She walked over to the window and better light.

"All I can make out is 'don't trust' and a name that looks like it begins with an F. The pen was dry and whoever wrote the note tried to get it to work by bearing down. See?"

Carol handed the receipt to Parsons, then immediately took it back.

"I think I can solve your mystery, Bill. The gas was purchased by the late Carl Keller."

She told him the story of encountering Carl, out of gas on the upper lake road, and taking him into Cumberland to purchase enough to get his car to a gas station. But it was the unfinished message on the back of the receipt that interested her. What was he trying to say? And why had he left the receipt in the passenger's side pocket? Was he trying to tell her something? Surely the message could not be for someone else. But why hadn't he simply told her what was on his mind instead of trying to write a message? There certainly hadn't been anyone else in the car who might have heard something Carl hadn't wanted him to hear.

"What do you think this says?" she asked Parsons.

"Something about not trusting somebody. At least I think it's somebody, and it looks like the name begins with an F before the pen failed him. You think he was warning you about someone?"

"It looks that way, but if so it doesn't look like he succeeded. Do you have a few minutes? Let's sit down and see if we can make sense of this."

Bill Parsons was all ears as Carol told him about her strange encounters with Carl Keller before his death. She'd talked a bit about it in squad meetings, but other than Sam, her team didn't know much about her experience of being stalked by a man she had finally recognized as a former attorney in her old law firm.

"He obviously wanted to make contact with me, but for some reason he didn't know how to go about it. It's like he wanted me to figure out what he was up to before he was even sure himself. I remember the day I picked him up and took him to the gas station. I knew he looked vaguely familiar, but that was the first time I realized who he was. He barely said anything, but I got the feeling he was in trouble. And as we know, he really was in trouble. This two word message, along with that F, also tells us that something was wrong. I'm not supposed to trust Mr., or maybe it's Ms. Or Mrs. F. Who's F? Why shouldn't I trust F?"

Carol stared at the receipt.

Parsons said he didn't know enough to be helpful.

"Knowing what I know, and it's not much, the only person I know whose name begins with an F who was an important player in Carl's life is Francis Foster."

"Who's he? Or is it a she?"

"It's a he, and he's a senior partner in my old law firm. Moreover, he runs the firm. At least he makes the big decisions that don't require a majority of the partners. And one of the big decisions he made recently directly affected Carl. He fired him. He fired him because he mishandled a case and was cited for contempt of court by the judge. So based on what little we know, my best guess - and it is a guess - is that I'm not supposed to trust Francis Foster."

Parsons, now aware of at least some of the backstory of Carl Keller's murder, left on his rounds after reminding Carol that she needed to keep a neater patrol car, especially when it was his. Carol, on the other hand, closed her door and spent the next hour brainstorming the receipt and its message. Why, whatever his problems were, had Carl not taken advantage of the situation to explain why he needed her help? And if he couldn't bring himself to spell it out verbally, why hadn't he simply handed her the receipt with its unfinished warning? It did her no good in the passenger's side pocket of Bill Parsons' patrol car. If Carl had had his wits about him, he would have realized that.

When she finally forced herself to get back to the day's agenda, it was with the knowledge that what she was facing was exactly the kind of challenge Kevin took delight in solving. It wasn't close to quitting time, but she was already anxious to head for the cottage, take a cooling swim, and let Kevin take a crack at deciphering the problem of the $4.76 gas receipt.

CHAPTER 27

The swim had been satisfying, but Kevin was unable to offer any useful ideas regarding the receipt which Carl Keller had left behind in Bill Parsons' patrol car.

They had had an interesting but ultimately unproductive discussion. It had demonstrated to Carol, if further demonstration were needed, that Keller was not the person she had known at Morgenstern and Brauchli. Kevin offered the suggestion that he might have been experiencing a mental breakdown before he was killed, and voiced the question of whether an autopsy could shed light on the matter. But of course the cause of death was not in doubt, and Carol was skeptical that an autopsy of the brain would be able to explain Keller's behavior. She did, however, promise to speak with Doc Crawford.

If Keller's unwillingness to talk about his problems defied explanation, the meaning of his abbreviated message on the back of the receipt was similarly elusive. They both knew what 'don't trust' meant in the abstract. But who was it that wasn't to be trusted? Presumably a person, whose name - either first or last - begins with an F. But what about F wasn't to be trusted? His ability to do something? His promise to do something? And what was that something?

They kicked this puzzle around for awhile, and were about to give it up and have supper when the phone rang. Force of habit led Carol to answer it.

"Carol, it's Gretchen. I hope you have a few minutes. There's something you ought to hear."

"Inasmuch as I assume it's the Keller case you want to talk about, the answer is I have lots of time."

"Darn! And here I was going to tell you about a new recipe I just came across. Of course it's about Keller."

"I recently deputized Kevin to run over to Albany for me. What I should be doing is deputizing you. It'd save us toll fees on the thruway. Just give me a minute to refill my wine glass and tell Kevin who's on the phone."

That done, Carol settled down to hear what her Albany eyes and ears had to report.

Gretchen began by passing along her sense that Francis Foster was very interested in what the sheriff was doing in the investigation of Carl Keller's death.

"You're very much on his mind, Carol. He's not exactly pumping me. That would be too obvious. But the case interests him, even if he wishes we'd concentrate on the practice of law, not speculate on what happened to a former member of the firm."

"I trust you've told him that I'm about ready to make an arrest," Carol said.

"I'd love to see his reaction if I told him that, but we're just going to have to wait, aren't we? No, what's most intriguing is what he had to say about something Tony Ferraro told him."

"Ferraro? Carl's friend at M & B?"

"That's the Ferraro I'm talking about, but according to Francis he was no friend of Carl's."

"Slow down. I was under the impression I should be talking with Ferraro because he's the closest thing Carl had to a friend at the firm."

"That's what I told you, and I thought I was right. But Tony - that's Ferraro - seems to think of the relationship rather differently. At least that's what he told Francis, and what Francis told me. In fact, I think Francis told me what Tony told him specifically so that I'd pass the word on to you. It seems to me that our dear leader is trying to disabuse you of the notion that Carl is something of an old friend. Okay, now I've passed the word onto you. I'm not saying I agree with Francis, you understand. All I'm doing is relaying the message."

"This is a bit confusing, Gretchen. You'd observed the two of them, Carl and this Ferraro, and thought they were close, or reasonably so. Now you hear otherwise. What do you believe, a second hand story from Foster or what you yourself observed?"

"I'll have to tell you what Tony told Francis before I try to answer that question. Remember that I haven't heard any of this from Tony, so I have to assume Francis isn't lying to me. But he says that Tony flat out accused Carl of having violated his fiduciary responsibility to a client in a case, and that that was a better reason for Francis to fire him than the contempt citation in the Truscott case."

"Carl was guilty of financial fraud?"

"That's what Francis said."

"That sounds unlikely, but what do I know. Let's hear the details."

"I know nothing about details. Francis left it at that, except to say that Ferraro had no intention of pursuing it now that Carl is dead."

"What did Francis say to that?"

"If you mean did he say he was going to look into it, the answer is no."

"Somehow this doesn't sound right to me. I know I'm getting this third hand. It's like that old game of telephone. And Francis probably knows more about the case than he told you. But we know him, and I can't believe he'd take a colleague's word for it - a junior colleague's word at that - and then simply let it go. So what if Carl's dead. You and I, we'd want to get all the details, book, chapter and verse. We'd want the judge in the case to know, even if it was too late for it to matter. We'd want to use it as a teaching lesson in the firm. Sorry, I must sound like a law professor."

"No, you're right. You ought to be here, acting as Francis's conscience. My guess is that Francis will take steps, but he'll do it quietly. After all, he won't want to have word get out that one of his attorneys violated his fiduciary obligations to a client. Do you think I should have a good heart to heart talk with Ferraro?"

"If you think you can do it without it ruining whatever relationship you may have with him as a colleague, go ahead. After all, this is an in-house matter where you and he are concerned, and it probably has nothing to do with what happened to Carl. But I suspect that I'm going to want to see him, too. My deputy has already talked with him, although they spent most of their time talking about that Sugar woman, the one whose abusive lover was defended by Carl. Ferraro seems to have taken an interest in Sugar. He says he'd been sleeping with her."

"I'll be damned," Gretchen said. "Whatever else Tony may be, I'd say he's pretty stupid."

"If it weren't for my husband and the officers who work for me, there are times when I'd be tempted to say that about men in general."

"You're becoming a real cynic, Carol," Gretchen said. "Surely it can't be that bad."

"No, I'm just being bitchy. But frankly, and I have nothing but intuition to go on, I don't believe Ferraro's story that Carl Keller was guilty of financial fraud where a client is concerned. I haven't followed his career since I left Albany, but I just can't picture him doing something like that. Can you?"

"I didn't really know him. I guess anyone can do something illegal or unethical in a pinch, but I know how you feel about Carl. Bad enough he got killed, but even worse if he goes to his grave with that kind of reputation."

"Well, thanks for making my day," Carol said, sounding slightly bitter. "But let me know if you talk to Ferraro about this and what, if anything, you learn. I think I'll take a sleeping pill tonight."

"Sorry, but I thought you ought to know."

"You did right. Thanks, and keep me posted."

Carol found Kevin reading, or pretending to read, the latest Brunetti mystery by Donna Leon. He set it aside.

"So, what's the good word from your spy in Albany?"

"It appears that this guy Ferraro you never talked to has accused Carl Keller of defrauding a client. Posthumously, of course."

"No kidding," Kevin said.

"He mentioned it to the firm's managing partner, who mentioned it to Gretchen. This is how I get my information these days."

175

"It sounds as if Ferraro and Keller weren't quite as cozy as we thought."

"Wait a minute," Carol said, suddenly sounding excited. "I got so carried away by Gretchen's story that I forgot to mention the message on the gas receipt. The message about not trusting F. How about Ferraro? That would be just as likely as Foster. Why didn't I think of him?"

"I don't think you should assume that F is Ferraro just because he's accused Carl of fraud. There could be lots of F's who don't deserve to be trusted - females, Frenchmen, fair weather friends, even faculty members."

"Let's be serious, Kevin. I'll make you a bet Carl was trying to tell me that I shouldn't trust either Francis Foster or Tony Ferraro. One of them kicked him out of the firm and the other one accused him of defrauding a client. That sounds like reason enough not to trust them."

"You're probably right, but now you've got two candidates where before you only had one. I'm not sure Gretchen did you any favor."

"We shall see. I intend to quiz Ferraro myself."

"Are you going to invite him over for lunch, or do you propose to further deplete department funds by taking a trip to Albany?"

"I'll be going to Albany, and I'll kill two birds with one stone. Make that two Fs with one trip, Ferraro and Foster."

"You wouldn't rather let me do it, would you?"

"You had your chance with Ferraro. Besides, I'm the lawyer and I know Foster. I knew I'd have to talk with him sooner or later. And I'm sure he's anxious to see me."

CHAPTER 28

Lindsay Hartman had abandoned his lake cottage and the pleasure that fishing for bass and bluegills gave him and returned to Albany. He had not been ready to do it, but duty called him in the form of a case in which he was to be the presiding judge. The case gave every indication of being an important one, but Hartman was more interested in a case which was now officially history, the case in which he had sentenced Randall Truscott to three years in jail for aggravated assault. The Truscott case may have become history in a legal sense, but in a personal sense it was still very much a pressing concern. He couldn't get it out of his mind.

At the moment he was seated in his study in an oversized leather armchair that seemed to be hugging his ample girth. Hazel had taken to warning him that one day he would no longer be able to escape the chair's grip and make it to the dinner table. The idea amused him, and he was grateful that his wife, who had done a better job than he had in maintaining her figure, still loved him in spite of the evidence that he was leading a much too sedentary life.

Judge Hartman still loved his wife as much as she loved him. They had now celebrated their fortieth anniversary, seen four children off to college and on into satisfying marriages and careers, and welcomed seven grandchildren into the world. His judgeship had capped off his own successful career as a trial lawyer, and he and Hazel were having ever more conversations about retirement. There was only one problem, and her name was Donna Sugar.

She had come into his life four years earlier at a conference he had not decided to attend until the last minute. Hazel had urged him to go - 'you need to mingle more with your peers' she had argued. What is more, the conference was being held, not at some downtown site in the state capital, but at the Mt. Washington Hotel in New Hampshire. He had finally given in to her entreaties and had set off for the White Mountains. Lindsay remembered how she had brushed aside his argument that, if he were to go, she should come along.

'This is a professional conference, Lindsay, not a social occasion. I'd just get in the way.'

The result was that Hazel was back in Albany when her husband met Donna Sugar during a cocktail party reception the first evening at the Mt. Washington. Never a social animal, Lindsay Hartman had taken his martini over to a quiet corner and was in the process of removing an olive from a toothpick when a young woman wearing basic black and pearls and sporting a friendly smile broke away from a cluster of people at the bar and joined him. There were a number of women in the room, a few of them judges, most of them spouses, but this particular woman stood out. She was both younger and smaller than the others, and she was unquestionably more attractive.

"Hello there," she said. "I can see that you're not a mixer. Me either. Care to sit down?" She had set out for a small nearby table with two chairs, assuming that he would follow her. He did. It seemed the polite thing to do.

"My name is Donna Sugar. What's yours?"

He had told her, trying his best to act as if he were used to impromptu conversations with beautiful women. He doubted that he had fooled her, but she hadn't seemed to mind. Ten minutes later she had lured him into a surprisingly easy discussion of such things as their likes and dislikes in music and movies. She took the initiative, but she was also a good listener, and Lindsay was surprised to discover that he was enjoying her company. Forty-five minutes later they were carrying on their conversation over dinner. When it came time to call it a night, he had said little more than 'hello' and 'see you at the morning round table' to any of his fellow judges. He had spent a delightful evening with someone named Donna Sugar, who hadn't seemed to be attached to anybody. She hadn't even been wearing a name tag, and when they said goodnight and headed for their respective rooms, he realized that he had no idea where she was from or why she was at the the Mt. Washington Hotel.

The round table the next morning had been boring, and Lindsay was experiencing his first reservations about having followed Hazel's advice to attend the conference when Donna Sugar appeared at his elbow.

"Let me guess," she said. "Judge talk hasn't been very scintillating this morning."

"Is it that obvious?" he replied with a smile.

"No comment,'" she said, "but what do you say we take a walk? The grounds are lovely."

And they had taken that walk. It lasted for more than an hour, including an interlude on a bench in the woods, where Ms. Sugar had explained that she was a professional model who was taking a brief vacation. Lindsay was under the impression that models were tall and emaciated; the woman beside him on the bench was petite and there was nothing about her figure that could be described as emaciated. He had also assumed that models were empty-headed things, whereas this woman was obviously both intelligent and articulate. Suddenly aware that he was staring at her well turned and well tanned legs, he mumbled an apology and said something to the effect that he didn't really understand the modeling business.

Ms. Sugar declined to enlighten him, but when they returned to the hotel she suggested that they do dinner again, adding an invitation to join her for a cognac afterwards. He accepted with alacrity. He had expected to have the after dinner drink in the reception area, but she argued that she had some cognac in her room, and that she'd rather get away from the bar crowd. Lindsay Hartman would never forget what followed when they reached her room at the end of the second floor corridor.

It had begun innocently enough. At her suggestion he had tossed his jacket and necktie on a chair, and she did the same with her scarf. The cognac, he noticed, was a top of the line VSOP. With the room's only chair now occupied by the coat, tie, and scarf, Lindsay accepted his drink and made himself comfortable on a handsome love seat across from the big bed.

"Now," she announced, "let me enlighten you about modeling."

Enlightenment consisted more of show than tell. Lindsay was too mesmerized by what was happening to offer more than a weak protest, which Donna silenced by running a finger gently across his lips. There would be half-hearted self recriminations the next morning, but that night he yielded, as if in a dream, to the lovely young woman who seemed to know exactly what to say and what to do as things came to their inevitable conclusion.

By the time he had to return to Albany, he had spent a second night in Donna Sugar's bed, and this time he didn't feel guilty about it in the morning. He rationalized that for some unaccountable reason he had been blessed with this exhilarating and totally unexpected experience, and that it had happened to him before he was too old to fully appreciate it. Why she had come to him he did not know. There were men in better shape, more charming - he could think of a dozen qualities these other men had and he lacked. But she had singled him out at the Mt. Washington Hotel and he knew that his life had been forever changed. What is more, she had told him that she, too, lived in Albany, and that she hoped - no, insisted was the word she had used - that they should see each other again. And again.

And they had. They had enjoyed each other's company many times over the intervening years. Of course he had learned that she was in fact a call girl. Which meant that other men shared a bed with her, and there had been fallow periods, some of them several months long, when they had not seen each other. But she always came back, and she always treated reunions as if they were a first time. She had never asked for money at Mt. Washington, but it became apparent that he was expected to compensate her when they were in Albany. After all, this was her profession. It also became clear to him that she was unfailingly discrete, that they had a secret that was not to be shared with anyone. It was she who planned their assignations, and she varied their meeting places, deliberately and creatively, a practice which provided a sense of security which had never been threatened. Not, that is, until the Truscott case and the emergence of a distasteful attorney named Carl Keller.

Until Keller had begun to suggest that Donna Sugar was not the angel she claimed to be, his principal fear had been that he would lose his interest in his wife. But it hadn't happened. Ironically, he and Hazel had become closer. He couldn't explain it, other than to acknowledge the obvious: the two women in his life were both wonderful people whose virtues complemented each other perfectly. Hazel was the comfortable best friend of a life time, the wife who had shared his good moments and his bad ones, and who had always supported him in the latter. Donna was the one who had come along when he was beginning to fear the prospect of old age; he recognized it as a cliche, but she had made him feel young again.

Lindsay Hartman sank deeper into his leather chair and closed his eyes. Carl Keller was dead. His relationship with Donna should now be safe. Hazel would never know. Why then was he so anxious? Was it because he feared that Donna would tire of him as he passed from late middle age to senescent old age? Was it because he feared that Keller's insinuations would take root in someone else's mind, bringing a halt to his secret life with the beautiful, charming call girl?

Hazel stuck her head into his study and asked if everything was all right. He realized that he must be looking distracted, even worried, so he hastened to assure her that he was just fine. He knew it was a lie.

CHAPTER 29

Lisa Simmons was having a difficult night. It wasn't the first. She had never been an insomniac, but it had now been several days since she'd had a good night's sleep, and it had everything to do with the man who had come to the *Treasure Chest* and asked her all those questions about Carl Keller. He had been investigating Carl's death, and his questions had put her on the spot. Lisa knew that she had not been responsible for killing Carl in that horrible way, but she was also aware that the man who was asking her those questions had not been satisfied with her answers. For that matter, she hadn't liked her answers either. Why hadn't she simply been truthful? Why hadn't she told the man what she had done and why and when she had done it? The reason, of course, was that she had been afraid that doing so would have made her a focus of his investigation. Yet by not being more straight forward, all she had accomplished was to make him more suspicious of her.

She looked at her alarm clock again. It told her what she knew it would, that it was still the middle of the night. 2:37 a.m. to be exact. Reluctantly she kicked off the covers and climbed out of bed. She used the bathroom and then went into the living room, turned on the light by the couch, and picked up a magazine she had been reading the previous evening. After five minutes of a desultory effort to become interested in an article about ADHD in children, she tossed the magazine aside and curled up with her thoughts.

Her problem had begun when she moved out of Carl's apartment, although at the time she could not have known what would follow. Had she stayed with him, Carl might eventually have put the Truscott case behind him or at least shared with her more of what was bothering him. He might even have stayed in Albany rather than decamping for the Finger Lakes. But she had become frustrated with his moodiness and petulance, and she had moved back into the flat she sometimes shared with Erin Cooley, at least when Erin wasn't bed hopping with the men who moved into and out of her life in what she referred to as 'Erin's musical chairs.' Lisa had thought of her life as more stable than Erin's, but recent events seemed to be proving her wrong.

It was Carl's unexpected phone call that precipitated a chain of events which were now keeping her awake at night - a chain of events which she had not shared with the man who had so insistently questioned her at the *Treasure Chest*. She hadn't heard from Carl since she had moved out of his apartment, and she hadn't expected to. She had no desire to talk with him, and then suddenly, on a night in late June, she found herself doing just that.

"Lisa, it's me." He didn't need to identify himself. "I know I've been a bit of a bastard lately, and I'm sorry. But I have a favor to ask. And it's really important. Can you forget that I've let you down and do this for me? Just this once?"

"Where on earth are you?" she had asked, ignoring his plea for help.

"It doesn't really matter, but I'm in a little God-forsaken place called Hopewell not far from Crooked Lake."

Lisa had never heard of Hopewell or Crooked Lake.

"What are you doing there? And where is there?"

"Trying to solve my problems. But let's not go into that. I'm still on the planet, probably no more than two hundred miles from where you are. What matters is that I need your help. For old times sake, okay?"

"I don't know what this big favor is, Carl, so how can I tell you I can or can't do it?"

"It's really simple, and it won't take more than an hour or two. When I left, I meant to take a file with me - a file of papers related to a case. Trouble is, I forgot it. It's still in the Woodmere apartment."

"And you want me to get it and mail it to you, is that it?" she had said, her voice in neutral.

"No. I want you to get it and burn it."

"Burn it?" Not surprisingly, Lisa sounded surprised.

"Get rid of it. It's no longer relevant. Like a lot of legal documents, it's privileged information, so I shouldn't leave it lying around."

"Why can't it wait until you come back?"

"Because it can't. Please, will you do this for me? Getting into the apartment's no problem. You still have your key. And it's right there on my desk in a red file. You can't miss it."

"Is there a label on the file?"

"Yes. It says it's the Hartman file. Anyway, it's the only one on the desk." Carl had begun to sound frustrated. "Come on, Lisa, please."

"Oh, all right. Like you said, for old time's sake."

"Thanks. I really mean it. One other thing. After you do it, please call me and let me know it's been taken care of. I'm a worrier, and I'll feel better if you call. You've got my cell number, and if there's a problem, I'm staying in the *Welcome Inn* in Hopewell. Okay?"

"Okay," she had said without conviction.

He had asked how she was doing, but it was obvious that he was simply going through the motions of showing an interest. The conversation lasted for only two more minutes.

She did as she was asked. She had never been interested in Carl's law practice, and she made no attempt to open and peruse the file. Carl had doubtless been sure that she wouldn't.

Things got even worse after that, at least in her account - or false account - of events to the man from Cumberland County. Having decided not to tell him of her mission for Carl Keller, it had become easier for her to say nothing about Carl's cousin, Richard Keller. Richard had arrived at her doorstep the day after she had retrieved and destroyed the file. His very appearance had been a shock. She had not, of course, known that Carl had had a cousin; they had rarely discussed their immediate families, much less more distant cousins, aunts, and uncles. But what had been shocking was Richard's heavily bandaged head, which made him look like a mummy in an old black and white movie. He had told her that the bandages and his belabored speech were the result of a bad fall in the shower of his health club, a fall that had knocked out several teeth and broken his cheekbone. He had dismissed the damage as considerably less than it might have been, and then explained his reason for coming to see her. It seemed that he wanted to visit his cousin, but that the deskman at the Woodmere had reported that Carl was away. Subsequent inquiries had led him to her, and he was now seeking her help.

When Richard Keller thanked her and left, he had been given the key to Carl's apartment and the address of the *Welcome Inn*. She had been pleased to be able to help him. It was not until later that she began to worry about his expressed reason to visit both the apartment and the motel. But wondering got her nowhere, and she proceeded to forget about Carl's cousin until a plain clothes officer from Cumberland County named Kevin Whitman told her that Carl had been murdered. She had been surprised when Cumberland County's sheriff had reported Carl's death, especially when the news had come so soon after her last conversation with him. But she had assumed that he had died of a coronary or an automobile accident. Why, she asked herself, had she taken that news so casually? Why hadn't she immediately asked about the cause of death? Was she really so anxious to put her affair with Carl behind her that she couldn't muster even that small a token of compassion? But murder, well, that was something altogether different. And it immediately prompted thoughts about what she had done. Thoughts about burning Carl's legal file. Thoughts about giving his cousin the key to Carl's apartment. Especially thoughts about giving him the location of where Carl was staying. Somewhere near a place called Crooked Lake. Someplace where a sheriff named Carol Kelleher and one of her officers named Kevin Whitman were seeking to discover who had killed Carl. And why.

Lisa stirred herself on the couch. She started to pick up the magazine she had tossed aside, thought better of it, and disappeared into the kitchen to heat some leftover morning coffee. She had no idea who had killed Carl, but she knew that one person who might have done so was his own cousin, Richard Keller. And it was she who had given him the critical information about where Carl could be found. She had told the man from Crooked Lake none of this. Instead she had lied about when she had last visited Carl's apartment. She had lied about why she had gone to the apartment on that occasion. She had lied about what had happened to her key to the apartment. She had lied by making no mention of Richard Keller because she had wanted to avoid being drawn into the investigation of Carl's death. But now she was having trouble sleeping because she might have made it more rather than less likely that she would become a target of that investigation. Lisa took a sip of the morning's coffee. It was bitter.

CHAPTER 30

"Do you feel up to company again?"

Carol and Kevin were steering the canoe around the point at Mallard Cove, heading back to the cottage after a leisurely paddle when she posed the question. The breeze was very light, and the last of the sun's rays lit up the crest of the bluff across the lake. It had been a relaxing post-dinner outing that had taken them almost two miles down lake, but now it was time to call it a day. Except that Carol had another idea.

"What do you have in mind?" Kevin asked.

"I'd like to talk with Francis Foster," she replied, "and I'd like to do it here if I could persuade him to take a short break from the demands of keeping the firm afloat."

"Why here? You just told me the other day that you planned to go over to Albany to interview the two F boys, Ferraro and Foster. Why the change of plans? Isn't Foster more likely to see you if he doesn't have to take a four hundred mile round trip to do it?"

"You may be right, but I've been thinking about it. I've got a hunch that he might loosen up, be a bit more forthcoming, if we were on the lake instead of that claustrophobic office of his. What if I could use some of my Crooked Lake witchery to sell the idea?"

"I wouldn't bet on it, but if you want to invite him over it's fine with me. Unless, that is, you plan to exclude me from your little tete-a-tete."

"On the contrary, I'd like you to meet him. And him to meet you, of course. I haven't seen Francis in years, and now that he's a party to the Keller case it's important that I reintroduce myself to him. If you're there, he might even be more inclined to see it as a social occasion."

Kevin stopped paddling.

"Glad to be of use if I can, but in what sense do you picture Foster as a party to the Keller case? Are you starting to make up a roster of suspects?"

"Nothing like that. Francis may be a a bit of a martinet at times, but he's no murderer. Besides, I can't think of a reason why he'd want to do away with Carl. All I'm interested in doing is playing catch up with Morgenstern and Brauchli politics. Gretchen's been helpful, but she's still one of the peons. Unless Francis has become prematurely senile, he'll know who's up to what. I just want him to relax and talk to me."

"When is this meeting with the firm's managing attorney supposed to take place?"

"I'll tell you after I call him, but I'd like to aim for this weekend. I'll make it for lunch, like I did with Gretchen."

When they beached the canoe it was almost nine o'clock. Kevin secured the canoe while Carol went on into the cottage to make the call. Gretchen's list of phone numbers simplified the task, and to Carol's relief the firm's senior lawyer was at home.

"Francis, this is Carol Kelleher. Remember me?"

"How could I forget you, Carol? Are you about to ask for your old job back?"

It was a silly way to launch a conversation, but Carol found Foster's effort at humor to be a good sign.

"I hate to disappoint you by saying no, but I hope you will say yes to my question. Can I talk you into coming over to Crooked Lake for a day of R & R, like maybe this weekend? Or if that's impossible, sometime soon? I'd really love to see you, and we'd enjoy letting our hair down over here better than Albany. Cool lake breeze, things like that. I'll do lunch."

"You sound as if you've already marked your calendar. Efficient as always."

"And optimistic as always. But seriously, we'd love to have you. By we, I mean my husband Kevin and me. I like to show him off."

"Well, Carol, you've caught me off guard here. I'm used to spending my weekends at one grindstone or another. Don't even play golf much anymore. Tell me, what is your agenda?"

It was obvious that Francis Foster was interested. Gretchen had said that he was curious about her in her post-M & B career as sheriff, especially now that another of his former attorneys had been killed over in her jurisdiction.

"I have two reasons for the invitation, Francis. The first is that I'd really like to see you again. As you may imagine, I have good memories of my time with the firm, and it's been too long since we've seen each other.

"My second reason is that I'd like to hear more about the firm. Who's still there, what are they up to. Let's say it's nostalgia calling."

"I must revise my earlier tribute, Carol. Not only are you efficient, you're devious. Surely the recent death of Carl Keller has something to do with your invitation. But you haven't mentioned it."

"That's true, but I don't want to talk about Carl's death, sad as it is. I am interested, however, in what kind of man - and attorney - he'd become since I knew him. I ran into him over here on the lake just shortly before his death, and he wasn't the Carl I knew when I was a part of the firm. He seemed withdrawn, unwilling to talk about - well, about anything. Frankly I was surprised to see him, but even more surprised by how much he'd changed. Anyway, it isn't just Carl. M & B's a stranger these days, and that's too bad."

"I understand that you're still in touch with Gretchen Ziegler. I'd assume she could bring you up to date as well as I can."

"We talk occasionally, but you and she would have different perspectives on things. And I really am anxious to see you again. It's been almost ten whole years."

"You're very persuasive, just as you always were with juries. So tell me, if I come over this weekend, should it be Saturday or Sunday? Frances is visiting her sister and I don't expect her back until next Wednesday."

"How about Sunday? For lunch. And a swim, if you'd like to test our waters."

"That's a nice thought, but I don't cut quite the figure I used to. Nothing uglier than a 70 year old man in a bathing suit. Now why don't you tell me just where on that lake you live."

Very pleased with herself and her salesmanship pitch, Carol relayed instructions. She almost added something about where they were in relationship to Judge Hartman's place, but thought better of it. Foster would anticipate that she might bring it up, but there was no point in her making the connection between the two men obvious.

"We're on for Sunday," she called out to Kevin, who had settled into a deck chair to watch the moon rise over the bluff.

"My persuasive wife," he said when she emerged from the living room.

"I doubt that he's coming because I talked him into it. He's curious about me. And about what he assumes is my investigation into Carl Keller's death. I thought he might try to talk me into meeting him in Albany, but I have a hunch he rather likes the idea of seeing us animals in our native habitat. So we have company for lunch, and I'll let you plan the menu. I'm sure Francis is a carnivore."

"Hamburgers on the grill," Kevin said, "just to let him know we have the common touch."

"By the way, his wife is visiting family, so I didn't have to do the courteous thing and invite her, too. That would have complicated things, don't you think? But get this. Her name is Frances, making them Francis and Frances."

"That's not all that strange," Kevin said.

"Considering that I'm Carol and our latest murder victim was Carl, I'd say we come pretty damn close to a pair of coincidences."

"If you say so. Let's watch the moon rise."

CHAPTER 31

They had picked up the Sunday *Times*, sections of which had been scattered about the deck and the living room, leading Carol to observe that the cottage 'looks like the wrath of God.' Kevin had built a bed of charcoal on the grill, and Carol had gone to the trouble of changing into a summery lemon yellow pant suit.

"What do you think? Will he be impressed?" she asked.

"With the cottage? With your outfit? You aren't really worried about impressing a man who was your boss ten years ago, are you?"

"It is sort of stupid, isn't it?"

"You always make a good impression, Carol. And if you're worried about me, forget it. I promised myself when I hit the big 5-0 that I'd no longer worry about such things, not even when the sweetheart of Sigma Chi stops by during my office hours."

"I just want him to feel relaxed. So don't start asking a lot of questions."

"Me ask questions?" Kevin said in mock horror. "This is your investigation, not mine."

"I know, but I also know how hard it is for you not to ask the questions I'm trying to finesse."

"Would you like me to sit beside you so you can kick me in the shin if I step out of line?"

"It'll be better if you just keep busy tending the grill, mixing drinks, doing useful things. Leave Foster to me."

After another ten minutes during which Carol paced the floor, straightening things that didn't need straightening, a bright red MiniCooper pulled up behind the cottage and a well muscled man with pattern baldness stepped out. To Carol's surprise, in light of his self denigrating characterization of himself as an ugly 70, Francis Foster looked good in blue shorts and a yellow polo shirt that almost matched her pant suit. Her former boss was still an attractive man.

"Francis, how good to see you," Carol said as she met him on the lawn.

"The feeling is mutual," he replied and proceeded to give her a big hug.

Kevin had hung back in the living room, leaving it to Carol to welcome Foster. The greeting outside lasted for several minutes. Carol's introduction went smoothly, although Kevin had the feeling that the managing partner of Morgenstern and Brauchli was sizing him up.

"You get to spend the whole summer here on the lake?" Foster asked, the implication being that academia was an undemanding profession. Carol intervened to assure him that a major part of a college professor's responsibility had to do with researching and writing books and papers that would advance the frontiers of knowledge.

"He does a lot of writing while he's here at the cottage," she said. Kevin chose not to correct her.

"I don't envy you those long months living so far apart," Foster said.

"It's better than the alternative," Carol insisted.

Kevin thought that enough had been said about who he was and what he did. He changed the subject by offering something to drink. This led to five minutes of expressing alcoholic preferences and dislikes. In the end, Foster agreed to sample the Riesling. Carol and Kevin stuck to their favorite Chardonnay.

They retreated to the deck with their drinks, and after ten or fifteen minutes of discussion of the lake's undoubted beauty and Albany's inevitable preoccupation with state politics, Kevin excused himself to tend the fire on the grill.

As if by mutual consent, Carol and Francis chose to defer her agenda until after lunch. Foster seemed mostly to be simply enjoying the view when he turned to Carol and asked her about her job.

"You like police work?"

"I love it. Most of the time anyway. There are exceptions, but all in all it agrees with me more than the practice of law did. Are you surprised? Or disappointed?"

"I thought I'd heard that you've been up to your neck in some pretty tough cases. Like that one involving a former state assembly woman. I'm talking about murder cases."

Carol smiled.

"That's true. But those are the exceptions. For the most part police work is routine. Mostly we're in the business of cultivating our reputation as the good guys."

"What happens when something like Carl Keller's death roils the lake waters?"

Carol had assumed that Foster would raise the issue of Carl's death. She was surprised that he had done it so soon, not more than half an hour after parking his car behind the cottage.

"What makes Carl's death so hard to think about is that I knew him and that it occurred over here. Otherwise I suppose you could say it was just another case of someone's life being snuffed out prematurely. Why Carl? Why here? But now that you've raised the question, it's my turn. Carl was with the firm a long time. Did you sense a change in him over the years he was with M & B?"

"In what way?"

"When he first came aboard, he was eager, conscientious, and, sorry, I should have put this first, a good lawyer. I didn't know him for long, but I had the impression he had a good career ahead of him. I was glad to have him as a colleague. Was that how you saw him?"

"He was always pretty low-keyed, if you know what I mean. He didn't talk a lot, but when he did he talked common sense. I guess you'd say he was a bit harder to know than most of our people. I only remember meeting his wife once or twice. That's his former wife. Word has it that he'd taken up with another woman recently, but I never saw her, don't even know her name. I probably don't pay as much attention to my colleagues as I should."

Carol was inclined to agree with Francis Foster's self assessment.

"Did Carl have close friends in the firm? People he interacted with more than the others?" She wondered if Foster would confirm Gretchen's view.

"Not to my knowledge." He studied his glass, took another drink, and abruptly changed the subject.

"Why do you think Carl was killed?"

"I wish I knew. That's why I've been trying to get a better picture of who he was. When something like this happens, we start thinking about people the victim knew, not strangers. For all I know, Carl was killed by a homeless vagrant, but all of the studies I've read suggest it's more likely to be someone he knew, and probably knew fairly well. If I were still with the firm, I wouldn't have to be asking these questions, would I? Of course if I were still with the firm I wouldn't be investigating Carl's murder."

"Do you think his death is somehow related to the firm?"

Obviously Francis would like an unequivocal assurance that the answer to his question was no. She was unable to provide such an assurance, yet the more questions she asked, the more likely it was that he would assume the focus of her investigation was indeed M & B.

Carol was considering how to answer Foster's question when Kevin appeared with news that lunch was ready.

The lunch was excellent but the conversation began to sag well before dessert was served. Efforts by both Carol and Kevin to shift the discussion to lighter matters than Carl Keller's death were unavailing. Francis showed no interest in talking opera or lake lore or even his own vacation plans. It gradually became clear that their guest believed that the sheriff of Cumberland County knew more about Keller's murder than she had acknowledged. By the time they had finished lunch and repaired to the deck, he admitted as much.

"Carol, please do not be offended, but it seems to me that you know more about Carl's death than you've told me. I know something about how the police operate, and after a decade in the business you're no novice. But I think you can level with me. If there's something about the Keller case that involves

M & B or any of our people, I think you should tell me so. I would like to help you, but I can't do that if you aren't willing to show me your cards."

An interesting way to put it, Carol thought. The language of a gambler.

But it was Kevin who spoke up.

"Carol's problem is that so far her investigation is running on rumors. That's like a car running on fumes. One of those rumors is that the judge in the Truscott case cited Mr. Keller for contempt of court because he was coming dangerously close to revealing something that might be embarrassing for the judge. Moreover, the rumor persists that because you and the judge are old friends you severed ties with Mr. Keller to show your support of the judge."

Both Francis Foster and Carol Kelleher looked sharply at Kevin.

"That's rude, Kevin," Carol said between gritted teeth. There wasn't much more she could say inasmuch as Foster would realize that if Kevin knew of this rumor, so would Carol.

"Is this why you asked me to lunch?" he asked Carol. "So you could accuse me of doing Judge Hartman a favor? The judge correctly cited Keller for contempt because he repeatedly ignored warnings that he was out of order. I like my attorneys to vigorously defend their clients, but there are limits and Keller was way over the line. Let me be clear. I have never fired anyone to please Judge Hartman or any other judge."

"I apologize for my husband," Carol said contritely.

"I enjoyed lunch, but I think it would be best if I were on my way. No, don't get up. I'll see myself out. If you are interested in further information about M & B, I suggest you ask your friend Ziegler, whom I assume is the source of your rumors."

Once Foster had departed, Carol turned her attention to Kevin.

"I hope you're pleased with yourself," she said as she started to take the luncheon dishes to the kitchen.

"Come on, let me do that," Kevin said, anxious to avoid a marital spat.

"You've done enough already. What on earth were you thinking? I thought we'd agreed I'd do the talking."

"But you saw what he was doing. All he's interested in is keeping the law firm out of your investigation. The firm and probably Foster himself."

"Yes, and you saw how far you got with your in-the-face approach. He's not some 20 year old college sophomore trying to explain a late term paper. You virtually accused him of unethical conduct. On top of that you put my friend Gretchen in one hell of a spot. What if he decides to fire her, too?"

"I'm sorry, Carol. But he asked you to show him your cards, and isn't that what I did? Besides, he's too smart to fire Gretchen. It would look like a cover-up."

Carol put the dessert plates in the dishwasher and started attending to the wine glasses.

"Do me a favor and take a walk. Or a swim. I need to be alone for awhile so I can give some thought to damage control."

Kevin knew better than to argue.

CHAPTER 32

The cause of Carl Keller's death had been so apparent that the sheriff had paid little attention to the autopsy. She had notified Doc Crawford as she always did in matters like this, but had not been concerned when he told her that he would be out of town for several days visiting an ailing sister in Vermont. Thus it was with some surprise that she picked up the phone that evening and heard Crawford's familiar voice on the line.

"Thought I'd let you know that I'm back in harness," he said, "and that I owe you a report on the Keller autopsy."

"To tell the truth, I'd forgotten all about it. Well, that's not quite the case, but I had sort of put it out of my mind. How's you sister?"

"Hanging in there. She doesn't get around very well, so she's weighing a knee replacement. Actually, two of them. I tell her she might be better off with a wheelchair, but she thinks that would make her look like an old lady. I remind her she's already 78, so why not enjoy the perks of old age."

"She's 78? I had no idea she was *that* much older than you are."

"Thanks for the compliment, Carol, but I'm 72. There were seven of us in the Crawford litter, and I fell exactly in the middle. My brother Harold's even three years older than Vinny. But you aren't interested in us Crawfords. I called about my latest autopsy for my favorite sheriff."

"Thanks for the call, but frankly I haven't been worried that I haven't heard from you. I'm pretty much able to diagnose a slit throat all by myself."

"Oh, yes, the slit throat. Mean thing to do to a guy. Thank goodness he didn't feel a thing."

This surprised Carol.

"How could he not?" she asked.

"It doesn't hurt if you're already dead."

"Wait a minute. Can you run that past me again?"

"Like I said, your man Keller was already dead when somebody took a knife to his throat. I knew it as soon as I saw him. He'd hardly bled at all. You don't bleed when you're dead because the heart's no longer pumping blood. I can tell you about the knife if you like. It must have been a pretty deadly weapon, sharp as they make 'em. But that's not what's important. It's the fact that he was already dead from an overdose of drugs."

"You're telling me that he committed suicide?"

"Obviously I don't know what was in his mind, Carol. But he had ingested a lot of stuff. You name it, he'd taken it. It's what you would call a very bad cocktail, and I'm not talking illegal drugs but a combination of prescriptions and stuff you can get over the counter. The toxicology report will provide some names if you want to follow up with his doctor or pharmacy. Oh, and he'd been drinking. So it was benzos or painkillers and alcohol in quantities that no doctor would ever recommend. Either Keller was bent on suicide or he was on some kind of a high and didn't know what he was doing. My guess is that it was the former."

Carol suddenly felt very sad.

"Had he been dead long when somebody took a knife to him?"

"I can't be sure how long, but it's likely the two events occurred not more than an hour or two apart."

"Why would somebody slit the throat of a dead man?"

"That's for you to find out, not me. I suppose the man with the knife just didn't realize his victim was already dead. Or maybe cutting throats was his signature, something he had to leave behind to let the world know he'd been there."

"That's terrible, Doc. I can't imagine somebody that sick."

"Human beings are capable of some pretty awful things, Carol."

"What you're telling me makes it even clearer that I didn't really know Carl Keller anymore."

"You knew him?" Crawford sounded surprised.

"I guess I forgot to provide you with a backstory on Keller when I reported that we needed you to perform another autopsy for us. But yes, I worked with him briefly in Albany before I was persuaded to come back to my roots and become a sheriff. The strange thing is that I ran into him - or maybe I should say he ran into me - down in Southport not long before his death. At first I didn't recognize him. I even thought he might be stalking me. When I finally figured out where I knew him from, I tried to draw him out. But he just went into his shell. Next thing I know the owner of a run down motel in Hopewell calls to tell me he's got a dead guest. It's Carl Keller."

"Sounds to me like it's not just the guy with the knife who's sick. This guy Keller must have been sick, too."

"It's beginning to look that way, doesn't it?" Carol said.

When she rang off she was feeling the beginning of a guilt trip. Why hadn't she made more of an effort to help Carl cope with whatever was troubling him? Was it what had happened in the Truscott case? Was it what Francis Foster had done to him? Or was it something deeper in his past or in his own psyche, something which might explain his alienation from his parents, his withdrawal into himself, his strange behavior in both seeking her out and simultaneously avoiding her?

Kevin, who was in her dog house, had retreated to the study where he was presumably immersed in a book. She was quite certain that he wouldn't be at the computer, creating the paper he was supposed to be writing. Creativity requires that the mind be focussed, and Kevin's mind would be distracted by thoughts of the recent unpleasantness with Francis Foster. She was still annoyed with him for the way he had 'showed Foster her cards.' But he had been right that Foster had some explaining to do. Perhaps she should venture to make him a peace offering. On impulse she retreated to the kitchen where she found a box of brownies that she had picked up at a bake sale in West Branch. She put two of them on a plate and poked her head through the study door.

"How about a brownie?" she said hopefully.

"I'd love one if it comes with a kiss," he said.

"Don't push your luck, buster."

CHAPTER 33

It was Monday, and Carol would have loved to take a day off and do nothing but putter around the house and take advantage of the weather to enjoy the lake. Her sense of responsibility made that impossible. Instead, she got up even earlier than usual in order to make the trip to the office when it was still cool and the traffic would be light. She even took a different route than usual, one that took her over tertiary back country roads. She made the trip with windows rolled down, the better to enjoy the breeze. By the time she pulled into the department's parking lot she was able to congratulate herself on not spending a single minute thinking about Carl Keller and the puzzling Keller case.

That changed almost as soon as she'd said hello to JoAnne Franks, her unfailingly cheerful assistant.

"Good morning, Carol. You won't believe this, but you've had a call already."

"I hope you told them I don't return calls until I've had my coffee fix. By the way, what are you doing here so early? I was sure I'd beat everyone here today."

"Truth of the matter is I kind of like to open up. I'm a morning person. My boyfriend thinks I'm crazy."

"It's Jason, isn't it? How's he doing?"

"Not bad. He thinks they're going to give him a raise."

Carol could not remember who 'they' were. She'd have to find time to sit down with JoAnne and learn more about what was going on in the young woman's life.

"That's great. Coffee ready? I mean it when I say I don't take phone calls before coffee."

"I think you did just last Friday. Remember?"

"No, but anyway that was Friday. Who called?"

"It's that woman over in Albany you call a lot. Ziegler's her name."

"Oh," Carol said, suddenly more serious. "Did she say anything was wrong?"

"No, just that she wanted you to give her a call as soon as possible. Isn't she somebody you used to work with?"

"Yes, she's a lawyer in the firm I used to work for. She's one of those people who still can't believe I ever abandoned the law to do what I do now."

JoAnne gave her boss a knowing smile and set off for coffee.

Carol was surprised that Gretchen would be calling so early. And from the office, according to JoAnne's note. She put the call through.

"Good morning, Ms. Ziegler here."

"It's Carol. You're the early bird, aren't you? I hope everything's okay."

"Everything's always somewhat okay and somewhat otherwise. But I wanted to catch you before things got too hectic over there and over here. I thought you ought to know a couple of things, not that I know what they mean. I would have called over the weekend, but I had to go over to Pittsfield for a funeral. No one really close, but I felt I should be there."

"So you're still my eyes and ears. Good. What seems to be up?"

"I got a call at home last night from Francis. He asked if he could see me at 10 a.m., but he didn't give me a head's up as to what's on his mind. I can't ever remember him calling me at home before. It probably has nothing to do with the stuff you and I've been talking about, but just in case I thought I'd let you know that something's brewing."

"I don't want to alarm you, but it just might have to do with us. I invited Francis to come over to the lake and join Kevin and me for lunch. I figured he'd be interested enough in the Keller affair that he'd jump at the chance. Anyway, he was here yesterday. Everything went smoothly until he got the idea I wasn't all that forthcoming about my investigation of Carl's death. That's when my darling husband got into the act and asked about rumors that Carl was about to blow Hartman's cover during the Truscott trial and that Francis helped his pal by sacking him. Your boss didn't exactly blow his stack when he heard this, but he was obviously pissed off. He scoffed at such rumors and walked out in a huff."

"I see," Gretchen said. "Let me see if I can connect the dots. You and Kevin had heard these rumors from somebody, and from what you've told me it wasn't from Carl. That makes me the likely suspect, right?"

"Francis didn't say so, but he's smart enough to have figured it out. So now he's angry with me *and* you. I can't tell you why he wants to see you a.s.a.p., but it wouldn't surprise me if it has something to do with what happened at our cottage yesterday. I'm sorry, Gretchen. We didn't handle it very well, and now you've got to deal with Francis."

"Don't blame yourself, Carol. Or Kevin. You've got a job to do, and chasing down rumors that could have a bearing on Carl's death is part of it. I'm certainly not going to pretend we aren't friends just to keep Francis happy. He'll probably want to know where I heard these things, and that's not hard to deal with. Just about everyone in the firm who's alive and breathing knew Carl was upset and why. Nobody knows, of course, whether Hartman really was involved with a call girl, and nobody knows whether he really leaned on Francis to get rid of Carl. And that includes me. The worst is that he'll call me a bleeping gossip who should keep her mouth shut."

"You don't think he'll want to axe you like he did Carl?"

"He'd better not try. That would be the dumbest thing he could possibly do. The air may be chilly for awhile, but I'm a damn good attorney, and he knows it. Besides, I'm the only woman here at M & B, not to mention the only out of the closet lesbian. No, my job's safe."

"I'm still sorry I've put you in a position like this, and I hope your ten o'clock meeting isn't full of fireworks. But you said you had a couple of things to tell me. What's the other?"

"Remember I told you Francis cornered me one day and told me that Tony Ferraro passed along information that Carl had been guilty of violating his fiduciary obligations to a client. I thought I'd like to hear it from Tony, so I raised the subject with him last Friday. Inasmuch as you'll probably want to be talking with him, too, I thought you'd like to hear what he had to say to me."

"I sure would."

"Nothing. Nada. He laughed, said it was a dead issue. Carl had made a mistake, but he was now dead and there was no point in trampling on the poor guy's grave."

"Were those his words?"

"I'm afraid so."

"Well excuse me, but if Carl did something fraudulent, somebody out there's got a financial problem and he's to blame. I'm not ready to accept Tony's word for this, but he surely knows that his accusation means that some client's escrow account is probably out of balance. He can't just wave the problem away by saying that Carl is unfortunately dead."

"That's pretty much what I told him, but Tony insists everything's fine. I asked him how he happened to know about this, and it seems that he inherited a couple of Carl's cases, including this one."

"I sure hope Francis looks into this," Carol said.

They chatted for another five minutes, at which time Carol said she had to get off the phone for her squad meeting. Gretchen lowered her voice and passed the word that Foster had just walked by her door on his way to his office.

"Good luck," Carol said, "and let me know how it goes."

"I have a hunch Francis will do all the talking. I'll give you a call tonight. Bye."

With her officers assembling in the squad room, Carol had no time to reflect on either Gretchen's meeting with Foster or Ferraro's charge that Carl had violated legal ethics. She hoped, however, that the rest of the day would be an improvement over the first twenty minutes.

CHAPTER 34

By Monday evening, Carol had a strong feeling that she was spinning her wheels. Francis Foster had stormed out of the cottage and back to Albany after having been placed front and center by Kevin in the rumor mill surrounding Carl Keller's death. When asked by Gretchen Ziegler, Tony Ferraro had declined to elaborate on his story that Carl had violated legal ethics shortly before his death. Everyone else whose name had surfaced in the discussion of the Keller case had been unable or unwilling to shed light on what might have happened, including Judge Lindsay Hartman, Carl's ex-girl friend Lisa Simmons, and the mysterious Donna Sugar.

By the time she had slipped into her nightgown, Carol had decided that, in spite of what had happened with Foster the day before, she needed to be more aggressively proactive. It was too soon to tackle Foster again, and for some reason she was reluctant to press the judge until she had acquired more information from the others. All of those others, however, were in Albany. Which meant that she would have to forget about the condition of the department's budget for a few days and spend some time in the state capital.

Sam had already spoken with Ferraro and Sugar, and Kevin had quizzed the immodest Lisa Simmons. But while their reports had helped her form a picture in her mind of these people, they all remained opaque. Whether deliberately so or not, she didn't know. But she knew that she had to see them for herself and try to wrest more information from them than Kevin and Sam had. She would call the three of them in the morning and set up meetings, hopefully in the next couple of days. If they tried to put her off, she would make it clear that they wouldn't want to find themselves charged with obstruction of justice.

Kevin wasn't that thrilled to hear of Carol's plan, but he promised to hold the fort.

By 10:15 the next morning Carol had persuaded a reluctant Tony Ferraro to see her that afternoon at four o'clock and a very nervous Lisa Simmons to do the same at her own flat at 7:30. She hadn't been as lucky with Donna Sugar, who had left a phone message saying that she had to be out of town for awhile. If, as seemed to be the case, she was a call girl, that might mean that her regular clients were somewhat dispersed. Saratoga Springs? Lake George? As it happened, Ms. Sugar was going to be on Crooked Lake soon, but Carol, of course, did not know that.

At shortly after 11 a.m., she became the second member of the Cumberland County Sheriff's Department to set off for Albany since Carl Keller's death and the third in all if Kevin's somewhat less official trip counted. It was doubtful if it would be the last.

There had been every possibility that she would encounter Francis when she visited Tony Ferraro, and not only did she run into him but they met within seconds of her walking through the firm's door.

"What are you doing here?" It was not exactly a friendly greeting, although Foster shook hands with Carol.

"I'm pursuing my duties as sheriff, and I needed to speak with Mr. Ferraro. He agreed to see me this afternoon."

"What's your business with Ferraro?"

"It's been suggested that he was one of Carl Keller's friends in the firm, and inasmuch as we still don't know much about Carl it seemed like a good idea to meet him. He wasn't with the firm when I was here."

"I think you're wrong about his being a friend of Keller's, but I guess you'll figure that out after you've talked with him."

"One way or another, it's good to see this place again. It's been a long time. It looks like the foyer has been redone."

"We try to be welcoming as well as professional. Anyway, Ferraro is down the hall to the right. Why don't you come by my office after you're through with him."

"Sure, I'd be glad to."

Carol had no idea whether Francis wanted to pick up where he had left off on Sunday or try to mend his fences. She gave her former boss a smile and set off down the hall to where Ferraro was located.

The man who met her did not match her expectations, other than that he looked to be in good shape. His Italian name suggested he'd have dark hair, but although he was still fairly young, it was prematurely grey. He had aquiline features, surprisingly rheumy eyes, and a voice that sounded slightly nasal.

"Mr. Ferraro, I'm pleased to meet you. I hope you're fully recovered from the appendectomy."

"I'm doing fine. I'm glad to see you, of course, but you know I talked with your deputy not that long ago. Some new development?"

"I wouldn't say that. But in my experience, investigations like mine are always well served by asking lots of questions. And then asking them again. Nuance is important, as I'm sure you know."

"Have a seat. Coffee?"

"No thanks."

"Well, if you don't mind I'll have some. I'm a real addict." He disappeared to wherever the coffee machine was located, then reappeared a short minute later.

"Well, fire away, sheriff," he said. "This is your meeting."

"My agenda is Carl Keller. You will have heard that I was with M & B years ago, and I knew Carl back then. But people change. We all change. If I'm going to find out what happened to him, I'm going to have to know a lot more about him. You worked with him. Suppose somebody asked you to produce a profile of the Carl you knew - an honest sketch in which you talked about his interests, his strengths, his weaknesses. What would be the things you'd want to be sure to include?"

"Like if I were writing his obituary?"

"In a way, but obits tend to emphasize the positive, unless of course they're about somebody who'd been notorious in some way or other. Let's just try some free association. What comes to mind as you reflect on the Carl Keller you knew?"

"In the first place, I didn't know him very well. I don't think anybody did. But I see what you're getting at."

Ferraro paused, as if to think about how to answer the sheriff's question. Then he began to offer his impressions. After about ten minutes, Carol interrupted him.

"What I'm hearing is generalities. Can you be more specific?"

He couldn't. Or wouldn't.

"I have heard," Carol interrupted again, "that Carl had violated his fiduciary obligations to a client. Not long ago, but quite recently. That would be a pretty serious matter. What's more, it's my understanding that you knew about it and reported it to Mr. Foster. Why don't you tell me about it."

Ferraro laughed nervously.

"Oh, that. It's no longer important. When Carl left the firm, I took over a couple of his cases. That's how I found out about it."

"Fair enough, but why is it no longer important? I would assume that the client wouldn't think it was unimportant."

"Well, Carl obviously had second thoughts about what he'd done and assured me he would reimburse the escrow account."

"So you haven't taken any action except to notify Foster?"

"That's right."

"But when I asked you to tell me what kind of a guy Carl was, you didn't mention this. I'd have thought it was a pretty revealing piece of evidence that he was a shady character, even someone in danger of disbarment."

"I suppose so, but like I said, we'd put it behind us."

Carol decided that if she wanted Ferraro to be more forthcoming, she might have to be a bit more candid herself.

"As I'm sure you know, Carl came to a really nasty end. Somebody slit his throat. Do you know anything that might suggest that this is related to his messing with a client's escrow account?"

"You mean did someone kill him for doing it?"

"That's my question."

"That would be a major overreaction, don't you think?"

"I do, but you never can tell. Let me change my scenario. Do you think Carl could have been so broken up over what he'd done that he might feel suicidal?"

"But you said he was murdered."

"I know. I'm not saying he committed suicide. I'm only asking whether he might ever have contemplated suicide. Did he strike you as the kind of person who was subject to depression?"

"I really can't say. He wasn't very demonstrative. But suicide - he certainly never said anything that you could interpret that way."

When Carol left Tony Ferraro's office, she knew more than when she arrived, but was still fairly sure that he was still not telling her everything he knows. She wondered what Ferraro would make of her question about whether Carl appeared suicidal. She had, of course, avoided saying that he had almost certainly committed suicide. Better to let people believe it had been murder.

As promised, she stopped briefly in Foster's office on her way out. He chose not to ask her about her conversation with Ferraro, but he had either gotten over his pique of Sunday or had at least decided that an olive branch was in order. When she was back in the car and on her way to a motel where she would be spending the evening, her thoughts were on Foster, not Ferraro. She was not only quite certain that Carl's unfinished note about F referred to one or the other of the two men. She also was quite certain that sooner or later Foster would be in touch with her to find out just what she knew about Carl's alleged violation of his fiduciary obligations to a client.

CHAPTER 35

Tony Ferraro went back to his apartment after another day at the office more anxious than he had been when he came to work that morning. He would have liked to stop off at *Bernie's* for a couple of drinks, but that would have meant an hour of idle chit-chat with the usual bar crowd in this hangout for lawyers, and his mind was too preoccupied with other things to enjoy that. He had now been visited twice by a representative of the Cumberland County Sheriff's Department, and he didn't like their attention. He needed to spend some time taking stock of his situation and thinking about just what he ought to do about it.

He was glad to have the apartment to himself, even if he occasionally missed Donna Sugar's presence. She had been a welcome diversion from the rigors of practicing law in the tightly run ship which was Morgenstern and Brauchli. But in important respects they had not been compatible. She was good in bed, but why wouldn't she have been? After all, that was where she earned her income. But to his surprise she had proved to be an intellectual, with interests that ran to fine art and the theatre and even to politics, whereas politics bored him and his cultural interests extended to a handful of prime time TV shows and little further. The result was that their relationship had gradually petered out and come to an end by mutual agreement. Unfortunately, it had been an expensive experiment, if not a long enduring one. He remembered the day he had been reconciling his accounts and discovered, to his horror, that his financial situation was not nearly as solid as he had assumed it to be. Donna was not the only culprit, but she was a major factor.

Tonight, however, she was not on his mind. Instead, he was thinking about Sheriff Kelleher and the questions she'd been asking and the worries which she had stirred up. The problem seemed to be that he had been identified, presumably by Gretchen Ziegler, as Carl Keller's closest friend in the law firm. That was a joke. Keller didn't have friends. He had largely kept to himself ever since Tony had known him. The familiar expression that 'there is no there there' applied to Keller better than to anyone else he had ever met. It wasn't that Carl wasn't a competent lawyer; he was a workaholic who was always prepared, and Tony wasn't aware that Francis, or any of the other attorneys for that matter, ever disparaged his courtroom skills.

In any event, he and Keller had not been friends. They had never even spent much time together at the office. Not, that is, until the day that Carl had been told that he was being let go by the firm and that two of his cases were being turned over to Tony. They had spent a couple of days together in virtually round the clock work sessions in their offices. One of the cases he was inheriting was only a few weeks old, and getting on top of it wasn't much of a problem. The other had a rather long and complicated backstory, and involved an escrow account for which Carl had been responsible. They had discussed it exhaustively and eventually taken care of the transfer of paperwork. When Carl had cleaned out his office and disappeared, Tony had put what he thought of as the Rasmussen case on a back burner, confident that there was nothing he had to do about it immediately. But one day about a week later, shortly after a troubling evening on his *Quicken* program with its revelations about his shrinking financial balance, his thoughts turned to the Rasmussen escrow.

He had gone through the file that very day, and it reconfirmed what he had learned from his sessions with Keller. The case had been going nowhere fast, and it didn't look as if that was about to change. Moreover, the amount in escrow was considerable. If he were to tap into the account, he would have to do it in such a way that no one would ever know he had done it. He had spent the better part of an hour studying the papers in the file before he made his decision. It would be possible to write checks to payees of Carl's (actually his own) creation, back date them, and sign them with Carl's signature. To do this would require some very careful planning, not to mention time spent practicing Carl's handwriting. But Tony was both clever and patient, and by the end of the week he had enriched his own bank account by quite a few thousand dollars.

Keller's death made the rest easy. He waited a few days and then went to Foster with a tale which he told with a mixture of sorrow and anger - sorrow that his former colleague had lost his moral compass and anger that he had been left with a mess to clean up. The managing partner had accepted his version of what had happened and even thanked him profusely for his assiduous detective work.

Sooner or later he would have to 'discover' that Keller hadn't reimbursed the escrow account. And when he reported this fact, Foster would reluctantly transfer funds to cover the theft and gradually the whole affair would become ancient history. He could think of no way that his bit of sleight of hand could be discovered. The only person who knew his story wasn't true was dead, the single fact that had made it all possible.

Yet he was uncomfortable. Something was bothering the sheriff. What if she prevailed on Francis Foster to investigate the Rasmussen case himself? What if Foster were to find something in the file that he had missed, something that might cast doubt on his story? He couldn't think what it might be, but he knew that the boss was smart, his knowledge of the law both broad and deep.

When he had come home he had been pleased to be alone. Now, much as he had tired of Donna Sugar, he wished she were there. Her conversation might not take his mind off his worries, but her body would. Unfortunately, he had burned that bridge.

CHAPTER 36

Carol grabbed a quick dinner at a restaurant she remembered from her days in Albany. She was actually surprised to find it, right where it had been ten years before. Unusual, for restaurants, with rare exceptions, seemed to change owners and cuisine with amazing frequency. To her delight she found that the kitchen still produced a commendable pad thai.

Her meeting with Lisa Simmons would not be, like Kevin's, at the *Treasure Chest*, but at the flat she shared with Erin Cooley. Fortunately, it was one of those nights when Erin was playing musical chairs.

"It's nice to meet you at last," Lisa said as she welcomed Carol into what looked more like a college dorm room than the abode of two women who were probably in their 30s. No effort had been made to spruce the place up for the sheriff's visit. Nor had Lisa thought it necessary to dress for the occasion. Her levis had a hole in both knees and her orange blouse looked like it could use an ironing. Her feet were bare, and her long blonde hair hadn't seen a brush recently.

"Hello, Ms. Simmons. I appreciate your willingness to see me on such short notice."

"Come on in, sheriff." She proceeded to sweep things off the couch and onto the floor and motioned for Carol to sit down. "Care for a coke?"

"No thanks. I've just come from dinner."

Lisa shrugged her shoulders and took a seat in a chair across from a coffee table covered with magazines and rings left by numerous glasses.

"I thought I'd told your officer everything I could think of when he was here," she said.

"I'm sure you did. Perhaps I'll have some questions he didn't ask, but first I'd like to know if you found the key you'd lost."

"The key?"

"Yes. Remember, my colleague asked you for your key to Carl Keller's apartment, but you told him you'd lost it."

"Oh, yes. I'm sorry, but it's really gone missing. As you can see, we aren't all that neat and tidy. We're always misplacing things."

Lisa gestured to the condition of the room to underline the point she was making.

"I've been thinking about that lost key ever since my officer told me you'd lost it. Sometimes we think we've lost something when in fact we've loaned it to someone. Do you suppose you could have done that?"

"I'm pretty sure I didn't. I mean, who would I give it to other than Carl?"

"Richard Keller?"

"Why would I give the key to Richard?" It was a careless mistake, and it gave Carol an opportunity to press her advantage.

"How does it happen you know Richard Keller?"

"I don't know him. I don't know any of Carl's family."

"But you know a bit *about* them, don't you. He told you about his parents over in Massachusetts. And about Richard."

"Yes, but I never met any of them."

"No, I'm sure you didn't. One reason you never met Richard is that Carl has no relative named Richard."

Lisa briefly closed her eyes and bit her lip.

"My colleague had the impression that you hadn't told him the truth. He's a good policeman. His only weakness is that he has a hard time telling attractive women that they're lying. Sometimes the female of the species is really tougher than the male, Lisa. You lied to Mr. Whitman and he didn't call you on it. Now you're lying to me, and I'm not going to let you get away with it. I'm not here tonight for a friendly chat. I'm conducting a murder investigation, and you're going to help me or face an obstruction of justice charge. So why don't you go to the kitchen and get me that coke you offered me, and then I want you to tell me just what's been going on since you walked out on Carl."

When Lisa handed Carol the coke, she was having a hard time holding back tears.

"Thanks for the coke. How about you? Will you have one, too?"

"No," she said, shaking her head."

"Okay. Then let's talk."

And for the next forty minutes Lisa Simmons unburdened herself of the things that had been bothering her ever since Carl had called her from a place called *Welcome Inn* and asked her to retrieve a folder from his apartment and burn it.

"Let me see if I have all of this right," Carol said. "Let's begin with Carl's call to you from the motel. He asked you to go to the apartment and remove a file that was on his desk. You were then to destroy it and call him back and let him know that you'd done it, just as he asked. He never told you what was in the folder. Right?"

"No, he didn't."

"Did the folder have a label on it, anything to tell you what it contained?"

"It said it was the Hartman file."

"Did you look into the folder at any time? Can you tell me anything about what was in it?"

Lisa looked decidedly ill at ease.

"If you did, that's perfectly all right. As you can see, I'm anxious to know what was in the folder."

"I thought about it, but he said it was legal stuff, and I wouldn't know what any of it meant. So I left it just as it was, with the cord still tied around it."

"And then you burned it rather than put it out it in the garbage?"

"That's right."

"Okay. Now about the man who said he was Richard Keller. He came here to your apartment because the man on duty at Woodmere told him you might be able to help him."

"That's what he said."

"He said he was Richard Keller, Carl's cousin, and his head was all bandaged because of some accident."

"Yes."

"Of course he was wearing that bandage so you wouldn't get a good look at his face. That way you wouldn't be able to remember him or see whether he bore any resemblance to Carl. Anyway, you took him at his word that he was Carl's cousin, and you gave him your key so he'd have access to his cousin's apartment."

"I'm afraid I did. And even worse, I told him where he could reach Carl. It seemed like a nice thing to do, them being cousins."

"I understand, Lisa. You had no reason to doubt his story. For what it's worth, we don't know that this phony cousin had anything to do with Carl's death. But it's a possibility, which is why it's important that you are now telling me about him. I know that the bandages made it impossible to get a good look at his face, but try to tell me as much as you can about this man. How tall was he? How heavy? What color hair? What kind of voice - deep, high pitched, accented?"

Lisa did her best to provide the sheriff with a verbal picture. She thought his hair was grey and that his voice was sort of nasal. But otherwise there had been nothing particularly distinctive about him other than the bandaged face.

"Do you remember whether he was right or left handed?"

"I don't think we ever shook hands."

Carol chose not to remind Lisa that both left and right handers shake with their right hand.

"Do you recall what he was wearing? Was he well dressed, or did he have on casual clothes, even work clothes?"

Lisa looked as if she were about to cry again.

"I can't really remember. I know he wasn't wearing a coat and tie, and I think he had a blue shirt, but I wasn't paying much attention to things like that."

"Can you make a guess as to his age?"

Lisa started wringing her hands.

"This is terrible. First I didn't tell the truth, and now I'm not being any help at all. His age? Quite a bit older than me, but probably not as old as my father."

Then she broke into an almost hysterical giggle.

"How stupid I am," she said, her voice out of control. "You don't even know my father."

"Lisa, please, don't do this to yourself. You've done very well, and I really am grateful that you decided to level with me. It will probably be necessary for you to make a deposition in due course. We shall stay in touch, and I want you to call me if anything occurs to you that might help us identify this man who called himself Richard Keller. Anything at all, no matter how unimportant it may seem to you."

"You won't be bringing charges against me because I told those lies, will you?"

"If what you've told me tonight is the truth, and you promise to stick to the truth, the answer is no. In the meanwhile be careful. If Richard Keller calls you or comes around to the flat here, don't talk to him or let him in. And call the Albany police immediately."

It wasn't likely that the bandaged man would bother Lisa again, but Carol had suddenly felt a twinge of anxiety. Unlike Carl Keller when he came to her library talk, Richard Keller or whoever he was might be a real stalker. And a dangerous one.

CHAPTER 37

Donna Sugar had taken the weekend off in order to do herself the favor of clothes shopping. Her wardrobe was still one of the finest in the business, but she was beginning to feel the need for a change in color. She'd spotted some things in a fashion magazine which had been described as periwinkle blue, but she'd been unable to find them in Albany. Two or three phone calls had been enough to send her off downstate to the city, where she had made a few purchases, taken in a show, and allowed herself to be picked up at a swanky bar on Madison Avenue. The dinner at a four star restaurant had been excellent, and a nearby upscale hotel had been a much better than average setting for some intimate late night calisthenics.

She had nothing on her calendar for Monday due to a cancellation by a very frustrated orthopedic surgeon who had missed a connecting flight somewhere between Denver and Albany. As a result she had done little more than call a few friends and get herself a manicure. It was almost 4 p.m. when she got back to her apartment. The day's mail was waiting for her, but it promised nothing of great interest - a few bills, a couple of catalogs, the latest copy of the *New Yorker*. There was nothing personal. But there was something unusual at the bottom of the small pile, a small sealed envelope that contained no name or address and no stamp. Someone must have stuck it through the slot. Perhaps it was a notice from the management, although they typically came in a house envelope and carried her name.

Donna took the mail into the living room, where she took off her shoes and began to go through it more carefully. She didn't expect the unaddressed envelope to contain anything of interest, so she actually took a peek at the *New Yorker* cartoons before opening it. It contained a single sheet of paper, folded twice, on which was a handwritten note. There was no date, no salutation, no signature, only a few lines of scribbled cursive writing with frequent exclamation points.

You probably think I'm out of your life for three years, but don't count on it! My connections with your world are very real, as you shall see! My former lawyer is dead, God rest his lousy soul, but the judge is another story. If he wants to stay on the bench, he's going to have to come up with a way to get me out of here. Not someday - NOW! You're going to convince him. I don't have to spell it out - you know what I mean? So do it! Don't make me play hardball!

Donna took a deep breath. And then another. She got up and went to the kitchen, where she opened her liquor cabinet, took out a bottle of Scotch, and poured herself quite a bit more than was her custom. This time she didn't bother with ice cubes.

The note had obviously come from Randall Truscott. She had assumed that he was whiling away the hours - and the days and the weeks and the months - in a place where he could do no one, least of all her, any more harm. Yet that very day he had thrust a note though the door of her apartment. It was inconceivable that he had escaped from prison, of course, although she thought it prudent to check the news to see if there had been any report of a jail break. Far more likely that he had loyal friends on the outside, friends with whom he stayed in touch, friends who were prepared to do his bidding. Today one of those friends had visited her apartment building, bearing a note from him. And there was no question about it. The handwriting was his. But even if the note had been typed, it was unmistakably Randall's - tough, blunt, impatient. And threatening.

Unlike some women in her business, she had made it a point to be extremely careful not to place herself in physical danger. The one exception had been Truscott, and when she had first met him there had been no hint of what was to come. Now there was further evidence that she had made the biggest mistake in what was otherwise a satisfying and successful career when she failed to recognize the dangerous volatility which underlay his reckless charm.

She knew that she would have to take Randall's note seriously, although at that moment she had no idea just what she should do about it. She set her glass of Scotch down and went down the hall to her dressing room with its big floor length mirror. She wasn't quite sure why, but Randall's threatening note prompted a sudden urge to take a good look at herself.

Donna didn't like the face that looked back at her. The puffiness and discoloration that had made it almost impossible for so long to stare into the mirror had disappeared, but today the face that looked back at her was not the face that she had always thought of as her best feature. Friends in the trade all had attributes that they treasured above everything else: their boobs, their legs, their derrieres. But her boobs were too small, her legs too short, her derriere, well, not bad but nothing special. Some call girls shared a belief with her that their face and its features were their ticket to professional success. Donna had had no doubt about it. She had the look of both a sophisticated lady and the girl next door, a face which permitted men to see in her whatever they wanted to see. But there was something in the face in the mirror today that wasn't quite right. Was it a hint of anxiety? A lack of self confidence?

Randall Truscott was to blame, of course. Thank God he was now in jail, paying the price for his brutal assault on her. In her mind there had never been any doubt that he would be found guilty, at least not until his lawyer had suggested in court that she herself was in part responsible for what had happened. She had been alarmed by the way this man - Carl Keller was his name - had slyly insinuated that she was not the innocent the prosecution had proclaimed. And then, just when insinuations were about to give way to specific allegations, Judge Hartman had interceded, siding with the prosecution that Keller's charges were out of order and eventually citing him for contempt of court. She had been grateful for the judge's ruling, but she was well aware that he had done what he had done not only for her sake, but because he feared for his own reputation. He surely knew that, had he not ruled against Keller, his own relationship with her might come out, thereby ruining his distinguished career.

Lindsay had prudently kept his distance during the trial. For that matter, he had said almost nothing to her about the trial once it was over, but gradually they had begun to see each other again. She had welcomed this return to the comfortable intimacy they had established at Mt. Washington, and she had no reason to believe that Lindsay didn't feel the same way.

But now she was in possession of a note from Randall Truscott in which he virtually ordered the judge to secure his release from jail. She didn't know much about such things, but she knew enough to be sure that it was highly unlikely that Lindsay would be able to do what Randall demanded. Even worse, Truscott had told her that it was her responsibility to make it happen. She could think of no way to do that, which meant that Truscott could take his revenge on the judge by spreading the word that he had been cohabiting with a call girl. Except he would probably call it shacking up with a whore. She could probably survive such a revelation, but Lindsay could not. It would very probably put an end both to his marriage and to his seat on the bench.

Of course it was possible that Randall didn't know for a fact that she and Judge Hartman were in a relationship. She certainly had never told him. Although attorneys were supposed to discuss strategy with their clients, Keller might not have been specific. He might not even have been sure that his sources were accurate. But Sugar realized that she was grasping at straws. The reason Lindsay had cracked down so hard and so soon on Keller was that he could see which way the wind was blowing. After all, his paramour was sitting right across the courtroom from him.

When Tony Ferraro told her that Keller was dead, she had been relieved to hear the news. She had felt guilty to feel that way, but it meant that the defense attorney would no longer be around to do what he had tried unsuccessfully to do in court. How naive she had been. If Keller knew - even if he had only suspected - that the judge and the defendant were sleeping together, there could be others who shared that knowledge and were in a position to go public with it. She had been so sure that her relationship with Judge Hartman was their own secret. She should have known better. The insatiable media scandal mongers had uncovered and trumpeted any number of dangerous liaisons between celebrities and prostitutes. Why had she assumed that her case would be different? Randall Truscott was now in the process of proving that it wasn't.

For the first time in several years, Donna Sugar found herself having second thoughts about her profession. It wasn't that she had regrets about not pursuing a career that her college major in chemistry had prepared her for. She knew herself well enough to know that the life of a research scientist at some place like NIH would have been boring. What was responsible for those second thoughts was the fact that had it not been for her, Lindsay Hartman would not be in trouble. She respected him; moreover, she was genuinely fond of him. And she was now powerless to help him.

CHAPTER 38

Donna was rarely nervous. At the moment, however, she was very nervous. Calling Lindsay at his home, even on his cell phone, was not a good idea, and they had long ago decided it was something she would do only in emergencies. There was no doubt in her mind that this was an emergency. Lindsay's office had explained that the trial in which he was to be the presiding judge had been postponed yet again. The woman who told her this didn't say so, but she had sounded annoyed that the parties in such cases seemed chronically incapable of moving the judicial process forward more expeditiously. Donna shared her annoyance. It meant that she would have to try him on his cell at home.

The judge picked up her call almost immediately.

"It's me, Donna. I didn't want to call you at home, but something's come up. We have to talk."

"Well, we're in luck. I'm over at the cottage. The Kretschman case has been put off for at least another week."

Donna was both surprised and disappointed.

"You didn't tell me you were going to the lake."

"I know, and I'm sorry. The truth is that Hazel's chosen this week to have some work done on the house. Kitchen remodeling mostly, but I decided I'd just be a nuisance while it was going on."

"You mean you're alone at the cottage? Hazel's still here in Albany?"

"Right. I think she's glad I won't be underfoot while the work's going on."

"Maybe it's all for the good. I've got to talk with you. If you're by yourself, I could come over there."

"Is it that important? We can't afford to be seen here anymore than we can at the house."

"I know that, Lindsay. I won't be sunning myself on the beach. I've had lots of practice staying out of sight. Tell you what. I'll rent a car, something inconspicuous, and turn myself into a long lost niece or something."

"I don't have any nieces, Donna. What seems to be the trouble?"

"I'm sure we can come up with a cover story if we have to. You can give it some thought while I'm on my way over. All I need is a few hours, and we can't handle it over the phone. It's too complicated."

"You're being awfully mysterious."

"I think you're in trouble because of me, Lindsay. I got a threatening letter from Truscott, the guy who beat me up and you sent down. He says he'll go public if you don't get him out of jail fast."

"What do you mean, he'll go public?"

"About us. That you've been seeing me, and he knows who I am and what I do."

Judge Hartrman was suddenly much less interested in keeping Donna away from the cottage than he was in the terrible news she'd just passed on to him.

"I can't do that," he said. His tone of voice left no doubt that springing Truscott from jail would be impossible.

"We have to do something. Tell me where to find the cottage and I'll arrange to get there right after dark."

The judge reluctantly gave her instructions.

"Do you think you'll be able to find it? These back roads aren't well marked."

"Not to worry. Remember, I'm not your average 30 year old."

"I thought you were 32," he said.

"Women have always been able to shave off a few years when it suits them, Lindsay. I'll be there no later than ten. You concentrate on a way to foil Truscott."

Neither of them knew it at the time, but they had just indulged in a bit of conversational banter for the last time.

Donna was confident that she could manage a few hours at the cottage without giving away their secret. But it was Lindsay she was worried about, so she took the extra precaution of renting a plain black Chevy, which was much less obvious than her bight red Ferrari Spider, and delaying her departure until after seven o'clock.

It was an anxious judge who met her at the back door of his cottage. The light over the door was off, and he used a flashlight to guide her to a sheltered parking spot under a large willow. He hustled her into the cottage, foregoing their customary welcoming kiss.

"You're staying the night, I assume," were his first words.

Donna had thought about this and concluded that it would be foolhardy to drive back to Albany in the middle of the night. She wanted a drink, preferably two, and she had no desire to risk becoming a thruway statistic. Besides, the prospect of sleeping in the bed that Lindsay and Hazel shared had a certain appeal. She was surprised at herself for having such a thought. She had never met Hazel and had no intention of meeting her. But she knew that, in spite of the double life he was leading, Lindsay truly loved his wife and she had no desire to further compromise that relationship. Perhaps he would be offended by the very idea of making love to her in Hazel's bed. Never mind. She'd let things take their course. It was quite possible that after discussing Truscott's message neither one of them would feel like making love. A strange phrase, wasn't it? Donna enjoyed doing it, but she never really thought of it as making love.

"I don't have much choice," she said in answer to Lindsay's question. "Try not to worry. I'll clear out by six a.m. at the latest. How about some Scotch?"

"Sure." He disappeared briefly into the pantry.

"Here you are," he said when he returned. "Now let's have it."

They took seats in what looked like a small library, its drapes pulled tightly shut, presumably so that the neighbors would be unaware that Judge Hartman was entertaining. Or urgently discussing how he might cope with Randall Truscott. Donna had never seen the cottage, of course, and in more normal circumstances she would have said nice things about it because in fact it was an attractive and comfortable place. But these were not normal circumstances. The conversation turned instead to Truscott's threatening message.

Donna explained that it had come that very day, not courtesy of USPS, but via a friend of

Randall's. The judge examined the envelope, extracted the letter, and quickly read it.

"This is very bad news, Donna," he said. His face was grim.

"I know. That's why I'm here. Can you think of any way to deal with him?"

"I'm afraid that in a matter like this there'll be no dealing with Truscott. I don't pretend to know much more about the man than what I learned from his case. But in light of what he did to you and the peremptory tone of his note, I suspect it's futile to assume he'll be willing to negotiate. I can try, but the odds are awfully long."

"So what do you think he'll do?"

"My guess is that he'll do just what he threatens to do. He has nothing to lose, and he probably thinks he's got a lot to gain. His motive is pretty clear - revenge, pure and simple. I'm afraid that if I could somehow get him out of jail, he'd still take his suspicions public."

"So what do we do?"

"*We* don't do anything, Donna. I'll have to do it."

"But do what?"

"Fight him. I don't know where he'll take his story, but there'll be some paper, some TV station, that'll jump at the chance to run with this. Used to be that the media wanted to do their homework first, check the facts, that kind of thing. That way we'd have a good chance of nipping his story in the bud. No more. Somebody over in Albany'll see this as a ratings bonanza, a front page headline with what journalists call legs. You and I are going to be in the news for weeks, Donna."

"But you said you'd fight him. How can you do that? After all, it's true."

"Is it?" Hartman had initially sounded resigned. Suddenly he sounded angry.

"I'll sue anybody that runs this. He may have forgotten that I can go public, too. A roughneck serving three years for aggravated assault is going to impugn the integrity of one of Albany's finest jurists? He won't be able to prove a thing. Before I'm through with him he'll be sorry he pulled a stunt like this."

"That's all well and good, Lindsay, but he knows something. We've been careful, but somehow he found us out. Keller probably told him."

"Keller is dead." The judge practically spit out the words. "He was just fishing. The court record makes clear that he was poking around, looking for a way to give Truscott a get out of jail card. He knew nothing. Even if he did, there's no Keller to back up Truscott's charges. He's just a criminal doing time, trying to embarrass the guy who put him away. Well, I'm not going to let him do it. So try to relax."

Donna did not share Lindsay's optimism. She also had another worry.

"What's going to happen to us? Once Randall goes public, how can we possibly see each other? They'll be watching our every move. They'll be camping at your house around the clock. I watched what was going on in the Levenger case. He couldn't pick up the morning paper without somebody putting a mike and a camera in his face."

Judge Hartman took a deep breath and managed to shut down the vitriolic anger of the previous few minutes.

"I know," he said, his voice now low and sad. "We'll just have to be patient for awhile. In time it'll all die down. They'll lose interest. We can start over, maybe back at Mt. Washington."

"Are you serious?" Donna asked. "Our relationship will be on life support until you drop dead and I'm way past menopause. You're really telling me it's over, aren't you?"

"No, Donna, no. That isn't the way it's going to be. Please bear with me. I love you."

Lindsay had never told Donna he loved her. She didn't believe him.

"We've never loved each other, Lindsay. You don't love me and I don't love you. You love Hazel, and I'm not the falling in love type. So, please, let's not turn this into a melodrama. It's a big enough mess without our losing our grip on reality. Look, I'm sorry to be sounding off. It's just that I can't pretend that this is just a little setback for us. It's really over. This is no time to play Pangloss - all's *not* for the best in this best of all possible worlds. Will you miss what we had? Sure you will. Will I? Absolutely. What you've got to concentrate on is Hazel and your judgeship. If anyone asks, I'll tell them we know each other only because we found ourselves in the same courtroom in the Truscott trial."

The judge sighed.

"Want another drink?" he asked.

"I do. Then we can discuss tactics."

They talked until close to one a.m. at which time Donna borrowed Lindsay's alarm clock and disappeared down the hall into a guest bedroom.

Neither of them even hinted at going to bed together. They both recognized that this was neither the time nor the place.

Lindsay Hartman remained in his library chair for another hour. He fully expected that even if he went on to bed, he wouldn't sleep. He had assumed that Randall Truscott's incarceration and Carl Keller's death had put an end to his fear that his relationship with Donna Sugar might become public knowledge. He was a smart man, and he should have known better. He, more than most men, should have known that jails can be incubators for fantasies of revenge. As for death, it was now apparent that it does not always have the last word.

CHAPTER 39

Kevin had never been interested in owning a power boat. He knew that this placed him squarely in the minority of Crooked Lake's residents. In fact, it probably guaranteed that most of his neighbors thought of him as a square. Had he had children, he would probably have given in to their entreaties to get a power boat so they could go water skiing. But there were no children by his first marriage, and he and Carol seemed comfortable with the fact that it was highly unlikely that they would ever be parents. Which meant that the canoe was their lake boat and the source of many of their happiest moments on the lake.

Carol had no problem with this arrangement. At least most of the time. But on occasions she found herself longing for an outing when the wind would come whipping by her face while she trailed her hand in the water as it rushed by the boat. The morning after returning to the lake from her visit with Lisa Simmons was one of those occasions. On her way to Cumberland and the squad meeting, she decided that she was going to accompany Officer Parsons on lake patrol for a change. She knew that she'd be bumping one of her colleagues off the boat and onto highway patrol, but it would just be for a couple of hours.

"Bill," she said, calling him aside when the meeting broke up, "I'd very much like to share the patrol boat with you this morning. You wouldn't mind, would you?"

Officer Parsons looked surprised.

"I thought you'd had your fill of what it's like to be one of us," he said, reminding her of the recent week when she and Bridges had swapped places.

"I'm not planning on giving patrol duty another whirl," she replied. "It's just that I'd like to feel the wind in my hair for a change. An hour or two would do. I know Grieves will be disappointed, but then I'll owe him one, won't I?"

"You're on. I'll even take her to full throttle if you like."

"Thanks, but no thanks. We'll still be enforcing the safety rules. No need to do any showboating."

"Sounds fine. Why don't you meet me at the dock, and I'll tell Grieves to meet us there at - what? Noon?"

"Let's make it eleven. No point in overdoing it."

And so it was decided. It proved to be an easy morning. There was but one small problem, involving a Scarab that had embarrassingly run out of gas about half way to Southport. Otherwise, Carol simply relaxed in the stern, chatting with her most senior officer while her hair went wild and she reveled in the spray. As was usually the case, she enjoyed the view of familiar cottages, large and small, from the lake, as well as the sight of happy vacationers water skiing, zipping along in their personal water craft, and taking advantage of a light breeze on their Sunfish. In spite of her worries about the Keller case, the thought uppermost in her mind as they circled the lake was how lucky she was to live where she did, do what she was doing for a living, and share it all with Kevin. She didn't expect Bill Parsons to understand just what she was feeling, but she told him anyway.

"I know just what you mean," he said. "I'd simply add that we're lucky you came long after we lost your Dad."

"That's the nicest thing I've heard in ages." Carol got out of her seat in the stern and gave Parsons a kiss on the top of his head.

The patrol boat ride had been a wonderful pick-me-up, and she traded places with Officer Grieves back at the West Branch dock considerably more upbeat. Now back to work, she said to herself as she set off for the office and her yellow pad full of random jottings about the loose ends of the Keller case.

And there were many loose ends. Carol read her notes, amending them as she went along when they didn't quite convey what she believed had been on her mind when she had first written them down.

Carol pushed the yellow pad aside, and sank back in her chair. The morning on the patrol boat had been far more satisfying, but it hadn't advanced her investigation an inch. There were many phone calls to make. Many face to face conversations to have, most of them in Albany on a rapidly shrinking budget. But Carol was now determined to interview people herself.

She got up and went to the window looking out over the parking lot. Not a particularly interesting view. She wished the department were located somewhere where she could see the lake, perhaps outside of Yates Center. But that was not possible. There was a greater likelihood, with expenses outrunning revenue, that her department might be moved to even more cramped headquarters with fewer amenities and no better an outlook. Even worse, she might be confronted with staff cuts. Carol shook this bad thought out of her head and went back to her desk and to her telephone.

The two people she was most anxious to talk with were Francis Foster and Donna Sugar. Talking with Francis ought not to be a problem, but she was sure it would be after the unpleasantness over lunch. Unfortunately, she wouldn't be having that conversation for at least a few more days. The person who took her call at M & B announced that Mr. Foster was unavailable, and when pressed said that he wouldn't be taking calls until Thursday. Carol explained who she was and tried to make an appointment, only to be told that that would be impossible unless Mr. Foster had been consulted. She suspected that Francis had left word specifically not to put the sheriff on his calendar.

Ms. Sugar was another story. The only reason that Carol wanted to talk to her was the vague rumor she'd heard from Gretchen, and Bridges had already questioned her. The woman could well find so much attention from the sheriff's department of Cumberland County both puzzling and unwelcome. In any event, Carol's call to her was as unsuccessful as the one to Foster.

"I'm not home," a woman's voice said and hung up. Strange. It would have been easier simply not to answer the phone, which suggested that Sugar didn't have caller ID and didn't want to speak with anyone associated with the sheriff's department. If so, that in itself was interesting. It made Carol even more anxious to meet the woman.

Frustrated by this inability to arrange meetings with Foster and Sugar, she turned her attention to other matters. One of them was Carl's suicide and whether those who knew him had thought of him as someone who could be suicidal. Lisa Simmons would be on her list. His parents would have to be called, although she doubted that they would be helpful. And then there was Carl's first wife. Carol consulted her notes; her name was Mary Louise Gallagher, and Carl's parents hadn't known where she was living. Possibly Pittsfield. At least she had lived there according to the Kellers. Even if she could be found, it was doubtful that she could speak to the issue of Carl's suicidal tendencies. But she'd have to try to locate her and raise that question. Finally, there were his colleagues at M & B. She'd already broached the subject with Ferraro, who'd been non-committal. But there were others at the firm, quite a few others. Was it going to be necessary for her or Bridges to open an office annex in Albany? Carol looked down at her yellow pad and muttered an expletive.

"Tommy," she said as she looked in on Officer Byrnes. "I need to locate the former wife of Carl Keller. Her name was Mary Louise Gallagher. No idea where she is now, or whether she's kept Keller's name, been remarried, or gone back to Gallagher. How about looking for a needle in a haystack and seeing if you can track her down. Keller's parents don't know where she's living, but they mentioned Pittsfield. Possibly Worcester or Burlington, but I think they were just taking a shot in the dark. Anyway, give it a try."

"What's this about?"

"I'm trying to find out if anybody who knew Carl thought he might be suicidal. I'm not quite sure why - after all, it looks like in the end he was."

"Just want to be thorough, is that it?" he asked.

"More like I can't get through to the people I really need to talk to." Carol went back to her office to call Lisa Simmons. If she, too, were unavailable, she'd try to talk Gretchen into querying Carl's old colleagues at M & B.

CHAPTER 40

It was going to be one of those days. The euphoria generated by the patrol boat ride had quickly vanished. Not only were Foster and Sugar unavailable. Neither were Lisa Simmons nor Carl Keller's father or mother. Byrnes was still pursuing the former Mary Louise Keller, so far without luck. Carol decided to defer imposing on Gretchen for the time being and call Marty Reece instead. She couldn't explain why she wasn't satisfied with what she had learned at the *Welcome Inn*, which meant that she had no idea what questions to ask Reece. But experience told her that it was better to pursue nagging doubts than summarily dismiss them.

Reece, unlike all of the others she had called that morning, answered the phone.

"You found the guy who did it?" he asked, sounding eager to hear all about it.

"I'm afraid not, but I'd like to come by and see how things are going at your motel."

"Well, sure, any time. When do you expect to let me have that room back?"

Carol had not been paying attention to the status of room 8 at the *Welcome Inn*. She was embarrassed to hear that, unlike the rest of the motel, it was still being treated as a crime scene, long after it had been meticulously searched for evidence. On the other hand, perhaps it was just as well that Keller's room had not been used since the night of Carl's death. Visiting it again might jar her memory of what was bothering her.

253

"I'm sorry about that, Mr. Reece." Carol was about to say that they'd just been too busy, but decided it would be better to argue that sometimes these investigations simply take time. In any event, she was quite certain that the *Welcome Inn's* business wasn't suffering from lack of another room. "How about it if I drop by sometime in the next hour or two?"

"No problem. I'll be here all day for that matter."

"Good. And thanks."

Carol busied herself with a few matters that had nothing to do with the Keller case, and was about ready to leave for Hopewell and her meeting with Marty Reece when Officer Barrett popped in.

"Have a minute?"

"Always. What's up?"

"It's that Crooked Lake grapevine," he said. "It may be unimportant, but I heard something this morning that I thought you might want to know about."

"Come on in, tell me about it."

Barrett was wearing a tentative smile as he took a chair across from Carol's desk.

"First, I'll have to confess I was taking a coffee break. Actually I'd stopped for breakfast at the Southport diner."

Carol was thoroughly familiar with the habits of her officers. Jim Barrett rarely ate breakfast at home, preferring to begin his working day with ham and eggs at the diner. She'd long since decided that this little social ritual was an important part of why he enjoyed his job.

"There were a couple of guys I know in the booth, and Joe Williams joined us. You know him?"

"Not well, but we've met."

"Anyway, Joe, he's not what you'd call a gossip, but he said he'd seen something he thought was interesting. Just this morning. It concerns one of those people you've been talking about because of that man who got his throat slit. He's a judge. Hartman, I think."

"Williams, is he a friend of the judge?"

"I don't think so. He happens to have a place next to him over on the East Lake Road. The judge doesn't live there. It's just a summer cottage. Anyway, Joe was up early like usual, and I guess he was in the kitchen making coffee or something when he sees this car coming out of the judge's driveway. He said it stopped just before it reached the road and a woman got out to do something. Wipe the condensation off the rear window, I think. That's all that happened, but what interested Joe was that he says the woman definitely wasn't the judge's wife, yet there she was leaving the cottage sometime before six in the morning."

"Did he speculate about the woman?"

"No, he mostly just thought it was strange. Seems the judge had just come back to the lake a few days ago. He'd said hello to Joe, told him he was going to get some fishing in while his wife redecorated their kitchen. "

"I take it you didn't ask a bunch of questions."

"No. Do you think I should have?" Barrett suddenly looked as if he might have let the sheriff down.

"It's better you didn't. No reason for people to think we're interested in Judge Hartman. Which, of course, we are. It was before six when this happened?"

"That's what Joe said."

"Did he describe the woman? The car?"

"No. It probably wouldn't have been easy. Too early."

"Well, what do you know." Carol looked pensive. "Do us a favor and keep taking breakfast at the diner. You never know what you'll learn."

Carol knew better than to start making assumptions about the importance of what Jim had just told her. There was probably some perfectly simple explanation for what Joe Williams had seen. On the other hand, she was much more interested in this news flash from the local gossip mill than she was in the trip she was about to take to the *Welcome Inn*.

————

The motel looked depressingly just as it had when she had arrived the morning after Carl Keller's death. The parking area still needed paving, the building still lacked a fresh coat of paint, and the absence of plantings and other amenities was guaranteed to discourage any but the most desperate of those searching for a place to spend the night. There were no cars in sight. Room 8 still bore the familiar yellow tape of a police crime scene plus a large official looking warning notice on the door.

Carol parked and was promptly met at the door to the office by Marty Reece. He looked much as he had when first they met: a balding man of average size who was probably in his 30s. He had a pockmarked face, and was wearing a gaudy sport shirt, surprisingly well pressed Levis, and sandals.

"Always glad to welcome our sheriff, although I'm sorry you haven't been able to discover who killed my guest in number 8."

"You aren't nearly as sorry as I am, Mr. Reece. This is proving to be a tough one. What do you say we go down to 8.

"Whatever you say."

He collected the key and led the way down the walk to where Carl had spent his last night on earth.

"I'm assuming that this is the first time anyone's been in this room since my men posted the sign."

"Absolutely. When the sheriff's department issues orders, I do exactly as I'm told. You didn't think I'd try to rent the room, did you?"

"No, but I'm a chronic worrier. At first I worried that we might have overlooked something, but that'd be hard to do, don't you think? I mean, it's a pretty bare bones room. No offense, but here isn't much of any place where something could have been hidden, is there?"

"No, ma'am, no frills."

No frills, Carol thought, not even a place for a Gideon Bible. Nonetheless, she went around the room, looking into corners, opening the drawers in the dresser, checking the toilet tank and the small medicine cabinet. The only thing that was different was that the bed had been stripped, revealing its old and stained mattress. It was thin and sagged in the middle. She lifted a corner; there was nothing there, of course, and she found herself thinking that Carl's nights at the *Welcome Inn* must have been uncomfortable.

Ten minutes later they were back in Reece's office.

"You told me that Carl didn't talk very much," Carol said. "But surely over the span of a week - I think you said eight or nine days - he must have talked some. Did he ever say anything about where he was from, why he was here in Hopewell or at Crooked Lake, what he did?"

"I wish I could tell you he had, but I can't. I asked him a few questions like that, but he didn't seem to want to talk about himself. All he said - and this I do remember - was that he was looking for something."

"Something or somebody?"

"I think it was something, but now that I think about it I'm not a hundred percent sure."

"Did he ever ask for directions to someplace in the area? I mean if he was looking for something or somebody, that would have been a natural thing to do. He didn't know the area, we know that."

"Nothing very specific," Reece answered, obviously trying to recall something that would not have struck him as very important. "When he first checked in he asked about the usual things, like where's a good place to eat and how's the fishing. Things like that."

"He asked about fishing?"

"I'm pretty sure he did, but maybe he was just trying to make small talk, not planning on doing any fishing."

"Did he ever mention any names? Names of people?"

"I don't recall that he did."

"Aside from not talking much, how did he strike you? Did he seem anxious, like maybe something was bothering him? Did he act nervous?"

"Now that's a funny thing," Reece said. "I'm not sure nervous is the right word, but there was something about him. Like he didn't really know what he was doing. Or maybe whether he should be doing whatever it was he was doing. That's doesn't make sense, though, does it? There was a day when I had a feeling he might have changed his mind, that he'd just jump in his car and take off, maybe without even settling his bill. There, that's the word I was looking for. He seemed jumpy. Do you know what I mean?"

"Yes, I think I do. People can get jumpy if they're afraid of something or somebody. Do you think Mr. Keller acted like he was worried about being followed?"

Reece shook his head.

"I'm not being very helpful, am I."

"There's no reason why you'd know what was on Mr. Keller's mind. Let me ask another tough question. Do you think he might possibly have been depressed?" This time Carol deliberately avoided the word suicidal.

"How in the world would I know if he was depressed?" Reece sounded unexpectedly irritated.

"There are certain warning signs," she said. She tried to explain to Reece some of the characteristics of depression. "I know you didn't know him, but try to think about it."

Marty Reece looked uncomfortable.

"I've got a brother who used to tell me he was depressed, but I could never quite figure out what he was talking about. He seemed normal to me. All

I can tell you about Mr. Keller is that he wasn't very happy. Or if he was, he just didn't know how to show it. I'm no shrink, but I think he was sort of down on himself. He said he was looking for something, but maybe it's closer to the truth to say he was running away from something."

Later, as she was driving back to Cumberland, Carol was also analyzing what she had learned from her visit to the *Welcome Inn*. She still wasn't sure what it was about the motel and Carl's death there that was bothering her. But she was pleased that she had spoken with Reece again. He's not a well educated man, she said to herself, but one of the last things he had said to her struck her as remarkably perceptive. Keller may have been looking for something or somebody, but it might be more important that he was also running away from something or somebody.

CHAPTER 41

Marty Reece had watched the sheriff back up and turn left and out of the *Welcome Inn* parking lot. The car disappeared from sight, but Marty remained at the door to his office, thinking about the conversation he had just had with the sheriff. Why had she found it necessary to come back to the motel? Her men had spent the better part of three days there after he had reported Carl Keller's death. He had thought that even two days were more than necessary, considering how small the room was, how spartan its furnishings. Of course the cops had to be thorough. He'd watched enough crime shows with their depiction of the 'scene of the crime' to know that. But three days at the most unprepossessing of motels, the *Welcome Inn*? And now she had come back. Her questions had been pretty much what they had been when she first talked to him. All except the one about Keller acting depressed. What was that all about?

Maybe it was time for him to think about moving on. He'd been at Crooked Lake for almost two years, which was almost as long as he had spent before at Pend Oreille. And he liked Pend Oreille much better. Unlike Crooked Lake, it was surrounded by real mountains, much of its shoreline was unpopulated, the fishing was superior, and you could actually see real wild animals, like moose and black bear and even grizzlies. All you had here were acres and acres of grapes. Grapes that would be turned into alcoholic grape juice with fancy names. He hated wine, couldn't understand the fuss about it. All this talk about vintages and oak and tannin and hints of pear or some other fruit. Wine. That's probably what Keller drank, although he also remembered finding a nearly empty bottle of scotch in his room.

He went back to his office and sat down at his desk. He tried to pull out the drawer, but as usual found it difficult. Something had been caught in it, something he had never tried very hard to remove. It was easier to jerk the drawer from side to side and utter the occasional curse. It always worked. The fact that it was hard to open gave Marty some satisfaction. It meant that his private papers would remain private, resting inviolate in the difficult drawer along with a few odds and ends of memorabilia, out of sight to prying eyes. Not that anyone would be tempted to poke around in his desk.

Or would she? He could think of no reason why the sheriff would be interested in him or his troubled background. Indeed, it would never occur to her that he might have a troubled background unless she somehow managed to yank the drawer open. For that matter, what would she know of that corner of the United States? It was possible, of course, that she had visited the American northwest at some time in her life. Seattle, possibly the Cascades, maybe Glacier National Park, just to see the glaciers before they all gave way to global warming. But the Idaho panhandle? Highly unlikely.

One more hard tug and the drawer responded. He had opened it many times, and knew exactly where things were. He ignored a small box containing a Purple Heart he had earned during one of his two postings to Iraq, as well as two letters earned by his prowess as a distance runner on his high school track team and a small collections of stones, rubbed round and smooth, which he had collected as a boy along the Oregon coast. What interested him - what always interested him when he opened the drawer - were clippings from a small town newspaper. They had been fastened together by a large paper clip, and they lay atop a small pile of assorted papers that took up most of the space in the drawer.

Marty did not remove the paper clip. He seemed satisfied simply to hold the clippings in his hand, as if by doing so he could temporarily be transported back to the time and place of the events recorded on them. It was not that holding the newspaper clippings gave him a sense of pleasure or pride in something he had done. Quite the contrary. They made him uncomfortable, bringing to the surface memories he wished would go away but knew he had to hang onto for dear life.

It was a typical day at *Welcome Inn*. There was nothing he had to do. He had already changed the bedding and towels in the one room that had been occupied the previous night. The carpet hadn't needed a vacuuming, so he had skipped that chore. He had, as he always did, examined the things that had been dropped in the wastebasket before emptying it. It was one of his many habits, like biting his finger nails and dropping his cigarette butts in the toilet. Today there had been nothing of interest in the wastebasket, if one were to discount the stub of a ticket to a recent game at Yankee Stadium. The man who had used the room had not looked as if he could afford the price of such a ticket. But one never knows.

Mr. Keller had obviously been a man of some means, yet he had chosen to stay at the *Welcome Inn.*

With nothing that had to be done, Marty Reece settled into his only comfortable chair to think. Had he been a reader, he might have picked up a book. But he wasn't a reader and there were no books in the small place he called home. Which left thinking. And what he wanted to think about was whether he should pack up his few belongings, load the car, and set off for another town, another life. One reason for doing so would be that he was restless. A more important reason was that he was convinced that he was safer if he didn't let himself put down roots, if he kept moving. Of course if he moved too soon, the sheriff might find it suspicious. Marty weighed the possibilities. He decided to give life at the *Welcome Inn* one more week. By that time the sheriff would surely have seen enough of the motel and its manager. The yellow tape and the notice on the door of room 8 would have been removed and he would have been given permission to rent it again to guests, assuming that there were any. But he wouldn't have to worry about that. In all likelihood, he'd be long gone and perhaps as much as a thousand miles away when a guest knocked on his door, asking for room 8.

He had momentarily forgotten the clippings in his hand. It was when he started to reach for a cigarette that he remembered. The sight of the clippings made him angry. He closed his fist, crumpling them into a ball, and threw the ball on the floor. There was no one in the motel, much less in the cramped room where he was sitting, to hear the vulgar oath he uttered. He got up from his chair and retrieved the clippings. The paper clip had come off and he spent nearly a minute searching for it, cursing as he ran his hands over the floor and under the TV stand. It was only a few inches away from his foot, rendered almost invisible by the dirty grey carpet on which it lay. When he found it, he resumed his seat and gently straightened the clippings, careful not to tear them, as he restored them to something like they had been when he took them out of his desk. That done, he put them back in the drawer and placed the box with the Purple Heart in it on top of them. Closing the drawer was not quite as difficult as opening it had been. Marty lighted his cigarette and leaned back in his chair. His eyes were closed, but tears ran down his cheeks.

CHAPTER 42

Kevin customarily met Carol at the door when she got home from work. This day was an exception. He was nowhere in sight. She called out his name, but he didn't answer. It was not until she went out onto the deck that she spotted him standing at the end of the dock. Had he been wearing his bathing suit, she would not have been surprised. What surprised her was that he was fully dressed and, somewhat awkwardly, casting a fishing line out into the lake. This was a sight the like of which Carol had never seen. Her husband was not, and presumably had never been, a fisherman.

She set out for the dock, curious about this strange new and totally unexpected development.

"What's going on?" she asked as she came up behind Kevin.

"I'm fishing," he said as he reeled in the line.

"I can see that, but why?"

"To catch a fish."

"Kevin, this is Carol. I'm entitled to an explanation, don't you think?"

She took a seat on the bench at the side of the dock where she could see his face. It wore a broad smile.

Kevin lifted the pole until the baited hook came out of the water, then turned toward his wife.

"I've been busy, as you can see. I bought a pole, that little tackle box over there, and got myself a license. You're looking at a new man."

"But you've never done any fishing. You wouldn't know how."

"Every red blooded American boy knows how to fish. It's a genetic thing, passed down over generations."

Carol waved that bit of nonsense aside.

"What, may I ask, prompted this particular mid-life crisis?"

"The lake trout we're going to have for dinner. Mike Snyder caught three of them this morning and gave us one. It's all gutted and cleaned, ready to put on the grill. All I have to do is tuck some thin sliced onions and lemons in it. Sound good?"

"I guess so, but what does this have to do with the sudden desire to take up fishing?"

"I figured I didn't need to depend on Mike. Why not catch them myself?"

"I hate to spoil your fun, but you can't catch lake trout off the end of the dock. They're deep water fish, and our canoe is no fishing boat. You hook an eight or ten pounder out in the middle of the lake and you'll be overboard before you can net him."

"Oh ye of little faith. Look, all I'm doing at the moment is perfecting my skills, catching a sunny or two for practice. I'll admit to being a little rusty."

"Rusty?" Carol said in mock derision. "I'll bet the only fish you've ever seen are the ones resting on your dinner plate."

The familiar pattern of good natured banter lasted for a few minutes, after which they headed back to the cottage, where Kevin exchanged the fishing pole for a bag of charcoal and a pair of tongs. As it turned out, the trout was good and the conversation eventually got around to Carol's day and developments in the Keller case.

"For the most part I've been spinning my wheels. No one wants to talk with me."

"Can't you tell them they have no choice? You know, that you're she who must be obeyed."

Carol laughed at this old joke of theirs.

"That's not it. The problem is that the people I need to see aren't available when I call. They'll come around, but it's been frustrating. But there was one interesting development. Officer Barrett ran into a neighbor of Judge Hartman's today. Not over in Albany, but at his cottage on the East Lake Road. I didn't know that Hartman was at the lake. In fact, I don't know for sure that he was. At least the neighbor didn't say he was. But this morning it seems this neighbor looked out his kitchen window sometime before six o'clock and saw a woman drive out of Hartman's driveway and head north. It probably means nothing, but, like I said, it's interesting."

"Why interesting? The judge is married, so why wouldn't you assume the woman was his wife?"

"Because the neighbor knows Mrs. Hartman and swears that the woman driving away from the cottage wasn't her. So what does that suggest?"

"Sugar!" Kevin suddenly remembered the rumor Gretchen Ziegler had reported. "Did he describe her?"

"It was pretty early, and she was some distance away. So we don't know it was Ms. Sugar. In fact, come to think of it, I don't really have a very good idea what she looks like. Bridges talked with her. I'll have to get him to fill me in."

"But who else could it be? If they have a cleaning woman, she wouldn't be leaving the cottage at that hour. Logically, the woman had spent the night there, and who is it that is rumored to be sleeping with the judge?"

"That's what it looks like to me, but we can't be sure at this point. Besides, we don't know if the judge was even at his cottage. He'd been there for a brief vacation when I visited him, but he was supposed to go back to Albany shortly thereafter. Of course Sugar could have been using the cottage even if the judge wasn't there. We have no idea what arrangements they have. Maybe none whatsoever. But until we learn something to the contrary, Sugar would seem to be the most likely candidate as the woman Joe Williams saw."

"Williams, he's the neighbor who told Barrett about this?"

"Right."

"I think I'd talk with him, see if he can't be more specific."

"I plan to do that. Tomorrow, while you're improving your ability to cast a fishing line. And while I'm at it, I intend to keep right on pursuing Ms. Sugar. I can't wait to talk with her and find out whether there's anything to this rumor about her and Hartman."

"It shouldn't be hard to find out whether the judge was at the lake last night," Kevin said.

"I'm not so sure. Let's see if we can find out. I'm going call the cottage. Right now."

Carol disappeared into the study. She reappeared five minutes later.

"He's there," she said. "It seems that a trial he was to handle was postponed and he took advantage of it to get in some more fishing. Like you, he's a dock, not a boat, fisherman. I didn't ask if he had company last night. No point in tipping my hand. But I've arranged to see him tomorrow."

"How'd he sound?"

"Cautious. I said I wanted to talk with him about a story I'd heard that Carl Keller was guilty of stealing from a client's escrow account. I may bring it up, but what I'm really interested in is Randall Truscott's ex-girl friend, Donna Sugar."

CHAPTER 43

Carol resorted to several forms of subterfuge in arranging her meeting with Joe Williams. In the first place, she could not allow Judge Hartman to see her at his neighbor's cottage, so she met Williams at the diner, just as Barrett had. In the second place, she left the official car, with its telltale markings, in the department's parking lot and drove her own much less conspicuous vehicle. She also left her uniform and gun at the cottage, opting instead for casual slacks and blouse. She didn't dare to pretend that she wasn't the sheriff; Williams knew otherwise. But she cooked up an explanation for meeting with him which was patently untrue. Carol did not like to make lies a part of her repertoire, but she had found them useful from time to time and she had become quite good at it.

Having warned Officer Barrett that he was to forego his breakfast with friends at the diner, she arrived as planned precisely at nine o'clock. Williams recognized her before she recognized him, and escorted her to one of the only two vacant booths.

"You're out of uniform," he said. It was as much a question as a statement.

"I'm taking a day off. Doctor's appointment, wouldn't you know. Just in case she wants me to slip out of my clothes for an examination, these things are easier to shed than that pesky uniform."

She wondered if Williams was imagining her disrobing for the doctor.

"Have some coffee if you like. I was told to skip breakfast, coffee included. They say it makes your blood work unreliable."

"I think I will," he said and signaled to a waitress.

"I suppose you're wondering why we're doing this," Carol said, making a point to keep her voice down. "Like I told you over the phone, it's all because Jim Barrett told me that he had breakfast with you yesterday and that you mentioned that your neighbor, Judge Hartman, might have had a visitor."

"That's right. Some woman was leaving his cottage just ahead of six. It seemed kinda strange."

"I'm sure it did. But I think the explanation is pretty simple. There's a woman from out of town who was looking for a relative here on the lake early yesterday. Somebody eventually steered her to my office for help. Her instructions were hopelessly complicated. It was no wonder she was having trouble. Anyway, she said she'd gone to cottages with the wrong number twice and was by then both thoroughly confused and more than a little embarrassed. It strikes me that there's a chance that the woman you saw is this woman. That's why I'm here this morning."

Joe Williams looked puzzled.

"How can I help?"

"I've talked to the woman who was lost, and I thought it would be helpful if I described her and asked if she sounds like the mystery woman you saw."

Carol had considered first asking Williams to describe the woman he had seen. But then it would be too easy for her to declare it a match, case closed. Williams might be smart enough to see the trap.

"The woman I talked to is quite short," she said, "and fairly young - maybe in her thirties, no older than 40, and she has dark hair."

"It was still pretty early, but that could be the woman I saw. She was definitely short, maybe five foot tall. And she had dark hair. I'm not sure about her age, but I could tell she wasn't an older woman, like Mrs. Hartman is."

"I think you can see why I'm asking you to try to remember the woman you saw. If she was the one who had simply gotten lost, it could hurt Judge Hartman's reputation if a rumor got around that some woman was spending the night at his cottage. Those of us in the law enforcement business aren't just interested in catching crooks. We also have to protect people from false accusations."

What she said was true, but Carol didn't like what she was doing. Hartman had very probably been entertaining Donna Sugar, but she didn't want a rumor to that effect to become common knowledge around the lake. At least not until she had had an opportunity to confront Hartman herself.

Joe Williams was now uncomfortable.

"I probably should have kept my mouth shut. I don't really know the judge, but they've been good neighbors. They're not here that much, but they're quiet, mind their own business. I wouldn't want to hurt him."

"We obviously don't know for sure who the woman was that you saw. But it's because we don't know that it's better not to talk to people about it. Of course if you hadn't said something to Officer Barrett, we wouldn't be discussing the problem this morning and things might have gotten worse. Anyway, I'd suggest that we assume the woman was the one who'd gotten lost and not speculate about someone visiting the judge. Okay?"

"Absolutely. I just hope I haven't started a false rumor."

Carol smiled and thanked him for listening to her. When she left the diner, he was thoughtfully stirring his coffee and looking off into space.

Her next stop was with Lindsay Hartman for a much more difficult conversation. She would have to be circumspect, but she wouldn't have to lie.

The appointment wasn't until 10:30, so she killed a bit of time by taking a roundabout route to the judge's cottage. It was just shortly after 10:30 when she pulled off the East Lake Road onto Dogwood Point. A woman who had not yet been positively identified had done just what the sheriff was doing less than two days earlier. Carol parked under the big willow tree and circled around the cottage to the lake side. The judge was on the dock fishing, as he had told her he would be.

"Good morning, sheriff," he announced, setting his pole down as he turned to greet her.

"Good morning to you, judge. No need to stop fishing. I'd hate to be responsible for you losing a big one. Why don't I just take a seat here?"

The end of the dock had what amounted to a spacious fan deck with four Adirondack chairs. Carol sat down in one of them.

"You really have a beautiful place," she said. "If it were mine, I think I'd spend most of my leisure hours right here on the dock."

"I'll have to confess I spend a good part of my waking hours here. Reading when I'm not fishing, although I fish more than I read. I'll just leave my line in the water, if you don't mind."

Hartman fiddled with his fishing pole for a moment and then took one of the other Adirondack chairs.

"So here we are, talking to each other for the second time in less than two weeks after not seeing each other for nearly ten years. I can hardly believe my luck. And speaking of luck, are you having any in solving Carl Keller's murder? No, I shouldn't put it that way, should I? I'm quite sure the secret of your success in law enforcement isn't luck."

"Actually, it isn't Keller I came to talk about." Carol had taken notice of the fact that the judge's bonhomie seemed forced. His tone of voice suggested that he was relaxed. Something about his face, especially his eyes, told a different story.

"Oh, yes. Something about stealing from an escrow account. Well, that isn't my bailiwick, but - say, I'm forgetting my duties as host. Would you like coffee?"

"That would be very nice. I take it black, unsweetened."

"Right back." Lindsay Hartman strode off in the direction of the cottage, leaving Carol to wonder just what kind of conversation they would be having. She stared at the pole and watched the line twitch. A fish was biting. Just as suddenly, the twitching ceased.

"Here you are," Hartman said as he handed Carol her coffee and resumed his seat. "Now about that escrow account."

"Have you always been a fisherman?" Carol asked, deferring her real agenda.

"Oh, yes, I'm a veritable Izaak Walton."

"My husband never fished a day in his life until yesterday. Now, all of a sudden, that's all he talks about." Carol suspected that within a week he'd have forgotten all about it. "But back to my question. Suppose a lawyer took money from a client's account for his personal use and then died. Who'd be responsible for making the account whole again, the lawyer's estate or the firm with which he was associated?"

"Is this a hypothetical question?"

"I don't really know. The facts aren't clear."

"It can be complicated, but the bottom line is that there's a lawyers fund to protect clients from an attorney who does what this one did. Do you think you know such an attorney?"

"I may."

For a moment neither of them said anything.

"Is there something you'd like me to do about it?" The judge finally asked.

"Not now," she replied, knowing that the judge was curious. But she had no intention of pursuing the matter. It was Francis Foster with whom she'd be discussing Carl's alleged violation of legal ethics.

"Do you mind if I ask a personal question?" Carol asked him.

"I suppose that depends on the question." Hartman tried to produce a smile, but failed.

"When we first met here at your cottage awhile back, we discussed the Truscott trial. I'm not making much headway in my investigation of Mr. Keller's death, but for some reason I keep coming back to the trial. I may have it all wrong, but I can't shake a feeling that the reason is that what happened to Mr. Keller has something to do with the Truscott case. After all, his life seemed to be pretty normal until he agreed to defend Truscott. But it didn't go well for him. He lost the case, he was cited for contempt, he was fired from his law firm. He seemed to fall apart. He comes over to Crooked Lake, checks into a third rate motel, and dies there."

"I can understand that what happened at the trial could be a real downer, even make him depressed, but I can't see what it could have to do with his death"

"I know. That's been puzzling me, too. It's what brings me to my question. A rumor has come to my attention, and it pertains to you, judge. I hesitate to bring it up, but I feel you should know about it. It has been suggested that you had been in some kind of personal relationship with the woman who brought charges against Truscott."

Carol paused to gauge the judge's reaction.

"I thought you were going to ask me a question. Is your question whether the rumor is true?" Lindsay Hartman's bonhomie had been forced. Now it had disappeared entirely.

"You don't have to talk about it. I just thought it would be easier if you could put the rumor to rest, one way or another."

"Well, of course I can put it to rest. I have never had what you call a personal relationship with that woman. Sugar is her name, as I'm sure you know. She was in my courtroom because she had been brutally assaulted by Truscott. It was not difficult for the jury to reach a verdict or for me to hand down a sentence. If you are implying that I somehow stage managed the whole affair in order to protect my relationship with the woman, you are a fool."

"Judge Hartman, I am not implying anything. I am investigating a murder, and in the course of my investigation this rumor - a rumor which you have just denied - has come to my attention. It seemed only fair that you should know what has been said about you and Ms. Sugar. I'm sorry to be the bearer of bad news."

The judge stared at the sheriff, stone faced, unaware that he now had a fish on his line.

"I'll accept that as an apology, sheriff. But you still haven't explained why Mr. Keller's failure as a defense counsel in the Truscott case might have led to his death. Had he committed suicide, I might call it a tragedy but I could understand it. But you told me his throat was slit. I fail to see how that could possibly have anything to do with the fact that he'd just gone through a rough patch in his career. It sounds more as if it's linked to some secret in the man's past or was just a random act of violence by a sick and deranged member of this troubled society of ours."

"That could be. But no matter what happened, I'd call it a tragedy. I knew Carl, and he didn't deserve to die like that."

Once again Carol had declined to mention that Carl had committed suicide. She had no reason to think the judge had slit Carl's throat, but if by some chance he had, it was better to let him think she was investigating a murder.

When Carol said good-bye and left the dock, the judge appeared to have lost his interest in fishing. She made that even more likely with her parting words.

"Oh, by the way, one other thing. A young woman was seen driving away from your cottage very early yesterday morning. It may be unimportant, but I thought you ought to know."

CHAPTER 44

Carol's afternoon wore on without any success in reaching either Francis Foster or Donna Sugar. Nor was Officer Byrnes successful in finding Carl Keller's first wife. But just ahead of four o'clock she did make contact with Lisa Simmons at the *Treasure Chest*.

It was immediately apparent that she was not at all anxious to be having another conversation with the sheriff. Carol thought she actually sounded frightened when she told her who it was that was calling.

"There's something I meant to ask you the other evening, Ms. Simmons. You've known Carl Keller for quite some time. You actually lived with him for several months before he left the law firm and you decided to move out. As I remember it, you said you left Carl because he wasn't much fun any more. Is that right?"

"Something like that. We weren't communicating, if you know what I mean."

"When he did talk, did he ever say he was depressed?" Carol had fallen into the habit of speaking of depression when what really interested her was whether Carl had been suicidal.

Lisa was obviously surprised by the question.

"Do you think he was depressed?"

"That's what I'm asking you."

"No, that never came up."

"Please think carefully, Lisa."

"I guess I never gave it much thought."

Carol once again trotted out her little lecture on suicide, even as she avoided the word itself.

"People who are often behave differently than usual. They are often moody, seem to lose interest in things. They can have trouble sleeping. In those days after he left the law firm, did Carl ever talk about himself as a failure?"

"Like I've said, he didn't talk much at all, but some of those things you mentioned - you know, like being moody - they sound like Carl. He definitely seemed to have lost his interest in most everything. Especially me. That's why I left."

"As you think back on it now, would you say he was depressed?"

"Well, I'm no doctor, but the way you describe it, maybe he was." It was Lisa who then made the connection between depression and suicide. "Didn't I read somewhere that people who are depressed are more likely to commit suicide?"

"I believe that's true."

"But Carl didn't commit suicide by cutting his own throat, did he?" Lisa made a face that perfectly reflected the picture in her mind.

"No, of course not. I'm calling because I figured you're the person who probably knew him best in his last weeks, which is why I need your help. We know that Carl kept his thoughts to himself for the most part. But even if he didn't talk a lot, he must have talked some to you, and I doubt that when he did it was all about the weather or what was in the refrigerator. How about names? Anything that gave a hint to what was on his mind?"

"It's like I told you, once in awhile he said something about getting another job, but he didn't do anything about it."

"So he never talked about the people he'd been working with, people who'd been a part of his life?"

"Now that you mention it, I think he did say something about a man he was working with. I don't recall his name. No, wait a minute, it was something like the name of a European car. Ferrari, that's it. I think it had to do with Ferrari taking over his cases after he was fired."

Carol mentally translated Ferrari to Ferraro.

"What did he have to say about this Ferrari?"

"It wasn't much of a conversation. But Carl said something about not trusting him."

Aha, Carol thought, F is for Ferraro.

"Did he say why he didn't trust Ferrari?"

"Not that I remember. Probably just that he didn't think Ferrari could handle those cases as well as he had."

"Perhaps. We may never know just what the problem was between them. How about other names? Like Foster. Francis Foster."

"Wasn't he the man who fired him?"

"He was, so Carl did talk a bit about what was going on at his old law firm."

"I guess so. Not much, but maybe I didn't pay as much attention as I should have. Carl thought the legal stuff would bore me, and I guess he was right."

Lisa Simmons, who could have - *should* have - been a gold mine of information about what was going on in Carl Keller's life, had obviously not been living with Carl because they were intellectually compatible. It had probably just been a physical attraction. Carol had not known Carl well enough to speculate on his tastes in such matters, but she had trouble imagining him in a relationship with Simmons.

"Now that you've dug back into your memory bank, is there anything else you can think of that might be of help to me?"

'I don't think so, but I promise I'll tell you right away if I think of anything."

"How's business at the *Treasure Chest*?" she asked.

"Not bad. I've had a hard time concentrating on the store lately. I've been worried about Richard Keller and telling him where to find Carl."

Carol wanted to say that Lisa might still have reason to feel guilty about not trying harder to understand Carl, but she let it go.

"We still need to find out who Richard Keller really is. That's pretty much my first order of business."

"Do you still think he could come after me? Why would he do that?"

"I don't know how his mind works, Lisa. But I do know that he'll remember that he used you to get to Carl. And if he's as smart as I think he is, he'll realize that that makes you a potential danger to him. I wouldn't be surprised if he's worried that that elaborate facial bandage of his might not have been an adequate disguise. In other words, he might worry that you could identify him. It's like I told you. Be alert. And don't hesitate to get in touch with the police if you see or hear anything suspicious."

"Do you think I should be in a witness protection program?"

"No, that won't be necessary." The woman has seen too many episodes of shows like 'Law and

Order,' Carol thought. "Just keep your wits about you and stay in touch."

When Carol got off the phone, she found herself wondering if it might have been wiser to admit that Carl had indeed committed suicide. As it was, she might have alarmed Lisa Simmons unnecessarily and then treated her anxiety too casually. She wished she knew more, much more, about the man who had pretended to be Richard Keller.

CHAPTER 45

"Catch anything today?" Carol put the question to Kevin as soon as she got home.

"Three sunfish, but they were too small. I threw them back. I'm going to have to go further out if I'm going to have a prayer of catching a lake trout."

"I thought we agreed that you don't have the right boat for it. In fact, I suspect you don't have the right equipment. If you're determined to be a real fisherman, why don't you talk to Mike Snyder, get a better picture of what you'll need to catch lake trout."

"I already talked with him, and I'm going to see if I can't pick up some of the proper gear tomorrow."

"I fear this is going to be an expensive hobby. And that's leaving out a power boat, which is way beyond our means."

"I told you I can use the canoe."

"That's insane, Kevin. I'm sure Mike would tell you the same thing."

"Well, we don't have multiple thousands to put into a bigger boat, so what choice do I have?"

"You could stick to sunfish, or you could ask Mike or somebody else if you could go out with them."

"Come on, Carol, I've got my pride. I don't want to impose on Mike, and guys my age don't fish for sunnies. That's kid stuff."

Carol could see that she had a problem on her hands. Her husband.

"Okay, let's test your plan. Why don't you get the paddles and we'll take the canoe out. I'll go get my bathing suit on."

"How are we going to test my plan? I don't have the right gear yet. And why do you need to wear your bathing suit?"

"Trust me. It won't be perfect, but it'll give us a reality check."

Kevin looked at Carol as if he were trying to decide whether she had an ulterior motive. But he did set off to get the paddles and cushions for the canoe.

It was a mismatched couple who set off for deeper water. Carol was barefooted and wearing a bathing suit. Kevin was still in slacks and a polo shirt, and was wearing his loafers. His fishing rod lay in the bottom of the canoe along with a can of worms.

"I know you don't catch lake trout with worms," he acknowledged. "But like you said, this is just a test run."

Veteran canoers though they were, Carol and Kevin typically paddled parallel to the shore. This time they were headed toward the bluff, across the lake from the cottage.

"This should be far enough," Carol said from her position in the bow.

They were short of the middle of the lake, but a good distance from the shore. They both stowed their paddles, and Kevin picked up his fishing pole and demonstrated his new found ability to bait the hook.

"Now I'll show you how it's done," he said as he got ready to cast.

"I'm watching," Carol announced over her shoulder.

The canoe rocked dangerously as Kevin's follow through shifted his weight.

"Got to be more careful," he said, laughing. His second and third casts were less exciting. Then to his surprise a fish took his bait. At least he thought that was what was happening. He twisted around the better to see his line, as did Carol. It was at that moment that the waves generated by a boat towing two water skiers in the direction of the bluff hit the canoe. Kevin impulsively grabbed the gunnel. The result, unfortunately, was not that of stabilizing the canoe but of propelling its occupants into the middle of Crooked Lake.

The next few minutes were spent in more or less purposeful thrashing around which eventually succeeded in righting the canoe with both of them back inside it. They sat there for a long moment, catching their breath. And then, as if on cue, they both broke into laughter.

"You should have seen yourself," Carol said "Very balletic."

Kevin was removing his water soaked loafers.

"You knew this was coming, didn't you?"

"No way. I had complete confidence in you. The bathing suit was just an insurance policy."

"I think I just flunked Fishing 101," Kevin said, acknowledging that canoes weren't meant for fishing. "So you don't have to tell me you told me so. What do you say we go down to *The Cedar Post*? I don't think I'm up to burgers on the grill tonight."

Half an hour later, back on shore and into dry clothes, they set off for dinner. As usual, *The Cedar*

Post was crowded, noisy, and unquestionably the most informal restaurant in the Crooked Lake area.

They did find a table, however, and once they were seated Carol urged Kevin to take a look around.

"See those guys at the bar? Fishermen, all of them."

"That's an unwarranted generalization, Carol."

"But they all look like they'd be right at home netting a lake trout. And I'll bet none of them would be doing it from a canoe."

"You must remember that I'm here to give the place a little diversity. Now why don't we study the menu."

"I already know what I'm having," Carol said.

They ordered and turned the conversation away from fishing to the more serious issues of the Keller case.

"I learned one thing today that's of more than passing interest," Carol said when the waitress served them and refilled their glasses. "It has to do with the mysterious F."

"The mysterious F?"

"Remember that note Carl tried to write on the back of the gas receipt?"

"Oh, that F. I'd forgotten. The person Carl didn't trust. You learned who he is?"

"I think so, thanks to Lisa Simmons. It's the lawyer Tony Ferraro."

"You think so, meaning you don't know for sure."

"I'm ninety percent sure, assuming Lisa is not part of a conspiracy to confuse me. I called her and tried to get her to tell me whether she thought Carl might have been suicidal. Her stock response is always that they didn't talk much, so she didn't know. But I pushed her to think hard about what they talked about when they did talk, and she remembered a conversation about somebody name Ferrari."

"Ferrari? That's an Italian car, not an Albany lawyer."

"I know, but I figured she'd just gotten the name confused. Anyway, she recalled that Carl had said he didn't trust this Ferrari guy. So all of a sudden I knew who F is. Wouldn't you agree?"

"It makes sense. She didn't say why Carl didn't trust him, did she?"

"No. She obviously wasn't interested in lawyer talk. In fact, she must have been pretty dull company. But when you're in my business, you take what you can get, and I got F's identity."

"What do you propose to do with it?"

"My first thought was to rush back to Albany and confront Ferraro," Carol said. "But that's a no go. These Albany trips are eating a big hole in my budget. To think I once thought I'd be able to handle it by letting you do it, off budget. How naive."

"But I did go to Albany, and I believe I did you some good."

"I know, but there are some things I can't delegate, and one of them is talking turkey to Francis Foster. So I'm going to call Francis, tell him what I know - or what I'm pretty sure I know, and try to persuade him that he's got to look into Ferraro's story about Carl stealing from a client's escrow account."

"Considering how angry he was when he was over here for lunch, do you think he'd listen to you?"

"Francis may be irritated with me - and you," Carol said, "but he's a good lawyer and a conscientious manager. I can't imagine him refusing to investigate a matter like this just because I'd ruffled his feathers."

"I hope you're right," Kevin said, sounding doubtful. "What do you think he'll discover?"

"I wish I knew. My instinct tells me that Carl wouldn't do what Ferraro accuses him of doing. Of course Carl was dead before Ferraro would have had an opportunity to frame him, but Carl may have had good reasons for thinking the man who was taking over his cases wasn't trustworthy. How, I don't know. Maybe Foster can tell us."

"What do you think this has to do with Carl's death?"

"Maybe nothing. Maybe a lot."

"Fishing is so much easier, isn't it?" Kevin suggested as he speared another forkful of eggplant parmigiana.

CHAPTER 46

Her swim the previous evening had been inadvertent. Not so the the one she was taking before heading for the office the next morning. Carol intended to try to reach Francis Foster again, and the best warm up for what was likely to be a difficult conversation was a dip in the lake.

Yesterday she'd been told that Foster was taking no calls, and would not accept any appointments he had not personally cleared in advance. He might still be reluctant to talk with her, but she intended to be more insistent. She had decided that there was no point in going back to Albany to make her case. She would do it over the phone.

The case which she would be making was that Francis should not accept Tony Ferraro's claim that Carl Keller had been stealing from a client's escrow account. Francis should look into the matter himself, and should do so with a healthy dose of skepticism about Ferraro's story. In effect, Carol said to herself, she had to persuade him that Ferraro was not to be trusted.

Kevin woke up just as she was finishing dressing, and it was with some difficulty that she was able to ward off his advances.

"Unlike you, I have a demanding agenda for the day and must put duty ahead of pleasure. So do something useful, like making the bed or putting my breakfast dishes in the dish washer. You're even welcome to take a swim. I did, and it was much more satisfying than the one I took last night."

"It's not enough that you're rejecting me," he said. "You're going to keep harping on our little canoe accident, aren't you?"

"The thought never entered my mind," she said as she strapped on her gun. "Barring some dramatic development, I'll see you no later than six."

She leaned forward to give Kevin a kiss and disappeared out the back door.

Carol had stopped providing updates on the Keller case at squad meetings. It wasn't that she had put it on a back burner. But in spite of the fact that the case was on her mind virtually every day (and more than a few nights), nothing had happened which enabled her to say with any conviction that she now knew just who the prime suspects were. In theory she thought she knew, but law enforcement, she realized, depends on much more than theory. In some respects the possible suspects were, if anything, too obvious, yet nothing had surfaced that made them more than people who might - again theoretically - have reason to want Carl Keller out of the way. Besides, Carl had been killed near Crooked Lake, whereas everyone who might be a suspect lived and worked in Albany, which was not exactly next door.

For some reason, her expectation of actually talking with Foster had improved. While he had not exactly been friendly when she ran into him on her visit to speak with Ferraro, he had not been as unpleasant as he'd been at their lake luncheon meeting. Perhaps on reflection he'd realized that his abrupt departure from the cottage had been an overreaction to Kevin's insinuation that he had axed Keller to placate Judge Hartman. But even if he were still angry, she was determined not to let him refuse to talk to her.

She killed some time to improve the chances that Francis would be in his office, and then took a deep breath and placed the call. The woman who answered the phone once again reported that he was busy, but Carol persevered.

"I'm sorry to be a nuisance," she said, "but it is extremely important that I talk with Mr. Foster. I have learned something important about one of his attorneys and a case he's handling. I know that he'll want to hear what I have to say."

"I don't know whether Mr. Foster will be able to talk with you now, but if it's important I'll let him know you'd like a call back."

"I think I should stay on the line," Carol said.

The woman, who had obviously been trained to be a tough gate keeper, said something under her breath which was hard for Carol to understand. But she didn't shut her off. Carol waited, looking at her watch to see just how long Francis Foster would keep her waiting.

"Good morning, sheriff," he said, picking up the phone more quickly than she had expected. "It appears that you have something to tell me that can't wait. Something regarding one of my attorneys."

"That's right, Francis. I can't say that I know how important it will turn out to be, but my instinct tells me that it is something you should be aware of."

"Who is the attorney I need to know more about?"

"Tony Ferraro." Carol chose not to rush into an explanation of the issue, but to let Francis ask questions.

"I think I already know all about it," he said. "It's the Rasmussen case. Carl Keller was handling it, and when he was let go I shifted the case to Ferraro. He subsequently reported to me that Keller had been stealing money from the Rasmussen escrow account. I don't think I'd ever had a colleague doing something like that in all my years in this business. Anyway, it seems Keller had reimbursed the account, so I decided to leave the matter alone. Keller'd had enough problems. Why drag his name through the mud posthumously?"

"I understand," Carol said. "But what if it wasn't Keller who'd been taking money from the account but Ferraro?"

"You can't be serious. Why would Tony do a thing like that?"

"I'm not sure he did. But I also can't imagine that Carl did. Now, to reinforce my doubts, I've come across a note that Carl left behind in which he says that Ferraro shouldn't be trusted. It's a brief note, and it doesn't say why he shouldn't be trusted. But it strikes me as important enough that someone other than Tony Ferraro should be investigating the Rasmussen account."

"And you're telling me that I'm the one to do it," Foster said.

"It's not for me to say. I suppose you could designate somebody else. But as an old friend of Carl's, I'd like better evidence that he's an unethical lawyer than Ferraro's say-so."

"So this is really about an old friendship with Keller, not a compromised escrow account."

"It's both, although the current status of the account isn't my responsibility. By the way, are you sure that Carl put the money he stole back in the account - assuming that he stole it in the first place?"

"That's what Tony says."

"But what if he didn't? What if the account is still short? How would you make it right with the client?"

"There's a fund for client protection in New York, sheriff. There's one in every state. The system makes sure that bad lawyers don't leave their clients holding the bag."

"I'd assume that you couldn't move money from this fund to a specific account, like Rasmussen's, without a serious investigative process by whoever manages the fund."

Foster didn't answer immediately. He didn't have to. But he was thinking of the possible consequences if he ignored Carol's unsolicited advice.

"I think I should look into it," he said.

Carol had gotten the attention of M & B's senior partner. An investigation by New York's Lawyers' Fund for Client Protection would not have a positive effect on the firm's image. She was sure that Francis Foster would at last be willing to intervene and scrutinize the Rasmussen case himself. She hoped that his investigation would exonerate Carl. If it did, there was a possibility that it would put Tony Ferraro's relationship with M & B in jeopardy. Perhaps even his membership in the New York bar.

It was only ten minutes after ten, and Carol leaned back in her chair, exulting in her successful conversation with her former boss. He would be no happier with her, but he would respect her more. He might even be willing to be more forthcoming in the investigation of Carl Keller's death.

CHAPTER 47

Buoyed by her apparent success with Francis Foster, Carol turned her attention to the elusive Donna Sugar. She had a good idea of what professional life was like for Francis Foster and Tony Ferraro because she had been there, done that. Her knowledge of the life of a judge was somewhat less precise, but she had been in court often enough to picture what Lindsay Hartman did when he was on the job. Donna Sugar was another story.

Carol thought she knew, at least in a general sense, what call girls did for a living. They were, not to put too fine a point on it, high class hookers. Rather than walk the streets, they made appointments by phone with men of money and then proceeded to entertain them and go to bed with them. But she suspected that their lives and sexual practices varied considerably from one of them to another. She remembered having once read an article by a sociologist that contrasted call girls with geishas. Or was it the other way around. In any event, she had a feeling that some call girls were bed hoppers, while others were virtually monogamous. Exactly where Sugar fell on this spectrum she did not know, but she did know that she had lived with Randall Truscott and cohabited briefly with Tony Ferraro. And was rumored to have had some sort of relationship with Judge Hartman.

The reason she was anxious to meet her and talk with her was to find out whether there was any truth to the Hartman rumor. Sam had been unable to get her to acknowledge such a relationship, but he had found her responses to his questions to be frustratingly just short of adamant denials. Perhaps that was due to a conscious desire on her part to maintain an aura of mystery. Perhaps it was because she enjoyed teasing Sam, whom Carol had always thought of as being slightly ill at ease in the presence of attractive women. It was even possible that Sam had misread Sugar.

One thing Carol knew for sure: she had no intention of discussing the woman's relationship with the judge over the phone. That was her preferred approach to questioning virtually everybody in any case. But in Sugar's case, it was essential. Which meant that if she were lucky enough to catch her at her apartment, the phone call would simply be a prelude to yet another trip over to the state capital. She briefly debated with herself the possibility of inviting her over to the lake, but just as quickly dismissed that idea. Inviting Francis Foster was one thing, even if it hadn't worked out as well as she had hoped. After all, they had been good acquaintances at one time and an invitation might even have been viewed as a thoughtful thing to do. Donna Sugar would almost certainly regard such an invitation as bizarre. 'You want me to drive all the way over to nowheresville so you can interrogate me about the death of a man I barely knew and my relationship with a judge I barely know? Sorry, sheriff, I'm a busy woman.'

Inevitably, Carol would be hitting the thruway again. And further putting her department's budget into the red. But if it had to be, so be it. She needed to meet the call girl. She tried her apartment.

"I'm not home." The same voice, the same words.

"Don't hang up." Carol spoke quickly, trying to keep the line open. "We must talk. This is Sheriff Kelleher in Cumberland County, and it's very important that I see you."

Donna Sugar did not answer, but she did not hang up.

"Thanks," Carol said. "Please listen to me. I won't take but a minute of your time. It is imperative that we talk. I'm calling to see if we can arrange a mutually convenient time for us to get together."

Again, silence. And then a question.

"Is it about Truscott?"

It wasn't the question that Carol had expected. She made a spur of the moment decision to say 'yes,' even if she had no idea what had prompted the question.

"Yes it is. I can make it by late this afternoon or evening. If that won't work, how about tomorrow?"

In her mind, Carol was trying to imagine what trysts Sugar had to work around if she were to agree to a meeting. She held her breath.

"Are you in Albany?"

"No, but I can be there within a little more than three hours. Like I said, it's very important."

"What about five o'clock? I have an evening appointment."

"I'll be there."

"Do you know the city?"

"I do, and my deputy gave me directions as to how to find your apartment."

"Oh, that's right," Sugar said, remembering that she had already had a visit from the sheriff's department. Carol thought she suddenly sounded less interested in seeing her.

"I'll see you at five," she said, and rang off before the call girl had a chance to change her mind.

Carol called the cottage and explained to Kevin that she would miss dinner and would be staying overnight in Albany.

"Why don't we inaugurate a shuttle service, Southport to Albany?" Kevin asked. "What's this make it - fifteen round trips in less than a month?"

"If it were that many, my department would be filing for bankruptcy. Hopefully, this will be the last one."

"You know perfectly well that it won't. Anyway, good luck with the delectable Ms. Sugar."

"Thanks. I may need it. She thinks I'm coming because I know something about Truscott."

"Why don't you drop by the jail and say hello to him?"

"That's probably not a bad idea, but I don't even know where he's been incarcerated, much less why Sugar thinks he's my reason for seeing her."

————

Carol made the trip to Albany in about a quarter of an hour less than she had expected to, but rush hour traffic in the city erased that advantage and she was close to ten minutes late for her appointment.

"Sorry, but the traffic was horrendous," she said when Donna Sugar opened her apartment door. "It's a pleasure to meet you."

"I'm sure that's not true, sheriff, but thanks anyway. This way." Carol followed her down the hall and into a living room which looked very much like a small greenhouse. There were plants on a small bookcase, in planters hanging from ceiling hooks, and in large ceramic pots in the corners of the room. All looked to be well cared for. Otherwise, the apartment, what she could see of it, looked attractive but not as elegant as Carol had imagined it would be. Donna Sugar, on the other hand, was quite simply beautiful. Sam had alerted her as to what to expect, but he still had not done the woman justice.

"I just poured myself some Scotch. What can I get for you?" Sugar asked.

"Officially I'm on duty, and drinking on duty is a no-no in my business," Carol said. "So I'll pass. I appreciate your willingness to see me on such short notice."

"It's not my usual practice to make people drive so far for a half hour of my time, but you seemed particularly anxious to see me. So here we are."

She tucked her feet under her on the couch, flashed Carol a smile which was more chilly than warm, and waited.

Carol knew she would be expected to talk about Randall Truscott, but she knew nothing about Truscott other than that he'd been sentenced to jail and had begun serving his time. She decided to talk about Truscott by inviting Sugar to do the talking.

"You expressed an interest in seeing me because of Randall Truscott. I'm aware that he was convicted of committing aggravated assault against you, but I assume that you are still worried about him. Why don't you tell me about it?"

"I thought you had something to tell *me* about Truscott."

"That would depend on what your problem with him is," Carol said, now aware that control of this conversation was slipping away from her.

Donna Sugar uncoiled herself, and with her feet back on the carpet got to her feet.

"You don't know anything about him, do you? You said you could tell me about Randall, but that was a lie."

"No, it wasn't a lie." Carol was thinking fast, trying to fill in the blanks. "I'm interested in Mr. Truscott because he was defended by a man who was killed over in my jurisdiction. I need to find out who killed him and why. You had a terrible experience with Mr. Truscott, but he's not in a position to harm you while he's in jail. Are you concerned that he'll come after you when he's released?"

"He's never going to be a physical threat to me again. Never!" The look on her face matched the tone of her voice. "It's his mouth, not his fists, I'm worried about."

Carol knew that Ms. Sugar might well be wrong on that score. Many an abuser has been known to return to his victim after a jail term or a judicial warning, often angrier and more violent than before. But she also realized that she had misread the reason for the call girl's anxiety. 'His mouth, not his fists.' It was something that Truscott might say, not what he might do, that was the problem. Carol thought she knew.

"You must understand," she said, "that my principal concern has been Truscott's attorney, not Truscott himself. Let me see if I can put myself in your shoes. Mr. Keller, the lawyer for the defense, tried to convince the jury that you were not simply an innocent victim. He wanted to do this by introducing evidence that you are a call girl, which would conjure up a negative picture of you in the minds of the jury. If my sources are correct, he might also have intended to plant the suggestion that you and the judge in the case had had some kind of relationship. Whether that was true or not, and whether it was his intent or not, the judge would not allow it and eventually held Mr. Keller in contempt of court. Keller is now dead, but that need not necessarily mean that his courtroom strategy is also dead. He may have shared his intentions with his client, Mr. Truscott. Would I be correct that that is what is troubling you? That Truscott, even though he is in jail, might choose to issue a statement that you and the judge had had an affair?"

Donna Sugar had listened with rapt attention to the sheriff's attempt to reconstruct what had happened, or might have happened.

"I have no idea what Mr. Keller intended to say in court, other than that he started to comment on what he referred to as my tawdry profession. But this business about my being in a relationship with the judge, that is preposterous. I find even the thought of it offensive."

"But if that is so, why did you agree to see me because I might know something about Mr. Truscott? Or perhaps I should ask what it is that you thought I might know?"

The call girl bit her lip. For the first time since Gretchen Ziegler had briefed Carol on the Truscott case and the rumors it had spawned, she felt reasonably confident that there was some truth to the rumors.

"Nothing in particular," Donna answered. "It's just that I can't get Randall off my mind. I still have nightmares."

"I can appreciate that. Unfortunately, you are now among a staggering number of women in this country who've been battered by men. I've been luckier, but I read the statistics and they tell an appalling story. While we're talking about Truscott, however, it may not matter to him that you deny a relationship with the judge. If he accuses you and Judge Hartman of having an affair, even if it isn't true, you'll find it very difficult to win the public relations battle that follows."

"That's what I'm afraid of," Donna said.

"Sometimes it's better to get out in front of something like this, admit it and deprive the rumor mongers of any advantage."

"What kind of advice is that? I should announce to the world that I did something I didn't do just to deprive Randall Truscott of a public relations coup?"

"No, of course I wouldn't do that if there is absolutely no evidence of a relationship with Judge Hartman. But I'd first want to be sure that there's absolutely no evidence."

"Why am I talking to you? You think I've been sleeping with the judge."

"What I think isn't relevant. What I know is that if you have been seeing the judge outside of a courtroom, it's going to be impossible to keep it a secret. We live in an age of gotcha journalism. You read the papers as well as I do."

"Here's the problem," Sugar said as she resumed her seat, apparent'y resigned to a longer and more detailed conversation with the sheriff than she had anticipated. "I received a message from Randall Truscott the other day in which he told me he wants out of jail, not in three years but right now. If I don't get Judge Hartman to get him released, he'll tell the world that the judge and I have been having an affair. And I believe that he'll do just what he says."

"How'd you happen to get this message?"

"Some friend of his must have pushed it through my mail slot."

"Does anybody else know about this?"

"I told Judge Hartman. I had to. It could ruin his career. Like you said, people will think it's true even when it isn't."

"And the judge, what did he say?"

"What would you expect? He says he'll sue any paper or TV station that prints or broadcasts it. He's definitely not going to take a big lie like this lying down."

"Which doesn't mean that he'll win. I'd say he's in a tough spot, a lot tougher than yours. And that's a shame. I know the judge, used to argue cases in his court when I practiced law. No reason why you'd know it, but some people you're familiar with were colleagues of mine in an Albany firm, including Truscott's lawyer, Carl Keller. Not to mention Tony Ferraro."

Sugar looked wide eyed at the sheriff.

"You know Mr. Ferraro?"

That bit of information obviously shocked her. Carol had now gained the upper hand in this sparring match over what was true and what wasn't in the rumor about Judge Lindsay Hartman's relationship with Donna Sugar.

"I do, and I understand that you do, too. It's a small world, isn't it?"

CHAPTER 48

Lindsay Hartman had tried unsuccessfully to reach Donna Sugar three times before she finally returned his call. He had been worried and on edge ever since she had surprised him by coming to his lake cottage with the news about Randall Truscott's impossible ultimatum. However, nervous wreck would have been a better characterization of his condition since the sheriff's visit the following day. It was bad enough that she had questioned him about the rumor that he might have had an affair with Sugar. But the sheriff had also told him that a young woman had been seen leaving his cottage early on the morning after Donna had spent the night. Donna had insisted that no one would know that she had been there, yet someone had seen her. Perhaps the person who had seen her leave did not know who she was, but that was small comfort. If word got around that a young woman had been spending the night in his cottage, it wouldn't be long before she had been identified. In all likelihood the sheriff already assumed it was Donna Sugar.

"Where have you been?" was the judge's first question. He hadn't meant to sound like an accusation, but it did.

"I can't always pick up or return calls right off the bat, Lindsay. Not even yours."

"No, I suppose not." He assumed that she had been with one of her other 'male friends,' and not in a position to answer him. They had long ago reached an agreement about situations like this, but at the moment he resented the fact that she was otherwise occupied.

"We have a problem," the judge said. "Another problem. You were seen leaving here the other night."

"That's not possible," Sugar said. "I was very careful, and it was early. Very early, as I told you it would be."

"I'm not blaming you for being careless. But that's beside the point. The sheriff over here told me that somebody reported seeing you leave the cottage."

"They know it was me?"

"I don't think so, but what difference does it make. Given all the rumors making the rounds, it won't take long before they put two and two together."

"What am I supposed to do? See if I can prove that I was watching a movie at the Landmark? Or coaxing Mr. Big into bed? I'll do what I can, but it won't be easy."

"I knew it was crazy for you to drive over to the cottage."

"Damn it, Lindsay, I had to tell you what Randall was up to. We're screwed, one way or another. And it's worse than you think. That sheriff over there dropped by tonight, - she drove all the way from Crooked Lake to see me. She doesn't come right out and say so, but I think she believes that you and I have something going. She's smart, and she thinks we'll lose if we get into a pissing contest with Truscott. She even suggested that our best chance is to beat him to the punch and admit we've been seeing each other."

"That's impossible, and you know it. She doesn't give a damn about us. All she cares about is nailing Carl Keller's killer."

"The problem is she's interested in our relationship because she thinks it's related to Keller's death. At least it looks that way to me."

"Did she tell you that?"

"No, but I don't like her questions. Why is she bugging us? We didn't kill Keller, so what difference is it to her whether we sleep together."

"Please, Donna, I hate that expression. It's so coarse. Look, let's just stick to the plan. If Truscott follows up with his threat, I'll fight back and you lay low. We're going to win this thing. Do you hear me?"

Sugar heard him, but she thought he was kidding himself. Moreover, she realized that events were putting a strain on what was left of their relationship. She couldn't recall a time when he had been so curt as he was this evening. What is more, she herself had been borderline unpleasant.

"Lindsay, let's try to be patient with each other. Okay?"

"I am patient. What choice do I have?"

The judge did not sound patient when he said good-bye. Donna set off for her 'date' with mixed emotions, unhappy about her conversation with the judge but relieved that the evening ahead with a hedge fund manager would take her mind off the problems they were facing.

———

Later that same evening, two old friends were, ironically, thinking about each other. One of them was Lindsay Hartman. The other was Francis

Foster. They hadn't talked recently, but both remembered well the last time that they had talked. Hartman had been concerned about Carl Keller, who had pursued a line of questioning during the Truscott trial that eventually led the judge to cite him for contempt of court. The judge had taken his frustration with Keller to Foster and had insisted that the managing partner of M & B do something about him. Foster, in turn, had honored his friend's request and sacked Keller. Now both Hartman and Foster found themselves having to contend with Carol Kelleher, the sheriff of Cumberland County, and the reason in each case could be traced to Carl Keller.

Keller was dead, and the sheriff, unfortunately, was not only investigating his death but was doing so with unusual fervor because she had once been a colleague of his and apparently had respected him as a friend and lawyer. Now she was virtually demanding that Foster investigate another member of the firm, Tony Ferraro, who had accused Keller of stealing funds from a client's escrow account. Although she was in no position to know what had happened, she was certain that Keller would never have done such a thing and that it was Ferraro who might be the guilty party. Hartman, on the other hand, was being badgered by the sheriff about a rumor that he had had an affair with the call girl against whom Randall Truscott had committed aggravated assault. And it was that affair, the judge was convinced, that Keller tried to have admitted into the record in Hartman's court.

Neither Francis Foster nor Lindsay Hartman was aware that the other was also thinking about Sheriff Kelleher that evening. It was the judge who took the initiative. He called his old law school friend shortly after ten thirty.

"Well, I'll be damned," Foster said when the judge announced himself. "I was just thinking about you."

"I hope this isn't a bad hour to be calling, but I'm having problems sleeping and I didn't realize it was this late."

"No problem at all. I've always been a night owl. Besides, I like to catch the eleven o'clock news, find out what a mess the country's in."

"That's why I called. I'm in a bit of a mess myself, and it's all because of an old colleague of yours, Carol Kelleher."

"Kelleher? What's she done to you?"

"It's a complicated story, and I needed someone to share it with. You up to this?"

"We go back a long way, Lindsay. You know how it is. Truth of the matter is Kelleher's been bugging me, too. I hadn't seen her in years, and all of a sudden she's trying to tell me what to do."

"Let me guess. It has something to do with Carl Keller."

"How did you know?"

"I didn't. Just an intelligent guess. She's investigating Keller's death, and I can't think of another reason why you'd be tangling with her."

"Actually, her problem has to do with another member of our firm. She thinks he's trying to saddle Carl Keller with a serious breach of legal ethics - taking money out of a client's escrow account. She's certain Keller is - sorry, was - innocent of any wrongdoing."

"That's rich," Hartman said. "The sheriff asked me about a case like that just the other say. I'll bet it's the same one. What in hell is she doing sticking her nose into your business?"

"I think she's on a crusade to turn the late Mr. Keller into a saint. I've always trusted the guy she think's is framing Keller, but frankly she has me worried. To make matters worse, she invited me over to her cottage last weekend for what I thought was old times sake. And damned if she didn't accuse me of firing Keller as a favor to you."

"She said that?" the judge sounded alarmed.

"Technically her husband was the one who said it, but I'm sure she put him up to it. He's nothing but a college professor - of music, if you can believe that."

"It sounds to me as if the sheriff has a problem with the two of us. For which we can thank your man Keller."

"He's not my man, Lindsay. I sent him packing, like you asked me to."

"Now that's not fair. I merely suggested you get him to shape up."

"There's no need for us to argue about it, but your words, if I remember correctly, were to 'take care of him.'"

"Be that as it may. The problem was that he was hell bent on challenging me in my own courtroom, and I had no choice but to cite him. You were his boss, I figured you were the one to wise him up, let him know you wouldn't tolerate such things."

Francis Foster wasn't about to pursue the matter further, but he was quite sure that what his friend the judge had been suggesting was considerably more drastic than a trip to the woodshed for Keller.

"So what's your problem with Sheriff Kelleher?" Francis asked.

"It goes back to that Truscott case. It's like I told you. Keller was doing everything but insinuating that Truscott's woman was also having an affair with me. You and I both know it's a lie, but the God-damned American public loves salacious stuff like that. The truth has a hard time catching up. That's why I wanted you to shut Keller up. But I was naive, figured Keller was the only problem. Now Truscott has told me to get him out of jail or he'll see to it that this phony story of my relationship with that Sugar woman goes public."

"But he's in jail, Lindsay. It'd take a lot of gall to pull a stunt like that. Besides, who's going to buy a bunch of malarky from a convicted felon?"

"You've been in this business long enough to know that the media love stories like this, no matter who's the source. What makes it worse is that he didn't contact me directly. He sent a message to the woman who's supposed to be my bed mate, telling her to see to it that I get him released from jail. She was as shocked as I was, and she had no idea what to do. Not surprisingly, she asked me. I told her I'd take care of it."

"How do you propose to take care of it?"

"I'll fight the son of a bitch, of course. I won't pretend it'll be easy, but I'll do it."

"Wait a minute. You haven't told me what this has to do with Sheriff Kelleher."

"She's heard the rumor that I've had an affair with Ms. Sugar. I'm sure she heard it first from Gretchen Ziegler, one of your partners and an old friend of hers. Ziegler probably heard it from Keller himself. I'm sure the sheriff will handle her investigation of Keller's death by the book. But because he was a friend back when they were both with M & B, she may be inclined to believe this rumor he started about me and Ms. Sugar. And wouldn't you know it, when the Sugar woman came over to ask me what she should do about Truscott's threat somebody saw her and told the sheriff about it. Of all the damned luck. Some days you can't win for losing."

"I'm confused, Lindsay. Who in Albany even knows who Kelleher is, other than you and me and maybe a few of my colleagues?"

"I was over at the cottage, and that's where Ms. Sugar came to warn me. Hell, everyone around the lake knows the sheriff. Crooked Lake's just a small pond, and she gets lots of press for cracking murder cases."

"I thought Crooked Lake looked a lot bigger than a small pond."

Hartman wasn't amused.

"Oh come on, Francis. It's just a figure of speech. The point is that somebody saw the Sugar woman leaving my house early in the morning, which of course suggests that she'd spent the night with me. Well, of course she spent the night - in my guest bedroom! She'd driven all the way from Albany, and I was damned if I was going to make a virtual stranger turn around and go back home in the middle of the night. She was trying to do me a favor, for God's sake."

"Sounds like you did the decent thing. But maybe it wasn't so smart."

"You're almost certainly right about that, because now I've got the neighborhood *and* the sheriff thinking I'm a philanderer. And with a call girl to boot. Next thing you know the press'll start comparing me with Spitzer."

"I don't know what to tell you," Francis said, verbally backing away from an offer to be more helpful than he had been at the end of the Truscott trial. "Maybe the guy's just bluffing."

"He's not bluffing, Francis, and neither am I."

Some time later, well after the eleven o'clock news had begun, the managing partner of Morgenstern and Brauchli was still slumped in his chair, thinking not about the state of the world but about his friend, Lindsay Hartman. The judge might not be bluffing about how he'd respond to Randall Truscott's threat. But he might well be lying about whether he had had an affair with Donna Sugar. Back at Harvard, Foster said to himself, I was the one who was always skating close to the edge. Perhaps Lindsay and I have reversed roles in our old age.

CHAPTER 49

While Foster and Harman were discussing the ways in which Carol Kelleher was making their lives difficult, Carol was sharing with Kevin her own frustrations. They had gone to bed early but had found sleep hard to come by. At least Carol had. The alarm clock, set for seven a.m., indicated that it was only 10:50. She turned over and poked Kevin on the shoulder.

"You still awake?" she asked.

"I always have a hard time sleeping when you punch me." Kevin sounded as if he, too, were wide awake.

"I hate these nights when I can't get things off my mind. Don't you?"

"It depends on what's on my mind. I was just about to turn over and see if you were in the mood."

"I wish I were," she said, "but right now all I can think of is the Keller case, and I'm coming up empty."

"Well, you know that old aphorism, 'if life gives you lemons, make lemonade.'"

"That's very helpful, Kevin. Why don't you go back to sleep."

"I'm not sleepy. And by the way, the best comeback to the 'if life gives you lemons' line is 'grab the tequila.' Can't remember who said it, but that's my philosophy in a nutshell."

"Instead of being a wisenheimer, why don't you tell me who killed Carl Keller."

"He did. Suicide, remember?"

"All right, who tried to kill him but got there too late?"

"That's one of those things I can't answer in the middle of the night."

"Or in broad daylight, I suspect. But come on, help me out. I'm spinning my wheels. The trouble with this case is that there aren't any good suspects. I've got that awful feeling that somewhere in Carl's past something happened that's festered underground, like 17 year cicadas, and it finally came to the surface in the last month. But his parents aren't any help, we can't locate his first wife, his live-in girl friend Lisa seems not really to have known him, the attorneys he worked with at the law firm saw him as something of a cipher - and so on and on. His life is essentially a mystery. Which means that we're left with the people who sat in the courtroom at the Truscott trial and a call girl about whom we know very little. Oh, I almost forgot, a fellow attorney who claims that Carl's moral compass leaves something to be desired. I've tried and tried, and I just can't picture any of these people as Carl's killer. Sorry, his would-be killer. So I keep coming back to the view that he died because of something we know absolutely nothing about."

Kevin sat up in bed.

"You really are having a bad night, aren't you? I thought things were going better."

"I think I did, too. But then I find myself thinking back to the days when we thought Carl was stalking me. He was like somebody I'd never known. And that's the point. I never really knew him. There were all those years before I met him, and then the years after I met him. We knew each other for about three months. What was he doing all the rest of that time? What did others do to him that left a scar? And what did he do to others that might have prompted an itch to even the score?"

"Come on, Carol. You'll never get to sleep if you spend the night wondering about Carl Keller's life story. I'll make you a bet that you already know everything you need to know. So why not take a Valium and give your imagination a rest."

"I've never taken Valium, and I'm not going to start now."

"Okay, tell you what *I'm* going to do," Kevin said. "Roll over and let me rub your back. A little foreplay to sleep."

"Only if you promise to keep your hands on my back."

"Of course. We're just talking about tonight, aren't we?"

"Just be quiet and start rubbing."

Carol turned over and closed her eyes. The massage produced the desired effect. Within less than ten minutes she was fast asleep.

————

When she awoke the next morning, Carol felt reasonably refreshed. But no sooner had she climbed out of bed than her mind began racing again. This time, however, it wasn't Carl Keller who was bothering her but the *Welcome Inn*. The motel had never been at the top of her agenda, but she had been aware for some time that there was something about it that disturbed her, something she couldn't quite recall.

She and Kevin were making a list of things for him to pick up when he went over to Yates Center, and for some reason that list brought the motel to mind again. Not immediately, of course, but as the list lengthened.

"Don't forget paper towels," Carol said. "We're almost out. And check to see if we have any light bulbs. The one in the pantry just went out yesterday. I'm pretty sure it's 60 watts."

"No problem," Kevin said, adding paper towels and light bulbs to his list.

"Hey, I think I've got it." Carol sounded excited.

"Got what?"

"The *Welcome Inn* puzzle."

"Well, I haven't. Want to enlighten me?"

Carol laughed.

"Tell you in a minute, then I'll be off." She went back to the bedroom to collect her jacket and holster.

"It's no big deal," she said as she buckled up. "Just something I've been trying to remember. Couldn't think of it for the life of me until we started talking about paper towels and light bulbs."

"You're still way ahead of me."

"It's a list the manager of *Welcome Inn* had tacked up in his office. I saw it the day he found Carl. There were stores and their phone numbers. Looked like places where he bought supplies for the motel, like Durgin's, a plumber - Wyrostek, I think it was, and Faulner's Hardware. You'd know them all. All, that is, except some place called Pend Orel or something like that. Anyway, the list was gone when I went back the next day and I haven't seen it since."

"On top of Carl Keller's life you've been worried about a list of phone numbers?" Kevin sounded as if Carol was misplacing her priorities.

"Not worried, just puzzled. And now that I've remembered what was missing, I realize that I can't recall any place of business around here named Pend Orel."

"Maybe it's new."

"That's not it. I can't remember the phone number, but I'm sure it wasn't in our area code. Something like 208." Carol looked at her watch. "Look, I've got to get out of here or I'll miss briefing. Don't forget the light bulbs."

She thanked Kevin for the back rub, gave him a peck on the cheek, and was gone.

Kevin was still in his pajamas and bathrobe and in no hurry to get ready for another day of leisure, much less a shopping excursion to Yates Center. He poured himself another cup of coffee and parked in front of the computer to check out headlines and baseball scores.

It was while he was waiting for his Mac to warm up that Carol's reference to Pend Orel came to mind. He had assumed that it was a local place of business rather than a national or regional chain. It wasn't important, but he was in no hurry so he decided to do some Googling. It was only a matter of seconds before he found himself staring at Pend Oreille.

Kevin's fund of knowledge was spotty. He knew a lot about music, especially opera. He'd been a birder since he was a youth, and at one point had compiled a list of over two hundred different birds species he had seen and positively identified. Regarding more practical things, his knowledge was not only more limited. It was embarrassingly sparse. But there was one other area where he really shined: geography. His parents had subscribed to

National Geographic, and he had read every issue voraciously. He had insisted that he needed both a globe and an atlas, and his parents had obliged with what many of his friends thought of as strange Christmas presents. Kevin knew what and where Pend Oreille was - a very deep lake in the far north of Idaho. He had never been there, but it was on his '1000 places to visit before you die' list.

It took only a few strokes of the keyboard and a few moves of the curser and he had located the area code. With it staring back at him from the screen, he was sure it was the one Carol thought she remembered.

So the manager of the *Welcome Inn* (Kevin couldn't remember his name) had posted in his office a list of names which supplied the motel's necessities. And on that list was a lake in Idaho, or perhaps a business somewhere in the Idaho panhandle which used the name of that lake.

Surely the *Welcome Inn* didn't order goods or services from a place practically clear across the continent. Why, then, was it on the list, a list that had disappeared from the office wall after Carol and her team had begun to use that office? Perhaps the manager's family lived there. Perhaps he himself had previously worked there. The possibilities were many and none of them would be of any importance to Carol.

Kevin went back to the baseball scores, but not for long. Now it was he, not Carol, who was bothered by something, and that something was the man who managed the *Welcome Inn.* The man who not only ran the motel where Carl Keller was staying, but the man who found his body and reported that fact to the sheriff. Carol was reluctant to call anybody a suspect in the Keller case, but it was obvious that her investigation was focusing on several people whom she was treating, however tentatively, as suspects. And none of those people had as good an opportunity to kill Keller as the manager of the *Welcome Inn*. He lived in the same small building, and he had a key to Keller's room. Why not think of him as a suspect? Of course there was one problem, and a fairly large one at that. What would have been his motive? Having a phone number in the Lake Pend Oreille area code on his office wall hardly qualified. *But.* Kevin began to do what he had often found himself doing since he had become Carol's de facto partner in solving Crooked Lake's annual murders. He began to imagine reasons why the man who ran the *Welcome Inn* might have decided to kill Keller. Could it have something to do with a lake in far off Idaho?

Such wild speculation occupied Kevin for much of the morning. It wasn't until nearly noon that he showered, dressed, and set off for Yates Center and paper towels and light bulbs.

CHAPTER 50

Tony Ferraro closed his office door and turned the lock. It was something he rarely did, but this morning he didn't want any of his colleagues to barge in, something the informal fraternity of M & B attorneys were inclined to do. He particularly didn't want Francis Foster to walk in on him.

He extracted the Rasmussen file from the cabinet behind his desk and sat down to study it for the umpteenth time. That he did so had nothing to do with the possibility that he would learn something that had previously escaped his attention. In spite of the thickness of the file, he had committed all of its salient issues to memory, especially those concerning the escrow account. Tony knew what the balance of that account should be. He also knew that it would be off by almost exactly seven thousand dollars, a very modest sum in view of the fact that the account as a whole ran into six figures. But the missing thousands would not seem negligible to the Lawyers Trust Fund for Client Protection if it were ever to investigate the matter. And it was his anxiety about just such an investigation that had prompted him to lock his door and reexamine the Rasmussen file.

Tony had told Francis Foster, the managing partner, that Carl Keller had replaced the money he had stolen from the escrow account before he had left the firm. It had, of course, been a lie. Carl would have had no reason to reimburse the account for a theft he was not responsible for and about which he knew nothing. And he himself, the real thief, would not have reimbursed the account; to have done so would have defeated the very purpose which had led him to violate this basic rule of professional ethics. No, the Rasmussen account was still short seven thousand dollars, a fact which had become worrisome ever since Carol Kelleher had begun to press her former boss, Francis Foster, to look into Keller's alleged act of defalcation.

Francis had been quite willing to take his word for what had happened as long as the escrow balance had been corrected. But then that busy body sheriff had embarked on her crusade to clear Keller's name, and it now looked to be not only possible but likely that Foster would be asking to see the Rasmussen file.

Tony leafed through the file until he reached the ledger that reflected the state of the escrow account. It told him exactly what he knew it would tell him. He briefly considered a careful doctoring of the bottom line, an entry which purported to show that Keller had indeed repaid the seven thousand. But if Foster's scrutiny was anything more than perfunctory, if it included a single check with the bank, this ruse would be discovered and he might find himself in even more trouble. Perhaps it would be a better idea to simply claim that he had accepted Keller's word for it that he'd had a crisis of conscience and paid back the money he'd stolen. He would be apologetic, profusely sorry that he had not been more skeptical. Better to be seen as incompetent than dishonest. It was doubtful that Francis would recognize his admission of incompetence as itself dishonest.

He spent the next twenty minutes thinking about what he would say and how he would say it were Foster to tell him that he wanted to borrow the Rasmussen file. He had put the file away and was about to unlock the door when he heard a sharp rap and the managing partner's voice.

"Tony, open up. I want to have a look at the Rasmussen file."

"The door's open," he said, fighting down a wave of panic and worrying that Francis would know what he was up to.

"It's locked!" The voice was stentorian. "What's going on?"

"Nothing," he said, opening the door. "I must accidentally have pushed the lock. Sorry."

"What is it these days? Ziegler's door's been closed since Monday. You're not sleeping on the job, I hope."

Foster wore a smile. Ferraro tried to reciprocate.

"If I ever nap, I deduct it from my billing hours." Tony was trying to make light of a situation fraught with potential danger.

"Better not to nap, Tony. I'm here to pick up that Rasmussen file. I'm sure you can handle it, but the buck stops on my desk, if you know what I mean. So I'm going to have a look at it. I hope it's not too complicated."

"If you skip over all those party of the first part clauses, I think you'll find it pretty straightforward. But there's one thing you'll need to know, and it's my fault. Keller never put back what he stole. I was giving him credit for seeing the error of his ways when I should have been paying more attention. Got caught up in that Fleischmann trial, and, well, you know how it is. I've been going through the file, and the escrow's still out of balance."

Aware that Foster might think that's what he'd been doing behind a locked door that morning, Tony amended his statement.

"Just yesterday, that's when I spotted it."

"Damn it, Tony. I'm counting on you to get us right with Rasmussen. We can't just write off thousands of dollars."

"I know, and I think I know how we can make up for what Keller did. He wasn't married, but it shouldn't be hard to get ahold of his parents. They won't want the family name soiled by something like this. It's not that big a sum. They'll send us a check."

Francis Foster's face reddened.

"That's a damned stupid idea, Tony. Don't you go anywhere near the Kellers. You don't even know if they're alive, and if they are, M & B's not going to ask them to pay for the sins of their son. Christ, what kind of people are we to do something like that? We'll find a way, and I'm sure as hell not going to the Lawyers Trust Fund. If we have to take it out of our own hide, we'll do it."

Tony's reaction to this diatribe was decidedly mixed. He was relieved to hear Foster make it clear that he wouldn't take the case to the Trust Fund. Were he to do so, the investigation would be much more thorough than one conducted in house. On the other hand, the boss was obviously unhappy with him, and he could only hope that that didn't presage any thoughts about his own complicity in the matter. He had enough to worry about without that. When Foster left, Tony wanted to close and lock his door again, but he didn't dare.

CHAPTER 51

The barbecued chicken, while just slightly burned, had been excellent, and the after dinner conversation - another 'let's really do it this time' talk about taking a cruise in the winter - had happily taken their minds off the Keller case. Carol and Kevin were having what both regarded as a relaxing evening when the phone rang. 9:26. Who would be calling at this hour on a week night? They looked at each other as if to ask 'who's turn is it.' Carol was usually the object of evening calls, but considering the hour, Kevin got up and disappeared into the study.

"Mr. Whitman, this is Francis Foster. I'm sure you remember me. Let me assure you that I'm not calling for a reprise of my unpleasant performance at that wonderful lunch you and your wife put on for me the other Sunday. I'm afraid I was quite unnecessarily rude. I'm also aware that it's rather late, but I really do need to talk with Carol. If she's there, could you put her on?"

"Of course, Mr. Foster, and I think I was the one who may have been rude on Sunday. Just give me a second."

Kevin set the phone down and went back to the living room to tell Carol she was wanted.

"It's Francis Foster," he said, sotto voce. "Surprised?"

"Nothing surprises me these days," she replied. "Can't imagine what he wants, but I'd suggest you should see what's on TV."

Carol doubted that this would be a quick conversation, so she took a seat in Kevin's favorite chair before picking up the phone.

"Francis! What a surprise."

"I apologize for calling at this hour. I normally wouldn't dream of doing it, but I need to talk with you and I couldn't break away until a few minutes ago and tomorrow's going to be impossible."

"No problem. Kevin and I were just planning the vacation we never seem to get around to taking. What's on you mind?"

"I'd rather talk about your vacation plans," he said, "but it happens to be a matter of more immediate relevance. And importance. It's Tony Ferraro."

"Oh." Carol had assumed that Francis was having second thoughts about the subject that had spoiled their Sunday lunch. "What about him?"

"Well, I hope you'll be interested in what I have to say. I've no idea whether you'll call it good news or bad news. I'm not entirely sure myself. Anyway, I took your advice that I involve myself in Carl Keller's violation of his fiduciary responsibilities. Probably should have done it sooner. I didn't challenge Ferraro, just told him I had a responsibility as senior partner to look into the Rasmussen case. So I took the file and spent a couple of hours familiarizing myself with it. I'm sure you aren't interested in the case itself, just the matter of a shortage in the escrow account. It's the shortage which Ferraro blames on Keller. To make what could be a long story short, I don't see anything in the ledger itself which disproves Tony's story."

Carol was disappointed and said so.

"But," Foster interrupted, "I don't quite like the look of it. The principal reason why I hadn't involved myself in it earlier was that Tony said that Keller had gotten religion or something like it and had sworn he had put the money back. Problem is, the account is still out of balance. When I took the file from him, Tony acknowledged that the account was short, that he'd simply taken Keller's word for it that he'd fix it. He admits that he should have been paying more attention, so maybe I should write it off to the fact that he was just busy or careless. Or both. But you'd think he'd have been more concerned, that he'd have mentioned the problem to me, instead of insisting that everything was just fine. After all, Keller's been dead for more than two weeks. If he never reimbursed the escrow while he was alive, how the hell was he going to do it once he was dead?"

Foster paused. Perhaps he was looking for an answer to his own question.

"It doesn't add up, does it?" Carol said, referring to Ferraro's story, not the Rasmussen escrow balance.

"It does if I'm ready to find Tony guilty of incompetence. Or a craven reluctance to share bad news with me. But I've seen his work for several years, and he's not incompetent. And if you know Tony, he's no shrinking violet. All of which make me a bit suspicious. And then there's your report that Keller had told you that he didn't trust Tony. I don't really know just what I should do next, but I thought you ought to know that I'm concerned about that escrow account. And, quite frankly, about Tony."

Carol had serious reservations about sharing her suspicions about one suspect in a case with another. Especially when they were only prospective suspects. It was too soon to treat either Tony Ferraro or Francis Foster as a suspect in Carl's murder - or, considering that he had committed suicide, in an intent to kill him. But why not take advantage of Francis's doubts about Ferraro and invite him to help her? If he had wielded the knife which cut Carl's throat, he should logically be willing to help pin the blame on someone else. If, on the other hand, he had had nothing to do with what happened at the *Welcome Inn,* he should be equally willing to help her identify the culprit.

"Francis, do you have a few more minutes?" she asked.

"Of course," was his reply, and it sounded genuine.

"I want you to understand that I have no evidence - none whatsoever - that Tony Ferraro had anything to do with Carl's death. But it has occurred to me that if Tony was trying to frame Carl for something that he himself had done, he might view Carl as a threat to his plan. Carl would inevitably challenge his story, and conceivably could disprove it. If that were to happen, Tony would face disbarment. That strikes me as a motive for murder."

"There are a lot of ifs in that scenario, Carol."

"I know, but let's start from the admittedly iffy premise that Tony has been framing Carl and would be safer if Carl were dead. I know, thanks to Carl's former girl friend, Lisa Simmons, that a man claiming to be Richard Keller, a cousin of Carl's, visited her and took away both a key to

Carl's apartment *and* the name and address of the place where Carl was temporarily staying - a seedy motel over here near the lake. I also know that this man was not Carl's cousin; Carl has no male cousins. What is more, the man pretending to be Carl's cousin had his head heavily bandaged. He claimed that he'd had a bad accident, but whether he had or not, the bandage was an effective disguise. We also know two other things. This man then went to Carl's apartment and proceeded to take away just about everything that would provide any clue to Carl's life and his plans. The other thing we know is that Carl was found dead shortly thereafter at the very motel where Ms. Simmons told this fake cousin he was staying. Wouldn't you say there's a possibility that Richard Keller was really Tony Ferraro, and that he was indeed planning to kill Carl? All of this assumes, of course, that Tony was guilty of stealing from the Rasmussen escrow account. For purposes of argument, Francis, I'm urging you to make that assumption."

Carol could hear Foster taking a deep breath before answering her.

"I suppose it's possible, but it's awfully circumstantial. And there's still that big if."

"Agreed. But if you were in my shoes, you'd surely want to do everything you could - within the law, of course - to find out if it's true. Just how would you do that? You could simply ask Ferraro point blank if he'd killed Carl. Or if that sounds a bit too bold, you could come right out and ask him if he had pretended to be Carl's cousin. We know he'd deny both allegations. Your questions would shake him up, no matter whether he was guilty or not. But I can't imagine him losing his grip and inadvertently giving himself away, and I'm sure you can't either.

"There is an alternative. You could take what we know, stress our suspicions, and get a warrant to enter his apartment and search for the things I'm convinced he removed from Carl's apartment. Things like a laptop, correspondence, financial records - anything that might undermine the charge that Carl had stolen money from the Rasmussen account."

"I see. And from whom am I to get this warrant, Carol? Don't tell me, let me guess. How about Judge Lindsay Hartman? Inasmuch as you seem to believe that I did him a favor by sacking Carl Keller, presumably he now owes me one. Pretty clever."

"Please, Francis, this has nothing to do with you and Judge Hartman. I'm simply trying to think about how we can best solve two mysteries: who stole from the Rasmussen account and who slit Carl's throat. I'm sure you're as interested as I am in getting to the bottom of both matters."

"Yes, of course. But as you're in a position to know, I'm what you might call a prudential attorney. I never leap before I look. Or do some hard thinking. So I'm sure you'll indulge me and let me give this some thought. And I'd very much appreciate it if you'd do the same. You don't want this mess to blow up in your face. At a minimum, I believe you have an obligation to keep me informed of anything and everything your investigation turns up. Do we understand each other?"

"I think we do, and I want to thank you for your call."

So, Carol thought as she hung up, I now have another partner. She doubted, however, that she'd trust him as far as she did Kevin.

CHAPTER 52

On the morning after Francis Foster and the sheriff had had their conversation about Tony Ferraro and what to do about him, Carol was feeling much better than she had in several days.

"Thanks again for another back rub," she said to Kevin as she got up from the breakfast table. "Let's make it a nightly ritual."

"Great idea. I think I'll add masseur to gumshoe on my rapidly growing resume," he said as she disappeared down the hall to get dressed.

"You're good, Kevin, but not that good. How about sticking to professor?" Carol said as she closed the bedroom door.

Kevin spread marmalade on his toast and settled back with a smile on his face. Carol's good moods were contagious. But the smile had more than a little to do with his own decision to keep quiet about his flight of fancy about the manager of *Welcome Inn*. What had gotten into him? Why had he suddenly become fixated on the possibility that Marty Reece might have killed Carl Keller? The very idea now seemed preposterous. It would never have come to mind had it not been for the fact that Pend Oreille had been on the list that Reece had posted in his office. Fortunately, common sense kicked in and prompted a big 'so what.' What if the list had included a phone number for Flagstaff or Toledo? Kevin reflected on the fact that he himself had been born in Holland, Michigan, had lived in Worcester, Massachusetts, and had friends in

Minneapolis and Sacramento and even Durango, Colorado.

No, he thought as he poured himself another cup of coffee, Carol will never hear of my crazy Pend Oreille brainstorm.

———

As the morning wore on, Kevin once again found himself perched in front of his computer, struggling with his annual case of writer's block. He'd type in a sentence of two, sit back and read what he'd written, and then delete it. At this rate, he'd finish the paper by Columbus Day, maybe Thanksgiving. Thoroughly frustrated, he got up to get himself his fourth cup of coffee of the day. He took it out onto the deck and for a few brief minutes watched a mallard duck and her brood of seven ducklings swimming along in a neat row past the end of the dock. Amazing, he thought. So young, yet so at home in the water. And I've been around for decades and still can't bring a twenty page article to fruition.

The ducks had disappeared and the coffee cup was empty, yet Kevin lingered on the deck. When he went back to the study, it wasn't the troubled article on opera to which he turned but the puzzle of Pend Oreille. He had said he wouldn't start that again, but here he was ignoring his own better judgment and once again googling Idaho's panhandle.

Kevin was no longer thinking of the *Welcome Inn* manager as someone who might have slit Keller's throat, but he set himself the task - anything was better than the paper that was going nowhere -

of seeing if he could figure out what Reece's connection with Pend Oreille might be.

By noon he had read almost everything he could find on the internet, including commentary on the area, with special attention to the lake itself and the many small towns that dot its shoreline. Much of what Kevin read (and the photographs that invariably touted blue skies and blue water) confirmed his belief that this would be a great place to visit; he even examined many of the recommended lodges and made mental notes of a few that looked especially promising. But the reason for these hours of browsing was ostensibly to discover what Marty Reece might have been doing out there, so after lunch he turned to the phone.

The logical place to start seemed to be the largest community on the lake, Sandpoint. There would be a chamber of commerce and the local police. The odds that anyone he spoke with would have heard of Reece were infinitesimally small, but he'd give it a shot. The person at the chamber was kind enough to scan a directory for him, but it turned up no Reeces. She suggested the local historian, who proved to be quite a talker but had no knowledge of the man Kevin was seeking. The police department, or at least the officer who answered the phone, seemed to resent a call that didn't fall within typical police business.

"You've got the wrong number," a grumpy voice informed him. "Unless this is a missing persons matter."

"No, the person I'm inquiring about isn't missing, and he may never have lived in Sandpoint. Or around your lake, for that matter. I'm just trying to track somebody down. Is there someone there who by chance has been on your force for quite some time?"

"Joe Joyce might be able to help. Just a minute - he just walked in."

He may just have walked in, but he was in no hurry to pick up the phone.

"Joyce speaking. What's this about?" he finally said. While he was abrupt, his voice was soft.

"Officer Joyce, my name is Kevin Whitman. I'm calling from another lake, clear across the country. This isn't police business as far as I know, but I'm trying to locate someone I believe has spent some time on Lake Pend Oreille. You know how it is - unless a guy has made some kind of a name for himself, it can be awfully hard to track him down. I've tried with no luck, so I thought I'd see if the local police could help. His name is Reece. Are there any Reeces in Sandpoint or somewhere nearby?"

"Well, we've got one that I know of. Pauline Reece. Lives down in Bayview. She's an old timer, must be 90 if she's a day. Pretty spry, though, and she's a bit of a character. But Pauline doesn't have any family."

"No relatives who might drop in on her now and then?"

"None that I've ever met or heard of. You say this isn't police business?"

"I hope not, but when someone goes missing you start to worry."

"Well, I don't know any more Reeces. Be glad to post a notice if you'd like. What's the first name?"

"Marty. Marty Reece."

There was a moment of silence.

"You sure it's Reece? Not Rice, by any chance?"

"No, it's Reece."

"I'm sure you know who you're looking for, but I had to ask. Just a coincidence, but the name reminded me of someone we're looking for. Murray Rice."

Marty Reece and Murray Rice. Kevin was reminded of the similarity between his own wife's name and Carl Keller's.

"I'm afraid it's a Reece I'm looking for, not a Rice."

"For a minute there I thought I might have gotten lucky."

"How so?"

"Two, three years ago we had a real bad case over near Trestle Creek. A guy got bludgeoned to death in his own cabin, and the case has never been solved. I thought about it because this guy Murray Rice disappeared not long after. There was no reason to suspect he'd killed the man, no evidence whatsoever, but he did know the victim and, well, his pulling up stakes and leaving the area without any notice seemed kind of funny."

Kevin was suddenly much more interested than when he had casually called the Sandpoint police station. He considered the name Murray Rice.

"What do you know about this Murray Rice?"

"Pretty close to nothing. He worked in a hash house, didn't mix much. What I know is mostly what Merrivale told me."

"Merrivale. Is he a fellow cop?"

"He is, and while nobody knew Rice well, I'd guess Ben knew him best."

"Is he where I could talk with him?"

"Not today, but sure, you'd probably catch him tomorrow. Why? I thought it was a guy named Reece you were looking for."

"It is, but I figure the more people I talk to, the better the chance I'll catch up with Reece. Do you have a home phone for Merrivale?"

"Better try him here at the department. You'll get him sooner or later."

Kevin was afraid it would be later. But what did it matter? The odds that Murray Rice was Marty Reese were somewhere between slim and nil.

Nonetheless, Kevin felt much closer to Lake Pend Oreille than he had when he first discovered that the area code out there in Idaho's panhandle was the same as the one on the wall of the *Welcome Inn* office. Still no point in sharing his new found interest in Pend Oreille with Carol. She'd see it as just one more bit of evidence that he had a secret hankering to exchange his cap and gown for Sherlock Holmes' deerstalker and calabash.

CHAPTER 53

Carol's alarm clock rarely needed resetting. It was set for 6:45 and had been, with few exceptions, since she had become sheriff of Cumberland County. All she had to do is flip the switch from off to on when she went to bed, and without fail she was awakened in time to make the squad briefing. Kevin was a much sounder sleeper and typically slept through the 6:45 wake up call. Unless, that is, Carol needed to remind him of something he had to do that day.

It was the first Friday morning in August, and neither the alarm clock nor the sun had announced that it was time to rise and shine. That function was performed by the telephone, which happened to be on Kevin's side of the bed. He reached out and stabbed ineffectually at the bedside table. The phone eluded his hand, and it was Carol who got up and went around the bed to pick up the phone. It was 6:28. It wasn't the 17 minutes of sleep she'd lost that concerned her; it was the possibility that some crisis had arisen that required her prompt attention. She had been sheriff long enough to know that challenges to local law and order weren't confined to the hours between sunup and sundown. Quite the contrary.

"Hello, Sheriff Kelleher speaking."

"Carol, it's Gretchen. I hate to bother you at such an ungodly hour, but there's something you need to know and I wanted to be the first to share the news. I'm assuming you haven't seen the *Times Union* this morning."

"The *Times Union*? It's as rare over here as *Pravda*. Whats up?"

"It's just a brief piece, page 7, only about five column inches. But the headline reads - get this - 'Judge Alleged to Fail to Recuse Himself.' Want to guess who the judge is?"

"I'm not awake, Gretchen, but I doubt you'd be calling me this early if it were an AP story from Montana. It's Hartman, right?"

"You've got it. Do you want me to read it?"

"If you've got a minute, yes. But I'd like to take it in the study. Otherwise Kevin will be badgering me for details."

"Go ahead, I won't hang up."

Still in her shorty pajamas, but now wide awake, Carol hurried down the hall to the study.

"Okay, let's hear it."

"It's short and it strikes me as cautious, as if the *Times Union* feels it has to publish but would rather not make a big thing of it. Anyway, here goes.

> It has been alleged that a prominent Albany judge, Lindsay Hartman, failed to recuse himself in a recent case in which he had a serious conflict of interest. The allegation was made by the defendant in the case, Randall Truscott, who claims that the judge was engaged in an intimate relationship with the woman who was the complaining witness in the case. Mr. Truscott was convicted of aggravated assault and sentenced by the judge to three years in prison.

The decision to recuse or not recuse oneself because of a conflict of interest is typically left to the judge's discretion. But Truscott claims that the trial was unfair, citing the judge's refusal to allow into evidence information regarding his relationship with the complainant. The name of the woman with whom the judge is alleged to have had an intimate relationship is being withheld by the paper pending further investigation.

That's the whole of it, and I'm sure it sounds pretty much like the rumor I passed on awhile back."

"Looks like the fat's in the fire, doesn't it? I wonder why the woman's name isn't used."

"No idea. It's a matter of public record, just like Truscott and Hartman. I'm sure the paper will identify her as soon as it's done a bit of digging. Which they'll be doing, starting yesterday. Besides, this is a story about the judge, not the woman. I'm betting that the *Times Union* isn't the only paper running Truscott's little bombshell. He'll want publicity, a lot of it, and that means starting a fire in one of those underground rags that don't get delivered to your door. People like you and me don't read them, but there's got to be an audience out there that keeps *The Broadside* and *Tattler* alive. I intend to see what they have to say, today and tomorrow. I'll be surprised if they aren't out ahead of the *Times Union*, putting nails in Hartman's coffin and turning his lady friend into this summer's celebrity."

"Do you think there's a chance that Francis will crop up in any of this?"

"It's possible, but I don't think so," Gretchen said. "If Truscott's pulling the strings, he'll be after the judge and that call girl. I have trouble picturing him trying to bring Foster down, too. After all, Francis got rid of Carl, and I'd assume that's just fine with Truscott."

"Well, this is certainly going to stir things up. I doubt that Francis will spend much time thinking about Tony Ferraro and that escrow account business while his friend Hartman's in the news. Sometimes I feel like I'm playing cards with half the deck missing."

"Anything I can do for you?" Gretchen asked.

"You're doing it, keeping me informed on what's going on over there. I appreciate it. Just keep on giving me updates. Obviously I'm interested in how the Hartman story plays out. And how Francis seems to be taking it. By the way, you don't happen to know, do you, where Randall Truscott is serving his time?"

"No, but I'll find out today and let you know, along with what coverage the story gets in other local media. Hope you have a good one - and sorry about my wake up call."

"Au contraire. I'd be upset if you hadn't called."

————

As was to be expected, many residents of the state's capital knew nothing about the charge against Judge Lindsay Hartman. Most of those who did got the news from a local TV station, which appeared to have picked up the story from the *Times Union*. But among those who learned that

Hartman had been accused of having an extramarital affair and of failing to recuse himself from the case were five people who were not surprised by the news.

One of those people was the judge himself, for the obvious reason that he was in the best position to know that the story, while incomplete, was factually true. A second was Donna Sugar, who was the unnamed woman in the case and the original recipient of a warning that the story would become public knowledge if she didn't convince the judge to release one Randall Truscott from jail.

The other three people who were not surprised did not know for a fact that the story was true, but they had had their suspicions. Francis Foster, senior partner of Morgenstern and Brauchli, was among them, and he had suspected his friend, Judge Hartman, since the day that the judge had called to tell him that Ms. Sugar - the innocent Ms. Sugar - had visited his lake cottage to warn him that Truscott was on the warpath. Also not surprised was Tony Ferraro, and his suspicions, while perhaps less well grounded than Foster's, were the result of conversations with Carl Keller and the ubiquitous Donna Sugar. The fifth and last person to learn of Truscott's charge from reading the *Times Union* or listening to the local news on TV was Hazel Hartman, the judge's wife.

In fact, Judge Hartman, who rarely turned on the TV set in the morning or did more than skim the front page headlines in the *Times Union* before leaving for his office, learned of the five inch long story buried on page 7 of the paper from his wife over breakfast.

They were seated in the newly redone kitchen, of which Hazel was very proud and which the judge agreed was a major improvement.

"There's something here which you ought to read, Lindsay," Hazel Hartman said as she passed him salt and pepper for his eggs, along with the morning paper. The paper was folded so that Lindsay was looking at page 7.

"You know me and the news," he said. "Most of it is too depressing for so early in the day."

"I know, but there's a piece down in the corner which you should look at."

Lindsay turned his attention to the corner of the page to which Hazel had referred. It took no more than a second before he forgot his eggs and scrambled to his feet.

"What nonsense is this!" he bellowed.

Hazel, having gotten his attention, said nothing. Her husband was a quick reader.

"This is outrageous. Lies. All of it, lies. Why in hell did they print scurrilous crap like this without ever speaking to me? Where's my cell phone?"

The judge went through his pockets, cursing his inability to locate his phone.

"It's under your napkin," his wife said.

"I'm calling that god damned editor. What's his number?"

"I've never called him, and I have no idea what his number is. Lindsay, please sit down."

The judge, suddenly aware that Hazel was surprisingly calm, looked at her suspiciously.

"I know, Lindsay. I've known for a long time, so don't have a stroke. We need to think, not holler. And there's no point in suing the *Times Union*. How about another cup of coffee?"

CHAPTER 54

Carol shared Gretchen' news with Kevin before she departed, but there wasn't time for anything but the most cursory discussion of this major development in the Keller case.

"Try not to dwell on it. I should know a lot more by the time I get home. See you at six, before that if I'm lucky."

She was out the door and gone before Kevin could pump her for more information. He spent half an hour scouting for word about Judge Lindsay Hartman's troubles on CNN and a couple of local stations in western New York, but quickly discovered that neither the judge nor the case had been deemed worthy of even a thirty second mention. By late morning he had abandoned this fruitless search and turned his attention back to police officer Ben Merrivale in Sandpoint, Idaho. He knew that the story of Hartman's alleged extramarital affair was far more important than the disappearance from the Lake Pend Oreille area of someone named Murray Rice, but in the absence of something better to do with his time Kevin placed a call to the Idaho panhandle.

As luck would have it, Merrivale was not available, although Kevin was assured that he'd be back before noon, pacific time. He tried to punch out another paragraph or two in the paper he was writing, but found himself as devoid of ideas as he had been for the past week. Frustrated, he made the bed, swept off the deck, and set up the hose to nourish a yard that needed watering. It was just five of three when the phone in the study rang.

"Kevin Whitman here," he announced hopefully.

"Mr. Whitman, this is Ben Merrivale, calling from Sandpoint in Idaho. I understand that you need to talk to me."

"I sure do, and I appreciate you calling back. Tell you what. There's no reason why this call should be on your nickel. Why don't you hang up, and I'll call you right back."

"That's good of you. I won't be going anywhere."

Two minutes later, the two of them were again connected, and Kevin was explaining his reason for talking to the Sandpoint policeman.

"Your colleague, Officer Joyce, tells me that you probably knew a Murray Rice better than anyone else out there. I don't know Mr. Rice at all. In fact, I was calling about someone named Marty Reece. I'd been led to believe that he had lived in the Lake Pend Oreille area, but Officer Joyce didn't know of anybody named Reece except for some elderly lady. But the name Rice is a lot like Reece, so I thought it'd be a good idea to ask you a few questions about Rice. They're probably not the same person, but - well, just in case. Why don't you tell me about Rice?"

"I'm not sure I can be of much help. He was a loner, if you know what I mean, not easy to get to know. I suppose I knew him only because I used to drop in at *Jimmy's Shack* where he worked. It's over near Trestle Creek. Don't suppose you know this area, just a lot of small places scattered around the lake."

"But about Rice. Big guy, short, dark hair, blond?"

"Actually he was close to bald. I guess you'd say average height, weight. You'd miss him in a crowd."

"How old would you say he was?"

"Quite a bit younger than me. Not far past 30."

"Had he been around Pend Oreille long?"

"Come to think of it, I don't think so. He was sort of a drifter. At least I think he was, though he didn't talk about it."

"What did he talk about?"

"Like I said, he didn't talk much. Once in awhile he mentioned he'd seen duty in Iraq. He hadn't liked the war, but he couldn't seem to get it off his mind. I think he might have had that thing you hear 'em talking about these days when guys come back from Afghanistan. Post something."

"Post traumatic stress?"

"That's it. Anyway, he'd be quiet, moody one day, angry, all riled up another. I think he'd won a medal or two while he was over there. I'm pretty sure he'd been wounded, had a Purple Heart. One thing he talked about was throwing his medals away. Don't think he ever did it, but I've got a hunch he was ashamed of 'em."

"Officer Joyce says he just left town one day, not a word to anyone."

"That's true. Just got in his car and drove off. Jimmy said he never even collected his last paycheck."

"I understand there was a murder back around that time."

"Joe tell you about that?"

"Just that somebody was bludgeoned to death. That's the way Office Joyce put it."

"Yeah. We never found out who did it. The victim was a guy from Pakistan named Malik. He'd been here for 20, 25 years. No idea why he settled here - far as I know there aren't any other Arabs out this way. His wife died a few years back, and his kids grew up and left. But he was harmless. Nobody could figure out who'd do such a thing."

Kevin chose not to tell Merrivale that Pakistanis were not Arabs.

"But what about Rice?" Kevin asked. "He'd been in the war, probably been shot at by Iraqis who supported Hussein. That'd be why he had a Purple Heart. Maybe he still hated people who looked like those guys. I'd have thought he might have been a suspect in Malik's murder."

"It makes no sense. Rice actually had a soft spot for Iraq. Used to say they were good people who'd had a bad leader. He spent more time with Malik than anyone else did. I never heard him say a bad word about the man. Besides, everyone remembers Rice crying like a baby when the story got out. People figured he decided to leave Sandpoint because of it."

"Did he leave right after Malik was killed?"

"Not exactly," Merrivale said. "I don't remember just when it was. About a month later, I think."

Kevin was obviously not satisfied with what he had heard, but that was only because he'd gotten it into his mind that Rice and Reece might be the same person. How likely was that? When he put on his skeptic's hat, the answer was highly unlikely. On the other hand there was the similarity in the two names. There the fact that bludgeoning and throat slitting were both cruel and unusual ways to kill a man. There was the fact that both killings - all right, a killing and an intended killing - had taken place in relatively remote places rather than in or near metropolitan areas. There was the disturbing fact that the crime on Lake Pend Oreille was, from what he could gather, a cold case, and that the investigation of the crime a scant two miles from Crooked Lake, while more recent, had slowed to a crawl. If only Marty Reece would suddenly abandon the *Welcome Inn* and simply vanish, the two cases would become near perfect replicas of each other.

Carol, of course, would remind him that the cases were actually unalike in dozens of ways. He could already think of several of those ways.

And he always came back to his problematic starting point, the similarity of Reece and Rice. Carol didn't like coincidences, but she would undoubtedly be quick to point out that any telephone directory would contain innumerable juxtapositions of similar names. Reece and Rice? How about Cohen and Cohn? Braun and Brown? He was in the process of compiling a mental list of such cases when Carol came bursting through the back door.

"What a day!" she exclaimed without pausing on her way to the bedroom to shed her uniform.

Kevin was sure it would have had to do with Judge Hartman, and he was as anxious to hear about it as Carol would be to tell him about it. There had been no time in the morning for her to do more than give him a brief account of Gretchen's call. By now she would have much more to report, and he wanted to hear it, right down to the last detail. Murray Rice would have to be put on hold for another day, or at least for another hour or two. Probably just as well.

"The wine's cold, I assume?" She asked as she came back to the kitchen.

"You know the old line that it's always five o'clock somewhere, which means the wine has to be chilled 24/7. What's more, I've already poured. Let's hit the deck."

Carol almost literally collapsed into her chair.

"I'm sure you're dying to tell me that you finished your paper, but if you don't mind, I'll go first," she said. "This has been one for the books. Why don't you bring the bottle out. I'll need seconds in about two minutes."

"You've caught my attention," Kevin said as he headed back to the kitchen.

"I don't know what you remember," Carol said as she held her glass aloft for a refill. "You were barely awake when I left."

"I remember that the Albany papers had told the world about Judge Hartman's dirty little secret. That's about it."

"The *Times Union* was cautious. Brief story, buried inside. They treated it as only an allegation, which of course it will remain until they put one of their reporters on it. I'm sure whoever gets the assignment will be tickled pink."

"So there's no late breaking news?" Kevin asked. "When you said it'd been a big day, I thought maybe Hartman had confessed to killing Carl Keller, something dramatic like that."

"I put in rough days, Kevin, even when the sun doesn't rise in the west. So no, Hartman hasn't confessed to anything, not even to having a mistress and failing to recuse himself in the Truscott case.

But - why don't you let me give it to you in order, beginning with Gretchen's second phone call."

"Oh, that's right. It was your lawyer pal who woke me up this morning."

"Yes, and she called back mid-morning to report an even bigger story than the one the *Times Union* ran. There's a local tabloid that's sort of a *National Enquirer* for bottom feeders. It's called the*Tattler*. I've never read it, and I suspect that Gretchen hadn't either until today. Anyway, it didn't bury its story about the judge. It's on page one, with a headline several times life size that reads 'The Judge and the Hooker: Justice Takes a Holiday.' I'll bet the editor and his cronies had a lot of fun cooking that one up."

"Any pictures?"

"Of course. They must have had a file photo of Hartman, and he looks like he's just been stung by a bee. Unlike the *Times Union,* they also identify Sugar and include a picture. I have no idea whether it's her or not. It's fairly dark, but whoever's in the shot is sitting on a bar stool, showing a lot of leg and rump. I wonder how they get such stuff."

"Where there's a will there's a way," Kevin suggested.

"Gretchen sent the article and the pictures through to my computer. I made copies so you can read all about it, but why don't we save that until after supper. I'd rather talk than sit here and watch you read what the*Tattler* did with Truscott's story. How much of the piece is taken verbatim from what he told them, I don't know. The paper gives him credit for exposing Hartman, but I'm pretty sure they gussied it up to satisfy the prurient interest of their readers. Sugar comes off as someone who went looking for a sugar daddy - as you can imagine, they milked her name for all it was worth and then some. And the way they tell it, she found a pushover in Hartman. If you believe the rag, he's simply pathetic, a puppy dog on a leash. On top of everything else, he's lambasted for taking the Truscott case when he clearly had a conflict of interest. All in all it's a nice piece of character assassination. Unless there's evidence that Truscott's making it all up, I'd say that Hartman's years as a jurist are over."

"You weren't entirely surprised, were you?"

"No, but it's still a shocking story. And here's the most interesting part. I'm not the only one who wasn't surprised."

"And who might that be?"

"Hazel Hartman, the judge's wife. Gretchen was my source, of course, but the really interesting phone call came around three this afternoon. It was Hartman's better half."

"Why would she be calling you?"

"That's what I wondered when JoAnne told me who was on the line. Mrs. Hartman had apparently spent much of the day since she'd read the *Times Union* arguing with her husband. Or maybe I should say reasoning with him. In the end she called me. Out of desperation more than because she thought I was the person who could handle her problem."

"I thought you were saying she knew what hubby was up to."

"She claims she did. She made that clear as soon as she'd introduced herself."

"And she'd lived for some time with that knowledge?"

"She had. The way she described the situation, she wasn't just pulling a Tammy Wynette. Far be it from me to understand people I don't understand, if you know what I mean, but she insists that she still loves her husband and I think she's sincere."

"Will wonders never cease."

"It wasn't clear to me just when or how Mrs. Hartman discovered that her husband was taking a call girl to bed, but she seemed to have suspected something along those lines shortly after he came back from some conference up at Mt. Washington a few years ago. In any event, she never told him of her suspicions. Not until today, following publication of the *Times Union* story. Apparently he tried to deny it, claimed he was going to fight a malicious falsehood. It must have been an odd argument. She says he eventually came around to accepting that she knew he was having an affair but that she still loved him. But it seems he's still determined to fight Truscott and sue the paper, and that he wants her to support him. And this is how I come in."

Carol took time out to pour herself another glass of wine.

"What is it that you're supposed to do?" Kevin was by now thoroughly confused.

"I'm supposed to persuade Judge Hartman to take the high ground. No law suits. No public displays of anger that will only make matters worse. In other words, simply ignore the issue and in time it will just fade away."

"Are you kidding?"

"That's what she wants me to do. Will it work? Of course not."

"Are you going to talk to the judge?"

"If you mean am I going to be her advocate, the answer is no. This is between them. Whatever he does, I suspect he's heading for an early retirement. But I would like to talk with him. For that matter we should also be talking with Ms. Sugar again, now that we know what she's been up to. Make that three people. As soon as we find out where he's incarcerated, Sam or I will be talking to the catalyst for today's excitement, Randall Truscott."

"One thing I don't understand is why Mrs. Hartman sought your help."

"I asked her that question, and I still don't have an answer. In view of their friendship, I thought Francis Foster would be the logical one and said so. She was quick to shoot that suggestion down. When I pushed back, she said something about my having a good head on my shoulders. Nice compliment, but we'd barely met. My guess is that her friends would have had a hard time understanding that she would forgive Lindsay for having an affair with a prostitute. She probably thought of me as someone who would have no reason to be judgmental."

It was nearly nine before they had dinner, and when they retired for the night another day had gone by without Kevin telling Carol about Pend Oreille and Murray Rice. Surely they'd get around to it the next day, unless, that is, Judge Hartman ignored his wife and went to the mat with Randall Truscott.

CHAPTER 55

Fortunately for the budget of the sheriff's department in Cumberland County, Randall Truscott had been transferred from a correctional facility in the far north of the state to the Mid-State facility between Utica and Rome. The reason for Truscott's transfer was not clear, and Sheriff Kelleher hadn't wasted her time seeking an explanation. What mattered was that Deputy Sheriff Bridges would not have to travel nearly as far for his meeting with Truscott. Mid-State was only one of many prisons in the system, and while it contained a small maximum security modular unit, it was primarily a medium security facility for men.

While Bridges had visited many of New York's correctional facilities over the years, he never felt comfortable doing so. He understood the red tape which every visitor had to go through, but he hated the process. More than that, he didn't like the looks he invariably received from the inmates. His uniform stamped him as the enemy; he may not have had anything to do with the incarceration of the inmates he passed, but he was a member of the tribe that was responsible for the fact that they had lost their freedom to move about like most of their fellow citizens.

Nonetheless, Sam was on his way to see a man who had beaten a woman to within an inch of her life and then exposed her affair with the judge who had sent him to jail for three years. Sam had no idea what to expect. Truscott might crow about what he had done, or he might simply refuse to talk with him. The word was that Truscott was capable of being a real charmer. Sam was prepared to believe it. How else to explain Ms. Sugar having consented to live with him? On the other hand, he obviously had a mean streak and he certainly knew how to manipulate the system, even from his jail cell. A veritable Jekyll and Hyde, and over the years Sam had come to regard such people as nature's most dangerous.

He had done his homework, not only determining visiting hours and requirements but identifying himself as someone who was investigating suspicious behavior by the person he was visiting. Not surprisingly, this last bit of information was of interest to the people in charge at Mid-State. Sam had had to mount a strenuous argument with one of the prison's authority figures to gain permission to see Truscott without being accompanied by the warden or one of his top aides.

Sam had only the vaguest idea what Truscott would look like. Carol had passed along a sketchy picture, courtesy of Judge Hartman, but he was still unprepared for the handsome man who joined him in the room where inmates met their visitors. The prison uniform detracted marginally from his overall appearance, and Sam had no idea whether he usually wore a beard or had grown one since being locked up, but he was impressed by the man who sat down opposite him. Truscott even had a smile on his face, although Sam thought it looked more smug than friendly.

"So, you're a law and order official from Cumberland County. Right?"

"I am. Sam Bridges, deputy sheriff." He wasn't and never had been exactly sure of the protocol when greeting prisoners, but he stuck out his hand. Truscott's grip was firm.

"You'll forgive me for not being entirely up to speed," Truscott said, "but I assume you know more about me than I do about you. If my information is correct, however, my former defense attorney was found dead over in your jurisdiction. Such a shame. He meant well, but I'm afraid I'd have to give his efforts on my behalf a failing grade. Your boss - her name's Kelleher if I'm not mistaken - I've been told she's a pretty sharp cookie."

Sam didn't like to hear Carol called a cookie, but he wasn't in the Mid-State Correction Facility to correct this man's vernacular.

"We're investigating the death of your attorney, Carl Keller. We thought it might help if we got to know each other."

"Well, of course. Ask away."

"You are aware, of course, about the stories in the Albany papers that deal with Judge Hartman and a woman he is alleged to have been seeing."

"I thought we were going to talk about Mr. Keller's shocking death."

"In my business," Sam said, "things aren't so easily compartmentalized. You are the source of the stories about Judge Hartman, aren't you?"

"I'm not sure where their information came from. But I can assure you that it agrees with my sources."

"Your sources. What would they be?"

"I wish I could say. Unfortunately, what the judge was doing was pretty much common knowledge, so it's really impossible to name a particular source."

"If it was common knowledge, I'm surprised that nobody mentioned it until the *Times Union* and the *Tattler* came out yesterday."

Randall Truscott shook his head.

"Maybe Judge Hartman had bought their silence."

"You can't be serious," Sam said. He was rapidly becoming irritated with Truscott. "Do you honestly think that a distinguished judge is going to bribe a respected paper like the *Times Union*?"

"Do you have a better theory?"

"How about your defense attorney as a source? Didn't you and he discuss strategy?"

"Of course, but it was rather vague. And the minute Hartman told him to lay off the girl he turned into a marshmallow."

"The way I heard it Keller kept pushing until the judge cited him for contempt."

"I was the defendant, remember. You'd think he could have pushed a lot harder."

Sam could see that this was a dead end. He changed the subject.

"Who do you think killed Keller?"

"I'd put Hartman on my short list."

"Forgive me for repeating myself, but you can't be serious."

"Why not? If he was so afraid of what Keller might say, why stop at citing him for contempt? Better to shut him up permanently, don't you think?"

"Do you think judges go around killing fellow attorneys? Even doing it by cutting their throats?"

"I'm sure it wouldn't be the first time it's happened," Truscott said. "If he had the balls to risk his reputation by shacking up with a call girl, taking the knife to someone who could rat him out doesn't sound like that much of a reach."

"To use your expression, you ratted him out. Were you ever concerned that he might consider killing you?"

Truscott broke into laughter. Virtually everyone in the room looked their way.

"Unlike the naive Mr. Keller, I watch my back. And I've got friends, a real band of brothers."

Sam leaned back in his chair and studied the man across the table from him. A former marine, he disliked Truscott's appropriation of the phrase 'band of brothers.' And then Donna Sugar came to mind. Whatever her profession, she was a beautiful woman and the smiling, mocking man he was talking with had blackened her eyes and broken her ribs. He decided that he hated Randall Truscott and that he was very glad that he would be behind bars for almost three more years.

He was ready to break off their conversation, when Truscott asked a question.

"You asked me, now I'm going to ask you. Who do you think killed Keller?"

"It had occurred to me that you might have," Sam answered.

"I'd resent that, except that I know you're putting me on," Truscott said. "As you will remember, I was in one of these places they call correctional facilities. They don't let us out so we can go around slitting throats."

"No, you're right about that. But as you've just pointed out, you have what you call a band of brothers. I'm sure one or more of them would have been more than happy to play hit man for you."

Sam motioned to the nearest guard, signed out, and headed for the exit and some fresh air.

CHAPTER 56

Judge Lindsay Hartman had long thought of Donna Sugar's entry into his life as the most remarkable event in his successful but largely uneventful time on this earth. Until, that is, his wife had calmly acknowledged that she had known of his relationship with Ms. Sugar for years and, what is more, had quietly and apparently without rancor accepted the presence in their lives of this woman she had never once met or spoken to. Her forbearance had been truly remarkable. Instead of having to deny the story in the *Times Union,* the judge had found himself struggling to overcome Hazel's insistence that to deny it would only keep the story alive and make matters worse. As he had expected, he and Hazel did have an argument, but it wasn't about the truth of Randall Truscott's charges. It was about how best to handle those charges. It was an argument that Lindsay could not afford to lose, yet were he to win it he feared it would cost him the wife he loved. For Donna Sugar, who was the reason for the terrible trouble in which he now found himself, was obviously, however regrettably, a closed chapter in his life.

It was while he was pondering this heart wrenching dilemma that the judge suddenly found himself facing another problem. It came in the form of a phone call from his old friend, Francis Foster.

"Hello, Lindsay. Please forgive this intrusion into what I'm sure has been a terrible day. I read the piece in the *Times Union,* and I don't envy you what you're going through."

"It's been tough, I grant you. If there's a silver lining, it's been Hazel. She's being a true soldier. We're still trying to figure out just what to do. I can't believe that our decent citizenry will pay attention to a guy who's doing time for beating the crap out of this woman. Trouble is, it's the kind of story that won't go away. The *Times Union* should never have published the damn thing. If I thought it would work, I'd sue. How about it? Suppose they said things like that about you, what would you do?"

"It depends, Lindsay, on what they know," Francis said, choosing his words carefully. "I can't believe they'd run a story like this if they thought Truscott was just some nut case. After all, he was dating the woman, living with her, whatever you want to call it. The public will assume that she told Truscott that there were other men in her life and that the judge was one of them."

"That's ridiculous, Francis. If the Sugar woman had told him she was having an affair with me, wouldn't you think he'd have demanded that some other judge take the case?"

"Of course, if he'd learned about it before the trial. But I'm assuming he heard about it during the trial - from his attorney, Carl Keller. By then it was too late, because you wouldn't let Keller go there - prejudicial, that's what you called it."

"Wait just a minute." The judge was angry. "Are you saying you believe Truscott? My God, what kind of a friend are you?"

"I'm not saying I believe Truscott. I'm only saying that a lot of people will believe him, and they won't spend a lot of time trying to figure out where he got his information. Think of all the people who've been in this kind of situation. Even our own governor. The public knows who he is, some of 'em know who his prostitute was. But how many people know or care how the press connected the dots? What I'm telling you is what you already know - you're in trouble, and you'd better hope that some investigative reporter doesn't turn up some incriminating evidence."

"You do think I was seeing Sugar, don't you?"

"Like I said, I don't know. We all do dumb things, Lindsay. Heaven knows, I've done my share. I just hope that you didn't mess around with that woman. But you know the old adage, where there's smoke there's fire, and what matters is what the masses believe."

The judge could be heard sighing. A sigh of resignation? Foster didn't know, but he was feeling sorry for his friend since Harvard Law School days.

"I want to sue the paper. Hazel to my surprise, says to leave it alone, figures it'll just turn it into a spectator sport that I'll lose. I don't know what the hell to do."

"Wish I could help, but -" Foster cleared his throat. "I never did tell you why I called, but there's something you can do. For me. Remember our conversation about one of my people? His name's Ferraro. He's taken over Keller's cases, and he claims he's found evidence that Keller'd been stealing from one of his client's escrow accounts. I've been looking into it, and there's something fishy. Nothing that pins the theft on Ferraro himself, but there's enough circumstantial evidence to suggest that he may be trying to frame Keller. It could be helpful if I had access to Ferraro's apartment. Which means I need a search warrant, and that's the real reason I called."

Lindsay had assumed that Foster had called to express his support for a friend. Not only hadn't he unequivocally done so. He'd called to take advantage of the judge's situation, to collect on an IOU.

"What makes you think I should okay a warrant? The way you describe it, your justification sounds pretty flimsy."

"Let me see if I can convince you," Foster said, and proceeded to lay out the case very much as the sheriff had presented it to him.

"Interesting," the judge said when Foster had completed his argument. "I can see that you'd be suspicious of Ferraro. But legally - well, it's rather thin."

"I need your help, Lindsay. Think of all the attention that *Times Union* story's going to stir up. Who'll ever know you've let me search the apartment of some attorney named Ferraro, much less do it on what you call flimsy evidence?"

"Maybe the local bar's going to be paying me a whole lot more attention *because* of the Truscott story, not less."

"Maybe, but not likely. In any event, granting a search warrant will cause you a lot less trouble than not recusing yourself from the Truscott case."

"Why are you doing this to me, Francis?"

"Come on, Lindsay. I'm not doing anything to you. You wanted me to take care of my trouble-maker, Carl Keller. And I did. All I'm asking is that you give me some cover so I can see if I've got a crook at the M & B firm. Keller hadn't done anything illegal, just used poor judgment in a case where you happened to be on the bench. Ferraro, on the other hand, may really have done something illegal. Neither of us wants to endorse that kind of behavior."

The silence which followed lasted so long that Foster began to worry that Hartrman had put down the phone and gone to the bathroom or to the kitchen to get himself a highball.

"Okay," the judge finally spoke. "Give the Albany PD a draft in which you lay out precisely why you need a warrant. Be as specific as you can. Treat it as if you see it as an open and shut case. No hint that I owe you one. Do you understand? And tell the PD that time is of the essence."

"That's really good of you, Lindsay. I won't forget it."

No, I'm sure you won't, the judge said to himself after he had hung up.

CHAPTER 57

Kevin had wanted to share with Carol his information about the murder at Lake Pend Oreille, but the fact that he hadn't done so was attributable both to the publication of the Truscott story and to his own concern that Carol would dismiss his report as wholly irrelevant to the Keller case. But that evening Carol had provided an update on the Hartrman-Sugar saga and Kevin had finally set aside his reservations about the importance of his conversations with the Sandpoint police.

"I think I have some news you'll find interesting," he said, not at all sure his wife would in fact find it interesting.

"Good. I need something to take the rancid taste of the *Tattler* article out of my mouth. What happened? You finished your article? No, that would be expecting too much. You *started* your article?"

"I've changed my mind. I don't think I'll share my news. At least not until I get a bit more respect."

"When have I ever failed to respect you?"

"Let me count the times," Kevin said, but by way of showing he didn't mean it he offered to get them another glass of wine.

"Okay, I'm all ears," Carol called after him. "I promise to be a good audience."

"It's about that list you saw on the office wall at *Welcome Inn*. Nothing as mundane as my article for *Opera News*. You were puzzled by a place called Pend Orel, which also had an unfamiliar area code.

As it happened, my article was going nowhere fast, and my mind started wandering."

Carol did her best to suppress a familiar 'I told you so' look.

"I'll try to keep this brief, but I got on the computer and almost immediately realized that you'd gotten the name wrong. It's Pend Oreille, not Pend Orel, and it's a lake in northern Idaho. I checked the area code, and sure enough all of Idaho is 208, the number you'd remembered. Well, one thing's for certain. The *Welcome Inn* doesn't order things from Idaho. Which would seem to mean that the motel manager had a more personal reason for listing a phone number from out there. You know me. One thing always leads to another, and in this case another thing turned out to be some calls to Pend Oreille, or more specifically to some of the towns on Lake Pend Oreille. They're none of them big, sort of like Southport and West Branch. I started with a place called Sandpoint, still small but it's got the biggest population of any place on that lake."

"Very enterprising of you, but who would you call? A family of Reeces?"

"As it happens, there seems to be only one Reece out there, a very elderly lady who could be over 90. No, I asked myself who I'd call if I wanted to find out about somebody here on Crooked Lake. Guess who I'd call? The sheriff's department. It didn't take long before I was talking to a police officer in Sandpoint. Sounded like a nice guy, just like Sam and the rest of your boys."

"It goes with the badge, Kevin. Us law and order types have to have wonderful personalities. It says so in the regs."

"Either that or I just happened on someone who's just naturally inclined to be helpful. I asked the obvious question, did he know or remember a guy named Marty Reece."

"And he did." Carol sounded interested for the first time.

"No, he didn't. But he came close. Seems that someone named Murray Rice lived there until fairly recently. He worked in a hash house not far from Sandpoint. Unfortunately - or perhaps it's fortunately - he left the lake without telling anybody he was going or where."

"Forgive the question, but so what? Why are we interested in a Murray Rice?"

"Two reasons, Carol, and the first one came to mind because your name and Carl Keller's are about as close as they can be without being identical. You've said so yourself, many times. So how about Marty Reece and Murray Rice? Is that just a coincidence? Anyway, the other reason is what really got me to thinking. Not long before Rice suddenly left Pend Oreille, there'd been a murder. A man from Pakistan who'd moved there with his family some time ago was bludgeoned to death in his home. And the cops have never been able to figure out who did it. You're going to ask if they suspected Rice, aren't you? Not according to my source. He claims that Rice and the Pakistani were good friends, that Rice broke down when he heard what had happened. But doesn't it strike you as - I'm not sure what I'd call it - how about strange? It's worth thinking about."

"I assume you asked some questions about this Murray Rice. Does he sound at all like Reece?"

"Hard to say. Probably around the same age. But what I found most interesting is that Rice had been in service in Iraq, had won a Purple Heart. Merrivale - he's the one I talked to - thinks he might have been coping with PTSD. You know, post traumatic -"

"I know what it is," Carol said. Kevin had now gotten her attention. "Did Merrivale say Rice admitted to the problem?"

"No, he just thought Rice's mood swings sounded like what he'd read about it."

"Sorry to keep quizzing you, but tell me what else this guy Merrivale had to say about Rice."

"Quiz away. I was hoping you'd find this interesting. For what it's worth, Merrivale says Rice didn't talk much. Sort of a loner. And somebody who didn't put down roots. A drifter, that's what he called him."

"How long have you known these things?"

"Not long. A couple of days. I'd have brought it up sooner, but the news about the judge and the call girl preempted me."

"It may mean nothing," Carol said pensively. "On the other hand, it may be important. By itself, Reece and Rice don't mean a thing. But put it together with the murder, the hasty departure from the Idaho lake, the PTSD - I'd say I had better get myself over to *Welcome Inn* and have another talk with Marty Reece."

"What would you talk about? You can't come right out and ask him if he murdered some guy on Lake Pend Oreille."

"I can't picture the whole conversation, but the first question I think I'd ask is whether he knows someone named Murray Rice. How about you? Does that sound like a good opening gambit?"

"It does. Will you need me as backup?"

"No thanks. I'm the sheriff, remember?"

———

Kevin was thoroughly pleased with himself when he rolled over and shut off the light. His 'news' not only hadn't been dismissed out of hand by Carol; it had led to a very satisfying use of their kingsize bed.

The following morning they were both all smiles. Kevin hoped that Carol would catch Marty Reece off guard and in the process introduce another suspect into the troublesome Keller case. Carol was not optimistic, but at the moment there was nothing she could do about the relationship between either Hartman and Sugar or Foster and Ferraro. Kevin's homework in distant Idaho had given her something to do, and she welcomed the opportunity to do it. Her good-bye kiss lasted longer than usual.

"You've made my day," he said, coming up for air.

"Wish me luck." And she was off for *Welcome Inn* by way of her squad meeting.

Had it not been for the fact that arriving at the motel too early might alert Reece to the possibility that something was troubling the sheriff, she would have turned the meeting over to Bridges. As it was, she dragged it out longer than her agenda actually required, and she did so without mentioning Kevin's phone conversation with members of the tiny Sandpoint, Idaho, police department. To bring her husband into her remarks would only further upset Sam and perhaps other members of her small staff.

It was nearly nine o'clock when she set off for the motel at the Hopewell by-pass. Not for the first time she wondered why Reece had chosen such an unpromising location when he moved to Crooked Lake. He seemed like someone who was capable of landing a job in any number of places on or near the lake. In fact, the more she thought about it, he would almost literally have had to search out the *Welcome Inn*. It wasn't located where he would have been likely to spot it had he been driving about looking for help wanted signs. Nor was it in a place likely to have come to the minds of people when he inquired about jobs.

Carol realized that she knew very little about the motel. It had once been fairly busy. But it was not part of any chain with a familiar name, and it had begun to show its age. Inasmuch as there weren't many motels in the Crooked Lake area, even a fading *Welcome Inn* would occasionally sport a No Vacancy sign in tourist season. But then the Hopewell by-pass had been built, and while the motel was still as close to the lake as it had been, its location was inconvenient. There were signs advising motorists which way to turn and how far to go, but they were unlikely to entice tired drivers.

Reece certainly did not own the motel. She couldn't remember who did, or why he hadn't made an effort to unload it when the by-pass ceased to be a rumor and became a funded project. Carol would have to do some research, learn who owned it and had hired Reece to manage it, and make an appointment to talk with him. But first she would be talking with Reece himself and asking the questions for which Kevin had laid the groundwork.

To her surprise, neither Marty Reece nor his car was at the motel. In their place was a handwritten notice on the door to the office, announcing that the manager was running an errand in Southport and would be back by 10. Reece had had enough experience to know that he would be unlikely to miss prospective customers, especially at an early morning hour. For a brief moment the thought occurred to Carol that perhaps Reece, like Rice, had simply hit the road, leaving behind, without a forwarding address, the place where he had killed a man. But just as quickly, she brushed that thought aside. I'm getting to be as bad as Kevin, she thought. The odds that Reece was Rice, that Rice had killed someone in Idaho, and that it was now happening all over again on Crooked Lake were so slight that even entertaining the idea was ridiculous.

Carol returned to her car and settled down to wait for Marty Reece to return from Southport. He didn't quite make it by 10, but he missed the time he'd put on his notice by less than five minutes.

"You're getting to be a regular here, sheriff," he said as he came over to her car.

"You must find it boring," Carol said. "Did you expect more business when you agreed to take the job?"

Reece laughed.

"No. Clemens was very above board. He told me he wasn't sure what he would do with the place, but that he needed somebody to run it while he made up his mind."

"So you haven't minded that business is slow?"

"Don't mind at all. I'm a bit of a loner. Always have been. I knew right away this place'd be lucky to cover what he pays me, much less the taxes and some new mattresses. I figure it'll be a tear down before Christmas. You've got some news for me? Want to come in?"

"I don't know about news, but yes, I'd like to come in."

"Good. Just give me a minute to unload a couple of things."

It didn't take long. A few minutes later they were seated in the dingy office, which looked just as it had on the sheriff's previous visit. And on her first visit as well, except for the missing phone list on the wall.

"So, what's up? Somehow I don't think you're here to tell me you've caught the guy who killed Mr. Keller. Big news like that, you'd have told me before you shut off the engine."

"You're right, of course. It's going to be one of those slow, frustrating days - you feel it the minute you wake up in the morning. So I thought I'd make a few stops, talk with some of the people I've met recently. I'm sure you'd rather not be one of those people, but we never know what lies ahead, do we?"

"I guess not," Reece commented.

"One question comes to mind. I don't think I asked it the last time I was here. Do you know a man named Murray Rice?"

Carol had assumed that Marty Reece's answer would be 'no.' So it wasn't what he said that interested her. It was how he reacted to her question. She was paying very close attention to the man behind the desk.

"Rice? Don't believe I've ever heard of him."

There had not been the slightest sign that the question had surprised Reece, much less that his answer might have been a lie. Either the man knew nothing about Rice or he was an extremely accomplished liar. Carol did not know whether to be disappointed or not. She had assumed that Reece and Rice were not the same person, but for some reason she had hoped they were. If they weren't, she was wasting her time. Kevin may have been having fun once again playing sleuth, but he, too, would have been wasting his time.

She turned to the next question on her short list.

"Have you ever spent time out in Idaho?"

"Afraid not." Once again there was no indication that this was other than an honest answer. "It's one of the four states I've never visited. You ever collect states? I started doing it when I finished high school, added a few while I was in the service. Getting those last four has been tough, though. Never did get to Idaho, Montana, North Dakota, or Vermont. That sounds like a couple of trips, doesn't it? One to the northwest, one up north of here. Maybe I'll take myself a long weekend and add Vermont to my list."

"You'd like Vermont. I don't know about the others. Never been there. So you were in the military. Ever see active duty?"

For the first time Reece's face registered something other than friendly interest in their conversation. It lasted for the briefest of seconds, but Carol was convinced the motel manager had let his thoughts drift to something in his past.

"I was," he answered. "Two tours in Iraq. I was just a kid. Let's not talk about it."

"Sorry. I didn't mean to bring up bad memories."

Reece's smile returned.

"That's okay. We're out of there now, thank goodness. Wish I had some coffee to offer you," he said, changing the subject. "But wouldn't you know it, I plumb forgot I was out when I went to Southport."

"No problem. I have to be moving on anyway. Just wanted to say 'hi.'"

It wasn't true, and Reece would have been aware that it wasn't. He got to his feet and walked the sheriff to the door.

"Let me know when you discover who did that awful thing to Mr. Keller. And thanks for taking down that yellow tape you people use. It doesn't make the place look all that welcoming. Of course we'll never know how much business we lost, will we?"

Not much, Carol thought as she backed the patrol car up and set off down county road 31. There hadn't seemed to be any point in asking more questions, but she couldn't quite get the presence of a Pend Oreille phone number on the *Welcome Inn* wall off her mind.

CHAPTER 58

When Carol got back to the office, she found both Officers Bridges and Byrnes eager to talk to her. Both were busy, but each quickly dropped what he was doing when he heard the sheriff's voice and hustled down the hallway to her office.

She was in the process of hanging up her jacket when the two of them appeared simultaneously at the door. An impromptu Alphonse and Gaston act ensued, but it was readily apparent that each sought precedence.

"The two of you must have had an interesting morning."

"Very much so," Tommy sad.

"Well come in, both of you. And shut the door. There may be spies in the corridor." It wasn't until they started to talk that it became clear to the sheriff that they had separate agendas.

"Okay, one at a time. Sam?"

Carol was still conscious of the deputy sheriff's sensitivity over the role Kevin always seemed to be assuming in the department's investigations. The very fact that she had just come from a meeting with the manager of *Welcome Inn* at her husband's suggestion underscored the point. Tommy looked to be the more excited of the two, but rank mattered and she turned to Sam.

"There was a call for you from Lisa Simmons in Albany. JoAnne thought she sounded anxious so I figured I ought to see what the problem is. She still wants to talk with you, but she says she's being stalked and that you'd warned her that it might happen."

"I guess I did, after she told me about her experience with someone she assumed was Carl Keller's cousin. Did she say who the stalker was?"

"She doesn't know. She just assumed that it's the man she'd told you about. I advised her to report it to the Albany PD, but she'd already done that and doesn't seem to have much confidence they'll take her seriously."

"She describe the man?"

"She'll try to give you an idea of what he looks like, but she says he's going out of his way to stay out of sight. I'm not sure that's the way she put it. More like he stays in the crowd, keeps his distance. But she's sure he's there, following her."

"There may be nothing to it but her imagination, but inasmuch as I warned her that something like this was possible I should get back to her right away. We don't want a witness in trouble."

"She's a witness? Of what?"

"It's all about that guy who used her to get into Keller's apartment. She knows this guy may have had something to do with Keller's death, and there's a very good chance that he knows she knows. Anyway, I'm feeling responsible for her safety. I'll call her as soon as I hear what's on Tommy's mind."

Carol turned to Officer Byrnes. There was no need for her to ask him what was on his mind.

"I found her, believe it or not. Finally. Keller's former wife, Mary Louise Kinsler, nee Gallagher. Pretty clever of her to marry a guy who's last name also begins with a K. She could still use the same old MLK jewelry. Or is it MGK?"

"I have no idea, and it doesn't matter. Where is she?"

"Keller's parents were wrong. It wasn't Worcester or Burlington or any other place they suggested. It's St. Cloud, Minnesota. I'd never heard of the place. But she's the one who was married to your friend Keller all right. Her current husband is a gynecologist. She obviously has a preference for professionals - first a lawyer, then a doctor."

"You're sure Kinsler is her second? Maybe Keller was the second. Maybe there was someone between the two Ks."

Tommy looked puzzled for a moment, then shook it off.

"For a minute I thought you were criticizing my research," he said, his face still betraying a hint of doubt.

"We aren't into family history here," Carol said. "I just need her to tell me what she can about Carl. When I left home this morning I had no idea what my day would be like. Now I know it's going to involve two phone conversations with people who probably knew my former law partner better than I did. Good work, both of you."

———

Getting in touch with Lisa proved to be very easy. She picked up on the second ring. Carol guessed she had been waiting expectantly, cell phone in hand, ever since Sam had told her the sheriff would call her back shortly. Unfortunately, the conversation which followed was a disappointment. Ms. Simmons seemed to be unnecessarily alarmed.

Her answers to Carol's questions were invariably vague. No, she had never had a good look at the man. No, he had never actually approached her. No, he had never called her at work or at home. The more they talked, the more it struck Carol that Lisa thought she was being stalked because Carol had suggested that it might happen. In fact, Lisa's fears had nothing to do with a familiar face, a person she had seen on a number of occasions. Her 'stalker' was, for all practical purposes, any one of a large number of people who happened to be going her way, people she was aware of because she had the habit of frequently looking over her shoulder.

"I know I urged you to be alert, Lisa, but nothing you have told me suggests that someone is deliberately following you, much less that the man who called himself Carl's cousin is doing so. Stalkers are typically much more obvious. They want you to know they are interested in you. I fear I may have alarmed you unnecessarily. Try to relax. Stay alert, but let's not assume that the phony cousin is following you around. The chances he would do so were never very great, but I felt I had to say it was a possibility. So, please, let the Albany police department know if and when you think a particular person is doing the following. And you can call me anytime."

Lisa seemed relieved when Carol said good-bye. Carol hoped she had not overstated her case. She had a well founded respect for the Albany PD, but she also knew that it wouldn't be assigning an officer to keep an eye on Lisa.

Reaching Mary Louise Kinsler was considerably more difficult. After all, she would have no idea that her first husband was deceased or that a sheriff investigating his death was trying to contact her. Carol arranged for JoAnne to try the St. Cloud number from time to time, and it was at 5:17, just as she was getting ready to leave for the day, that one of those calls was answered.

"This is Mrs. Kinsler," she said. Carol appreciated it. She wished that more people would let you know who was answering the phone.

"Mrs. Kinsler, I hope you can give me a few minutes of your time. My name is Carol Kelleher, and I'm the sheriff of Cumberland County in western New York state. This is not an emergency, so please don't be worried that you're talking with a policeman. Do you have a few minutes?"

"I guess so. It depends on the problem."

"Of course. I'm calling about Carl Keller, whom I understand was once your husband. I have something to report and a question to ask. Carl died recently. His death occurred in my jurisdiction, which is why I'm the one who is calling."

"I'm sorry to hear that," Mrs. Kinsler said. "You must understand that we went our separate ways quite a few years ago, and I haven't seen Carl since."

"It might interest you to know that I knew Carl when you and he were married. We both worked for the same Albany law firm for a few months. Like you, I hadn't seen him in years until a few weeks ago when he died quite unexpectedly on nearby Crooked Lake."

"I'm sorry, but I don't seem to remember you."

"There's no reason why you should. We never met. But I'm calling because the circumstances of Carl's death are somewhat unusual, and it would help if you could try to remember him and help me get a better picture of him. I'm sorry to be bothering you, but I wouldn't have called if it weren't important."

"Well, sure, as long as you know it's been some time and we never maintained contact of any kind."

"Thanks. My questions don't depend on staying in touch with Carl. They are more about how you remember him. For example, did he ever act suicidal or talk about suicide?"

"Did he commit suicide?" It was the obvious question.

"We think so," Carol said, hedging the truth of the matter, "but we aren't one hundred percent sure."

"I don't remember ever talking about it. In fact, Carl didn't talk much about anything. His law practice was his life. I always thought he enjoyed it, but he never brought it home with him. We sort of inhabited the same house, but didn't share a lot else. I suppose that's why we divorced."

"You make Carl sound sort of introspective. How about moody? Did you ever get the impression that he was quiet because he was depressed?"

"I really don't know. He just wasn't someone who was easy to know. It's funny, but something just came to me. First time in years. I'm not sure exactly how to put this, but things embarrassed him, things you wouldn't expect a man his age to be embarrassed about. Like he didn't much like sex. He was uncomfortable whenever we did it."

Mrs. Kinsler paused, and when she spoke again it was clear that she wasn't sure she should have commented on something so personal.

Carol assured her that she had no intention of repeating any of this conversation to anyone.

"By the way," she asked, "how would you describe the divorce?"

"I think he wanted it as much as I did. It was amicable. There weren't any kids, there weren't any money problems. It was almost as if we'd had a trial marriage, discovered it wouldn't work, and simply walked away. John is wonderful. I just made a mistake the first time."

John was presumably the gynecologist.

Carol turned to another question, one she hadn't originally planned to ask.

"I mentioned that we think Carl's death was a suicide. But we aren't entirely sure. Which leads me to raise another question. Can you recall anything in Carl's life when you were living together that might have given someone a possible reason to kill him?"

"That's a terrible idea. Who would want to kill Carl? You don't kill somebody because he's dull."

"What about the people in his law practice? Or people he prosecuted?"

"It's like I said, he never talked about his cases. Unlike John, it was almost like I didn't really know what Carl did for a living. I don't remember ever meeting any of his colleagues. I may have, but we certainly never socialized."

It had been a dispiriting conversation. Carol apologized for interrupting Ms. Kinsler's day and thanked her for her time and information.

"Not much information, I'm afraid," the woman said. Carol reluctantly agreed.

CHAPTER 59

On her way home to the cottage at the end of the day, Carol found herself thinking about alibis. Who among possible suspects in the Keller case had an alibi which would have made it impossible to visit the *Welcome Inn* on that fateful summer night? It was a serious subject, but for no apparent reason Carol seemed to be in a jocular mood. Those who did have an alibi technically numbered in the hundreds of millions, overwhelmingly because they lived too far away: the shopkeeper in Istanbul, the gondolier in Venice, the sherpa in Nepal, the physician in London's Harley Street. She smiled to herself. Needless to say, her investigation had no interest in such people. Nor was she interested in people who lived their lives in such places as Fresno or Cheyenne, Kalamazoo or Toledo, Clearwater or Baton Rouge. She wasn't even concerned with residents of such relatively nearby places as Rochester, Binghamton, and Syracuse They lived close enough, and had they known Keller and for some reason bore him sufficient animus, they might have made the trip to Crooked Lake and crept into the *Welcome Inn* with knife in hand. But they were not on her list of possible suspects.

By the time she reached West Branch and turned down the West Lake Road, her thoughts about alibis had turned serious. Everyone who might be a legitimate suspect came from one of two places: the area around Crooked Lake and the state capital, Albany. If they were locals, coming to the motel, dispatching Carl, and returning home to snuggle down for the night would have posed no problem. The only local on her list was Marty Reece, and he lived only a few yards from *Welcome Inn's* room 8. It was at least conceivable that he had an alibi, such as being involved in an all night poker game with friends, but Carol's real problem with Reece had nothing to do with whether he had an alibi. She simply could not imagine that he had a motive for killing Keller.

Albany was another story. There were at least half a dozen people who both called it home and had had their problems with Carl. Leaving aside the matter of motive, Carol knew of only one of these persons of interest who had an iron clad alibi. Randall Truscott would have been disappointed with his defense attorney, of course, but she could not imagine that he would have been tempted to cut Carl's throat. In any event, he couldn't have done it for the simple reason that he was serving time in jail, and Carol had no reason to believe that security at the Mid-State Correctional facility was lax.

Unless there was someone else whose name had not yet surfaced in her investigation, this left Francis Foster, Lindsay Hartman, Tony Ferraro, Donna Sugar, Lisa Simmons, and a man pretending to be Carl's non- existent cousin. Carol had trouble picturing any of them except for the impostor slashing Carl's throat, and she was in no position to hazard a guess about him. Each of the others may have had a reason to dislike Carl, but motive for murder was another matter. Nor did she have any idea whether any of them had an alibi that would pass muster. Moreover, all of them would have found it more difficult to make the round trip from Albany than it would for Reece to walk the short distance from his office to motel room 8 and back. And Reece was the most marginal of marginal suspects.

By the time Carol reached the cottage, she knew that she was going to have to pursue the issue of alibis. Which posed a problem. She could not ask these potential suspects to account for their whereabouts on the night of Keller's death without explaining why, and doing so would immediately make it clear that they were suspected of something. Every one of them would know, without asking, that what they were suspected of was killing Carl Keller. She could (and probably would) argue that it was all simply pro forma, that she had no reason to believe that they had anything to do with Carl's death, but none of them would be fooled. What is more, when it came to Foster and Ferraro, it would not be sufficient to single them out and not question other members of the M & B law firm. It would be a waste of time and would surely irritate a few people, but not to interrogate the others about where they were and what thy were doing on the night of Keller's death would focus undue attention prematurely on Foster and Ferraro.

Kevin was not in the study nor was he on the deck. He was on the dock, and once again he was fishing.

"I thought you'd given this up as a bad idea." Carol said as she joined him on the dock.

"I thought so, too."

He set his pole down and gave his wife a hug.

"Unfortunately, everything else was going wrong. I thought maybe a sunfish or two would cheer me up."

"What is this about everything going wrong?"

"The car battery died - I'd left the lights on. I also forgot a medical appointment and they're going to charge me for a no show. Two trips to the supermarket and I still forgot the barbecue sauce. And you don't want to hear about the progress I'm not making on my paper."

"Considering what I face every day, that sounds like a walk in the park. What did you do about the battery?"

"Mike came home for lunch and gave me a jump. Anyway, my luck is still bad. The fish aren't biting."

"Why don't you put the pole away and join me for a drink. I'll fill you in on what I didn't accomplish."

"You had a bad one, too?"

"No, it's just that in the law enforcement business the stakes are higher. Just give me a few minutes to change."

It was on the second glass of wine that they got around to the subject of alibis.

"Who do you think paid a visit to the *Welcome Inn* with the intention of killing Carl Keller?" Carol asked. "Come on, who's at the top of your list?"

"You mean other than Marty Reece."

"I've already told you we can forget him. I'm talking about my Albany connection."

"If I gave you a name," Kevin said, "it'd be a shot in the dark. I'd feel a lot better if I knew what kind of alibis all those lawyers and call girls had."

"And how would you propose to get those alibis?" Carol asked.

"I'd ask them. You know, where were you when Mr. Keller met his maker?"

"You'd just corner the sweet Ms. Sugar and demand that she tell you with whom she'd shacked up that night and where?"

"Why not?" Kevin asked. "And I'd pay the easily offended Francis Foster a visit and tell him you'd get off his case if he could account for his every move the night Keller was killed."

"We do try to be a bit more subtle than that, Kevin. It wouldn't be so hard if I could rank order my suspects from most promising to least promising. Unfortunately, none of them looks all that promising. Which is why it would be helpful to know who has an alibi that would take him off my list. But where do I start?"

"Just a hunch, but how about Ferraro?"

"I've been leaning that way, too," Carol said, "but we still don't know whether Keller stole from that escrow or Ferraro's framing him. Which would mean that the only way to do it without practically accusing him of lying would be to quiz all the M & B lawyers about their alibis for that night."

"Yeah, I see what you mean. I'll concede - you have had a tougher day than I have."

CHAPTER 60

Hazel Hartman walked purposefully into her husband's study, waving a copy of Albany's number one newspaper, the *Times Union*.

"You weren't going to do this," she said. Both her voice and her face betrayed the fact that she was upset. "You told me you'd ignore the story."

She tossed the paper down on the desk, upsetting a small cylindrical pot that held a number of pens and pencils.

"Hazel, please. I didn't say I'd ignore it, I said I would give them a simple denial. In fact I thought my statement was appropriately non- belligerent. I didn't get down in the gutter with Truscott. But I just couldn't let anyone think Truscott's story was true."

"What's the matter with you, Lindsay? It *is* true. You know it and I know it. If we have to we'll stand up together and say we're a loving couple, that what happened was a mistake and we've put it behind us. But now look what you've done. People are going to think you're not just a philanderer but a liar as well."

"You really don't understand, do you?" Lindsay said. He looked and sounded like a defeated man, trying without much success to set things right. "I can't admit it, which is what I'd be doing if I said nothing. We've been all over this before. I didn't take myself off the Truscott case because I would have to have explained why - that I was having a relationship with one of the parties. That's something judges don't do. It's a conflict of interest, and a serious one. I can hardly pretend it didn't influence the way I conducted the trial. I was on Sugar's side from the outset, and anybody who was following the trial would know it. The bar doesn't take kindly to what I did, Hazel. I'd be lucky to get a severe reprimand. Chances are it would be worse. My colleagues wouldn't speak to me."

Hazel sat down in her husband's recliner. She now looked resigned.

"I wish you hadn't burned your bridges, Lindsay, but let's face facts. You're going to have to retire. It's what people do when they reach your age. Maybe we should buy an RV and find some places where the fishing is better than Crooked Lake."

"There's nothing wrong with fishing over there," he said, but he knew they would probably be selling both the house and the cottage and moving to some place where he wouldn't be remembered as the judge who threw his career away for a call girl.

———

It was somewhat later that morning that Gretchen Ziegler was on the phone, updating Carol on the latest development in the Hartman-Sugar story.

"Judge Hartman has responded to Truscott," she said. "I had no idea what to expect, and as denials go, this one is pretty tepid. I think Hartman wants people to believe he's a gentleman, not a street brawler. Here's what he says, short and sweet: 'I am very sorry that Randall Truscott has chosen to attack my character and integrity. It saddens me to have to respond to his charges, but I want the readers of this newspaper to know that there is no truth in what he alleges.'"

"I'd have been a bit more cautious if I were in his shoes," Carol said. "The judge sounds civil, but he also sounds as if he's convinced that Truscott hasn't a shred of evidence. But why would he have gone after the judge unless he had some reason for thinking he could make a case? What's your opinion?"

"I'm a lawyer, remember. I haven't seen the evidence - or the lack of it. Why don't you pick up the details on line? I'll keep you updated on local scuttlebutt, including whatever the *Tattler* has to say."

"I can't wait." Carol sounded sarcastic.

She read what the *Times Union* had reported on line. If anything it made it even clearer that the judge was accusing Truscott of character assassination. For some reason, this made her uneasy. Sam's report on his meeting with Truscott had only heightened her instinctive hostility toward the man. On the other hand, given the fact that she was investigating Carl Keller's death, she knew she had to withhold judgement. Truscott could not have slit Keller's throat; he was already in jail when Carl died. Hartman was another story. He would inevitably end up on her short list of suspects in the Keller case, especially if it turned out that he had indeed been having an affair with Sugar.

———

Other than Hazel Hartman, the person who was most interested in the judge's riposte to Randall Truscott's charge in the *Times Union* was of course Donna Sugar. He had sworn to fight back, and she had not doubted that he would. But while she didn't know exactly what Randall knew of her relationship with the judge or how he had come by that knowledge, she was quite certain that he knew enough to guarantee that her affair with the judge was at an end and that his tenure on the bench was probably over as well. Inevitably, she read the piece in the *Times Union* with mixed feelings.

She wanted to call Lindsay, but she knew that she couldn't do that. It briefly crossed her mind that they might be able to establish some form of communication whereby they could at least send each other private messages from time to time. Perhaps via a mail box drop. She pushed that thought from her mind. This was not the kind of relationship they had enjoyed. They had had stimulating conversations about everything from the Tea Party phenomenon to their mutual fondness for *Downton Abbey*, but they had never corresponded, not to mention communicating via Facebook or Twitter.

Donna folded the *Times Union* and stuffed it into the wastebasket.

———

Francis Foster also paid attention to his friend's challenge to Randall Truscott. He was almost morally certain that Lindsay had been in some kind of relationship with the call girl, which made his denial of such a relationship in the *Times Union* particularly painful. He could understand the denial, but he could not imagine a happy ending for the judge. How had it happened that Lindsay, always the straight arrow, the one who shook his head in amazement at his classmate's notorious indiscretions, had gotten himself into such a mess. It made him realize that he didn't know his friend nearly as well as he thought he did. Moreover, he didn't know the call girl at all. That was likely to change as the story played out in the media in the days ahead.

CHAPTER 61

Carol put her alibi campaign into operation that morning, beginning with what was likely to be the most difficult part. She called Francis Foster.

"Good morning, Francis, Carol Kelleher here."

"I was afraid that I hadn't heard all the bad news," he said. "First it's Judge Hartman in the *Times Union*, now it's you reminding me about that warrant to search Tony Ferraro's apartment. Or maybe you haven't seen the *Times Union*."

"I read about it on line. It looks as if the judge is going to fight Truscott's charges."

"I feel sorry for Lindsay. No matter how it turns out, it's going to be unpleasant. But about the search warrant, he agreed to authorize it and it looks like Albany's finest will be executing it in a day or two."

"That's good, and I appreciate your help. Actually I didn't call about the search warrant, but I'm glad you brought it up. I'm assuming that the warrant covers everything we discussed, and that the Albany PD knows what it's doing. Do you think I should have one of my men come over and join the search party?"

"It shouldn't be necessary, but I'll get in touch with a friend in the department and see if they're receptive to ringers."

"Thanks. Now, if you're on your feet, let me suggest you sit down. I've got another request."

"What have I done to deserve this?"

"It's because we both believe in seeing that justice is done. You're helping M & B by searching Ferraro's apartment. You'll be helping me catch a killer if you say 'yes' to what I'm proposing."

"What if I don't?"

"I think you will. Somebody slit the late Carl Keller's throat, and I've got a number of people who are hypothetically suspects. It would be enormously helpful if I knew which of them have an alibi which makes it impossible for them to have done it. What I would like you to do is help me track down those alibis. Unfortunately, it's going to entail getting each and every one of your lawyers to tell you what he or she was doing the night Carl was killed."

Carol let that sink in for a few long seconds before elaborating. Francis beat her to it.

"Tony Ferraro and the escrow account I can understand. I don't like the idea that *any* of my people might have killed Keller, but really - a dozen of the best attorneys in Albany? Your list of suspects includes my whole staff? Or are you willing to leave out the secretaries and interns?"

"I'm only interested in the lawyers, at least for now," Carol said, seeking to defuse the shock of this latest appeal for help from the Cumberland County Sheriff's Department. "The truth of the matter is that I'm not at all interested in most of your people. Let me be more specific. I'm not interested in any of your people except Tony Ferraro. But I don't want Tony to know that. Not yet. Frankly, I don't have hard evidence that I should even be treating him as a suspect. If I check everyone for alibis - yes, even my friend Gretchen Ziegler - it will look like I haven't singled him out for special attention. At least that's what I hope Ferraro will be thinking."

"And how am I supposed to go about this alibi hunt?"

"You'll find a way to do it without ruffling feathers, I'm sure. Maybe something like calling a staff meeting, saying you know everyone is innocent as a new born babe, but insisting that helping the law and order people is our civic responsibility. All you need is a statement of where people were, what they were doing, and who can vouch for them. Oh, and you can put an end to all the whining by saying that you'll be making a statement of your own, just like everybody else."

Francis Foster laughed out loud.

"You enjoy this sort of thing, don't you, Carol?"

"I do if it helps us nail the bad guys. You'll notice that I've just taken you off my suspect list by putting you in charge of this little exercise. And you'll be pleased to know that I'm going to be soliciting alibis from a few people myself. My list of suspects isn't limited to Morgenstern and Brauchli. May I count on you?"

"You don't leave me with any choice. When do you want the results of my little survey?"

"Let's see. Today is Tuesday. How does Friday sound?"

"Come on, Carol, give me a break," Foster was no longer laughing. "I'm not even sure what I was doing the night Keller was killed. Why not give us the weekend to get it right? Let's say Monday morning."

"Okay, Monday. And good luck."

———

It had gone better than Carol had expected, but she still had to deal with Lindsay Hartman, Donna Sugar, and Lisa Simmons. The judge would be a tough sell. Not only would he be preoccupied with Randall Truscott's accusations, he would see her request as a not very subtle way of treating him as a prime suspect in Carl Keller's death. He might well tell her to go to hell, and she wasn't quite sure how she should respond if he did. The call girl, whose status as a suspect was rather shaky, might also hang up on her. Only Simmons could be expected to cooperate. She already was feeling guilty for having let the false Richard Keller know where Carl was staying; better to be eager to help the sheriff than to indignantly claim a right of privacy.

Carol chose the easier path, and called the *Treasure Chest*.

Lisa's colleague answered, but promptly called out something to the effect that 'your friend the sheriff wants you'.

"Hello." Carol wasn't sure whether the word betrayed hope or anxiety.

"Ms. Simmons, I'm glad you're at the shop today. I have a favor to ask of you."

"A favor?" Anxiety won out this time.

"Yes, and it's really quite simple. As you know, I'm conducting an investigation into Carl Keller's death. It's common practice in cases like this to create a record of what everyone who's been involved in a case was doing when the death we're investigating occurred. So I'm calling to ask that you think back to the night of Carl's death - it was July 2nd - and put together a statement that explains just where you were and what you were doing. We also need to know the names of people who can verify what you report. I know it's just a piece of busy work, but it's part of our job. What I'd like you to do is write out such a statement and and send it to me. Okay?"

"That sounds like what they call an alibi on cop shows. Why do you think I need an alibi?"

"It's routine, Lisa. I do not suspect you of anything, but a case record is a way for us to tie together lots of things, things that may not seem to be related but which might help us better understand what happened."

"Well, if you say so. I don't remember off hand, but I keep a diary and I'll check it out tonight. It was after I moved out of Carl's, but you know that. Erin and I usually just hang out, unless she's out with some guy."

"I appreciate your help. Just be as specific as you can, and if Erin was with you that evening, be sure to let me have her full name. Or the name of anyone else who will remember that night."

"I take it you still don't know what happened to Carl."

"We're getting close," Carol said, declining to be specific. "I promise to let you know when it all comes together."

———

The call she dreaded the most was the one to Judge Hartman, which is why she tried Donna Sugar next. The call girl might refuse to cooperate, but Carol was less concerned about offending her than she was the judge. To her surprise, Sugar was at home and answering her phone.

"Ms. Sugar, this is Sheriff Kelleher from over on Crooked Lake. How are you doing? You can't be very happy with the news in the *Times Union*."

"No one I know would like to have her name dragged through the mud like that. Civility seems to be at a low ebb at the moment, don't you think? Now what is it you want of me?"

Carol explained the reason for her call. In order to do so, she had to plead twice with Ms. Sugar to let her finish.

"This is very difficult for me," she said. "My job is to learn how and why Carl Keller died, and I need your cooperation. I have absolutely no reason to believe that you had anything to do with his death. But in my business, investigating a case like this is very much like putting together a jigsaw puzzle. Call it trial and error. You never know when some seemingly unimportant piece of information will prove to be critical. What I would very much like you to do is try to recreate in your mind what you were doing the night when Mr. Keller died. I'm not asking for an alibi. Like I said, you are not a suspect in Mr. Keller's death. But everything you can tell me about what you did that night, whom you met, whom you talked with, might point me in the right direction. For what it's worth, I'm making this same request of everyone whose life intersected Mr. Keller's recently."

"I'm sure what you're doing makes sense to you, sheriff. But you are asking me to divulge information about my private life and the lives of others, and that I cannot do. You are quite right, of course, that I had nothing to do with Mr. Keller's death. The very idea is, well, let's call it absurd. So I think you can simply forget about me and concentrate on those who may have had their reasons for killing Mr. Keller. I hope you are successful. Unfortunately, I have an appointment for which I am already late, so I must say good-bye."

The line went dead. It was very much as Carol had expected. Donna Sugar would not provide her with an alibi. If she had spent that evening with Judge Hartman, the reason for her not saying so was obvious, even if it would have provided the judge with an alibi. Carol was unfamiliar with the modus operandi of call girls, but she thought it highly unlikely that they would voluntarily share the names of any of the men in their little black books with the police.

———

Which left Judge Lindsay Hartman. Not surprisingly, he answered at neither his home nor his office. In all likelihood there were many people who were trying to reach the judge, and she could hardly blame him and his wife for refusing to answer their phone.

CHAPTER 62

The search of Tony Ferraro's apartment took place without any of the sheriff's men on hand to help out. The Albany PD had not liked the implication that they might not do a thorough enough job. By the time that Foster got back to her with word that she or one of her officers was not needed, the warrant had already been served and the Ferraro apartment searched. The police had arrived at 6:45 in the morning, apparently to make sure that the occupant would be there, thereby avoiding the necessity of a repeat visit. Thank goodness, Carol thought, they didn't knock the door down.

It was Foster himself who called her to report that the search had taken place and what had been found. She had never expected that the Albany police department would be calling her directly. After all, the search officially had had nothing to do with the death of someone named Carl Keller or the possibility that Ferraro had killed him. It was all about what had happened to the Rasmussen escrow, and it was Francis Foster who needed to know which of his two attorneys had been stealing from it.

"Well, it's done," he said. "I'm sorry you weren't there, but I think they did a good job. I haven't had time to take stock of everything they found - and didn't find. But it looks as if you may have been right. No question about it, there were things belonging to Keller in Tony's place, and I

411

very much doubt that Carl gave them to Tony out of the goodness of his heart. The whole business looked a bit fishy before. Now it stinks to high heaven."

Carol was eager to hear what of Carl's had been found, but she was even more interested to hear how Tony had behaved when he opened the door - still in his pajamas? - to find two police officers standing there, search warrant in hand.

"First things first," Francis said. "Tony didn't come in this morning. There was a message on my office phone which he left at around 7:20 saying he'd be late. No mention of why he'd been detained or how long he'd be gone. Of course I hadn't heard from the PD, so I didn't immediately put two and two together. It wasn't until close to noon that they called to ask if I could come down to headquarters and take a look at what they'd found. Oh, and Tony is still among the missing. No follow-up word from him. Unless he's planning on representing himself, he may be running around town looking for a lawyer who can put a different spin on the evidence."

"Nothing in his phone message to you about the search?" Carol asked. "I'd have thought he'd be angry."

"No, not a word that he'd had visitors before breakfast. He's smart, must have figured that he was in trouble and shouldn't make matters worse with some lame, spur of the moment excuse. But I don't like the fact that he said nothing about why he wouldn't be coming in. Detained. Hell, that could mean anything."

"He's probably buying time to cook up a good explanation for Carl's stuff being in his apartment.

Fortunately for him, Carl's not available to challenge his story. Anyway, what was it of Carl's that the PD found?"

"I just said he's smart, but I'll have to qualify that. He wasn't smart enough to get rid of any of the stuff that was Keller's. He'd stacked it in a clothes closet, all of it. It looks like he took everything that might possibly have told us something about Keller's finances and plans. Bank records - even some old ones. It looks like Carl never threw stuff out. His laptop was there, too. I haven't had time to see what's on it, but Tony probably figured he had a *Quicken* program. Tony wasn't particularly selective, just vacuumed up everything that wasn't nailed down. That includes a pocket calendar for every year going back to 2009. Can't imagine why he thought they'd be important."

"Did you go through the calendar for this year?"

"It's on my to-do list."

"I was wondering what it could tell us about people he saw, when he saw them. Phone numbers. Do the calendars have a place for addresses and phone numbers?"

"I think so, but I haven't taken time to look."

"Let me make a suggestion. Everything that pertains to the escrow account is yours, but the other odds and ends that Ferraro took from Carl's apartment, I'd appreciate it if you let me have them. Particularly the 2013 pocket calendar. I'm still investigating Carl's death, and I need to take a look at anything he wrote down about meetings, phone calls, things like that. I'm not optimistic. He probably used his iPad, and whoever did a job on him at the motel would have taken it away with him. But maybe I'll get lucky, so I'd like to see that calendar."

"That'll be okay, but I'm in no position to come over there. How about I package them up for UPS?"

"I'm sure UPS never loses anything, but I can't risk it. I'll make the trip myself. How's tomorrow morning?"

"I'll be here."

Carol was both pleased and disappointed with Francis's report. In the first place, it made it almost certain that the person who had told Lisa Simmons he was Richard Keller was in fact Tony Ferraro. The fact that many of the items lifted from Carl's apartment pertained to Carl's financial records made it almost equally certain that Tony had tried to frame Carl for the theft from the escrow account. Unfortunately, nothing she had heard from Francis reinforced her suspicion that Tony might have killed Carl. Or had planned to, only to find that Carl had already committed suicide. Now more than ever she was anxious to subject Tony Ferraro to some tough questioning, but neither she nor Foster had any idea where he was.

She tried to focus on other things, like pursuing Judge Hartman, but was finding it hard to take her mind off Ferraro. Why had he not complained to Francis about his apartment being searched? Why had he not explained why he had been detained and when he expected to return to work? Where was he? Carol couldn't overcome her fear that Ferraro, faced with the knowledge that 'they were onto him,' had decided to bolt.

It was at 1:52 after a hasty take-out lunch that JoAnne informed her that Mr. Foster was on the line from Albany. He wouldn't be calling for the second time in less than two hours if it weren't important.

"Francis!" she practically shouted his name. "You have more news, I hope."

"I do, and I don't know what to make of it. Tony called me just ten minutes ago, said he was driving and shouldn't be on his cell, so I was to listen and he'd be brief. I wish I'd been able to record him, but basically it went like this. He says he's experiencing terrible abdominal pains, thinks it may be related to some problem with his recent appendectomy surgery. Rather than go to an emergency room, he decided to get in the car and drive straight to Johns Hopkins."

Carol interrupted.

"Johns Hopkins? That's in Baltimore. If my gut were acting up that bad, I can't imagine driving all that way for help."

"My thought exactly. I started to argue with him, tell him not to be foolish, but he just said he had to get off the phone. I started to ask when he'd be back and he just said 'sorry' and that was that."

"He never said anything about the police searching his apartment?"

"Not a word. I didn't get around to mentioning it when I called this morning, but the PD said he was irate when they showed up at his door. He apparently threatened to call the cops before he remembered that they were the cops. Anyway, he backed off, except for some choice expletives, got dressed, and made one call, which was probably the one to my office. The guy I talked to said that as these things go, it was an easy search. You know, small apartment, basically neat, not much stuff to sort through."

"If Ferraro is on his way to Baltimore, he's going to be detained for more than a few hours. Frankly, I'd take his stomach pains and his trip to Johns Hopkins with a grain of salt. It's just a guess, but it wouldn't surprise me if he's on the lam. And if he is, he won't be easy to find. What do you propose to do?"

"Good question, and I don't have an answer. I suppose I should give him a chance to prove that his story about going to Hopkins is true. But considering what happened to him today, he knows he won't be facing a happy homecoming when he gets back. *If* he comes back."

"I've never done one of those all-points alert bulletins," Carol said, "and I doubt it would be effective in a case like this. He could already be in Cleveland or Richmond, even Miami if he ditched his car and caught a flight. Damn! It never occurred to me that he might run. How could I have been so stupid."

"It's not your fault, Carol." Foster was trying to sympathize with the sheriff, but what he had to say next was sure to upset her even more. "I hate to be the bearer of more bad news, but about those alibis you asked me to get from my people. So far only four have responded, and Ferraro is one of them. Unfortunately, he makes no attempt to provide an alibi. I've got his statement right here in front of me. Let me read what he says. 'How can you expect me to remember what I was doing a month or more ago? I live alone, I'm not what you would call a social animal, and I've never kept a diary or understood people who do. If it helps, you can say I read a lot - typically historical fiction, watch forgettable TV, and occasionally spend an hour or two on M & B homework. If necessary, I'll make something up, but rest assured that I had nothing to do with Carl Keller's death.'"

"Did he say anything to you when he handed in his non-alibi?"

"No. He left it with Marge in the front office. According to her, he said something about it being a waste of time."

"Wonderful," Carol said. "Look, if you can get his license plate number and relevant information on the car - make and model, color, the usual info, I'd appreciate it."

"I'll do what I can. Oh, you should also know that your friend Ziegler can't provide an alibi either. I think she's standing on principle."

CHAPTER 63

Kevin's offer to be the one who would go to Albany to pick up Carl's calendar didn't surprise Carol. Her rejection of his offer didn't surprise Kevin. Not only was it her case; she looked forward to the opportunity to talk further with Foster about Ferraro's sudden disappearance and to gauge the reaction to it of some of the firm's lawyers.

In spite of her need to make yet another trip to Albany, Carol doubted that it had ever been so frustratingly long a drive. It was as if the trip was but a mile by mile reminder of how slowly the Keller case was moving toward what she hoped would be its denouement. Nothing was going right. Tony Ferraro, who couldn't come up with an alibi for the night of Carl Keller's death, had now left town, ostensibly to receive medical treatment in Baltimore. Donna Sugar had declined to provide an alibi, even if evidence of where she had been was almost certainly as near at hand as her purse or boudoir. Judge Hartman wouldn't even answer his phone. And Randall Truscott's charges against the judge continued to generate much heat but little light in the *Times Union* and its downscale rival, the *Tattler*.

The trip actually took no longer than usual, and by 11:20 Carol was sitting in Francis Foster's office, drinking coffee and listening to M & B's senior partner sharing the day's mounting frustrations. He had learned that Johns Hopkins was not simply another hospital, but a large complex of medical institutions that dealt with everything from cardiac research to treatment of the many problems that can affect the human eye. There was no central site which could say that a man named Anthony Ferraro was in room X in building C. Francis had spoken with seven different people, some anxious to help but unable to do so, others impatient with his inability to answer the simplest questions about Ferraro's scheduled appointment, doctor, or specific ailment. It had become increasingly apparent that Tony Ferraro had either lost his way in the byzantine maze of Johns Hopkins or had never sought its help with whatever his problem was. Or, Carol thought, he had no medical problem and Johns Hopkins was but a red herring to keep Foster occupied while he put miles between himself and his pursuers. By this time, Ferraro would probably have realized that those pursuers consisted not only of the M & B Law firm but the Cumberland County Sheriff's Department as well.

Their conversation eventually shifted to the question of what could be learned from the things Tony had removed from Carl's apartment. Foster had already assigned one of his staff the task of seeing what information could be gleaned from Carl's laptop. Carol would have preferred to take it home with her and give that assignment to Officer Byrnes, but it was too late for that. She settled for the pocket calendars. The one for the current year was of greatest interest, but she took them all in the hope that she could learn more about what Carl had been thinking and doing since she had left the firm.

When Carol left Francis, she paid brief visits to several people she remembered from her days with the firm, but they seemed reluctant to discuss

Ferraro. Perhaps they were uncertain just how things stood between him and Foster. Or perhaps they were simply uncertain of her role in the matter. Only Gretchen was willing to be more forthright, but it quickly became apparent that she actually knew less than Carol did about the search of Tony's apartment.

Much as she would have liked to go through Carl's 2013 pocket calendar, Carol decided to save that task until she got back to her office. She hoped that Carl had made entries which would shed light on his reason for coming to Crooked Lake and the *Welcome Inn*. Perhaps there would be names and phone numbers which would provide clues to what he had been doing and with whom in the weeks leading up to his death. Perhaps. But she was pessimistic. Carl had been very opaque the few times she had seen him. Marty Reece at the motel had commented on how uncommunicative he was. There was little reason to believe that the small black calendar would reveal a different man.

———

Back in the office, Carol had a couple of hours before calling it quits for the day. She closed her door and opened the 2013 calendar. She turned first to the rear of the little black book, the section devoted to names and phone numbers. Most of the entries meant nothing to her. Four of them did, including, of course, Randall Truscott. But one of the four surprised her.

It was not listed under the letter H where it belonged. H was filled with the names of people about whom she knew nothing, names like

Henderson, Hancock, and Hutchinson. The name that surprised her had been added to the underused page devoted to names beginning with the letter Q. It was that of Lindsay Hartman. No address was listed, but two phone numbers were. One had an Albany code, presumably the judge's home phone. The other had an even more familiar area code, Carol's own. It was obvious that Carl had known how to reach the judge before he took up his brief and ill- fated residence at *Welcome Inn*, both at his home in Albany and at his cottage on Crooked Lake.

Carol found this more than mildly interesting. Carl had discovered that the judge had a cottage at the lake and had either called there or planned to do so. Was it possible that Carl had not come to the lake to 'stalk' her but to see the judge? The fact that he had left his calendar with the lake phone number in his apartment would not have been a serious problem. What was important was that Carl knew that the judge had a lake address; a local directory would have his phone number.

Enough speculation. She flipped the pages of the calendar back to a date prior to the beginning of the Truscott trial and began to work her way to the day he had left Albany and come to the lake. It quickly became apparent that Carl rarely made entries. Either he only had a few appointments or a memory so reliable that he didn't need reminders. The first familiar name he came across was Truscott's. She had expected this. After all, Carl had been his counsel. But even appointments with the defendant had apparently been few and far between, and it wasn't until the trial was over that another familiar name showed up. Francis Foster.

The entry made no reference to the time of an appointment; it consisted only of three angry words, boldly capitalized: FUCK YOU FRANCIS. Carol made a mental note to remember the date. It must have been the day that Foster had sacked Carl. The calendar didn't say so, but the absence of other entries with Francis's name suggested that Carl had been peremptorily dismissed.

There was a brief gap before another familiar name appeared. It was Tony Ferraro's. In this case it was clearly stated that the two of them were meeting to discuss the Rasmussen case. And then, two days later, came the final familiar name, Hartman. There was nothing about an appointment, only a brief note saying 'call Hartman'. Carol sat back in her chair and tried to imagine what had prompted this entry in Carl's calendar. Had Carl had a phone call from the judge asking him to return the call? Had Carl himself decided he wanted to call Hartman and used the calendar to remind him to do so? Each of these possibilities invited a second question. Why would the judge have wanted to speak with Carl? Why would Carl have wanted to speak with the judge?

Carol again set aside the urge to speculate and leafed through the remaining pages of the calendar, looking for evidence that there had been further efforts of the men to communicate. And there had been two such efforts. The first was identical to the earlier one: 'call Hartman'. The other was even less specific. It read simply 'Hartman'. This final reference to the judge was also Carl's final entry in the calendar. The date was the day before Carl had checked into *Welcome Inn*. Carol had no way of knowing whether Carl and the judge had actually spoken with each other. But one of them, perhaps both of them, had sought such a conversation.

Carol went over the relevant calendar pages a second time. Something had been going on between Carl and the judge, but she had no idea what it was. Carl would never be able to tell her. But when she left at the end of the day, she was determined that Judge Lindsay Hartman would. And he would do it tomorrow, even if it meant another trip to Albany. This time she didn't even pause to reflect on the consequences for the department's budget of such a trip.

CHAPTER 64

"Hello, this is Hazel."

Carol had feared that her call would once again go unanswered.

"Good morning, Mrs. Hartman. This is Carol Kelleher."

"Oh, thank goodness. I was afraid that it would be that reporter from the *Times Union*."

Poor woman, Carol thought. She thinks her husband's only problem is the call girl.

"I'm hoping your husband is there. I very much need to talk with him."

"I'm sorry, but you missed him by about half an hour. He's on his way to the lake. These stories in the Albany papers are making life miserable for Lindsay. I've told him he ought to stay at the cottage for awhile instead of commuting back and forth. At least he can breathe over there. Trouble is, he's got work to do here."

Hazel Hartman was worried about her husband. Carol was elated that she wouldn't have to drive to Albany again.

"Actually, Mrs. Hartman, I'm glad he's on his way the the lake. I really must see him, and I won't be talking about anything in the *Times Union*. Did he tell you how long he expects to stay at the cottage?"

"I wish he'd take a week or two, but knowing Lindsay he'll be back here by Tuesday. He can't sit still. Try to get him to relax. Can you do that for me?"

"I'll give it a try," Carol said, knowing that what she would be talking about with the judge would not help him to relax.

She had taken the trip to and from Albany so often that calculating when Judge Hartman would arrive at his cottage was no problem. She'd give him an extra hour, no more, and then knock on his door. There was little to gain and much to lose by calling and seeking an appointment.

The judge was obviously not happy to see who was at his door.

"Hello, Carol. You'll forgive me for not greeting you with a big smile. I've just arrived, hoping to have a couple of days of peace and quiet, and who do I find at my door but the sheriff."

"For which I apologize," Carol said, "but it's very important that we talk, and your wife said you were coming to the cottage."

"I won't pretend to be pleased to see you. But come on in. I'd rather spend a few minutes in your company than with those nosy reporters."

He stepped aside to let her in. She thought he'd want to talk about whatever she had on her mind down on the dock, or at least on the deck, but he stopped in the living room, urged her to take a seat, and offered something to drink.

"I'm not quite sure what we have. I haven't had time to make any iced tea. Let me take a look."

"Please, don't bother. I don't plan to stay long."

"Whatever you say, but I'd like a beer. Sure you won't join me?"

"No thanks."

Carol had expected Hartman to be out of sorts. But she was surprised that he didn't look well. He was under strain, and it showed. When he returned with a beer, he took a seat across from her and promptly took a long drink from a bottle of *Sam Adams*.

"I'm sure you know about the charges against me which have been running in the *Time Union*. I hope you never have to face something like this. If I look or sound distracted, it's because I am distracted. Now, perhaps you can tell me why you're here."

"You have my sympathy, Judge, and I can assure you that I have no intention of talking about what the *Times Union* is publishing. What concerns me is the recent death of Carl Keller. You recently authorized a search of the apartment of one of Francis Foster's attorneys, a man named Anthony Ferraro. The search found, as Francis suspected it would, a substantial number of things belonging to Mr. Keller. It looks very much as if Mr. Ferraro had removed these things from Keller's apartment without his permission. It is for Francis to take whatever action regarding Ferraro he thinks is necessary, but what concerns me is a pocket calendar belonging to Keller that was found in Ferraro's apartment. I thought it might provide information which would help our investigation into Keller's death."

Carol paused. The judge waited.

"This calendar, which covers the period of the Truscott trial, contains three entries in which Carl Keller mentions your name. They do not appear to be appointments, but rather suggest that you were calling him and requesting a call back. The dates on which Keller made these notes all come after the end of the trial and before he left Albany to come to Crooked Lake. I'm obviously interested in your reason for calling Keller and whether you and he spoke with each other after the trial and after Francis severed Keller's ties with Morgenstern and Brauchli."

Hartman's face was hard to read. When he spoke, his voice was level. Perhaps a bit tired.

"It's really quite simple, sheriff. I did call Mr. Keller after the trial. I had learned that Foster had dismissed him, and felt badly that he had lost his position with the firm. It was understandable that he might blame me, and I thought it was appropriate to offer my regrets for what had happened. There was never a question of apologizing for having cited Keller for contempt. What he was trying to put on the record was both prejudicial and hearsay. But I was shocked by Foster's action, and I wanted Keller to know that."

"Did Keller ever return your calls?"

"No. That's why I tried to reach him several times."

"So you and Keller never spoke with each other after the trial?"

"Unfortunately no." Was it Carol's imagination or had Hartman hesitated briefly before answering her question? She decided to press the matter.

"The pocket calendar I'm referring to contains both your Albany phone number and the number here at the cottage. I've been wondering if perhaps you and Keller did speak at some time, perhaps when both of you were here at the lake."

"I've already answered your question, and I have no idea why this calendar you're talking about had my cottage number in it." Lindsay Hartman no longer sounded tired. He now sounded annoyed that the sheriff was having trouble accepting the fact that he hadn't talked with Carl Keller since the Truscott trial.

It was time for Carol to ask the judge about an alibi. If he didn't like her questions about having spoken with Keller, he would surely be offended by a request for an alibi.

"Judge Hartman, I hope you will not be offended by another question. It is one I shall put to quite a few people. I do not believe that you had anything to do with Mr. Keller's death, but in my business it is not only a good idea to be thorough, it is rule number one. So I would appreciate it if you would tell me where you were and what you were doing the night of Keller's death. That would be July 2nd."

"I can't imagine why you would think I might have killed Keller. I'll give you the benefit of the doubt and accept your justification that you're only being thorough. As for where I was that night, it is impossible for me to answer your question off the top of my head. It was at about that time that I was so busy that I frequently stayed overnight at my club. That would be the Harvard Club."

"We can check that out, or you can let me know if you recall something else you were doing. I know how difficult your days have been, and how much you enjoy fishing. Perhaps you were taking a break and spending some time at the cottage. Why don't you take a look at your calendar and let me know when you were over here in the weeks after the Truscott trial."

The judge rose from his seat. He smiled, but it wasn't a pleasant smile and he didn't intend it to be.

"You do not come right out and say so, but it is obvious that in your mind I am a suspect in Mr.

Keller's death. I am sorry that this unfounded suspicion is causing you to waste so much of your valuable time. As for me, I came over from Albany today to do some fishing. Do you suppose we could wrap this conversation up so that I can go down to the dock and bait a hook before the storm clouds open up?"

"I'm sorry to have bothered you, Judge. I've said it many times to good people like you, and I'll say it again. I'm only doing my job, and there are times when it's painful. Much like your finding Carl Keller in contempt of court."

Carol let herself out with a parting 'good luck' to the fisherman judge.

———

By the end of the day, Carol still had no alibi from Lindsay Hartman, nor had she expected one. What she did have, after some delicate negotiating over the phone, was information that the judge had not spent the night of July 2nd at the Harvard Club in Albany.

CHAPTER 65

The blue Honda Accord idled in a long line of traffic on Route 87 north of Plattsburg. In fact, it had been idling most of the time for half an hour, creeping forward, car length by car length, every so often. The driver, Tony Ferraro, was frustrated. There had to be some problem at the border crossing into Canada. Tony had taken this route many times to ski at Mont Tremblant, and he couldn't recall an instance when there had been a problem at customs.

He shut off the engine, got out of the car, and walked up to the vehicle in front of him in the long backup.

"This is crazy, isn't it?" he said when the driver rolled down his window. "Any idea what's wrong?"

"I think it's that terrorist scare they had yesterday in Montreal. The Canadians are probably going through every car with a fine tooth comb."

"There was a terrorist attack in Montreal?" Ferraro asked, clearly surprised.

"You didn't hear? Somebody was going to blow up a mall, but it seems they foiled the plot in time."

"Shit. If that's the problem, it'll be over an hour before we even get to the border."

Ferraro went back to his car and took stock of his situation. He'd been driving around ever since the police had confronted him with a search warrant, and he was both tired and increasingly worried that he was making his situation worse.

His decision to hit the road rather than go to work had been a spur of the moment one, and in retrospect not all that wise. It hadn't taken him long to recognize that the Johns Hopkins story wouldn't fool anybody, and now he was having second thoughts about the Canadian alternative. What if he finally got to border customs and they asked to see his passport? Unfortunately it was back in the apartment. But even if he'd had it on him and his bladder held out until he got across the border, what was he going to do? He wished he'd taken the time to think things through before precipitously leaving Albany.

Perhaps his situation needn't be so dire as he'd assumed. He hated Foster for searching his apartment, and he knew that his stash of Keller's things had been found. But he could still claim that the reason he'd gotten into Keller's apartment and taken those things was to find evidence to support his belief that Keller had been stealing from the Rasmussen account. He'd be contrite about the break in, an irresponsible error of judgement, but there was no way Foster could prove that he had done it to frame Keller.

It still wasn't too late to return to Albany and to Morgenstern and Brauchli. He'd never been to a specialist at Hopkins, but Foster needn't know that. He could claim that the pains in his stomach had been diagnosed as the result of a kidney stone. Foster might well ask why he had gone all the way to Baltimore to learn this, and he could simply say he'd panicked, thinking that he might have an infection where he'd just had surgery and needed top flight medical attention.

Tony considered his options, and finally decided he'd be better off to return to Albany. An unpleasant chat with Foster would follow, but he was sure he could hold his own. Once again he would have to admit to bad judgment, but Foster could not afford to lose two of his attorneys in a single month. A little groveling and some practice on his apology should do it.

That decision made, he carefully maneuvered the Honda until it was possible to get out of the long line of cars and head back down 87. He had roughly a three hour drive ahead of him, which was nothing compared to the time it had taken from Baltimore to the Canadian border.

———

Ferraro stopped off at the apartment to grab a shower and a shave and to put on a fresh suit. He arrived at the office much later than was his custom, physically and emotionally exhausted. But he made it a point to act as if nothing unusual had happened. He hoped that Foster hadn't said anything to his colleagues about the fact that his apartment had been searched and that he had been mysteriously detained. Fortunately, the only person he saw was Gretchen Ziegler. Unfortunately, seeing her reminded him of her friend the sheriff, which set off another wave of anxiety. But he pushed that out of his mind and rapped on Francis Foster's door.

"Yes?" The managing partner's tone of voice was not welcoming.

"It's me, Tony. I need to see you."

It was only a matter of seconds before the door opened. Foster looked neither angry nor surprised.

"Our prodigal son has returned," he said.

"You might say that," Tony replied, trying his best to act as if he were glad to be back. "But I thought you'd want to see me, and, well - here I am."

"Why don't you take a chair and tell me whether your medical problem is under control."

"Oh, yes. It turned out to be nothing but a kidney stone. But I'd much rather talk about what happened at my apartment day before yesterday. You never told me you'd authorized a search. It sure took me by surprise, and, to be quite frank, I was hurt that you'd do it without telling me."

"I didn't tell you, Tony, because if I had I suspect you would have gotten rid of all those things you'd stolen from Keller's apartment."

"Francis, please. I am not a thief. I would have returned them, all of them, but of course I couldn't because Carl is dead. I visited Carl's apartment and borrowed a number of things because I hoped they might prove what I told you - that Carl had taken money from the Rasmussen account. I'm sure you can understand why I didn't ask Carl for them."

"Don't you have a question for me?"

"A question?" Tony looked and sounded puzzled.

"You say that you 'borrowed' all of these things so that you could prove that Carl was not honoring his fiduciary obligations. I have studied what the police found in your apartment. Very carefully. Why don't you ask me if it proves that Carl was a thief?"

It was a very uncomfortable Tony Ferraro who coughed and tried to answer his boss's question.

"I suppose different people might interpret things a bit differently. What is your opinion?"

"Let us just say that there is nothing on Carl's computer or in his financial and other papers that points to his having stolen anything from the Rasmussen account. You obviously spent time going through Carl's things, just as I did. And I'm sure you didn't find anything to back up your charge, anymore than I did. So how is that you know that Carl stole from the account?"

"He told me. It's like I told you, he did it and then had a bad conscience and promised to replace the money."

"It's too bad he isn't here to confirm that, isn't it?"

"Francis, you have to believe me. I know it looks bad, but I swear that it happened just like I told you it did."

This homecoming of the prodigal son was not going as Tony had hoped it would.

"What I don't understand," Foster said, "is why if Carl had a crisis of conscience and told you he'd repay what he'd stolen, you would still go ahead and break into his apartment and look for proof. Why would Carl confess to stealing from the account if he hadn't done it?"

Tony took a deep breath. He'd almost forgotten how tired he was.

"I know it was wrong, but somehow I didn't trust him. It was the way he talked about things, at least to me. It was like he always had an agenda of his own."

Francis Foster got up and went over to the window which looked out on a busy commercial street in Albany.

"I suppose you could be right about Carl, but I think you've made it very clear that you, too, have an agenda of your own. And that has made me very unhappy. Do you understand?"

Ferraro sensed that he had better leave well enough alone.

"I understand. Where do we stand, you and me?"

"I honestly don't know. I didn't expect you to show up at my door a few minutes ago. In fact, it had occurred to me that maybe you had decided to cut your ties to M & B, to all of us, and had simply gone off to create a new life for yourself. It would seem that you haven't done that."

"No, I would like to stay with M & B."

"What I think we have, Tony, is a problem of trust. I'm sure that -"

Tony started to interrupt.

"No, not now," Francis continued. "I have a suggestion. If I were you, I'd get in touch with the sheriff of Cumberland County. I know that you have met her. I think it's more important that you discuss your relationship with Carl Keller with her than with me."

"Of course, if you think I should."

"I do, and if I were you, I'd talk with her more frankly than you have with me."

It was clear that their conversation was at an end. Ferraro was in no mood to go back to his office and pretend to be at work. He was even less eager to call the sheriff.

CHAPTER 66

Although she had discussed Carl Keller's mental state with virtually everybody connected with the case, she had never told anyone that he had committed suicide. It was possible that the person who had slit Carl's throat knew that he was already dead, but not likely. Therefore, she still had an advantage. She decided to use it.

Her efforts to reach Donna Sugar were, as she expected they would be, initially unsuccessful. But she persevered, and eventually found herself speaking to the call girl.

"At last," Carol said. "I was afraid you might have gone on vacation."

"No such luck. Your call surprises me. Off hand I can't think of anything we need to talk about."

"There's one point where I may have to differ with you, Ms. Sugar. When last we spoke, I was interested in whether you could tell me what you were doing the night of Carl Keller's death. You declined to tell me, citing the importance of your privacy. Normally I would simply leave it at that. Like you, I respect my privacy. But sometimes situations arise in which it becomes necessary to make an exception. I thought I should share one such situation with you. It concerns Judge Lindsay Hartman."

"I would rather not talk about the judge. As you know, the papers are full of nasty allegations about the judge and me. Frankly, I'm fed up with it and in no mood to spend my time discussing the judge and our so-called relationship."

"I can appreciate your reluctance, but please bear with me. As you know, I am investigating Mr. Keller's death, and in doing so I have had to consider who might have killed him. Quite obviously, people who initially look like suspects may turn out to be absolutely innocent. In all probability, Judge Hartman had nothing to do with Mr. Keller's death. I am certainly not assuming that he did. I am only being thorough, as law enforcement officials must be. In any event, I am asking these hypothetical suspects to provide alibis for where they were when Mr. Keller was killed.

"Let's look at Judge Hartman's situation. He took action during the Truscott trial to exclude information he thought Carl Keller wanted to introduce. I think we both know that that information, whether true or false, concerned the rumor that you and the judge were in a relationship. After the trial, Carl still possessed that information. I am not assuming it was or is true, but what if Carl thought it was. If he did, he might have been willing to go public with it. None of us is now in a position to know what Carl might have done because he was killed not long after the trial ended. Put yourself in the judge's shoes. Might he not have considered getting rid of Carl to prevent his suspicions from becoming public?"

"That is ridiculous. Why am I listening to you? You're as bad as Randall."

"Let me repeat. I am not suggesting that you and the judge were in a relationship, nor am I suggesting that the judge killed - or even considered killing - Mr. Keller. But Judge Hartman is an intelligent and rational man. Is it inconceivable that he would have entertained the thought that Carl might go public with his suspicions?"

"But the judge knew the rumor was false," Sugar said, ignoring the sheriff's question.

"Ms. Sugar, please think about it. Let us assume that the rumor had no foundation. Rumors have a way of taking root in the public's imagination. The fact that a rumor is false doesn't mean that people who would be hurt by a rumor wouldn't try to squelch it. That is what Judge Hartman did during the trial. Hypothetically he might have tried to do it after the trial as well, except that by then another citation for contempt was impossible. Killing the person who could spread the rumor was not."

For the first time since she had answered the phone, Donna Sugar said nothing.

"The judge has told me," Carol continued, "that he isn't sure where he was the night Mr. Keller was killed. He thinks he was at the Harvard Club. Unfortunately, I know for a fact that he was not at the Harvard Club. So you see, the judge needs an alibi, something - excuse me, someone - to prove he could not have been anywhere near Mr. Keller when he was killed. Unfortunately, the judge has a cottage on Crooked Lake, only a few miles from where Carl was staying, which adds to his problem. I know that you have great respect for the judge. I was hoping that you could offer proof that Judge Hartman was nowhere near the *Welcome Inn* on the night of July 2nd."

"But how can I possibly do that?"

"I have done my best to stay as far away as possible from the rumor that you and the judge have had a relationship. But it seems to me that if there is any truth to that rumor, this may be the time to come forward and give the judge his alibi by admitting that he was with you. I would have to leave it to you to specify just where the two of you were that evening, but I'm sure you could take care of that."

"I can't believe this. You are demanding that I announce to the world that the rumor about the judge and me is true, that we've been sleeping together. How does that help him?"

"In the first place, your alibi for the judge need not be announced to the world. Its value would lie solely in the fact that my department would then have a good reason to cross the judge off our list of suspects. But more importantly, I should think the judge would rather have it revealed that he's been in a relationship with you than run the risk of being tried for murder."

If Hartman and Sugar had indeed been sleeping together, the call girl faced a problem. She could stand by the judge, supporting his rejection of Truscott's allegation in the *Times Union* and the *Tattler*. But so could she support him by admitting that he had spent the night of Carl's death with her, thereby giving him an alibi. She'll have to decide which of the two positions she should take. Before Sugar said anything, Carol gave her something else to think about.

"I must warn you that it wouldn't be a good idea to claim the judge was with you that night if it isn't true. Prosecution lawyers are bears when it comes to alibis. They love to tear them down, and they frequently find a way to do it. I assume that you'll be calling the judge to discuss strategy."

Donna Sugar laughed.

"If it's only a nasty rumor, it would be rather presumptuous, don't you think?"

It was a clever answer, but Carol suspected that Sugar would be in touch with Hartman. How they chose to handle the problem should logically depend on whether the judge had visited *Welcome Inn* the night of July 2nd. Carol was treating him as a suspect because he had a motive for killing Carl, but she still had no idea where he had been that fatal night. She wasn't close to the judge, but for some reason she hoped that he had been with the call girl.

———

JoAnne had been taking call after call for the sheriff all day long. As of late afternoon, none of those calls were what Carol considered urgent. When what she considered an urgent call did come through, it was from Tony Ferraro in Albany. He was the last person she had expected to be calling. Francis Foster had not given her a follow up report on Ferraro's 'disappearance,' so she had assumed that he was somewhere many miles from Albany and still incommunicado.

"Mr. Ferraro. What a surprise. To what do I owe the pleasure?"

"Francis," was his one word answer. "When I got back he urged me to call you. Said it was more important that I discuss my situation with you than with him."

"Your situation?"

"To be quite frank, I'd say he wasn't pleased that I missed a couple of days at the firm. I presume you know that he arranged to have my apartment searched. I was miffed, as you might imagine, and before I'd thought it out carefully I got into the car and drove to hell and gone. It's obvious that Francis doesn't trust me. And I've got a hunch you don't either. At least I'm assuming this business of establishing alibis for the night Keller got killed is your doing. So I guess I'm calling because I need to get back in Francis's good graces and because I must assure you that I had absolutely nothing to do with Keller's death. There, does that sum up my situation?"

"I take it that you did, in fact, pay a visit to Carl's apartment and remove a number of things."

"I did, and they helped me establish that he was illegally taking money from an account."

"This is between you and Francis, not me. Unless you'd like to tell me what it was that confirmed your suspicion of Keller."

"It's complicated," Tony said. "What is it that you need from me?"

"I'd appreciate it if you'd explain your unusual meeting with Lisa Simmons. Why did you tell her your name was Richard Keller?"

"You know about that?"

"Mr. Ferraro, my business is to find out things. Things such as people's use of phony names. You pretended to be Carl's cousin so you could get a key to his apartment from Lisa Simmons. Not to mention getting her to tell you where you could find Carl. Why don't you tell me why you thought it was necessary to do these things - and to wear bandages on your face when you did them?"

"It's like I told Francis, so I could prove what Keller was doing."

"Surely there are ways of making a case other than by sneaking around, wearing what amounts to a mask, using a false name. And why did you need to know where you could find Carl?"

Carol wished she could see Ferraro's face. If he'd had his wits about him, it should have occurred to him that, sooner or later, the sheriff would learn about Lisa's experience with the man in the mask who called himself Carl's cousin.

"I guess I thought I might be able to persuade him to pay the money back," he said.

"The way I heard it, Carl is supposed to have had a change of heart and had already reimbursed the account before he left for Crooked Lake."

"That's what he said, but it was a lie. I figured it was worth my time to talk with him again."

"And did you do that?"

"I was going to, but I never got to talk with him."

"Why not?" Carol asked. "You knew where you could find him. Why not go over to the motel and reason with him?"

"That's what I tried to do," Ferraro said, beginning to sound defensive. "I went to see him. But he wasn't there."

"And when was it that you went to the motel and he was't there?"

"Late June, early July. I don't remember the date."

"Day or night?"

"I couldn't go until after work, and it was a long day. I drove over one evening."

"You could have made the trip on a weekend."

"What is this? It sounds as if you're cross examining me."

"Mr. Ferraro, somebody visited Carl Keller at the *Welcome Inn* just off Crooked Lake on the night of July 2nd. When he left, Carl was dead. His throat had been slit. Francis Foster asked each of M & B's lawyers for an explanation of what they were doing that night. Let's call it an alibi. He asked you and your colleagues for an alibi, but you didn't provide him with one. I am investigating Carl's death. Your interest in Carl is of interest to me. I really do need to know where you were the night of July 2nd."

Carol could hear Tony inhaling, all the way from Albany to Cumberland.

"You think I killed Keller, is that it?"

"I'm sure if you asked around you'd find that what I am about to say to you is almost always my answer to a question like that. I do not know who killed Carl. I am conducting an investigation, the purpose of which is to find out who killed him. The way I do it is by asking questions and listening to what people have to tell me. That is what I have been doing. So, no, I do not think you killed Carl Keller, but I would be more certain of it if you would supply me with a verifiable alibi."

"I see," Tony said. "Okay, I promise to see what I can do about pinning down the date."

"Let's go back a bit. You say you went to see Carl, but he wasn't there. How do you know he wasn't there?"

"It was obvious," Ferraro said. "The place was dark, and I got no response when I knocked on the door."

"Did you speak to the manager?"

"Why would I do that?"

"Carl told Ms. Simmons he was staying at *Welcome Inn*, but it's less likely that he also gave her his room number. So it occurred to me that you'd get that information at the front office."

"Well, yes, that might have been necessary if Keller's car hadn't been there. People usually park in front of the unit where they're staying unless the place is all parked up. And it wasn't. His car was the only one I saw."

"His car was there but he wasn't? That seems unlikely. The motel isn't close to other houses or to a restaurant or a gas station. It's fairly isolated. If he'd been going out, I'd think he'd take his car."

"So you think maybe he was in his room and asleep?"

"That's a possibility. Did you try the door?"

"At 10:30 at night?"

"If I'd driven several hours just to see somebody, I don't think I'd have given up so easily."

"You're right, sheriff," Ferraro finally admitted. "I did wonder if Keller had fallen asleep and was sleeping so soundly he couldn't hear me. But the door was locked. There was no way I could have gotten in. Do you think Keller might have been dead while I was out there banging on his door?"

"It would depend on what night we're talking about. If I were you, I'd do some very hard thinking about your trip to the lake. You admit you came over to the *Welcome Inn*. You have made it clear that you came for the purpose of talking with Carl Keller. Your conversation was to have been about the Rasmussen escrow, concerning which there seems to be some disagreement between you and Francis Foster. One way or another, your life and Carl's seem to have become very much intertwined during the early summer, which makes you - and please note my adjective - a *tentative* suspect in

Carl's death. You could change that by producing a water proof alibi for the night Carl died."

I think they're the ones, Carol said to herself when she got off the phone. The person who had slit Carl Keller's throat was going to be either Judge Hartman or Tony Ferraro. There were other possibilities, of course, but she could think of no one else who had a motive as powerful as theirs. Yet she knew that neither of them would ever be convicted of murder.

CHAPTER 67

Kevin had made a trip into Southport to mail a few letters (bills to be more precise), and had discovered that the town square was to be the site of an evening concert by the town band. It was June Pringle, who was on duty at the post office, who had informed him of the event.

"Are you going to the concert tonight?" she asked.

"What concert are you talking about?"

"The town band. There'll be a good crowd, but the band is getting kind of thin. Losing Sean Jordan and Amy Meacham really hurt."

Kevin and Carol had once been regulars at the town square concerts, but they had gotten out of the habit of attending. He didn't know the names June had mentioned.

"Who are they?"

"They graduated high school last year, went off to college. She was their only flute, and Sean, he was the only good trombonist. That's the way it is now days. A handful of old timers, most of the rest high schoolers. I think they'd stop doing concerts if it weren't for Gus."

Kevin realized that he hadn't been much involved in the local scene lately.

"Gus?"

"Mathers. He must be all of 75, but he still plays a mean trumpet. You should be ashamed of yourself, music teacher that you are. There must be some instrument you could be playing in the band."

447

"I'm afraid not. Town bands don't need pianos. But I could join the crowd. Thanks for reminding me."

When Carol got home, the first thing she noticed when she walked into the cottage was the picnic hamper on the kitchen table.

"What's this? A picnic?"

"Sort of," Kevin said as he gave her a hug. "We're going to the band concert down in the square. I haven't heard a bad rendition of the national anthem since the super bowl."

"What prompted you to do this? We haven't been in ages."

"That's the point. I figured the least we can do is support our amateur musicians. There are a couple of ham and cheese sandwiches and a bottle of Chardonnay in the hamper. We've still got some time, so you won't have to go in uniform."

"I'd rather be late than show up for a picnic in this outfit."

Carol headed for the bedroom to change into something more comfortable. It was a warm night, so she opted for shorts and a T-shirt with a Crooked Lake logo.

"How's this?" She asked when she joined Kevin on the deck.

"Very sexy. You don't suppose you'll be violating the town square dress code, do you?"

"No way. They even allow bathing suits."

An hour later they had spread a beach towel across from the band stand and were nibbling the ham and cheese when the band launched into Rossini's *La Gazza ladra* Overture.

Kevin leaned over to whisper to Carol.

"The drummer's good. He doesn't look older than 15."

"He isn't," she whispered back. "That's the Carletons' kid. They grow talent around Crooked Lake like they grow grapes."

It was a pleasant evening, although Kevin had to agree that the band was a bit thin and could have used a good flutist.

It was 9:20 when they settled down back at the cottage with a respectable raspberry pie.

"How's it feel to spend an entire evening without a word about the Keller case?" Kevin asked.

"The evening isn't over yet," Carol said. "There's still time for me to tell you that I've finally come up with my final slate of suspects. Two of them."

"No kidding? Only two? What happened to all of those other Albany denizens?"

"No motive that would pass muster. Carl got his throat cut by either Judge Hartman or Tony Ferraro. I've been giving it a lot of thought, and I can't see how it could be anybody else."

"What ever happened to Marty Reece? Our man from Pend Oreille?"

"No motive."

"After all the work I did over the phone with the Idaho police."

"Sorry. Reece - or, if you prefer, Rice - just doesn't make sense. And the judge and Ferraro do. Ferraro wanted to make sure his plan to frame Carl for stealing funds wasn't exposed, and Hartman wanted to be sure Carl didn't expose his affair with Ms. Sugar. Considering the stakes, I'd call those a couple of persuasive motives. And as far as we know, both of them had an opportunity to pull it off. It'll be interesting to see what kind of alibis they come up with."

They talked about the problems facing the judge and the M & B attorney. It was while they were considering Carol's conversation with Ferraro that she brought up the issue of access to room 8 at *Welcome Inn*.

"He says he couldn't open the door. And it's obvious that new locks were installed at the motel. Just about the only thing that is new over there. I'm sending Sam over there tomorrow to see how tough it would be to get into a dead man's locked room."

"Sounds like a good move, but don't forget that Marty Reece had an extra key. It may be hard to find his motive, but there's no question he had by far the best opportunity to use a knife on Keller."

"You can't agree to delete Reece from the suspect list, can you?"

"I'm sure you're right, but I think it would be a pretty dramatic ending to your friend Keller's case if his killer turned out to be a wild card from Idaho."

"For a moment there I almost forgot," Carol said. "Keller's killer was Keller. We're still looking for somebody whose rap sheet won't include Keller's murder."

———

"Got something I'd like you to do first thing," Carol told Sam Bridges as the squad meeting broke up the next morning. "Are you feeling unusually strong? Or if your strength fails you, unusually creative?"

"Now how am I supposed to answer questions like that? If it's strength you're after, maybe you should ask Grieves to do it. As for creative, I'd recommend that you do it yourself."

"Tell you what. Take Grieves with you. I can't go, so I'll let you and him also be the creative team on the theory that two heads are better than one. I'm getting the feeling that whether someone could have broken into the *Welcome Inn* is going to become an issue in the Keller case. I'd like you to go down to the motel, tell the manager what you're up to, and then see whether you can get into one of their locked rooms without a key. No need to break down the door, but pretend you're a burglar if muscle doesn't do the trick. Those doors have been upgraded fairly recently, so it probably won't be easy."

"Some new development in the Keller case?"

"I don't know, but I have a hunch that things may start popping within the week."

"Good," Sam said emphatically. "I'm beginning to get tired of this one, just like I did last year with all the Mobleys and their Cessna."

"Patience, Sam. Try to remember that this time you got to interrogate a real live, bona fide call girl."

CHAPTER 68

"I think you'd better get over here." It was Sam on his cell phone, calling from the *Welcome Inn*.

"What's the problem?" Carol asked.

"I'm not sure. But something's wrong. Nobody's here, Reece's car is gone. For that matter, there aren't *any* cars here."

"That's typical. And Reece could have gone into town to get supplies. I had to wait for him just the other day."

"Yeah, but the place is empty. The office door is unlocked, and the place looks like it's been cleaned out. Reece seems to have used the room back of reception as his living quarters - bed, little fridge, microwave, stuff like that. Well, there's nothing there. No clothes in the closet, bed stripped. There's a few things in the fridge, but otherwise nothing."

Carol, who had been studying the department's financial ledger and worrying about what she saw there, was suddenly worried about something that promised to be even more important.

"You're telling me that Reece has packed up and left."

"It looks that way. There's no note explaining what he's doing, but my guess is that he decided that he'd had enough of this fleabag."

"Okay. I'm on my way. Are the keys to the rooms still there?"

"It looks that way, although I haven't checked to see if any are missing."

"While you're waiting for me, take a look in each of the rooms. I doubt you'll find anything, but we'd better be sure."

"You're thinking of more bodies?"

"Force of habit, I suppose. After all, the last time I got a call from the motel there was one in room 8. I should be there in half an hour."

———

Carol, unlike a couple of her officers, had never liked to exceed the speed limit unless it was absolutely necessary. She believed in setting a good example, not taking advantage of the fact that she was driving a car with the words 'Sheriff's Department' emblazoned on the side panels. This morning was different. She made it to the motel in 23 minutes.

Grieves was leaning against the door to the office. Sam was nowhere in sight, but he emerged from one of the rooms just as she closed the car door behind her.

"Find anything?" she asked.

"No bodies this time. You'd never know something's amiss if you hadn't been in the office."

Grieves stepped aside and Carol walked into the office, her deputy sheriff right behind her. At first glance, everything looked as she remembered it. But evidence that things were different was apparent the minute she entered the back room which had been Marty Reece's home on Crooked Lake. Her men had left the door to the closet open; it contained nothing but a dozen empty clothes hangers. Only an old mattress covered the springs on the cot sized bed. The drain rack beside the small sink contained a used coffee cup. Carol touched the coffee maker. There were still grounds in the filter, but it was stone cold.

"It looks like he left some time ago," she said. "Unless this is left over from yesterday."

Carol opened the fridge and found nothing but a nearly empty milk carton, a jar of mayonnaise, a partially consumed tube of braunschweiger, some marmalade, and a package of cheese.

"The cupboards, they're bare?" she asked.

"Not quite," Sam said, opening one above the sink to reveal what was left of a loaf of bread, a bottle of cooking oil, a box of shredded wheat, and some pasta. There were also, Carol noticed, a couple of jars of things that had been opened and should have been refrigerated.

"The dishes and silverware are over here," Sam said, turning to the left of the sink. "And there's a couple of pots and pans down there on the lower shelf. Pretty spartan living, if you ask me."

"About what I'd have expected. Did you look in the desk?"

"Not yet. We started with the personal stuff."

"Let's take a look."

Carol sat in the desk chair and pulled on the handle. Nothing happened.

"It's stuck." She gave the drawer another tug with the same result.

It was obvious that Sam wanted to take over, but he knew better than to suggest that Carol might not have the strength to do it. It took about two minutes, but by alternately yanking first one end and then the other, Carol was able to overcome whatever was jamming the drawer. Now it was open - and empty.

"Something's caught in there," Carol said. She reached a hand into the desk and felt around. "I think it's just paper, caught in one of the guide tracks."

"Anyway, there's nothing in the drawer," Sam said. "Whatever Reece kept in there he must have taken with him."

"Maybe he didn't keep anything in there because it was so hard to get it open." Officer Grieves was pleased to contribute to the discussion of the 'desk problem'.

Carol knew what Bridges and Grieves didn't know, that Kevin suspected that Marty Reece had once worked on Lake Pend Oreille in Idaho and had left that job without giving notice after the brutal murder of one of the locals. She had been dismissive of his theory. Now she wasn't so sure.

"I want to get that paper out of the drawer," she said and proceeded to try to loosen it without tearing it apart.

"You think it's important?"

"I've no idea. Probably not. For all I know it could have been jammed in there for years. But I'm curious."

Of course you are, Sam thought, remembering the many times when his boss had become obsessed with some aspect of a case that he was convinced wasn't worth pursuing.

It took several minutes, but eventually Carol was able to remove the paper from the drawer. It turned out to be not a single piece of paper, but three sheets which had been stapled together. While the papers had been bent and torn by their time in the desk drawer, they were still readable. Carol flattened them out as best she could and found herself looking at a typed document with the following heading:

May 13, 2008
From: Dr. Matthew Cooper, Psychiatrist

To: Whom It May Concern
Subject: Murray Rice

Carol quickly flipped to the third and final piece of paper. About a fourth of the way down the page was Dr. Cooper's signature, followed by an address in Bend, Oregon. Kevin's guess had been right. Marty Reece was in fact Murray Rice. Or was he? Carol told herself to calm down, not to jump to conclusions. She hadn't even read what Dr. Cooper had to say to 'whom it may concern' several years ago.

"Thanks for bearing with me, but I have the feeling that this paper is going to be important, well worth the time and trouble of removing it from that drawer. You have no idea what I'm talking about, but it just may be germane to the Keller case. If you'll bear with me just a few minutes longer, I've got to read it."

Officer Grieves looked puzzled. It was harder to read the deputy sheriff's face.

"Let's go outside," Sam said to his colleague. "She'll fill us in when she's done reading."

Carol was so busily engaged in studying Dr. Cooper's statement that she said nothing as they stepped out into the empty parking lot.

This is what she read.

Murray Rice is a 29 year old patient of mine, who has returned to his home in Oregon after two tours with the army in Iraq. He graduated in 1999 from high school here in Bend, where he was an outstanding athlete. After two years in community college, he enlisted in the marines. He planned on a career in the military, and in due course, like many young men of his age, he found himself on duty overseas in Iraq. His military record demonstrates that he was an exemplary soldier. He saw combat during both tours, and earned a Purple Heart during the second battle of Fallujah in Iraq.

His combat experience in Fallujah, and to a lesser extent elsewhere while on duty overseas, left its mark on Murray. He was involved in fire fights which resulted in many casualties, both to his own comrades and to many Iraqis, including Iraqi civilians. We have discussed on several occasions what he saw in those encounters, and especially what he felt when he realized that he had been responsible for the deaths of innocent non-combatants. As a result of this experience, Murray has suffered from post traumatic stress disorder. I have treated several men who have had this problem, and can confidently say that the problem is very real, and that it affects those suffering from it in different ways.

Murray has suffered from nightmares and, on occasions, from violent outbursts that appear to have been triggered by persistent memories of the traumatic situations he faced in combat. He has been advised and treated by military doctors who specialize in PTSD, but over the last year he has become my patient here in his hometown of Bend. I have placed him on medications which have had the effect both of reducing his experience of nightmares and controlling episodes of anger and occasional violence. He now regularly takes what are known as SSRI meds, and his response has been positive.

I believe that Murray has brought his PTSD disorder under control to the extent that he is both able and willing to assume a job which calls for the assumption of workplace responsibilities and good relations with his supervisors and co-workers. This is a good man who has served his country well and is in the process of recovering from war-induced trauma. If you need further information about Mr. Rice, please contact me at the address below.

Carol reread Dr. Cooper's statement, and found herself thinking about the terrible costs of war, even among those who survive it to return to civilian life. But her mind quickly turned to what this might mean for her investigation into what had happened to Carl Keller. Could Marty Reece - or Murray Rice - have slit Carl's throat? What black mood or painful memory might have triggered such an act of violence? Was PTSD the alibi for the manager of the *Welcome Inn*?

It was at that point that Carol's penchant for sober second thoughts kicked in. There was no evidence that Carl's throat had been slit by Reece. Lindsay Hartman and Tony Ferraro were still the most likely suspects. For all she knew, the motel manager had been confronted with some crisis that necessitated an abrupt departure. She would have to call the owner of the motel and see if he knew anything about Reece's plans. She searched her mind for his name, and it came to her. Clemens.

But she could not dismiss the possibility that Reece, or Rice, was a mentally or emotionally ill man who needed help before his demons again took possession of him. Which meant that it was essential that she alert state highway patrols to be on the lookout for him. Once more a good memory helped. She had always enjoyed license plate poker while driving, and while she couldn't recall Reece's plate number in its entirety, she remembered that it had a 5, a 6, a 7, and an 8. The numbers weren't in that order, but according to her rules that constituted a run.

"Sam, I didn't mean to send you out to the parking lot," she called out as she went to the front door. He and Officer Grieves were using the time to do what they had originally come to *Welcome Inn* to do, testing the locks on the motel room doors.

"No problem. I hope you learned something. What we're learning is that you'd have to be a professional burglar to open these doors if they're locked. Maybe it doesn't matter any more."

"I think it still matters. But I've got something else for you to do. The owner of this motel is a man named Clemens. I don't remember his first name. See if you can find him and talk with him. Did Reece let him know he was pulling up stakes? Does he know anything about what's going on with Reece? Any problems? What's his impression of the man? My guess is that they didn't see much of each other, but let's find out. I'm heading back to Cumberland to see what I can do to alert the state police in New York and nearby places where Reece could still be. I just hope he didn't leave last night. If he did, he could be in North Carolina by now."

"Those papers from the drawer, they tell you anything?"

"They did, but whether it's relevant to the Keller case or to Reece's disappearing act I have no idea. They aren't even about Reece, but a man named Rice. So maybe Reece is really Rice, and if he is he's suffering from post traumatic stress due to his experiences in the Iraq war. Make of that what you will."

"Anything you want us to be doing besides tracking down Clemens?"

"Just let me know what he tells you. I'll be at the office."

"Here's to no more surprises today," Sam said as he and Grieves climbed into the patrol car.

"Good luck."

Carol decided to take one more look around the motel office and mini-apartment. It proved to be a wise decision. When she squatted down to peer under the bed she thought she saw something under an old radiator behind it. She used a spatula from the kitchen to reach what turned out to be a plastic bottle containing a prescription for Murray Rice which had been filled at a pharmacy in Sandpoint, Idaho. The name of the capsules in the bottle was Risperdal. Carol had never heard of it. But if it was a drug prescribed to help people with PTSD, it wasn't doing the manager of *Welcome Inn* any good collecting dust under an old radiator.

CHAPTER 69

With Officer Byrnes' help, Carol was able to contact the state police in New York and several adjoining states and ask that they be on the lookout for a brown Chevy, probably six or seven years old, with a New York license plate number Tommy had produced with the help of the MVA. The odds that Reece would be picked up weren't all that good, but the effort had to be made.

Sam had called to report that Vergil Clemens was not at his home, although a housekeeper was fairly sure he'd be back at 'a reasonable hour,' whatever that meant.

Carol was about to call Kevin to let him in on what she had discovered at the motel when Tony Ferraro surprised her with a call from Albany.

"Ferraro here, sheriff," he said, "and I thought I should give you an update. It's the alibi issue."

"I didn't expect you to get back to me so soon."

"Nor did I. And I'm not calling to report that I've remembered what I was doing on the 2nd of July. I'll have to be frank about things, but I've done everything I can to clear the cobwebs and give you something definite and I can't come up with anything. The best I can do is tell you that it was some day close to that date that I finally got around to seeing the latest Woody Allen movie. I wish I could say it was the 2nd, but I can't. My brain is aching from the effort to help you. You'll just have to believe me. Besides, it's like I told you. When I did try to see Carl, he didn't answer the door and I couldn't get into the room because it was locked."

"You didn't try one of those tricks with a credit card or something to unlock the door and get into Carl's room, did you?"

"Do you honestly believe I'd have tried to break into the place?"

"We both know that you've been finding ways to get into other rooms, Mr. Ferraro. Your track record in matters like this isn't a very good one. Speaking of which, how do things stand between you and Mr. Foster?"

"They could be better. I think he'll keep me on until I finish up a particularly nasty case, and then bye-bye. He just won't believe me about Keller. God, am I naive. You think you'll be praised for being a whistle blower, calling attention to a colleague's dishonesty, but no, that's not the way it works."

Carol was tired of Ferraro's martyr complex. And his lies.

"Considering what we both know about what you've been doing - faking your identity with Lisa Simmons, taking all that stuff from Carl's apartment, running off to Baltimore, or was it Canada - I'd say that Francis has been remarkably patient with you. Don't just blame him alone. I'm also from Missouri."

It was obvious that Tony was never going to come up with a story that put him somewhere a long way from the *Welcome Inn* on the night of Carls death. She was surprised that he hadn't tried to make up an alibi. Why not pick that night to have seen the Woody Allen film? It was highly unlikely that someone at the theatre would remember. But he hadn't done so. Ferraro was an enigma, much like the judge with his call girl and Marty Reece with his troubled background in Iraq and Idaho.

Carol tried Kevin, only to find that he wasn't at the cottage. Oh, well, her report of what had happened at the motel would keep until evening. She was in the process of reordering her priorities for the afternoon when JoAnne buzzed to report that she had a visitor. Her office manager's voice sounded almost breathless, as if the visitor might be a celebrity.

"I thought our practice was for you to tell me who wants to see me," she said.

"It's Donna Sugar."

Carol mumbled something which JoAnne would interpret as 'Ill be damned'.

"Sorry. I'm surprised, that's all. Send her in."

Donna Sugar did look like a celebrity, at least when compared with most of the people who came knocking at the sheriff's door.

"Hello. I had no idea I'd be seeing you today. Perhaps you came over to the lake to see the judge and thought I'd make it a twofer."

"No, I'm here specifically to see you. I know I ran the risk that you'd be on vacation or out of the office, but it's very important that I talk with you in person. I know I've done my best to keep you at arm's length, but things are different now."

"Please sit down. And take your time. I have the whole afternoon if need be."

Sugar started to put her purse on the desk in front of her, but pulled it back into her lap.

"Go ahead, put it on the desk. May I get you coffee?"

"If it won't be any trouble. Just black, no sugar."

"I'm sure it won't be. We're a heavily caffeinated group here."

Carol asked JoAnne to bring them two cups of coffee.

"Now, what is on your mind."

"It's what we talked about on the phone. How I could help provide Judge Hartman with an alibi for where he was when Mr. Keller was killed. This is very awkward for me, and I want to be absolutely sure that nothing I say or do will hurt the judge."

"As I told you, an honest, verifiable alibi should make it impossible for Judge Hartman to have killed Mr. Keller. Frankly, I have always respected him, and am uncomfortable even thinking of him as a potential suspect in a murder case. I suppose I have been hopeful that he has a good alibi."

"But you must understand that his wishes and mine may not be the same." The woman had looked poised when they had met before. Now she was conspicuously nervous. "I'm not really sure why I'm having so much trouble saying what I must say, but the problem is that if I provide the judge with an alibi he might well be devastated."

Carol watched as Sugar fumbled for something in her purse. She felt sorry for the woman.

"I think you are here to do what you have to do," she said. "I'm sure it will not be easy."

"I have agonized about it since we last spoke. I think this is one of those situations where the truth is the best option. The irony lies in the fact that neither of us has been truthful up until now, and he prefers to keep it that way. But to use that distasteful but ubiquitous expression, Francis and I have been in a relationship for several years. It began at Mt. Washington, where he was attending a conference, and it appears that it has now come to an end thanks to Randall Truscott. I feel quite certain that Randall has no hard evidence of our so-called affair. Nor do I believe that his attorney, Mr. Keller, had hard evidence. But Mr. Keller thought he was helping his client, and Randall thinks he is getting his revenge on both the judge and me. To make my long story short, Judge Hartman and I were together the night of July 2nd. He was nowhere near Crooked Lake, and he most certainly could not have killed Mr. Keller."

Carol was fascinated by what she heard. She had almost expected it, all of it except the reference to Mr. Washington, but the way it had been presented cast the call girl in the chair across the desk from her in an entirely different light.

"Thank you. I think I can appreciate why this has been so difficult for you. As I told you the other day, I have no intention of rushing off to the *Times Union* with news that Truscott's story is true. I cannot stop the paper from running articles about it, and I cannot guarantee that sooner or later an investigative reporter will not find evidence that supports Truscott's claim. But I can assure you that I will say nothing about what you have told me unless the judge were actually to be put on trial. And with an alibi, that is extremely unlikely. It is up to you whether the judge knows that you have come to me."

"I can't help worrying about what I have done," Sugar said. "In any event, I know that I shall not be seeing Judge Hartman again. He knows it, too, but is having trouble admitting it to himself."

"I must ask you a question, Ms. Sugar. How do you know for sure that the judge was with you the night of the July 2nd?"

The call girl smiled a wan smile.

"Someone in my position has to keep a meticulous record. The media like to speculate about names in little black books. Well, I have a little black book. The judge is MW in that book - MW for Mt. Washington. If you like, I will show you the book. And I have taken seriously your admonition not to falsify any of this. The judge was with me that night."

"Do you have the black book with you?" Carol asked.

"I do." She reached into her purse and withdrew the book. "If you don't mind, I'd prefer that we look only at July 2nd. I'm sure you understand."

She stood up and came around the desk. Carefully covering the dates surrounding the one the sheriff was interested in, she showed Carol the book.

Carol nodded.

"Is there anything else you want to tell me?"

Donna Sugar replaced the book in her purse, and proceeded to answer the sheriff by asking a question.

"Is there something else you'd like to hear?"

"No, I don't believe there is. But I'd like you to sign a statement certifying that what you have told me is the truth. Don't be alarmed. It's common practices in cases like this."

It took another fifteen minutes to type up the statement for her to sign, and then Donna Sugar was on her way, obviously both relieved and anxious. Carol went to the window and looked down into the parking lot to watch as the call girl climbed into her car and disappeared into Cumberland's afternoon traffic.

She could not understand why women would choose to do what Ms. Sugar did for a living. But she sympathized with her dilemma and with the way she had decided to handle it. She hoped that whoever was investigating Randall Truscott's story for the *Times Union* and the *Tattler* would never be able to produce the smoking gun that would cost Judge Hartman his place on the bench.

CHAPTER 70

"So that's where we are," Carol said. "I've been the sheriff for over ten years and I can't remember anything quite like this one."

Kevin had been listening to Carol's recapitulation of the day's developments for nearly three quarters of an hour, interrupting only with the occasional 'interesting' or even 'no kidding'.

At Carol's suggestion, they had had a swim first, and were now sitting on the deck, still in their bathing suits, having forgotten all about dinner and having each finished off two glasses of Chardonnay.

"It sounds as if the Keller case has been solved," Kevin said.

"It's been solved in that I don't have to nab a killer. Carl took care of that by committing suicide. The question of who slit Carl's throat is another matter. Whoever did it obviously intended to kill Carl, and that *is* a crime. So it won't do simply to say 'nice try, better luck next time' and let it go at that. Which leaves us with the question of who took a knife to Carl's throat. That's the crime that may never be solved."

"I know, you want the guilty party in custody, a fool proof case ready to go to trial. But even if that doesn't happen, you know who did it. The case has been solved, right?"

"You're convinced it was Reece who slit Carl's throat, aren't you?"

"I am, except that I think his name is Rice. And you agree with me."

"You've been betting on Rice ever since you first talked to the Pend Oreille police. I've had to wrestle with the stubborn fact that there have been other suspects, people with much better motives than Rice, people who could well have been the culprit. I had to convince myself that they didn't do it before my default candidate became Rice."

"So you first had to eliminate Judge Hartman and this guy Ferraro. What is it that decided you they couldn't be guilty?"

"I ruled out the judge," Carol said, "when Donna Sugar admitted that she and Hartman had spent that night together."

"How do you know she didn't make it up?" Kevin asked. "Can you prove she's on the up and up, not just protecting her sugar daddy?"

"I can't prove it, but I know I'm right. You'd have to have listened to her, to have seen for yourself how difficult it was for her to contradict the judge. Every time we'd talked she had been the epitome of cool and confident. She's a woman who's accustomed to being in control. But when push came to shove, her confidence disappeared. She faced what was for her a very difficult moral dilemma. I think she was actually frightened. I'm sure there's no third person who can confirm that Sugar and Hartman shared a bed in Albany the night Carl's throat was cut, but I'm satisfied that they did."

Carol was a stickler for evidence. If she was this certain about what Sugar had told her and hence about the judge's alibi, Kevin had no intention of challenging her.

"Which leaves Ferraro," he said. "Why are you willing to take him off the hook?"

"He's nowhere near as cool and confident as Sugar. Nor as smart. He's been much more concerned about being caught stealing from the Rasmussen account than about being charged with killing Carl Keller. It wouldn't be too much to say that he's acted more like an innocent man than a guilty one. Innocent of slitting Carl's throat, that is. He admitted going to the *Welcome Inn* when he didn't need to admit it. There was no evidence that he'd been there. There wasn't even any solid proof that he was the man who'd gotten the motel address from Lisa Simmons. Yet he handed me what could be considered the most damaging evidence against him. He didn't offer us an alibi for the night Carl died, yet he told me he'd seen a Woody Allen movie that week. Why not say he'd seen the movie that very night? It's doubtful we'd have found someone who could put him in the theatre some other night. Frankly, Ferraro just hasn't acted like a guilty man covering his tracks. He lied, or at least I'm pretty sure he did, about the escrow account, but he's made no effort to do so regarding Carl's death. He may have had a motive for killing him, and for all I know he went to the motel with that in mind. But I'm accepting his story that he never entered room 8."

"So, having eliminated Hartman and Ferraro, you've come around to Murray Rice as your killer. Sorry, your throat slasher."

"When you've ruled out the other suspects, why not? Moreover, it makes sense. Two brutal acts, one on Pend Oreille, the other here on Crooked Lake. In both cases a man who knew the victim disappears just a few weeks later. The evidence points to the probability that the two men are actually the same man. What's more, the doctor's statement makes it clear that Rice had served in Iraq and had PTSD, which is pretty much what you heard from a policeman out on Pend Oreille. I don't presume to know all the characteristics of PTSD, but I'm sure I've read that there are cases when it may cause people to wig out, become violent. And just a layman's guess, but wouldn't that be more likely if they stopped taking their meds? We've established that the pills I found at the motel are used to treat symptoms of PTSD, and they weren't doing Mr. Rice any good while they were collecting dust under the radiator."

"Funny, isn't it," Kevin said. "I really shouldn't want the man who slit Carl's throat to be a war vet who can't help it that he's still fighting the war."

"I know," Carol agreed. "On the other hand, I like the judge and I'm happy I can rule him out as a suspect. As for Ferraro, Foster will very probably fire him for stealing from the escrow account. If somehow he were also tried for killing a dead man, that would look like piling on."

"You've got another problem: you don't know where Rice is. It won't be easy to prosecute a man if you don't even know where to find him." Kevin then had another thought. "And what if you find him and bring him back? Don't you suppose that a jury would have a hard time convicting a veteran whose PTSD makes him irresponsible for his actions?"

"It would depend on a lot of factors," Carol said, "not to mention the testimony of medical specialists. But you're probably right. After all, he didn't actually kill anybody, had no motive, and acted on an impulse he couldn't control."

"So you see, it's like what I've been saying. So what if the crime is never *officially* solved. There's more than one way to look at justice in this case, right?"

"I suppose my problem is that I liked Carl. Or that I liked the Carl I was getting to know over a decade ago. It doesn't seem fair that it should end this way."

"It was only about six weeks ago that you thought he was stalking you, Carol. The truth is that you're investing too much of your time and emotions in someone you don't really know at all. And maybe never did."

CHAPTER 71

It had been nearly a week since Marty Reece had disappeared, and the machinery of law enforcement had largely ground to a halt around Crooked Lake. That is not, of course, technically true. Speeders still received tickets, fishermen were still reminded that they needed a license to catch lake trout and bass, and the sheriff's team of officers was still busy helping local residents in trouble on the lake and on the local highways. But when compared with developments in the Keller case over the previous weeks, stasis was the name of the game.

The highway police in New York and nearby states had had nothing to report on Reece's car, and it was becoming more and more unlikely that they would be calling to tell Carol that Reece had been found. Vergil Clemens, the owner of *Welcome Inn*, had finally called back, but what he had to report was not very helpful. Reece had not given notice of his intention to quit, nor for that matter had Clemens learned much about his manager since hiring him. It appeared that rather than hire a replacement, he was finally going to bite the proverbial bullet and unload the motel to a developer who was prepared to take the white elephant off his hands.

Tony Ferraro had not provided an alibi for the night of Carl Keller's death, and it didn't look as if he were going to. Randall Truscott's allegations about a relationship between Judge Lindsay Hartman and Donna Sugar had not been enhanced by any new evidence and the story had gradually gravitated to the back pages and shorter columns. Both the judge and the call girl had disappeared from public view. Rumor had it that the judge and his wife had rented a place on Cape Cod, but Carol was betting that they had taken up residence at their Crooked Lake cottage. There had been no phone calls from Albany, a clear signal that Francis Foster was spending most of his time seeking a replacement for Keller and, in all likelihood, for Ferraro as well.

The weather, which had been hot and dry, had taken a hit from a front that came rolling in from western Canada, bringing rain and cooler temperatures. Summer renters had begun to complain, and even Kevin and Carol had done less swimming and more reading than was their habit for mid-summer. They had even gotten out of the habit of discussing the Keller case for several nights. And then the unexpected letter arrived.

"Ready for a surprise?" Carol asked as she came into the cottage through the back door and began to shed her jacket and holster.

"Always," he answered. "It's been pretty quiet lately."

"Don't I know. And now I have a letter, right out of the blue, from Carl Keller."

"Keller? You're putting me on. He's been dead for over a month."

"A voice from the grave. Believe me, I haven't been attending a seance. It came this afternoon, courtesy of Marty Reece."

"Wait a minute." Kevin suddenly sounded excited, as Carol had been sure he would. "The letter's from Keller, but it came from Reece. That requires a bit of explaining. Why don't you change and I'll uncork the Chardonnay."

Ten minutes later they had taken up chairs on the deck and Carol was in the process of trying to make sense of this unexpected development.

"What it is is a message from Carl, carefully folded up and tucked into an envelope addressed to my office and accompanied by a brief note from Marty Reece. I could let you read it, but I'd rather read it again myself.

"Let's hear it. How about Reece's note first?"

"Okay. Like I said it's brief. The postmark says he mailed it just four days ago. And get this. He mailed it from Marquette, Michigan. That's way off in the state's Upper Peninsula. I don't know where I thought he was going when he left here, but it sure wasn't someplace on Lake Superior. I've already contacted the police up there, and they promise to keep their eyes open. But I wouldn't bet he's still there."

"Well, in a way it's consistent. Lake Pend Oreille, Crooked Lake, Lake Superior. He seems to like water."

"Perhaps. Anyway, here's his note:

'Mr. Keller left what looks like a suicide note for you. I meant to give it to you, but forgot. Sorry. Don't worry about me. It was just time to move on. Reece.'

"Laconic cuss," Kevin said. "At least he's told you where he went. If he's Murray Rice, he didn't even do that when he said good-bye to Idaho."

"I doubt he's hunkering down in Marquette. Let me read what Carl wrote. It's kinda strange, but

I agree, it looks like a suicide note. Wish Reece had given it to me sooner."

"I'll bet he didn't *forget* to give it to you. I notice that he didn't send along Carl's car keys or any other personal belongings. He obviously wants you to believe that Carl committed suicide, and his timing is convenient."

"Carl's message is strange, but I'm sure he wrote it, and I think it says quite a bit about the man. Ready?"

"And eager to hear it."

'For Carol Kelleher -

To be or not to be - that is the question:
Whether 'tis nobler in the mind to suffer
The slings and arrows of outrageous fortune
Or to take arms against a sea of troubles
And by opposing end them. To die, to sleep -
No more - and by a sleep to say we end
The heartache, and the thousand natural shocks
That flesh is heir to. 'Tis a consummation
Devoutly to be wished. To die, to sleep -
To sleep - perchance to dream: ay, there's the rub,
For in that sleep of death what dreams may come
When we have shuffled off this mortal coil,
Must give us pause.'

I've agonized over this for weeks, and now have decided that I can no longer suffer those slings and arrows of outrageous fortune. Do not think less of me that I have chosen 'not to be.' My only regret is that I never got to know you better. Good-bye.

Carl

"That's it?" Kevin sounded disappointed.

"I'm afraid so. He was obviously familiar with Hamlet and used his soliloquy to lay out his dilemma. It's terribly sad."

"That's an understatement," Kevin said. "Not only did he know Shakespeare, he as much as says that he was something of a Hamlet himself."

"It says so much about 'what if.' What if he had come to me and told me about his problems instead of following me about and never sharing his thoughts with me. We even thought of him as a stalker, remember?"

"He was obviously a troubled man, and I'll bet it had to do with more than being let go by the law firm."

"He probably spoke with me for a total of ten minutes. And wrote me twice - a message urging me not to trust F and a suicide note. And I'd never have seen the note if Reece hadn't decided to mail it to me. He could just as well have dropped it in a trash can."

———

It was two weeks later, and Carol and Kevin had just mailed off a deposit for a January cruise in the Caribbean.

"We actually did it," she said. "Can you believe it?"

"I just hope we don't have second thoughts around Christmas time."

"There aren't going to be any second thoughts. Both of us have needed a break for I can't remember how long. Everybody seems to be doing something else. Why not us?"

"Everybody? Whom are you talking about?"

"I was thinking of the people who were involved in the Keller case, people like Judge Hartman, Donna Sugar, you know, the whole kit and kaboodle of them."

"I guess I haven't been paying attention. What's this about the whole kit and kaboodle?"

"Take the judge," Carol said. "He's announced his retirement, put his home on the market, and he and his wife are reportedly starting to look for a place on the west coast of Florida."

"You didn't tell me about that," Kevin said. "What's he doing with the cottage?"

"The way I understand it, they'll hang on to it and spend their summers on Crooked Lake. Not quite as hot as Florida. As for that other suspect of mine, Tony Ferraro, Foster tells me he resigned from the old firm and plans to go into practice with a friend in Scarsdale. Seems he cobbled together a check to cover the theft from that escrow account. He hasn't admitted that he's the guilty party, but claims he feels obligated to cover for his friend Keller. In any event, he got out of M & B before Francis booted him out."

"I love that 'friend Keller' bit."

"You haven't heard the best story about trying something new. Gretchen tells me Francis has now replaced both Carl and Tony. Want to guess with whom?"

"Now how would I know something like that?"

"Not their names, their sex. Two women. All of a sudden Gretchen's got company. Somehow I have trouble picturing Francis doing something like that. Maybe he came around to the view that Gretchen was his best attorney, figured he might be smart to hire a couple more gals. Speaking of the fair sex,

Lisa Simmons has moved in with her latest boy friend, and Donna Sugar - there's another surprise move. I got news about the others from Gretchen, but Sugar actually wrote me herself. She's going to get her master's in chemistry and see about a career at NIH."

"While moonlighting in her old profession?"

"She didn't say, and I'm certainly not going to ask her a question like that."

"It sounds as if you know what's going on in the lives of all the principals in the Keller case."

"Not quite. Reece or Rice remains a mystery. Nothing out of Marquette's police department. He'll probably remain just as much of a mystery to us as he did to the police on Pend Oreille. I've even tried that Oregon doctor out in Bend; he remembers Rice, but hasn't heard from him in several years. Much as I hate to say it, I've got a hunch we finally have our own cold case here on Crooked Lake."

"Your batting average is still pretty damned good," Kevin said.

"How's yours? I haven't heard a word about your luck with rod and reel in weeks."

"Oh, haven't I told you? Fishing is no longer my thing. The Southport Chamber of Commerce is sponsoring a BBQ Invitational Cook Off for Labor Day, and I've already put down my entry fee."

"You've given up on that article you're supposed to be writing?"

"No way," Kevin insisted. "Like Ms. Sugar, I'll be doing some moonlighting."

"Really? I'll bet Sugar finishes her master's degree before you finish your article."

Kevin got up and headed for the study.

"What are you doing?" Carol asked.

"I'm paying my computer a visit. Let's call it moonlighting. I have no intention of losing a bet like that."

"I didn't expect you would. Come here and let me give you a kiss. Maybe it'll inspire you."

CPSIA information can be obtained at www.ICGtesting.com
Printed in the USA
BVOW05s1139180515

400812BV00007B/16/P